The AVIATOR'S WIFE

DELACORTE PRESS *New York*

The

AVIATOR'S
WIFE

A Novel

MELANIE BENJAMIN

Copyright © 2013 by Melanie Benjamin

All rights reserved.

Published in the United States by Delacorte Press, an imprint of The Random House Publishing Group, a division of Random House, Inc., New York.

DELACORTE PRESS is a registered trademark of Random House, Inc., and the colophon is a trademark of Random House, Inc.

LIBRARY OF CONGRESS CATALOGING-IN-PUBLICATION DATA
Benjamin, Melanie.
The aviator's wife: a novel / Melanie Benjamin. 1st ed.
p.   cm.
ISBN 978-0-345-52867-4 — ISBN 978-0-345-53469-9 (ebook)
1. Lindbergh, Charles A. (Charles Augustus), 1902–1974—Fiction.
2. Lindbergh, Anne Morrow, 1906–2001—Fiction.   3. Air pilots—Fiction.   I. Title.
PS3608.A876A43 2013
813'.6—dc23   2012017014

Printed in the United States of America on acid-free paper

www.bantamdell.com

9 8 7 6 5 4 3 2 1

FIRST EDITION

Book design by Barbara M. Bachman

To Alec

"But the eyes are blind.
One must look with the heart."

—Antoine de Saint-Exupéry

The AVIATOR'S WIFE

E IS FLYING.

Is this how I will remember him? As I watch him lying vanquished, defeated by the one thing even he could not outmaneuver, I understand that I will have to choose my memories carefully now. There are simply too many. Faded newspaper articles, more medals and trophies than I know what to do with; personal letters from presidents, kings, dictators. Books, movies, plays about him and his accomplishments; schools and institutions proudly bearing his name.

Tearstained photographs of a child with blond curls, blue eyes, and a deep cleft in his chin. Smudged copies of letters to other women, tucked away in my purse.

I stir in my seat, trying not to disturb him; I need him to sleep, to restore, because of all the things I have to say to him later, and we're running out of time. I feel it in my very bones, this ebbing of our tide, and there's nothing I can do about it and I'm no longer content simply to watch it, watch *him* rush away from me, leaving me alone, not knowing, never knowing. My hands clenched, my jaw so rigid it aches, I lean forward as if I could *will* the plane to fly faster.

A stewardess peeks over the curtain separating us from the rest of the passengers.

"Is there anything I can do?"

I shake my head, and she retreats after one worried, worshipful look at the emaciated figure breathing raspily, eyelids flickering as if he's still searching, still vigilant, even in his drugged sleep. And knowing him, he probably is.

Still the unanswered questions, so many I can't gather them to me in any order, in any list, oh, his damned, disciplined *lists*! Now, finally, I have need for one and I can't even pick which question with which to start. So many demand answers. Why them? Why *all* of them? Did he love them? Has he ever loved me?

Have I always loved him? I left him once, long ago. So long ago but I can still remember the color of the suitcase I was carrying, the shoes I was wearing when I walked out the door. The same pair of shoes I was wearing when I came back. Has he ever suspected that he almost lost me then? Is that why he has betrayed us all?

I yearn to shake him awake, make him tell me, but I can't, not yet. So I force myself to focus on the one question only I will be able to answer. I will leave the rest for later. After we land; after our children have said all they need to.

After only I am left.

Sipping some tepid water, I look out the window and ponder, once more, how to remember this man who was never merely a man, least of all to me. We are above the clouds now, winging our way west across the continent.

Flying.

He is forever captured in photographs and newsreels waving jauntily from the cockpit, lean and bronze in his oversized flying suit, his sandy hair cut so short, boyish Buster Brown bangs in front, his neck shaved in back. Or he is leaning casually against his plane—*the* plane, the one of which he always spoke so reverently that I knew it was a part of him in a way, it turned out, I could never be. That single engine monoplane, the *Spirit of St. Louis.*

Even now, I think of flying as a refuge; gliding with the birds on the currents, the sky a great silent cathedral surrounding you. And although I know differently—my ears sometimes ring with the memory of the roaring of those early engines—I imagine him crossing that ocean in silence, a young man, his hand on the control stick and his foot on the rudder, alone with just his thoughts; for the first and only time in his life, free from expectation. Free from the burden of living up to the legend that awaits him a mere twenty or so hours away, in a primitive airfield just outside of Paris.

And if I finally choose to remember him like this, will I see his face? Or will I be seated behind him, as I was so many times, so that I can see only the fine, reddish-blond hairs that the razor didn't quite reach, his neck straining forward in a taut column of concentration? Will I recognize his shoulders, broad and tense beneath that bulky flight suit?

It will not be him flying, then; it will be *us.* Somehow, I will be in the tiny cockpit of the *Spirit of St. Louis* with him, a fly on history's shoulder.

No. Abruptly, I tug down the blind so that I can no longer look down upon the clouds. *No.* He should soar alone across the ocean that first time, just like in the history books, and he should be young and he should be boyish and his entire future, unimaginable, unsullied, should be his only passenger.

Despite all the pain, the bitterness, the betrayal—his and mine, both—I pray to the God of my childhood that this is how, finally, I will remember him. An intense yet hopeful figure so finely chiseled he is almost part of the machinery of the plane itself, willing it across the ocean with a couple of sandwiches, a thermos of coffee, and unwarranted arrogance. His blue eyes will glint like the sun on the ocean that is so close outside the cockpit window he can almost touch it. *Everything* will be ahead of him, including—especially—me.

Only he won't know it yet. And so he'll soar toward us all, so innocent he is still capable of capturing, and breaking, my heart.

CHAPTER I

December 1927

D OWN TO EARTH.

I repeated the phrase to myself, whispering it in wonder. *Down to earth.* What a plodding expression, really, when you considered it—I couldn't help but think of muddy fields and wheel ruts and worms—yet people always meant it as a compliment.

" 'Down to earth'—did you hear that, Elisabeth? Can you believe Daddy would say that about an *aviator*, of all people?"

"I doubt he even realized what he was saying," my sister murmured as she scribbled furiously on her lap desk, despite the rocking motion of the train. "Now, Anne, dear, if you'd just let me finish this letter . . ."

"Of course he didn't," I persisted, refusing to be ignored. This was the third letter she'd written today! "Daddy never does know what he's saying, which is why I love him. But honestly, that's what his letter said—'I do hope you can meet Colonel Lindbergh. He's so down to earth!' "

"Well, Daddy is quite taken with the colonel. . . ."

"Oh, I know—and I didn't mean to criticize him! I was just thinking out loud. I wouldn't say anything like that in person." Suddenly my mood shifted, as it always seemed to do whenever I was with my family. Away from them, I could be confident, almost careless, with my words and ideas. Once, someone even called me vivacious (although to be honest, he was a college freshman intoxicated by bathtub gin and his first whiff of expensive perfume).

Whenever my immediate family gathered, however, it took me a while to relax, to reacquaint myself with the rhythm of speech and good-natured joshing that they seemed to fall into so readily. I imagined that they carried it with them, even when we were all scattered; I fancied each one of them humming the tune of this family symphony in their heads as they went about their busy lives.

Like so many other family traits—the famous Morrow sense of humor, for instance—the musical gene appeared to have skipped me. So it always took me longer to remember my part in this domestic song and dance. I'd been traveling with my sister and brother on this Mexican-bound train for a week, and still I felt tongue-tied and shy. Particularly around Dwight, now a senior at Groton; my brother had grown paler, prone to strange laughing fits, almost reverting to childhood at times, even as physically he was fast maturing into a carbon copy of our father.

Elisabeth was the same as ever, and I was the same as ever around her; no longer a confident college senior, I was diminished in her golden presence. In the stale air of the train car, I felt as limp and wrinkled as the sad linen dress I was wearing. While she looked as pressed and poised as a mannequin, not a wrinkle or smudge on her smart silk suit, despite the red dust blowing in through the inadequate windows.

"Now, don't go brooding already, Anne, for heaven's sake! Of course you wouldn't criticize Daddy to his face—you, of all people! There!" Elisabeth signed her letter with a flourish, folded it carefully, and tucked it in her pocket. "I'll wait until later before

I address it. Just think how grand it will look on the embassy stationery!"

"Who are you writing this time? Connie?"

Elisabeth nodded brusquely; she wrote to Connie Chilton, her former roommate from Smith, so frequently the question hardly seemed worth acknowledging. Then I almost asked if she needed a stamp, before I remembered. We were *dignitaries* now. Daddy was ambassador to Mexico. We Morrows had no need for such common objects as stamps. All our letters would go in the special government mail pouch, along with Daddy's memos and reports.

It was rumored that Colonel Lindbergh himself would be taking a mail pouch back to Washington with him, when he flew away. At least, that's what Daddy had insinuated in his last letter, the one I had received just before boarding the train in New York with Elisabeth and Dwight. We were in Mexico now; we'd crossed the border during the night. I couldn't stop marveling at the strange landscape as we'd chugged our way south; the flat, strangely light-filled plains of the Midwest; the dreary desert in Texas, the lonely adobe houses or the occasional tin-roofed shack underneath a bleached-out, endless sky. Mexico, by contrast, was greener than I had imagined, especially as we climbed toward Mexico City.

"Did you tell Connie that we saw Gloria Swanson with Mr. Kennedy?" We'd caught a glimpse of the two, the movie star and the banker (whom we knew socially), when they boarded the train in Texas. Both of them had their heads down and coat collars turned up. Joseph Kennedy was married, with a brood of Catholic children and a lovely wife named Rose. Miss Swanson was married to a French marquis, according to the *Photoplay* I sometimes borrowed from my roommate.

"I didn't. Daddy wouldn't approve. We do have to be more careful now that he's ambassador."

"That's true. But didn't she look so tiny in person! Much smaller than in the movies. Hardly taller than me!"

"I've heard that about movie stars." Elisabeth nodded thoughtfully. "They say Douglas Fairbanks isn't much taller than Mary Pickford."

A colored porter knocked on the door to our compartment; he stuck his head inside. "We'll be at the station momentarily, miss," he said to Elisabeth, who smiled graciously and nodded, her blond curls tickling her forehead. Then he retreated.

"I can't wait to see Con," I said, my stomach dancing in anticipation. "And Mother, of course. But mainly Con!" I missed my little sister; missed and envied her, both. At fourteen, she was able to make the move to Mexico City with our parents and live the gay diplomatic life that I could glimpse only on holidays like this; my first since Daddy had been appointed.

I picked up my travel case and followed Elisabeth out of our private car and into the aisle, where we were joined by Dwight, who was tugging at his tie.

"Is this tied right, Anne?" He frowned, looking so like Daddy that I almost laughed; Daddy never could master the art of tying a necktie, either. Daddy couldn't master the art of wearing clothes, period. His pants were always too long and wrinkled, like elephants' knees.

"Yes, of course." But I gave it a good tug anyway.

Then suddenly the train had stopped; we were on a platform swirling with excited passengers greeting their loved ones, in a soft, blanketing warmth that gently thawed my bones, still chilled from the Northampton winter I carried with me, literally, on my arm. I'd forgotten to pack my winter coat in my trunk.

"Anne! Elisabeth! Dwight!" A chirping, a laugh, and then

Con was there, her round little face brown from sun, her dark hair pulled back from her face with a gay red ribbon. She was wearing a Mexican dress, all bright embroidery and full skirt; she even had huaraches on her tiny feet.

"Oh, look at you!" I hugged her, laughing. "What a picture! A true señorita!"

"Darlings!"

Turning blindly, I found myself in my mother's embrace, and then too quickly released as she moved on to Elisabeth. Mother looked as ever, a sensible New England clubwoman plunked down in the middle of the tropics. Daddy, his pants swimming as usual, his tie askew, was shaking Dwight's hand and kissing Elisabeth on the cheek at the same time.

Finally he turned to me; rocking back on his heels, he looked me up and down and then nodded solemnly, although his eyes twinkled. "And there's Anne. Reliable Anne. You never change, my daughter."

I blushed, not sure if this was a compliment, choosing to think it might be. Then I ran to his open arms, and kissed his stubbly cheek.

"Merry Christmas, Mr. Ambassador!"

"Yes, yes—a merry Christmas it will be! Now, hurry up, hurry up, and you may be able to catch Colonel Lindbergh before he goes out."

"He's still here?" I asked, as Mother marshaled us expertly into two waiting cars, both black and gleaming, ostentatiously so. I was acutely aware of our luggage piling up on the platform, matching and initialed and gleaming with comfortable wealth. I couldn't help but notice how many people were lugging straw cases as they piled into donkey carts.

"Yes, Colonel Lindbergh is still here—oh, my dear, you should have seen the crowds at the airfield when he arrived! Two hours late, but nobody minded a bit. That plane, what's it called, the *Ghost of St. Louis,* isn't it—"

Con began to giggle helplessly, and I suppressed a smile.

"It's the *Spirit of St. Louis,*" I corrected her, and my mother met my gaze with a bemused expression in her downward-slanted eyes. I felt myself blush, knowing what she was thinking. *Anne? Swooning for the dashing young hero, just like all the other girls? Who could have imagined?*

"Yes, of course, the *Spirit of St. Louis.* And the colonel has agreed to spend the holidays with us in the embassy. Your father is beside himself. Mr. Henry Ford has even sent a plane to fetch the colonel's mother, and she'll be here, as well. At dinner, Elisabeth will take special care of him—oh, and you, too, dear, you must help. To tell the truth, I find the colonel to be rather shy."

"He's *ridiculously* shy," Con agreed, with another giggle. "I don't think he's ever really talked to girls before!"

"Con, now, please. The colonel's our guest. We must make him feel at home," Mother admonished.

I listened in dismay as I followed her into the second car; Daddy, Dwight, and Elisabeth roared off in the first. The colonel—a total *stranger*—would be part of our family Christmas? I certainly hadn't bargained on that, and couldn't help but feel that it was rude of a stranger to insinuate himself in this way. Yet at the mere mention of his name my heart began to beat faster, my mind began to race with the implications of this unexpected stroke of what the rest of the world would call enormous good luck. Oh, how the girls back at Smith would scream once they found out! How envious they all would be!

Before I could sort out my tangled thoughts, we were being whisked away to the embassy at such a clip I didn't have time to take in the strange, exotic landscape of Mexico City. My only impression was a blur of multicolored lights in the gathering

shadows of late afternoon, and bleached-out buildings punctuated by violent shocks of color. So delightful to think that there
were wildflowers blooming in December!

"Is the colonel really as shy as all that?" It seemed impossible,
that this extraordinary young man would suffer from such an ordinary affliction, just like me.

"Oh, yes. Talk to him about aviation—that's really the only
way you can get him to say more than 'yes,' 'no,' and 'pass the
salt,'" Mother said. Then she patted me on my knee. "Now, how
was your last term? Aren't you glad you listened to reason after all, when you thought you wanted to go to Vassar? Now
you're almost through, almost a Smith graduate, just like Elisabeth and me!"

I smiled, looked at my shoes—caked with the dust of travel—
and nodded, although my mouth was set in a particular prickly
way, my only outward sign of rebellion. After almost four years,
I still wished I'd been allowed to go to Vassar, as I'd so desperately wanted.

But I swallowed my annoyance and dutifully recited grades
and small academic triumphs, even as my mind raced ahead of the
two sleek embassy cars. *Colonel Lindbergh.* I hadn't counted on
meeting him so soon—or at all, really. I'd thought his visit was
merely an official stop on some grand tour of Latin America and
that he'd be gone long before my vacation started. My palms
grew clammy, and I wished I'd changed into a nicer frock on the
train. I'd never met a hero before. I worried that one of us would
be disappointed.

"I can't wait for the colonel to meet Elisabeth," Mother said,
as if she could read my thoughts. "Oh, and you, too, dear."

I nodded. But I knew what she meant. My older sister was a
beauty—*the* beauty, in the parlance of the Morrow family, as if
there could be room for only one. She had a porcelain complex-

ion, blond curls, round blue eyes with thick black eyelashes, and a darling of a nose, the master brushstroke that finished off her portrait of a face. Whereas I was *all* nose, with slanty eyes like Mother's, and dark hair; while I was shorter than Elisabeth, my figure was rounder. Too round, too busty and curvy, for the streamlined flapper fashions that were still all the rage this December of 1927.

"I'm sure I won't be able to think of a thing to say to him. I'm sure I won't be able to think of a thing to say to *anyone*. Oh, what a lot of bother this all is!" Gesturing at the plush red upholstery, the liveried driver, the twin flags—one of the United States, the other of Mexico—planted on the hood of the car, I allowed myself a rare outburst, meeting Mother's disapproving frown without blinking. Christmas was special. The rest of the year we might all be flung about, like a game of Puss-in-the-Corner. But Christmas was *home*, was safe, was the idea of family that I carried around with me the rest of the year, even as I recognized it didn't quite match up with reality. Already I missed my cozy room back home in Englewood, with my writing desk, my snug twin bed covered by the white chenille bedspread my grandmother had made as a bride, bookshelves full of childhood favorites—*Anne of Green Gables*, the *Just So Stories*, *Kim*. Stubbornly, I told myself that I would never get used to Daddy's new life as a diplomat, his ability to attract dashing young aviators notwithstanding. I much preferred him as a staid banker.

"Anne, please. Don't let your father hear you say this. He's very fond of the young man, and wants to help him with all his new responsibilities. I gather Colonel Lindbergh doesn't have much of a family, only his mother. It's our duty to welcome him into our little family circle."

I nodded, instantly vanquished; unable to explain to her how I felt. I never was able to explain—anything—to my mother.

Elisabeth she understood; Dwight she entrusted to my father. Con was young and bubbly and simply a delight. I was— Anne. The shy one, the strange one. Only in letters did my mother and I have anything close to true communion. In person, we didn't know what to do with each other.

And duty I understood all too well. If a history of our family was to be written, it could be summed up with that one word. *Duty.* Duty to others less fortunate, less happy, less educated; *less.* Although most of the time I thought there really couldn't be anyone in this world less than me.

"Now, don't worry yourself so, Anne," Mother continued, almost sympathetically; at least she patted my arm. "The colonel is a mere mortal, despite what your father and all the newspapers say."

"A handsome mere mortal," Con said with a dreamy sigh, and I couldn't help but laugh. When had my little sister started thinking of men as handsome?

But at her age, I had started to dream of heroes, I recalled. Sometimes, I still did.

The cars slowed and turned into a gated drive; we stopped in front of an enormous, showy palace—the embassy. *Our* embassy, I realized, and had to stifle an urge to giggle. I followed Mother and Con out of the car and hung back as Daddy marched up a grand stone staircase covered in a red carpet. A line of uniformed officers stood on both sides of the staircase, heralding our arrival.

"Can you believe it?" I whispered to Elisabeth, clinging to her hand for comfort. She shook her head, her eyes snapping with amusement even as her face paled. The flight of steps seemed endless, and Elisabeth was not strong, physically. But she took a deep breath and began to climb them, so I had no choice but to follow.

I couldn't look at the uniformed men; I couldn't look at the landing, where *he* was waiting. So I looked at the carpet instead, and hoped that I would never run out of it. Of course, I did; we were done climbing, finding ourselves on a shaded landing, and Mother was pushing Elisabeth forward, exclaiming, "Colonel Lindbergh, I'm so glad for you to meet my eldest daughter, Elisabeth!"

Elisabeth smiled and held out her hand, so naturally. As if she was meeting just another college boy, and not the hero of our time.

"I'm happy to meet you, Colonel," she said coolly. Then she glided past, following Daddy into the embassy.

"Oh, and of course, this is Anne," Mother said after a moment, pushing me forward as well.

I looked up—and up. And up. Into a face instantly familiar and yet so unexpected I almost gasped; piercing eyes, high forehead, cleft chin, just like in the newsreels; a face made for statues and history books, I couldn't help but think. And here he was suddenly right in front of me, amid my family in this unexpected, almost cartoonish, opulence. My head swam, and I wished I had never left my dormitory room.

He shook my hand without a smile, for a smile would be too ordinary for him. Then he dropped it quickly, as if it stung. He took a step back and bumped into a stone pillar. His expression never changed, although I thought I detected a faint blush. Then he turned to follow Elisabeth and Daddy into the embassy. Mother bustled after them.

I stood where I was for a long moment, wondering why my hand still tingled where he had held it.

COLONEL CHARLES LINDBERGH. *Lucky Lindy. The Lone Eagle.* Had there ever been a hero like him, in all of history?

Breathless, reeling from the blinding, golden brilliance of his presence, I could not imagine there had. Not even Christopher Columbus or Marco Polo in their time—a time when the world was different, larger; people, countries, entire continents hidden from one another. But suddenly the world was another planet entirely; much more compact, everyone now within reach. And it was all because of one young man from Minnesota, only four years older than me.

I had been in the library at Smith last May, writing a paper about Erasmus, when a total stranger grabbed me by my arm, laughing and crying both. "A man named Lindbergh flew across the ocean!" she shouted, and that was the first time I heard his name. She pulled me from my desk and we ran out into the quad, where the entire student body and faculty had gathered to link arms, whoop, and yell as we celebrated this person unknown to most of us until just half an hour before. It seemed incredible, like something from mythology, or from H. G. Wells; this boy flying across the Atlantic Ocean like a bird, like an eagle—and doing it alone. At the age of twenty-five, he had conquered not only the entire planet but all the sky above it.

I lived in a world of remarkable thinkers and dreamers; people whose greatest achievements usually involved the writing of books, the handshake of diplomacy, the paper chase of academia. Heroes were figures from history or from literature: knights errant, brave explorers crossing oceans fully aware that there might be dragons at the end of the rainbow. There were no heroes in these modern times, I had sincerely believed—until I found myself bumping elbows while doing the Charleston in a sea of collegiate humanity, shouting "Lucky—Lucky—Lin—DY!" at the top of my lungs.

And now, because I was the ambassador's daughter— miraculously! astoundingly!—I was going to spend my Christmas holiday with him, this doer of all doers, this hero of all heroes, amen.

That first evening, he and Daddy left immediately for an official reception, while the rest of us unpacked on the second floor of the embassy; the "family quarters," Mother explained, sotto voce, as she showed us all to our respective rooms.

"We have fourteen servants," Con enthused, as she followed me into my grand suite, complete with a private bathroom. "Fourteen! Mother doesn't know what to do!"

"I'm sure she'll find something to occupy her time," I said wryly. Our mother was as tightly wound as a bedside clock; gongs going off every hour as she filled her days with meetings and charitable dinners and fund-raisers and writing letters upon letters. I envied her energy, even as I resented it for taking her away from us. But it seemed to me that the hot, pulsating force of it affected me negatively when we were together, as if the two of us were a science experiment. It pushed me away so that I was always looking for dark corners and silences, space to think and feel and worry but never, ever, to *do*, despite—or, perhaps, *in spite* of—my mother's shining, bustling example. Contemplation, rather than action; that seemed to be my lot in life, and I was ashamed of it even as I craved it.

"Oh, she does! There's a party tomorrow, you know."

"On Christmas Eve?"

"Yes, she says it's intimate, just for the staff and all of us, but that probably means fifty, at least!"

"Oh, bother!" I sat down in a heap, putting the finishing disastrous touches to my crumpled traveling dress. A party. With Elisabeth. Old worries and doubts and paralyzing fears stole over me; no one would pay any attention to *me*, the colonel would dance with *her*, she'd look exquisite, I'd be a brown lump next to her, I wouldn't be able to think of anything to say, maybe the colonel would dance with me, but it would only be out of pity . . .

But it wasn't Elisabeth's fault, I scolded myself. My sister was simply one of the golden people, like Colonel Lindbergh: effortless, graceful creatures, like unicorns. The rest of us could only look at them in awe, through no fault of their own.

"What are you going to wear?" I asked Con wearily. She wrinkled her snub little nose.

"Something glamorous," she said, with such assurance that I had to laugh, even as I envied her as well. Why couldn't confidence be bottled, like perfume? I'd sneak into my sisters' rooms at night and steal a few spritzes, just as I sometimes stole their clothes.

"Well, you'd better help me find something," I told Con, moving toward my trunk.

"Something to catch an aviator's eye?" she retorted wickedly.

I shrugged. But I didn't contradict her.

THE NEXT EVENING, I hesitated outside the entrance to the formal reception room, calming my breath. For the first time since arriving, I noticed that the embassy wasn't really as glamorous as it initially seemed. It was like a grand dame's moth-eaten dress desperately covered in jewelry and gay scarves; the shining chandeliers and elaborate velvet portieres did not quite disguise the worn upholstery, the faint, spidery cracks in the ceiling. It was clean—I was sure Mother had something to do with that!—but shabby. I wondered how Mother liked her new home, or even *if* she did. She'd been planning a grand new house in Englewood when Daddy got his appointment; they were still going ahead with the building of it, but it would be years, now, before they could live in her dream home. Typically, she never allowed herself to voice a moment's remorse about it.

As I held my breath, I could hear her fluty laugh, Daddy's excited voice, Dwight's hoarse chuckle, Elisabeth's throaty murmur, and Con's bubbly giggles. Also, a strange new instrument: a high-pitched yet masculine voice, offering only monosyllabic answers. Colonel Lindbergh. I felt my face flush, the bodice of my evening frock strain tightly against my breasts, flattened down as much as possible by a very hot, very uncomfortable rubber brassiere that Elizabeth Bacon, my roommate at Smith, had convinced me to buy.

"Wherever can Anne be?" Mother asked, and I imagined her looking at her watch, her mouth a thin line of impatience. So I took a deep breath—but not too deep in that cursed brassiere—and cleared my throat before entering the room.

"Here I am, Mother. I'm sorry—I'm afraid I got lost."

The room was brilliant—so many chandeliers and candles—that at first I had to blink, adjusting my vision. Then I saw the forms of my family huddled around an enormous grand piano at the far end of the room. I had to cross that room somehow, and I blushed to think that they would all be staring at me. Oh, why hadn't I arrived earlier? I could have slipped in unnoticed, not causing such a fuss—I felt the heat of their collective gaze upon my cheeks as I hurried toward them, my eyes staring only at my brocade evening shoes, the heels sinking into the plush carpeting. At last I reached them—I felt my father grasp my hand—but when I looked up, I saw that no one was watching me. And then I almost giggled at the absurdity of my vanity. I had made no grand entrance, after all. How could I, when *he* was in the room?

For every member of my family was turned toward Charles Lindbergh, and so I could easily slip behind my father, taking my usual place at the edge of the crowd. As I did so, Mother murmured, "Then leave a little earlier next time, dear."

"Yes, sorry, Mother." I peeked over Daddy's shoulder; Colonel Lindbergh was standing on the other side of the piano, next to Elisabeth. While Daddy was all pink and round in his evening clothes, and my brother, Dwight, a solid brick, the colonel was tall and slim as a knife. He looked uncomfortable in black tails with white waistcoat; he stood stiffly, his elbows askew, his shoulders pinched. In almost all the newsreels and photographs I'd seen, he'd been in his flying clothes. An entire nation had memorized his worn jacket, jodhpurs, helmet with the goggles tucked under his arm, the scarf around his throat. It was jarring to see him out of this costume, away from his airplane.

But the face was the same—the heroic brow, stern chin, high cheekbones. His eyes were so blue as to be startling; I decided I'd never seen blue eyes before, until that moment. They were the color of morning, the color of the ocean; the color of the sky.

He caught me looking at him, then he looked away and began to tap his fingers nervously on top of the piano, as if playing a tune only he could hear. That was when I noticed his hands, his fingers long and tapered. I imagined them gripping the control stick of his plane, steering it across that endless ocean; I thought them more than capable of the task.

"Aren't you, Anne?"

Someone had asked me a question and I had no idea what it was, or who had asked it. So I nodded like an idiot and said, "Yes," and was amazed at the sound of my own voice. It sounded normal, while inside, my heart was still beating so wildly I felt my entire body throb with each pulse.

"That's nice," the colonel said after a very small, very brisk nod, affirming the answer to the unheard question. Again, he could barely meet my gaze. His fingers began to tap even faster.

At that, my heart began to slow down. Was it true? Was the heroic Colonel Lindbergh as nervous around girls as Mother and Con said?

Apparently, he was. For as we milled about, sipping lemonade and nibbling at sandwiches brought in by an army of butlers, conversation progressed in a series of starts and stops; hesitation followed by sudden, unexpected bursts of chatter that were over before they'd had a chance fully to take off. Only once—when Daddy asked the colonel about the difference between a monoplane and a biplane—did our guest relax. With grace and confidence, he explained the differences in a long monologue that left no room for interruption; his somewhat reedy voice smoothed into a rhythm not unlike, I imagined, the purr of an airplane engine. He leaned forward, his blue eyes glistening, his fingers finally at rest, as he expounded on the differences and advantages of one set of wings (the monoplane) versus two (the biplane).

As none of us, naturally, could contribute anything to this subject, small talk resumed—tossed out easily by Elisabeth and my mother, while Daddy beamed and Dwight devoured enormous quantities of sandwiches. Con even dared to tease the colonel now and then, and he didn't seem to mind. Meanwhile, I studied my surroundings, achingly homesick for Englewood. Nothing in this cavernous hall was familiar to me, save for the tattered American flag draped over the gilt fireplace mantel: the flag my grandfather had carried, as a drummer boy, in the Civil War. There weren't even any framed family photographs, like there were on every surface back home. Yet I was curious about the embassy, in the way that one is curious about a museum; I promised myself I'd go exploring later, after everyone else was in bed.

"I understand you're at Smith?" someone asked, and after a

moment it dawned on me that the questioner was Colonel Lindbergh.

Surprised—I had found a corner, a good one, out of the range of any light, and had fancied myself hidden from view—I nodded. Then I realized he probably couldn't see me, cloaked as I was in shadows. "Yes. I am."

"Elisabeth graduated from Smith two years ago," Mother said brightly.

"Yes, you see, Colonel, it is decreed by proclamation. All the Morrow girls go to Smith, and all the Morrow boys go to Amherst," Elisabeth explained, and I couldn't help but admire the dry, almost bored tone of her voice, the exact same tone she used with lesser specimens of the male species. "Where did you go to school?"

The colonel stiffened, and thrust his chin out. "The University of Wisconsin. Although I did not graduate."

"Really?" Dwight's voice cracked with incredulity. "You didn't graduate? How extraordinary—what did your parents say to that? I can't imagine what Pa here would say if I don't graduate!"

I watched the colonel's face as my brother nattered on. It was as if his features had settled into a mask; I had never seen a man so immobile—yet so proud. And, I suspected, so humiliated.

"Oh, Dwight! Hush!" I blurted out, surprising myself and my brother, who gave me a gravely wounded look. "How could the colonel have graduated and still learned to fly and accomplish what he's done?"

"Yes, yes, Anne is correct. Young man, if you accomplish a tenth of what the colonel here has, I'll be satisfied. Surprised, but satisfied," Daddy said, as he patted the colonel heartily on the back—and gave my brother a familiar disapproving look. And

I sucked in my breath and felt a pang of guilt. Poor Dwight! There would be yet another "talking to" behind the closed door of Daddy's study, followed by the return, in full force, of my brother's stutter.

Colonel Lindbergh didn't reply. Instead, he looked at me in a curious, almost clinical way—until our gazes met for a confusing second that pushed me back in my corner and him back to studying the top of the piano.

Suddenly, thankfully, there were musicians setting up at the other end of the room, even more candles were lit, a fire started in the fireplace, and Mother, Father, the colonel, and Elisabeth were standing in an informal receiving line. Soon enough the room was full of people; women in fashionably short long-waisted gowns, jeweled bands about their bobbed or marcelled hair, elbow-length white gloves; men in black tie and tails, some with brilliant sashes gleaming with diplomatic medals across their chests. Several of my cousins had also traveled down, keen to see their uncle the ambassador. This grand affair had no relation to the intimate Christmas Eves of my childhood, when we would go to church, then come home and sit in Mother and Daddy's bedroom, listening as she read from the gospel of Luke, before praying silently while the snow fell, like a benediction, outside.

Now musicians were playing snippets of Bach and, in honor of the season, Handel. I floated along the edges of the crowd, content to watch; no one really knew me, so as long as I stayed away from the receiving line, I was spared having to be introduced to all these strangers.

But none of them had eyes for anyone in the room except for our guest of honor; Colonel Lindbergh was the star on top of the Christmas tree. No, he *was* the Christmas tree. There was an actual fir tree stuck in a corner, lit up brilliantly, decorated all in gold—but no one paid any attention to it.

"The poor man," Elisabeth whispered in my ear. I spun around, surprised that she had found me, half hidden as I was by a heavy gold velvet portiere. I had expected her to remain in the receiving line. "I'm sure he's miserable."

"He doesn't look it," I replied, watching the colonel. He smiled pleasantly as he grasped each hand thrust eagerly his way.

"But look. His face—it doesn't change."

"No, I guess it doesn't. It's like a mask." It was true; his smile never varied, never deepened or diminished, and his brow remained smooth. But it was impossible not to be awed by his poise, the unflinching way he looked at the long line of people in front of him. Had it been me at whom people were staring in that way—that rather frightening, mindlessly adoring way—I would not have been so calm!

"You know," Elisabeth continued, amused, "all the men want to be him. All those lawyers and diplomats, look at them just hanging on his every word! They all wish, secretly, that they had the same courage he does, but they all know, just as secretly, that they don't. It's sad, when you think of it."

"And the women?" I asked impulsively.

"Oh, for the older women, he's the son they never had. For the younger women, he's the husband of their dreams!"

"It must be hard to live up to that. Why did he come here, then—surely he's tired of all this?" I turned to Elisabeth; as she watched the colonel, a small smile played about her Kewpie doll lips. She was, I realized with a sinking sensation in my breast, interested in him, as Mother had most likely hoped—and as some of the gossip articles had hinted, when news of the colonel's impending Mexico visit had first appeared.

I shook my head, trying to rid myself of any feelings of jealousy; of course, the colonel barely knew I existed. How could he notice me, next to my sister? Me, a dull brown pinecone amid all this tinsel and polish and gilt?

"Oh, some of Daddy's colleagues formed a commission to promote aviation as diplomacy, and the colonel is the finest ambassador they could get. And, of course, you know Daddy met him at the White House when he first returned from Paris."

I nodded; Calvin Coolidge was an old school chum of my father's, and the reason why we were here in Mexico.

"Daddy offered to advise the colonel about all the money being thrown at him, and when the colonel asked what he could do by way of thanks, Daddy said, 'Fly down to Mexico!' "

I laughed. "That's just like Daddy!"

"And it was brilliant, because he couldn't have asked for a better public relations coup. The president of Mexico is over the moon, you know. And, really, central casting couldn't have found a better man for the job. Just look at him. The colonel is quite handsome."

"You really think so?"

"Well, of course! Don't you?"

"I suppose, in a way," I replied carefully. But I felt my sister's bright, hard gaze turn on me anyway. Oh, she was so like Mother at times!

"Anne, there's something I want you to understand," she began, in a strangely ominous tone. But before she could continue, Mother swooped down upon us.

"Why, girls, there you are! Hiding over here! I told you I want your help with Colonel Lindbergh. He's being mobbed by people—oh, those women! You'd think he was the second coming of Valentino!—and the dancing is about to start. He insists that he won't dance, and so I thought that you could sit with him, Elisabeth, and keep some of those horrid women away—did you see the countess? She's twice his age, at the very least. And, of course, Anne, you can help, dear. No one expects *you* to dance. Now I must go talk to the president. Señor Calles, it's such an honor!" And just as quickly, Mother glided over to greet the president of Mexico (whom I recognized from a newspaper photo).

"What if *I* wanted to dance?" Elisabeth said, in as close to a grumble as I'd ever heard from her. I followed reluctantly as she weaved her way toward Colonel Lindbergh. He was still standing next to my father, that grimly gracious smile on his face.

"Do you?"

My sister stopped, spun around, and looked at me. "No!" We both laughed, united, once more, in exasperation at our mother. "But she might have asked me first!"

Still laughing, she tugged on Colonel Lindbergh's sleeve and tilted her face up to his; she was so pretty, her face flushed, her fair curls bouncing, that I knew the colonel would be helpless. I'd never met a man who hadn't first fallen for my sister before being rebuffed and finally noticing me.

But Elisabeth wouldn't rebuff Colonel Lindbergh; she was famously particular, defiantly unmarried despite my parents' best efforts, but even she couldn't find fault with the most famous man on earth.

And realizing this set me free. Why should I be concerned about any impression I might make on the colonel, when I knew I would make none? Soon I was seated on a sofa in front of the fireplace next to Elisabeth, Colonel Lindbergh on her other side; I knew I was invisible in this situation, and so I behaved as such. I let Elisabeth take up the ball of conversation, while I indulged in my favorite pastime—people watching.

Daddy was in the center of a group of men his age, some of whom I recognized from the board of directors at J. P. Morgan & Co., where he had previously been a partner. They were all talking animatedly—but Daddy was the most animated of all. The smallest one by at least a head—he was only five-foot-three inches tall—he more than made up in energy what he lacked in height and background. He was the only one of his crowd who came from poverty, a fact he never bothered to hide; he was fiercely proud of his humble background, and never let any of us children forget it. *Education, education, education:* those were his watchwords; so much so that once, a family friend asked me, puzzled, "What is it with you Morrows and education?"

But education had served my father well as he graduated with honors from Amherst, then Columbia Law School, where he met many of the sons of the bankers who would summon him to J. P. Morgan. And now, he was a diplomat; at the beginning of what many felt was a promising political career. Some even predicted he could reach the White House!

Mother was swimming about, soothing and greeting and smoothing over any turbulence caused by Daddy's occasional outbursts. It was her usual role. She was as silky as he was rumpled; even tonight, his tuxedo looked two sizes too big. Daddy always claimed that he had married up, and nights like this gave merit to that claim. I was proud of my mother, despite our misunderstandings; she looked every inch the diplomat's wife in her tasteful green gown, long gloves, and ability to be everywhere at once without seeming to break her slow, regal glide. She always appeared taller than Daddy, even though she was an inch shorter. Both of them were graying now; Daddy's hair was thinning, while Mother's wiry curls were captured in an old-fashioned Edwardian sweep. She claimed she had no time for the weekly visit to the hairdresser that the newer styles required.

Assured of my invisibility, I didn't even mind the stares, not entirely furtive, that continued to be directed toward Colonel Lindbergh. He really was a magnet; a raw, yet strangely charismatic figure, direct and true. No polish, no practiced weariness;

watching him, you couldn't help but sense the impossibility of what he had accomplished—and yet also the inevitability of it. He exuded such a quiet self-confidence; every movement he made was so graceful, so deliberate. Even if his speech occasionally faltered while conversing with my sister, his eyes never did. They seemed fixed, always, on something important, something serious, just beyond the horizon.

"Would you like to, Miss Morrow?" The colonel was leaning forward, addressing me; surprised, I instinctively moved away from him. I couldn't help but notice that he colored a little when I did.

"Would I—would I like to what?"

"Go up in an airplane. Your sister has requested that I take her up, and naturally I would like to extend that courtesy to you. If you'd like to."

"Flying? Me?" I couldn't help it; my mouth flopped open like a fish. But I had never even imagined such a thing!

"Don't worry, it's perfectly safe," the colonel said with a smile—the first genuine one I had seen from him. Suddenly he looked quite boyish; he ducked his head, and his hair fell out of its careful part so that it brushed his forehead. "Flying is perfectly safe. Up there on the currents, like the birds—it's a holy thing. Nothing has ever made me feel so—so in control of my own destiny. So above all the petty strife and cares of the world. It's down here where the danger is, you know—not up there."

I had thought the colonel capable of many things, but not of poetry. And listening to him, I realized, with a thrill, that I did want to fly; to experience this holy thing, to soar above the earth as he had done. To be above all; to be above worry and fear and, yes, petty strife, but mainly, simply to be above *myself*—this awkward body, this mind full of doubt and heart full of longing.

"Oh, I would—" I began, but then realized a mob of people

was standing in front of us, listening to our conversation as if we were actors in a play. Suddenly my tongue felt thick and clumsy in my mouth, and I simply shook my head, knowing that I was disappointing him, but unable to respond as I wished with so many people watching.

But this time, he didn't color or withdraw; his blue eyes looked at me with a curious expression. Literally *curious*—as if I was a new species he had just discovered. Blushing, I turned away, and was grateful to see Mother hurrying up to us, a tight smile on her face—imperceptible worry in her eyes.

"What do I hear? Are you going to take my daughters up in your plane, Colonel?"

"If they would like to go. Naturally, I extend the invitation to you, Mrs. Morrow."

"What an honor! Elisabeth, are you quite sure? Anne?"

"Of course!" Elisabeth laughed and tossed back her head. "I can't imagine anyone I'd rather have take me up for my first flight!"

"I'm not—I'll think about it," I mumbled, wishing that all eyes weren't still on me; knowing that were I to go up in his plane, even more eyes would be watching: newspapermen, photographers, newsreel cameras.

To my relief, the music started up again—songs from *Show Boat,* the most popular show of the year—and instantly the entire attitude of the room relaxed. Waiters were busy running to and fro with trays of cocktails—there was no Prohibition in Mexico!—and people were beginning to pair up and dance. Dwight pulled me off the sofa, squeaking, "Come, Anne—let's do a Virginia reel! I'll get them to play one, just like we used to." And I, too, was out on the dance floor, linking arms with my brother and cousins as we flew about to a Mexican trumpet attempting to warble its way through "Arkansas Traveler."

I loved dancing! I loved the freedom, the silliness of the

Shimmy, the absolute joy of the Charleston; for some reason I could lose myself to the music and the rhythm in a way I couldn't lose myself otherwise. The more crowded the dance floor, the more fun I had, and soon Dwight and I were bumping into bodies, tripping over feet, but we didn't care. We used to perform this silly little dance at birthday parties when we were young; Elisabeth would pound the piano, playing some Stephen Foster song, and Mother and Daddy, seated side by side on the sofa, with Con on Mother's lap, would laugh and applaud as if they'd never seen us before.

But it had been ages since the last time we'd danced like this; ages in which we had both grown up, gone to school, attempted to leave behind our childish ways. I flashed a grateful smile at my brother for giving me this gift of a self I had just recently begun to mourn. And for helping me imagine, if only for an instant, that we were all back home in New Jersey.

Only for an instant. I was in the middle of a turn, one arm linked in my brother's, the other arm holding up my skirt, when I caught Colonel Lindbergh watching me. He wasn't smiling; he was studying me, a faint frown creasing his forehead. Even from all that way across the room, I felt the weight of his obvious disapproval. Of course, I was being ridiculous! A girl my age, dancing a child's dance, when he, not so much older, had crossed an entire ocean!

Suddenly my face was so hot I felt as if an aura, like the sun, was encircling my head; dropping my brother's arm, I whispered, "Oh, Dwight, how silly we are! We're not so little anymore; we're not children."

"So what, Anne? We're just having fun!"

Just then my cousin Dickie threw a black lace doily on my head, like a mantilla, and stuck a rose in my hair; pulling me by the arm he dragged me in front of Colonel Lindbergh.

"Doesn't Anne look like a señorita, Colonel?" He laughed. For a moment, I *felt* like a señorita in my red dress, flushed skin; I had a fragmentary glimpse of my hair in a mirror, dark and shining with that red rose against it, and I tilted my chin to meet my gay reflection, smiling.

But in that mirror I saw the colonel sitting there, watching me. He looked uncomfortable, as if his shirt collar was too tight; when our gazes met, he turned away, frowning.

"Oh, Dickie!" I pulled the flower out and threw it to the floor. "How silly!" And then I stumbled off, leaving them all to laugh at me. It was absurd, carrying on like that—what was I thinking? Embarrassed tears filled my eyes, and I pushed through the crowd, ignoring a matron who peered, fish-eyed, at me through a crystal wineglass and intoned, "Goodness, I've never seen a face so scarlet!"

Was it? I pressed my hand to my cheek as I fled; it was like touching an oven door. Finally finding myself in an empty hall, I ran as far away from the reception room as I could until I discovered a back staircase. Stumbling up the stairs to the second floor, I wildly bounced from hall to hall, room to room, like a billiard ball. I was so lost as to be truly frightened. All the doors looked exactly the same. How on earth would I find mine? Oh, I wished I was back home! And that I had never met Colonel Lindbergh, so smug, so arrogant—yes, that was it! His *arrogance* as he stared at me, as if he were God or Calvin Coolidge himself, sitting so stiffly on that sofa—"I don't dance," he'd told Mother, and immediately made everyone else in the room feel silly for wanting to. How dare he?

My heart was a furnace, fueled by my anger. Stopping to fan myself with the doily, which somehow had clung to my head through my mad dash, I found myself in front of a mirror with a cracked silver frame. The same mirror that I had consulted to make sure my nose wasn't shiny when I left my room earlier this evening. With a hysterical little hiccup, I pushed open a door that revealed my familiar red wool slippers laid out next to a four-poster bed, the flowered kimono I used as a dressing gown spread out on the coverlet.

Once inside, I flung myself down on the bed, dry-eyed. But now my anger was gone, leaving room for the familiar, heavy weight of uncertainty and guilt. Had I hurt Dwight by leaving him in the middle of the dance floor? Had I made a spectacle of myself, running from the room? But as time went by and no one knocked on my door, and still I heard the gay sounds of the party below—the music, the tinkling of glass, the sudden bursts of laughter—I realized that I hadn't. No one was going to come looking for me, after all—and I wasn't entirely sure how I felt about that.

I was sitting on the edge of my bed, calm now, my cheeks no longer burning, my skin no longer plastered to that awful rubber brassiere, when I heard footsteps pause outside my door. An envelope was thrust beneath it, and then the footsteps went, rather hurriedly, away.

Thinking it was a message from Dwight or Con, I ran to pick it up. It wasn't from either; I could tell that from the lack of ink-blots and thumbprints on the envelope. My name was written very neatly in a foreign hand: the precise, measured handwriting one would expect from a military man.

Or an aviator.

I felt a rush of excitement pummel me, punching my heart into high gear, buckling my knees. But I wouldn't allow myself to open it.

When I was a little girl, I had pleased my father most by being the child who could make a lollipop last the longest, who never asked for an advance on her allowance. "Anne's the disciplined one," he always bragged to his friends. It was the only character-istic I had of note. And like any person with only one talent, I cherished and guarded it. I no longer knew what it was to sneak a cookie before dinner, or buy a new frock just because.

I placed the envelope on the bed, then began my nightly ritual of slipping out of my dress, my step-ins, unsnapping my garters, rolling my stockings down, unbinding my chest, folding my lin-gerie and placing it all in a little silk bag hanging from the door-knob. I chose, after a long moment of grave contemplation, a long-sleeved pink lisle nightgown from a cupboard, where all my clothes, miraculously brushed and pressed by one of those fourteen servants, were now hanging. Sitting down at my dress-ing table, I unpinned my long brown hair and brushed it one hundred times, the brush occasionally getting caught in my wiry tangles, tugging my scalp until my eyes watered. And even though, all this time, I could see the white envelope waiting on the bright red coverlet of my bed, like an unopened Christmas present, I still took the time to smooth some Ponds Night Cream carefully on my forehead and cheeks, with a few extra pats for my throat.

Only then did I go to bed; pulling the coverlet up over my knees, I finally reached for the envelope. My hands were shaking, but in a delicious way; for once in my life, I wasn't afraid of what I might find waiting for me. Never before had I opened an enve-lope without being sure it contained some dire piece of news.

Miss Morrow,

I looked for you, but was told you had left the reception early. I cannot say that I blame you. I don't enjoy such gather-ings myself although, naturally, I much appreciate your fa-ther's hospitality on my behalf.

After our brief conversation on the sofa, I could not help but think that despite your silence concerning the matter, you did want to be taken up in my airplane, after all. I believe I understand your hesitation. I would not have liked to have taken my first airplane ride surrounded by newspaper reporters and photographers, either. Hence my proposal.

If you would like to fly with me, meet me in the kitchen at four-fifteen a.m. We can go up and be back here before breakfast is served, and no one will ever be the wiser.

I do, however, acknowledge the possibility that I have misinterpreted your intentions. I will not be offended if you do not choose to meet me.

> *Sincerely,*
> *Charles Augustus Lindbergh*

By the time I finished reading, my hands were no longer shaking, although my rib cage was—for I was laughing. Silently, prayerfully—but I was laughing, nonetheless. *If you would like to fly with me* . . . oh, miraculous words! Intended for me and me alone!

Colonel Lindbergh had looked for *me*—and, finding me, had understood me. He had known everything that I was thinking but could not express with all those people listening—that even as I longed to experience flying as he had described it, just beneath my longing was the fear that somehow I would fail this test, this test of gravity and expectations. And if I did fail—if I embarrassed myself by crying or being sick or chickening out at the last moment—I did not want it reported on the front pages of every newspaper in the land!

Elisabeth was cut out for that kind of publicity. She would not fail, for she had never failed at anything in her life. Yet I suspected that my desire to fly was more sincere than hers. Despite her obvious interest in Colonel Lindbergh, I was certain she had asked to be taken up primarily because it was expected of her.

There was a certain safety in being the plain one, I realized, not for the first time. Dwight was the heir apparent, expected to graduate Amherst magna cum laude simply because Daddy had done so on scholarship. Elisabeth was expected to be dazzling and beautiful and marry brilliantly. Con was too young yet, and too spoiled, anyway; she was the pet of the family, loved and unquestioned.

I was expected to be—what? No one had ever articulated it to me; I knew only that I wasn't to disappoint or disgrace my family, but beyond that, no one seemed to care.

Or—did someone care?

No, of course not; with a stern little shake of my head, I reminded myself that in real life, heroes were not interested in girls like me. It was simple politeness that compelled the colonel to ask; after all, I was the daughter of his host.

Still, he *had* asked, and that was enough to make me grin stupidly at my own reflection in the mirror opposite the bed for a long moment, before suddenly becoming aware of the lateness of the hour. Slipping the note—*his* note—inside my pillowcase, I wound my alarm clock tightly, setting it for four a.m. My stomach was so full of butterflies and other insects with busy, brushing wings—entirely appropriate under the circumstances, I couldn't help but think!—that I could hardly fall asleep. And when at last I did, I know I slept lightly.

As if I remembered, even in my slumber, that I had a dream beneath my pillow that I did not wish to crush.

CHAPTER 2

THE NEXT MORNING, I was almost late. Not because I overslept—
I was awake a good half hour before the alarm went off—but
because, for the first time in my life, I couldn't decide what to
wear.

Normally I didn't fuss with all that. I had an ample, if somewhat boring, wardrobe that I purchased in New York with my
mother every season, mainly from Lord & Taylor. Day dresses,
skirts, sweaters, tea gowns, one or two modest evening gowns,
tennis dresses, golf skirts.

But not a single flying garment among them! Sorting through
the clothes I had brought with me, I could not decide what would
be appropriate to wear while soaring through the sky. I had seen
photographs of a few aviatrixes, but they all had been dressed in
clothing similar to what Colonel Lindbergh usually wore:
jodhpur-like pants, snug jackets, helmets with goggles, scarves.

My only pair of jodhpurs was back at school; there were no
stables at the embassy, so I hadn't thought to bring them. I had
brought my golf clothes, however, and finally I decided on them:
sweater and pleated skirt, flat rubber-soled shoes, knee socks. I
braided my hair and pinned it up, and at the last minute, grabbed
the wool coat I had worn on the train. I then ran, on tiptoe,
down the private stairs I had discovered the night before. After

going the wrong way down a hall, I turned around and found myself in the large kitchen, empty at this hour with all the white enamel cookware scrubbed and gleaming, waiting to be called into service. There wasn't a single sign of the party from the night before; no unwashed trays or even a stray lipstick-stained glass.

But then I realized the kitchen wasn't empty. Colonel Lindbergh was standing stiffly by a stove in worn brown flying clothes, a leather jacket, his familiar helmet with the goggles in his hand. As I dashed into the room, he looked at his watch, a faint frown creasing his forehead.

"You're late."

"I know—I'm sorry. I didn't quite know what to wear. Will this do?" Ridiculously, I held my skirt out as if I were a German milkmaid.

"It'll have to, although trousers would probably be best."

"I didn't bring any."

"I didn't think of that. It shouldn't matter, anyway. The coat's good."

"Thank you." The inadequacy of my words rang stupidly in my ears.

Without another word, he turned to go out the kitchen door. Without another word, I followed.

Outside, in a wide graveled drive at the back of the embassy, were a chauffeur and a waiting car; how he had arranged for them, I had no idea. We both got into the backseat—he opened the door for me—and the car sped off.

At this hour, only the edges of sky were turning pink; still, it illuminated the streets of Mexico City so that I could get a better look than I had on our way from the train station. The narrow streets were empty. The buildings were almost all the same white, either stone or flimsy slats, with arched doorways and windows, reddish-orange clay roofs. Flowers spilled out of every corner, from window boxes, around signposts, even horse troughs. Vivid reds and pinks, showy flowers that I'd seen grown only in hothouses—orchids and hibiscus and jasmine. We passed an enormous square with a fountain in the middle that looked like a gathering place; I imagined it filled with dancing señoritas in long black mantillas and trumpet-playing men in sombreros.

Mixed in with the old and quaint was new; modern buildings—hotels, mainly—were going up on every corner. Prohibition had helped turn Mexico City into a pleasure place for the rich, and the money they were willing to spend in order to drink freely was in abundant evidence.

So absorbed was I that I almost forgot Colonel Lindbergh, mute as he was beside me. It wasn't until we headed out of town on a dirt road that I became aware, once more, of his masculine presence. After I finally ran out of things to gape at, I settled back only to find the colonel had wedged himself into the farthest corner of the seat away from me. He was still frowning. Blushing, I tried to explain my rudeness.

"I'm sorry—I haven't had a chance to see Mexico yet, except from the train."

"I understand," he said. Then he turned and stared straight ahead, his chiseled cheekbones and smooth brow immobile.

I thought and thought of something to say; something important enough for him. But I couldn't, and so we rode the rest of the way in silence. It wasn't long; soon the car turned off the road and bumped across a wide, flat field dotted with several outbuildings. The platform where Daddy and all the dignitaries must have stood, waiting for his landing days earlier, still remained; now-tattered bunting featuring the colors of both the Mexican and United States flags was suddenly illuminated by the headlights of our car.

Outside the largest structure, a horse stood, tethered to a railing.

The car stopped, and we both got out; I followed the colonel into that building, so large it resembled a barn. Instead of being divided into stalls, however, the place was cavernous. Instead of horses, planes were housed within it. And instead of the fragrance of sweet hay and horse manure, the air was noxious with the fumes from oil and gasoline.

"Good morning," the colonel called to a man wearing mechanic's coveralls who scrambled hastily from a camp bed. There was a rifle next to the bed. The man yawned, but then his face creased into a proud grin as he recognized his visitor.

"Oh, it's you, Colonel!"

"I trust there's been no trouble?"

"None at all! But of course, you see, I have my weapon. Just in case, Colonel."

Nodding briskly, the colonel grabbed a wrench and strode in the direction of an airplane parked at the far end of the barn. It took me a moment to realize that this was his plane; *the* plane. The *Spirit of St. Louis*.

I took off after him, glad for my flat golf shoes, as there were treacherous puddles of slippery grease dotting the ground. "Oh, Colonel, may I see it?"

"Please, call me Charles," he called over his shoulder.

"If you'll call me Anne."

My escort stopped for a moment. He nodded slowly, as if mulling over the proposition. Then he said, "Anne."

It was a good thing he didn't say anything else, as suddenly my ears were filled with the roaring sound of my own pulse. How can I describe how it felt, to have *him* say my name? Oh, it was rubbish, ridiculous, I knew, but for once I felt as if I might understand the literal definition of the word *swoon*.

Then he continued toward his plane. "I just want to tighten an axle. I noticed it was loose when I landed."

"Why did that man have a rifle?"

Charles sighed. "To protect my plane from souvenir hunters. They tore off pieces of it when I landed in France. Since then, I've had someone guarding it at all times."

"Oh." I scrambled to keep up with him; he was so tall, his stride so long. And I was so short. We passed several planes, and I wondered which one we would fly in. Of course I knew, even before I saw it up close, we couldn't fly in the *Spirit of St. Louis.* It was famously built just for one; one courageous, lone flyer.

Who was now on his hands and knees, crawling under his machine. I watched, awed; I had seen this plane only in newsreels. So while I recognized the wide, blunt wings; the cockpit built so that its pilot could see only out the sides, not the front—there was some technical reason for this, I remembered, but couldn't recall it; the jaunty *Spirit of St. Louis* painted on the nose, black against the silver of the body; still, I couldn't help but think that it was so much smaller in person. Just like a movie star; just like Gloria Swanson—I giggled, remembering. How odd to think that this plane was now even more famous than she was!

"What's so funny?" that reedy voice demanded, from beneath the plane.

"Nothing."

"When I landed the other day I thought I felt something give. I thought—aha! There it is!" And after a few methodical grunts, the colonel emerged, still on his hands and knees, from beneath the plane; his face was greasy, and his hair flopped down into his eyes. He had a grin on his face as he remained on the ground, resting his back against the wheel of his plane.

He looked so relaxed now, not the stiff, uncomfortable figure in evening clothes from the night before. I hadn't realized how tense he had been then. Now his limbs looked loose, lanky; he patted the plane in the same manner as a cowboy caressing his favorite horse. I almost felt as if I was intruding on an intimate scene.

"May I touch it?" I asked, surprised by my boldness.

"Of course!" Charles leaped to his feet. "Go on—you can't hurt it!" He grinned again, this time so wide that his entire face relaxed, his eyes crinkling up boyishly.

"Why, it's fabric!" I couldn't believe it; this machine that had carried him all the way across the ocean was made of nothing but cloth and wire!

"Yes. Fabric covered in dope—that's a kind of strengthening liquid. That's what makes it strong enough but also light enough to fly."

"Is the plane we're going up in made of fabric, as well?"

"Yes. But don't worry, Miss—Anne. I assure you, it's perfectly safe."

"Oh, I'm sure it is." I wanted to explain to him that I wasn't afraid; how could I be? There was no one I trusted more than Charles Lindbergh, even though I had just met him. Who else could I trust to launch me into the sky?

The next minutes were full of activity; after Charles inspected it, the guard hooked up the nose of a different plane—a biplane, I recognized from Charles's discourse the night before—to a tractor. This one was painted blue with a vivid orange trim, not the monochromatic silver and gray of the *Spirit of St. Louis*. With a startling roar that scattered the swallows gathered near the entrance, the tractor fired up and towed the plane out of the building. Charles found a helmet and goggles for me, and I followed him—again, running to keep up—out of the barn and to the plane, which was now at the end of a narrow, closely cropped strip of grass in the middle of the field. In the faint morning light,

I could barely make out a flag at the end of this runway, waving in the gentle breeze.

The air was warm and smelled sweet, like rock candy. There were a few white, puffy clouds high above, and I couldn't believe that in a few moments I would be among them.

Buckling my helmet beneath my chin, I eyed the plane; the two seats were in tandem, the one in back slightly higher than the one in front. They were both open to the sky.

"How do we get in?"

"We climb up on the wing," Charles answered. Then he leaned toward me and tightened the helmet strap. "There." He studied me solemnly, nodding, as if assuring himself that I was as snug as possible. I felt the careful weight of his attention yet knew, at the same time, that I was merely part of his preflight checklist, represented by a piece of paper he had tucked in a pocket; he had already measured the fuel, tested the throttle, wiped the smudges off his goggles. Then he busied himself with pulling on his leather gloves.

"It's very loud and very windy up there," he told me, his voice suddenly all business, brisk and gruff. "We won't be able to communicate. There are controls in your seat, but don't worry, they're not operable. I'll be in back, you'll be in front. Make sure you buckle your harness strap when you get in. I'd keep my hands inside if I were you. Oh—and chew this." Reaching into the pocket of his jacket, he pulled out a stick of gum.

"Why?"

"It'll pop your ears. You'll see."

"All right." Obediently, I removed the wrapper and popped the gum in my mouth. "Anything else?" I mumbled, chewing away until my jaws ached.

"No. Just relax. And have fun."

Then I was being helped up onto the wing, made of that same

fabric as the *Spirit of St. Louis*, but it felt sturdy, stable, beneath my feet. Climbing into the small seat in front, I found a harness that reached across my chest, and secured it. The top wing of the plane formed a kind of canopy above me. There was a stick and a round instrument panel in front of me: the controls Charles had told me about. There was also a pedal at my feet. I was cramped in this cockpit and couldn't have stretched my legs. I wondered how he had stayed in such a place for forty hours, even in the larger cockpit of the *Spirit of St. Louis;* his legs were so long.

I felt, before I heard or saw, the propeller turn in front of me; the plane shuddered, and a slap of wind hit my face. The engine sputtered, then roared to life, and I chewed my gum vigorously to drown out the surprisingly loud whine. Then we were rambling down the field, picking up speed; I could feel every rut and bump in the ground as we tumbled over it, still clumsy, so clumsy—how could we ever take wing? The ground came toward me faster and faster, bumpier and bumpier, until suddenly, it was smooth; no more clumsiness, no more friction. It was as if I were suspended in time, suspended in air—and then, as my stomach decided to test its own boundaries, I realized that I was.

I was *airborne*. My heart was rising in my throat, my stomach first leaping, then tumbling, as we went up, up, up . . . the tips of trees, green, leafy, so close I was sure I could touch them. Then they were below me.

The plane banked toward the right, and suddenly I was looking back down at the airfield, the buildings, the horse getting smaller and smaller until it turned into a toy. The air slapped and then tore at my face; my eyes stung, even behind the goggles. My ears felt as if they were full of water. This pressure in them built until I remembered the gum. Chewing furiously, I felt first my left, then my right ear pop, and I could hear again the reassuring groan of the engine, the wind whistling past my face.

The plane leveled out. Now I couldn't stop looking, craning my head this way and that; below, on my right, were hills. Tops of hills! And houses that looked like dollhouses. Fields were laid out neatly in geometric shapes, squares and rectangles.

The clouds remained above us; it appeared we wouldn't be touching them, after all. But it didn't matter; there was too much to see, anyway. Too much for me to absorb—I didn't feel weightless; there was no danger of me floating out of the plane, as I admit I had feared. Although I did feel curiously light, *above*. Above all the troubles of the world, above all my fears and doubts. Just as Charles had said.

Charles! My heart thrilled at my casual memory of his name, as if, for a brief moment, I was one of the golden people, too. And he was behind me! Again, I had almost forgotten about him even as I trusted him completely. Without a single doubt, I had placed my very being in his hands, certain he would take care of it, of me. And in that moment, that first moment of flight, of my breaking of the rules of gravity—I broke the rules of my heart, as well. For I had strictly governed it until this moment; this moment when I gave it, literally and figuratively, to the man seated behind me. The man steering me through the air, making sure I didn't fall. No longer did I need to be responsible for my own destiny, to worry about what to do today, tomorrow, next year. I needed only to give in and *be*, like the simplest of creatures. Like the birds flying miraculously below me.

I wasn't frightened. Hadn't I always wanted to be carried away by someone stronger than me? As much as I had told myself that life was no fairy tale, I had always hoped, deep down, that it was. What young girl doesn't dream of the hero rescuing her from her lonely tower? I had been no different, only more diligent, perhaps, than others in constructing that ivory tower of my own design—a foundation laid of books, the bricks formed of the duty drilled into me by my parents; dreams may have been the paintings on my walls, but doubts and fears were the bars on my windows.

Yet here I was, swept away through the very atmosphere— higher than any tower, far beyond any bars—by the most heroic one of all.

Fiercely, urgently, I needed to see his face, to see if he was real, after all. I didn't dare turn around, however; I didn't know how I *could*. The wind was pinning me to my seat. It took all my strength to look left or right; up or down. It was easiest simply to look ahead.

And so I did. I relaxed, gazing in delight at the rolling land coming up beneath us, marveling at the shadow of the plane racing us on the ground even in this half-light, like a tagalong friend. My ears adjusted to the engine until it was simply background noise. My eyes still stung and watered, but I was used to the cold now. My limbs were stiff, but I didn't care. I would have been happy to remain up in the sky forever, circling this valley. I was glad for the smooth ground below, the fields in which we could land, if necessary. I couldn't imagine how he had flown across that endless, forbidding sheet of water for all those hours. How could he have landed, if there was trouble? He couldn't have. Yet he had taken off anyway, knowing that.

At some point, I became aware that we were gradually descending; what had been blocks and ants were becoming houses and even a few people, once more. Now I could see that the people were jumping up and down and waving; I laughed, they looked so joyous and strange, like primitive cave drawings come to life. I tried to wave back, but my hand was almost ripped from my wrist; sheepishly, I stuck it back into the cockpit, and hoped that Charles hadn't noticed.

The airfield was now on the horizon, far ahead but getting closer, closer, as the trees began to grow again, the tips just below us, now even with us, now higher . . . and now we touched the ground. We sped down the runway as swiftly as when we'd taken off; once more I felt the ground, the bumpy, rutty ground, and my teeth rattled in my head. Even though I had been chewing the gum the entire time—it no longer had any flavor, and was the consistency of rubber—my ears popped again.

We slowed; the engine sputtered, and then, with a shudder, the plane came to a stop. It took me a long moment to realize the engine was silent, save for a stray hiss; my ears continued to ring with the noise of it.

I heard a vague sound behind me, as if the wind were speaking. But I was afraid to move, afraid to break my enchanted spell; I was suddenly overwhelmed by sadness. I didn't want to be back on the ground, back to being cautious, careful Anne. I loved the carefree, even wild, girl I had felt myself to be in the sky. Like a lover, I didn't want to say goodbye to her.

Someone was talking to me; someone was shaking my shoulder.

"So? Did you like it?" It was Colonel Lindbergh; he was standing on the wing right next to me, reaching in and unbuckling my harness so that his face was just inches from mine. The sudden warmth of his nearness, his hands on my shoulder, then grasping my own as he pulled me from my seat—I was abruptly dizzy, my stomach bouncing about as if it were still riding the currents.

Then my feet were somehow on the ground and a babbling, laughing voice filled the air; it took me a moment to recognize it as my own.

"Oh, did I! I never had such fun nor felt so free—oh, it was wonderful! I wasn't afraid, not a bit! It was like church, better than church, like being close to God, like seeing the earth the way He intended. Everything looked so different, so much more manageable from up there, didn't it? And did you see the people waving? Do you think they knew it was us? I can't wait to go again—oh, will you take me up again? Will you?"

Charles's mouth was open this entire time; finally I had to take a breath, giving him a chance to speak. There was something new in his eyes; not that faint arrogance from last night, nor that probing scientific gaze. "You don't feel sick? You're not dizzy?"

I shook my head, for now I was not. "No, not a bit!"

"Good girl. I'd better get you back home before your parents wonder where you are. But I would be honored to take you flying again, Miss—Anne."

"Oh, good," I said, falling silent again. I couldn't think of anything else to say; for once in my life I'd said all that I knew, all that I'd felt.

We walked back to the building in silence; we got in the car in silence. We rode back through the awakening streets of Mexico City in silence.

What need was there for words, when we had just shared the sky?

———————

CHAPTER 3

Back to earth.

I fell, with a thud, back into my life. After leaving Mexico—on a train once more, such pedestrian means of travel; I couldn't help but imagine flying back north, like a migrating bird, instead—I returned to Smith. Classes, papers, the frenzy of that last semester before graduation, with all the meetings and forms to fill out and final projects to plan—all reached out to me, like clinging tendrils of ivy, pinning me to the ground.

I told no one but my roommate about my secret solo flight with Colonel Lindbergh. Elizabeth Bacon didn't believe me. Why should she? The newspapers had been full of accounts of the official flight the next day; the one in which Elisabeth, Con, Mother, and I had gone up in the large Ford Tri-Motor plane that had brought his mother south to Mexico City. Studying the grainy newspaper photographs, I couldn't help but smile at the rather grim look on Elisabeth's face in some of them; she had been a bit green when we landed. She had still managed to face all the photographers and reporters with graceful aplomb, while Charles had stood, smiling that slightly frozen smile I was beginning to recognize as his public face, beside her. It had seemed to me he was happy to have someone else to share the spotlight, and how I wished, then, that it had been me! But I was too paralyzed by all the cameras and people; I had hung back with Mother and Con, dull, dry Anne once more.

So I cherished the memory of our private flight together, and tried to convince myself it meant more to him than the staged, public exercise with Elisabeth and Con and Mother. But as time went on, and winter melted into spring, I heard no more from the colonel. The newspaper interest in him had not abated; if anything, it had only escalated as he continued to fly around the country and Latin America, linking countries and spreading the gospel of passenger flight, mapping out routes, breaking new speed and distance records with almost boring regularity. And every other day there were rumors of an engagement. For now that the world had found its hero, it was impatient that he find his heroine.

Elisabeth's name appeared more than once as a likely candidate. Mine never did. Apparently, Ambassador Morrow had only one daughter worthy of notice.

So I immersed myself in my work and did my best to ignore the newspapers and newsreels. I turned, even more hungrily than usual, to my diary. I had always been like this; only able to recognize my world by reassembling it on the page. Everything felt topsy-turvy; overnight, long-held notions, dreams, ideas were alien to me, now that I had flown with Charles Lindbergh, trusted him with my body, my soul—my heart.

My fears, however, remained the same; after the astonishing intimacy of my flight with the colonel, the rest of our time together over the holiday had been one of marked politeness, nothing more. I was certain he had forgotten all about me, even as I clung to a memory growing wispier by the hour until I couldn't remember which parts I had dreamed and which parts had truly happened.

One Saturday in April, tired of books, tired of papers, tired of myself, I borrowed Bacon's Oldsmobile and drove to the tiny airfield outside of Northampton. I paid a man five dollars to take me up in a biplane smaller than the one I had ridden in with Charles. I strapped myself inside, fastened a pair of goggles around my head, and still it felt as if I had never done this before. But then—that dance, that balletic moment when the plane leaped from the bumpy ground and, as if it were holding its breath, hovered a moment before pulling up, up, up . . .

That moment brought back everything I had felt during my first flight with Charles. As tears rolled down my face, I tried to convince myself they were happy tears; happy because I hadn't dreamed it, after all.

That flight was shorter than the first—merely a quick pass over the college, during which I imagined all my friends scurrying around in the buildings below like a colony of ants—but when we landed, I felt better about life. I retrieved the heart I had given to Charles Lindbergh so impulsively, and tucked it safely inside my earthbound bones once again. One day I would be able to give it to someone else. Someone who wanted it.

"Anne? Anne—hello, Anne?"

I shook my head and shuffled in my hard desk chair; reflexively I stretched, only now aware that my entire body was stiff, my fingers cold. I must have been sitting, dreaming, for ever so long.

"What time is it?" I asked Bacon.

"Five o'clock," she said, turning on a lamp, twirling her ubiquitous strand of pearls, just like Clara Bow's; she even styled her thick auburn hair like the movie star's. "The announcements are here." And she tossed a small white cardboard box down on my desk.

"Oh." I opened the box and removed a card; it was bordered in our class color, purple, with the seal of Smith: *Education is the key to the future.*

"Can you believe it's almost here? Graduation? Gee, I didn't think I'd ever graduate, really!" Bacon plopped down on her narrow bed, the ancient mattress springs creaking like old, rusty door hinges.

"No, I'm sure you didn't," I said wryly. "I have no idea how you made it through French literature!"

"I might not have, if it hadn't been for you! Anne, do you think you'll win any prizes this year? I bet you win one of the writing ones!"

"Oh, I doubt it." Biting my lip, I tried not to think of it. I *had* been asked to try for both the Elisabeth Montagu Prize for essays and the Mary Augusta Jordan Literary Prize for prose or poetry. But, of course, I wouldn't win. "I'm sure I won't be known for anything other than being the ambassador's daughter," I mused out loud. "The ambassador's *other* daughter, at that."

"What?" Bacon looked up from the latest copy of *Vanity Fair.* "What on earth are you talking about?"

"Oh, you know. After college—after everything. What happens next, Bacon? I can't imagine it. I can't imagine that I'll ever be known for anything great, like—" I caught myself just in time; I didn't want to say his name, say "Charles" out loud, as if I had a right. I didn't want to let it slip that perhaps, for the first time, I was tempted by feats grander than literary prizes and ambassadorships; those staid, respectable feats endorsed by my parents.

"Well, who does imagine that?" Bacon said, returning to her magazine. "No one I know."

"That's just it!" It burst out from me, this unexpected passion and desire stirred up by that slim, tall boy with blue eyes and a hero's laurel in the shape of a flying helmet. "No one I know ever

does, we're all so, so—content! But what's it all about—what's it
all for? The studying and the reading and the trying so hard?
What are we supposed to *do* with it all, other than be exactly like
our mothers?"

"We get married. That's what we bright, promising young
Smith girls are supposed to do. That's what it's all for. We marry
equally bright, promising young men from Princeton or Cornell
or Harvard or Yale. We collect silver and china; we begin to entertain, modestly at first, you know! Then we have babies and
bigger houses and more silver and more china and entertain lav-
ishly. Our husbands come home every night at the same time, and
we get bored looking at their faces over the dinner table. Maybe,
if we're very lucky, they take us to Europe once in a while. If
we're very unlucky, they become politicians and we have to move
to Washington. Meanwhile, we play tennis and golf and try to
keep our figures and our sanity."

"It all sounds so awful!"

"Well, it is. And it isn't. I wouldn't mind a house on Long
Island and a charge account at Tiffany!"

"But what about love? What about passion? What about—
more?" I flung my pencil down with a dramatic gesture that surprised both of us. Bacon picked up the pencil and handed it back
to me, her eyebrows—dramatically darkened, just like a film
star's—arched in amusement.

"What about it? What's gotten into you, Anne?"

"Well, I don't know about you, but I don't want to be one of
those dried-up matrons you see at bridge parties, scowling at the
younger generation. *I* want to be one of those marvelous old la-
dies covered in scarves who rock in their chairs with mysterious
smiles, remembering the scandalous affairs of their youth!"

"Why, Anne Morrow!" My roommate's green eyes deepened.
"You sly creature! I guess still waters really do run deep!"

I shrugged, blushing, and Bacon returned to her magazine with a chuckle.

Tapping the pencil against my teeth as my briefly soaring soul returned to my normal, earthbound body, I couldn't help but wonder. As awful as Bacon's scenario sounded, at least she had some kind of vision for her future. Whereas I—fanciful thoughts of scandalous affairs aside—did not. I saw myself drifting about, like an actress in a play, waiting forever for her cue.

Beyond graduation, I truly couldn't see; I had always possessed some vague notion of "writing," but what on earth would I write *about*? Didn't one have to have experiences first? While the short essays and poems—many of them, lately, singing of wind and clouds and sky—I had written for the *Smith Review* had been well received, my words seemed like fluff to me; dandelion fluff, ephemeral, not substantial enough to remain in anyone's memories, let alone mine. Already, I couldn't remember half of them.

And where would I do this so-called writing? I had no plans except a smattering of invitations to classmates' summer homes for a weekend of sailing or tennis. Which was one more reason to envy my sister; as soon as Elisabeth graduated two years ago, she'd made a real life for herself with Connie Chilton. Between the two of them—and with Mother and Daddy's quietly proud blessing—they were single-handedly going to revolutionize early childhood education. They were already planning to start their own nursery school.

Unless, of course—or rather, *until*—Elisabeth married. Which suddenly seemed a very real possibility, one I couldn't bear to contemplate.

Seized with an impulse to act instead of think for only the second time in my life—the first time having taken place in an airplane—I grabbed a fountain pen. Scribbling quickly, before I lost my nerve, I signed my first graduation announcement with a short note, then slipped it into an envelope. For a sickening moment I realized I had no idea where to address it—until I remembered, my heart soaring with joy and empowerment, that we were *dignitaries* now. All I had to do was pick up the telephone and someone would find out for me.

Privilege, I was not ashamed to admit at that moment, had its perks.

OF COURSE, HE DIDN'T COME.

During the entire graduation ceremony, even when my name was announced not once, but twice, as the winner of both the Montagu and Jordan prizes, my only feeling was of disappointment; childish, selfish disappointment. What were those prizes to me when the one I desired the most was withheld from me? I searched and searched the crowd for his lanky, yet imposing, figure, those blue eyes that had *seen* me, and I searched in vain.

To make matters worse, after I received my diploma and joined my family, I was told that he had recently visited our home in Englewood.

"Colonel Lindbergh came to call two weekends ago, just after we got back from Mexico City," Mother said, after she hugged me and whispered how proud she was. She was wearing her alumni pin; so were Elisabeth and Connie, who, naturally, had driven up together.

"He—he did?" I tried to conceal my hurt by opening up the sheepskin cover and studying my diploma. *Anne Spencer Morrow.*

"Yes, he did. Elisabeth and Constance happened to be home, so they were able to entertain him."

"Ah."

"The colonel was as loquacious as ever," Elisabeth said, with a wry smile for Connie, who returned it, wrinkling her broad, freckle-splattered nose.

"I've never met a more boring man." Connie sniffed disdainfully.

"Oh, he's not boring, he's just—careful," I said. Being very careful, myself.

"There's my girl!" Daddy ambled up; he had been detained by a crowd of admirers and a couple of members of the press. "We're so proud of you, Anne!"

"Yes, we are," Mother assured me with another hug. Con, my little sister, took my two prize certificates and studied them. Then she sighed dramatically.

"Marvelous. Yet another Morrow achievement I'll have to live up to!"

"I wish Dwight were here," I blurted out, surprising us all. Naturally, we were not to mention my brother's recent "troubles" in public. But Con's little joke reminded me that there was at least one Morrow who was having difficulties living up to his heritage.

Dwight had been hallucinating, delirious, at school. Daddy's stern letters exhorting him to "buck up" had not helped; finally Mother arranged to place him in a rest home in South Carolina. It was merely a "temporary" situation, she reminded us all—but a necessary one.

There was an awkward silence at the mention of my brother's name; Mother fiddled with her gloves while Daddy tugged at his necktie.

"We thought it best for him to remain—for him to get some strength back, before traveling," Mother said, her eyes glazing over, giving her an odd, faraway air. She had turned away from my father, who suddenly seemed very interested in a clump of damp grass clinging to the top of his white shoe. Con and Elisabeth stared at the ground, while Connie Chilton retreated a few steps, as if unsure whether or not she should hear any of this.

"You're coddling him," Daddy grumbled—but he would not look at my mother, and for the first time ever, I sensed a crack in their partnership. My parents' overwhelming closeness was as much a part of my childhood as my beloved Roosevelt bear with its missing eye. My parents never argued or contradicted each other; they decided and spoke in one unified voice, and at times I had felt lonely in the face of it. Loved, always—yet sometimes lonely.

But now—

"We are not coddling him, Dwight. The boy is in *pain*," Mother snapped—the first time I had ever heard her raise her voice to my father. Then she turned away, as if collecting herself, while Daddy strode off to the car, his cheeks scarlet, his shoulders pinched so that his suit coat appeared even baggier than usual. Con blinked away a few bright tears before trotting off behind Daddy.

I turned to Elisabeth, to gauge her reaction to all this; she simply pressed her lips together and shrugged, then held out her hand to her friend. Connie Chilton looked as if she wanted to say something, but I saw Elisabeth squeeze her arm in warning.

After a moment, I followed Mother.

"You're doing the right thing," I whispered to her. "Dwight does need professional care. I've seen it. What can I do? I don't care if Daddy doesn't approve. I want to help."

"My daughter." She smiled gratefully. "You're such a rock sometimes, Anne, so quiet yet so steadfast. I don't know if you're aware of how much I rely on you."

I turned away, tears in my eyes; all my life, I'd wanted my mother to recognize me, alone; outside of Elisabeth's shadow.

Knowing that she had was my greatest graduation present, more precious to me than any awards.

"Now, I know you probably have loads of plans." Mother's voice was back to its normal soothing tone. "But if you could stay in Englewood this summer to oversee the building of the new house, instead of coming back with us to Mexico City, it would be such a help, Anne. Elisabeth and Connie have their school plans, and I would feel better knowing you were home, so that Dwight might be able to—well, if he's up to travel, I know he'd like to come home for a while. You don't mind, do you?"

I shook my head, grateful, actually, to have been asked. I still had no idea what I was going to do with myself. Watching over builders, helping my brother, even in his fragile state; both seemed a blessed alternative to sitting around, brooding and reading newspapers full of articles and photos of a certain Colonel Charles Lindbergh. And wondering what on earth I was going to do with the rest of my life.

"Of course I don't mind—I said I would help," I assured my mother, and was surprised to see a tear in her eye. She blinked it away almost before I could convince myself it was there, and she called, gaily, to Elisabeth and Connie—who were walking so close together that their heads, both so blond, nearly touched—"Now, what are you two whispering about? Connie, is Elisabeth telling you secrets about the colonel?"

Elisabeth and Connie sprang apart, laughing—too loudly, it seemed to me. As if my mother had accidentally touched a nerve.

"Yes, Mrs. Morrow, that's exactly what we were doing," Connie called out brightly, as she squeezed my sister's hand. And I couldn't help but notice that Elisabeth's face was suddenly scarlet, her eyes shining, as she squeezed Connie's hand in return.

Mother turned to me with a smile that suddenly crumbled, like a sand castle overwhelmed by an unexpected tide. She pretended to read my diploma, but then gave up and hugged it briefly to her chest, squeezing her eyes tight, and this time I knew there were tears.

But when she opened them, her gaze was clear and bright as always; what was startling was how it was focused entirely on me. For once, I didn't have the feeling she was thinking of someone or something else as she looked into my eyes. "Anne, dear, I really am very proud of you," she said, so strangely earnest. "Very. I tried for the Jordan prize, you know, when I was a senior. But I didn't win, and you did."

I smiled, touched and humbled by her confession. My mother didn't often let slip a disappointment; it simply wasn't in her nature to dwell on the past. She was changing, it seemed to me, almost before my very eyes. Maybe it was Dwight's illness, forcing her to stop and reflect, consider, maybe even to blame.

Or perhaps it was just my graduation; another childhood milestone over, my very last one. Maybe she felt older, more vulnerable, clutching my college diploma as if she could clutch all her children to her one more time before we all scattered and flew away.

Whatever accounted for this rare vulnerability, I didn't question her. I didn't feel privy to know what was in my mother's heart, despite my new college degree. I didn't want that much knowledge just yet, and the responsibility that must come with it.

But neither did I want to let go of her hand, for I sensed she needed someone strong to cling to; we held on to each other as we walked to the waiting car.

"DWIGHT, DO YOU WANT ANYTHING special for dinner tonight?" I stood in the doorway of the study; my brother was sitting at my father's empty desk, staring out the window.

I didn't like him staring in silence, but it was better than the strange, forced laughter that too often took its place these days. Since I had last seen him at Christmas, something had changed inside him, although on the outside he appeared much as usual. Still solidly built, low to the ground like a football player, with hair some indeterminate brown shade that was halfway between my dark tresses and Elisabeth's blond. He dressed the same, groomed himself as ever, was interested in the same things—he followed the Yankees and would have argued the respective merits of Lou Gehrig versus Babe Ruth all day with me if I had even an ounce of knowledge about either.

But his stutter was worse. That odd, strangled laughter burst out of him at the most inappropriate times—usually when he was in session with his tutor—and he sullenly stared out of windows far too often. Sometimes, I actually shook him; I told him to snap out of it or at least tell me what was wrong, for no one else seemed to be able to. The only thing he had said so far that was *true,* that wasn't part of the typical Morrow family banter, had been, "It's awful being Dwight Morrow Junior. You don't know, Anne. It's just too much for me."

I didn't know. I was becoming painfully aware that there was so *much* I didn't know. Now an adult, allowed a glimpse of these first cracks in my family's perfect surface, I couldn't help but wonder what else I didn't understand about us all. My childhood had seemed charmed, privileged, and not only because our parents took pains to remind us that it was. We were always together, never farmed out like other children of wealth, although naturally, governesses and nurses took care of our everyday needs. Our parents, we understood from an early age, were dedicated to more important pursuits than ensuring that our teeth were brushed and our scraped knees bandaged.

But Mother read to us an hour a day, every day, no matter how

busy she was. Even when we were so small we had to sit on encyclopedias in order to reach the mahogany table, we children dined
with our parents in the evening, and were expected to understand
the politics and philosophies discussed. There were picnics on
the sound and summers in Maine; travels abroad where Daddy
read from Shakespeare in London, Voltaire in Paris. Somehow,
though, we never were allowed to feel rich or special. Our
money—how much? It never even occurred to me to ask; it was
a cushion on which we could land, if necessary, once we reached
for ourselves. But we were, always, expected to reach. Maybe
that was the key to Dwight's troubles; perhaps, being the son, he
was expected to reach higher than Elisabeth or Con or me.

"Dwight, I asked you what you wanted for dinner." I repeated
the safest question of all that I wanted to ask my brother, as he
gazed at a robin hopping on the terrace, just outside the study
window. At least he had the draperies open today; the room
wasn't quite so gloomy and stuffy with all its dark paneling.

"Whatever you want, Anne."

"Isn't it odd, just the two of us here?" I sat down on an over-
stuffed chair, picking up a pillow and holding it to my chest. "Like
we're playing house or something. How did we get so adult?"

"You'd better get used to it—playing house. Once you're
married, that's all you'll be doing. Lucky."

"Oh, don't say that—what's lucky about it, anyway?"

"That's all you're supposed to do, Annie. That's all they expect."

"I don't think that's particularly lucky—even if it was true."
Although I knew, of course, that it was; already I had received
five wedding invitations from my just-graduated classmates.
"Anyway, I'm not going to get married." I shook my head defiantly.

"Nobody good enough for you?" Using his stocky legs, my

brother propelled the swivel chair around so that he was facing me; there was a glint of his old, teasing smile on his face.

"Nope. Not a soul. I'm far too rare a gem for any mere mortal man."

"You always wanted to marry a hero, Anne—don't you remember?"

"Oh, Dwight—that was just little-girl talk. Every little girl wants to marry someone heroic. It's silly now. I couldn't get a proposal from the milkman. But I don't want to get married, I've decided. I'd much rather stay independent."

"You? Independent?" Dwight hooted, and it was only because of his strange, fragile state that I didn't get up and leave in a huff. "As what? A teacher?"

"Well, I could be, I suppose." I didn't like this line of questioning, because it was too much like the questions I asked myself at night, alone in my narrow girlhood bed. "Anyway, it's Elisabeth who'll marry the hero, not me."

"You mean Colonel Lindbergh?"

My heart sank at how quickly he supplied my sister with her logical beau. But I nodded.

"Well, Father'll be pleased, anyway," Dwight said, frowning. "He gave me the dickens when I was rude to the colonel over Christmas. He read me the riot act after that." My brother's face darkened; his eyes dulled.

"Dwight, he loves you, you know."

"He'd rather have Colonel Lindbergh for a son."

"No, he wouldn't. You're being silly."

"Am I? When was the last time he was proud of me, Anne? When?"

"When—when you—now, Dwight, stop it! There were plenty of times!"

"Name one." Dwight was so calm, not agitated at all; his

voice didn't rise and crack, his face didn't turn from purple to scarlet and back again, like it usually did—and that was what frightened me the most.

Yet at that moment, I could not recall the last time my father had said he was proud of his son. He told Elisabeth and me he was proud of us, all the time. Often for no reason other than that we looked especially pretty, or had written a particularly pleasing letter to him.

"Dwight, I can't suddenly be expected to come up with examples! Heavens, I can hardly remember what I had for breakfast this morning! All I know is that you're wrong. Daddy loves you. We all love you."

"Well, sure, you do. What's that matter? You're only a girl."

"Only a girl? Dwight Morrow Junior, that's a ridiculous thing to say!"

"Oh, you know what I mean, Anne. It still doesn't matter— you'll go off and marry your hero some day, and then you won't have any time for me, either. Just like Mother and Father."

"Dwight, you know they'd rather be up here. But this is Daddy's job now. He has to be in Mexico City."

"Don't I know it. 'Dwight, you must remember, we have duties now, obligations.'"

I had to laugh. My brother's voice perfectly mimicked our father's excited, breathless staccato.

"'*You* have duties,'" Dwight continued. "'Your sisters have duties. Remember, young man, remember, *education*—'"

"*Education, education,*" I chimed in—but then the phone on Daddy's desk rang, startling us into silence. We both jumped, then giggled guiltily; had our father somehow heard us, all the way from Mexico? I don't think either one of us would have been surprised.

Dwight was the first to recover. Picking up the receiver and leaning toward the transmitter, he said, "Hello, Morrow residence," still in that urgent, high-pitched voice that sounded just like Daddy's. I giggled again, and Dwight rewarded me with a sly smile. Then my brother suddenly colored, sat up straight in his chair, and said, "Miss Morrow? No, she's away. Oh—are you sure? Yes, *she* is," and thrust the receiver and transmitter out to me.

"It's your hero, Anne," he said, his eyes twinkling.

"Oh, sure, sure." I stuck my tongue out at him, enjoying the teasing, wishing to prolong it for as long as possible. I pushed myself out of the chair with an exaggerated sigh. "It's probably that milkman." I sashayed to the desk, wiggling my hips just like Theda Bara, and took the receiver from him; holding it up to my ear, I leaned into the transmitter and crooned, in a deep, vampy tone, "Hello, this is Anne Morrow. Is this my hero?"

There was a pause; static crackled down the line into my ear. Then I heard a reedy voice say, "Miss Morrow? This is Lindbergh himself. Charles Lindbergh."

I wanted to drop the phone; I wanted to hit my brother—who was leaning back in his chair, shaking with laughter. I wanted to do anything other than somehow think of a proper reply.

"It—it is?"

"Yes. I'm sorry, did I catch you at a bad time?"

"No—no! My brother—Dwight—you met him, remember? He was just teasing me. I'm so sorry—I mean, no, I'm glad you called. Very glad. That is—wait—this is *Anne* Morrow. Not Elisabeth. I'm Anne."

"Yes, I know. I had been led to believe that you would be at home today. I called yesterday, but you were out."

"You did?" By now my knees were shaking and I had to sit down on the edge of the desk; Jo, my mother's secretary, had said that he had called. But she'd said he'd called for Elisabeth, not me.

Finally Dwight had the good sense to get up and leave me alone in the room, his eyes still shining with merriment. For a moment I forgot all about his condition; I stuck my tongue out at him, just like any big sister would.

"Miss Morrow? You are still there?"

"Yes—oh, yes, I am!"

"I'm very sorry I could not make it to your graduation. It was nice of you to ask me. But I was afraid that if I came it would cause a stir, and that wouldn't have been fair to you or your family."

"Oh." How thoughtful of him! "That was very thoughtful of you," I said, my tongue just a few beats behind my thoughts.

There was a silence; I could hear him breathing, softly. Then he cleared his throat, and I was reminded, suddenly, of the engine of the plane that we flew in together, sputtering to life.

"I understand that you're home for the summer?" There was a hesitation—like the catch of that motor before it finally found its groove—in his voice.

"Yes. I'm taking care of—I'm staying with Dwight while he's home for the summer. Mother and Daddy are back in Mexico City."

"The reason I called," he said hastily, as if he regretted having done so, "is to ask if you would like to go up again? I promised you I would take you back up in a plane, I'm not sure if you recall. I do not break my promises."

"Oh! Yes, I do remember—that is, I have some recollection of it." Cradling the receiver between my cheek and my neck, I grasped the edge of Daddy's walnut desk, grateful for its ballast; without it, I was certain I would have floated up to the ceiling.

"Then it's settled. I'll call for you tomorrow at ten o'clock in the morning, if you don't have other plans."

Of course, I had no other plans. Even if Mother had asked me to entertain the king of England, I would have canceled! But then I thought of how Elisabeth would have replied, and so I was able to say, coolly, "I believe I can rearrange things."

"Well, if it's any bother . . ."

"Oh, no! No bother at all! No, truly, there's nothing I'd like more, if you really are sure you have the time."

"I said I did." Did I detect annoyance now?

"Yes, of course."

"So. Ten o'clock, then?"

"Yes."

"Well, then, goodbye," Charles Lindbergh said in a faint, almost strangled tone, and he hung up the phone.

I did not. I remained holding the receiver to my ear, the transmitter to my mouth, for at least a minute; long enough for Dwight to knock softly and stick his bushy head—he was in dire need of a haircut; his hair stuck up all over his scalp—inside the doorway.

"Anne? Was that really Colonel Lindbergh?"

"I believe so." In a daze, I replaced the receiver.

"What did he want?"

"He wanted me."

"You? I thought he was supposed to be interested in Elisabeth."

"I know—I thought—I told him she wasn't here! Right off! Dwight, I think he really wanted to speak to me, but—oh, it's only because he once made a promise to me. That's it."

"What kind of promise?"

"He promised to take me flying again. He's coming tomorrow at ten."

"Ten? Huh. You sure he meant you?"

"Yes, Dwight!" How many times did I have to say it before we both believed it? I couldn't even count that high.

"Hmmm." Dwight scratched his head, then patted his stomach. "Anne, now I'm hungry. What were you going to have Cook make for dinner?"

"Dinner?" I stared at my brother. *"Dinner?"*

"Well, Anne, you were just asking me—"

"Oh, go ask Cook to make you a sandwich." Finally sliding off the desk, I brushed past my brother. "I can't help you; I must find something to wear!"

"But he's not coming until tomorrow morning!"

"I know! I hardly have any time!"

I left Dwight standing in the hallway, still scratching his head and saying, in a disgusted tone, "Women."

"Men!" I called over my shoulder, already mentally going through my closet.

But I paused once, on my way to my room, to shake my head in wonder at my brother. How on earth could he think of food at a time like this?

"HELLO," I SAID, opening the door. Then I looked up. Charles Lindbergh was standing before me, blocking out the bright morning sun. I'd forgotten how tall he was.

He had changed. He didn't look like a boy any longer; he had a slightly wary look in those piercing blue eyes, and he appeared much more comfortable in civilian clothes—tweed trousers and a white shirt and tie, although he did have that battered leather jacket over his arm. In place of his helmet, however, he wore a fedora that was just like every fedora I'd ever seen on any banker, my father included.

He also had a pair of sunglasses in his pocket; he donned these quickly as he led me to his car.

"I'm afraid it's a bit strange," he explained, as he held the door open for me. Once I was settled, he went around and slid into the driver's seat; as he did so, he pulled his hat brim low over his eyes.

"What is?"

"This—this getup." He gestured to his face. "Sometimes I can manage to fool the press, if they're not already on my tail. I don't think they are today, fortunately. The moment they see you with me, they'll have us engaged. I've been engaged to any number of women lately."

He then appeared to think about what he had just said; his hand, poised to flip the ignition switch, froze. "I didn't mean—"

"That's all right," I said hastily. "I understand."

"Yes." He nodded, then started the car; with a roar he drove down the circular driveway to the private road that led to the main street. We were in a new cream-colored Ford open roadster, so I pulled my cloche hat farther down on my head, holding on to it, praying it wouldn't fly off. His hat remained mysteriously tethered to his head.

He did not drive fast, much to my surprise. For a man who loved to fly, he appeared cautious and careful on the ground, constantly looking over his shoulder in case cars approached from behind. Nor did he talk; after a few minutes of total silence, I began to feel as superfluous as the small green spider that had hitched a ride on the windshield. And so, as we drove through the city, then out into the country of Long Island, down roads I'd never before discovered, I had a long time in which to wonder if, indeed, he had called the wrong Morrow sister. Half an hour passed, then forty-five minutes, and still he spoke not a word to me, nor even looked my way. Months had passed since we'd seen each other, but obviously he did not feel compelled to explain what he had been up to, and so, out of defiance and a prickly sense of pride that made me set my mouth a certain way, neither did I.

I glanced at my wristwatch, then at the immobile face beside me, the eyes hidden by those round smoky lenses, the brow obscured by that magical hat.

But if he didn't talk, neither did he give any indication that he expected me to. So I gave myself over to the purity of simply being, with him, on a fine summer day. Only once did I break the silence; it was when we drove along a lane bordered on either side with young birch trees.

"Oh, look! It's like they're bowing to us!" I couldn't help but laugh, pointing as the tops of the trees shimmied ahead of us, bending in the light breeze. Charles nodded but kept his eyes on the road, and so I retreated once more, embarrassed by my outburst.

Finally we turned down a long gravel road that led to an open field. There, two planes were waiting; an enormous white French Normandy–styled house rose up in the distance, along with several barns and smaller dwellings.

Charles braked the car, and the engine sputtered off. He turned to me.

"Well, that was fun," he said with a sudden, surprising grin, and I had to laugh.

"You like to drive?" I fingered the leather upholstery, dusty now. But it was certainly a fine automobile.

"I'm afraid I do. I used to have a motorcycle—an Indian— back when I was barnstorming. She was an extraordinary little machine, but I sold her to pay for my first plane, a Jenny."

"Do you name all your machines after people?"

"I—oh, no. A Jenny is a type of plane—war surplus, they were used overseas and then refitted. We used them to fly the mail."

"Oh."

"Anyway." He removed his sunglasses and his hat, and ran his hand through his sandy-colored hair. "Here we are."

"Where are we, exactly?"

"Friends of mine happen to have a private airfield. So far, none of the press has found it out."

"Oh." I could see the water of the sound glittering in the distance, beyond a thicket of slender trees. "It's lovely."

"Yes. The Guggenheims have been good to me in all—this." He waved his hands vaguely, and I understood him to mean everything that had happened to him *after*. After landing in Paris. "Harry lets me use his planes; I have a new one on order. The *Spirit*'s in mothballs now, I'm afraid. The Smithsonian has her." There was a definite note of sadness to his voice, a wistfulness; like a small boy who had been forced to part with his favorite treasure.

Then he cleared his throat and got out of the car. "It's a good day for flying," he said, pausing for a moment to survey the sky before he walked around to open my door. "Clear sailing, as far as we might want to go."

"Good." I scrambled after him as he strode toward the two airplanes, both silver and gleaming in the sun. He did not shorten his stride for me, and so once again, I had to run to keep up.

"You've not been up since I took you?" We reached the larger of the two planes, an enclosed monoplane with a longer wingspan. It was already pointed toward the flat airstrip.

"No." And then I remembered that I had. I wondered why that memory had escaped me. Was it because it didn't count, without him? Or because I felt oddly disloyal for flying with someone else?

"This is different than what we went up in before—more comfortable. For long-haul passenger flight, this is the type of plane we'll be using, only even bigger. You don't have to wear goggles." And he opened a small door and helped me climb up into the cabin. The interior was hot—baked, actually, from sitting in the sun, and so I slipped out of my jacket, grateful for the short sleeves of my cotton blouse. I needn't have worn jodhpurs; there were four wicker chairs bolted to the floor, two in front, two in back, all cushioned. I took my place in the front passenger seat as daintily as if I were at a tea party.

Charles climbed in on the pilot's side and took a quick look at all the controls, pushing a few buttons, playing with some toggles and pedals on the floor. Then he handed me a stick of gum— that awful spearmint, but I accepted it gratefully, and started chewing away. He started the engine and it sputtered, the propeller whirling, but this time it seemed so far away; not at all like my first flight, when I could feel the choppy air on my face. Enclosed as we were, I could see only out the front and a limited bit to either side. The whine of the engine was muffled, although still loud; already my head was pounding with it.

"Here we go," Charles said, and moved the control stick gently; the plane taxied down the field, picking up speed bit by bit until, once more, I felt suspended in a grand leap—before the wind caught us and propelled us up, up, up.

The moment we took flight, I noticed that Charles looked quickly out the side of his window, did a double take, and looked again. His hand gripped the stick, muttering something under his breath.

"What?" I asked, trying my best not to squeal in delight as we skimmed the tops of pine trees, so close I could have sworn I felt them tickling the soles of my feet.

Charles didn't reply, so I shrugged and enjoyed the scenery; the sound, glittering with white birds—sailboats, that is; the vast estates, many of which I recognized now as the homes of some of Daddy's banking associates; the vivid green undulating below. The plane bumped and bucked as it gained altitude, causing my stomach to do its own jittery acrobatics, but then it smoothed out so suddenly that my heart soared. My worries about Dwight, questions about my future, doubts about my purpose in life, all fell away. I was light, translucent; luxuriously, I stretched my arms and legs, wondering if the sun's rays could pass right through me.

Then I turned to my companion. Instead of the sure, carefree grin I expected to see, Charles's mouth was set in a straight line, and those startling blue eyes were narrowed in steely concentration.

"We lost a wheel," he shouted over the pulsating drone of the engine. I realized conversation was going to be difficult, if not impossible.

"What?" I shouted back.

"On takeoff. I thought I felt something. We left one of the wheels on the ground."

"So?" We were up in the air now; what did we need wheels for?

"Landing. A bit challenging," was all he said. Then he flicked some switches with his thumb, muttered something that sounded like a complicated mathematical equation, and nodded to himself.

I wanted to ask more but felt ridiculous, shouting so.

"Loud!" I said instead, pointing to my ears.

Charles nodded. "Some people use cotton. In their ears." He pointed to his. "I don't. That's not flying."

I nodded, as if I understood.

We flew for a while in silence. Then he turned to me again, his brow wrinkled in concern, as if something had just occurred to him. "We should stay up awhile to burn off fuel so landing is safer," he shouted. "Do you have other plans today? I'm not keeping you from something?"

For some reason, this last question struck me as hilarious; he seemed more worried about my social schedule than he was about the plane! And so I surprised us both by laughing.

"No!"

"Good," he said, his eyes widening and his grin deepening. "Although that means you're stuck with me for a while."

"I can't think of anyone else I'd rather be stuck with," I replied. And although I said it flippantly, I meant it. Who else would I rather be with in this situation? No one.

Was I afraid at all? It's incredible to believe now, but I was not. I had such confidence in Charles; as we flew on and on, the relentless clamor of the engine giving me a slight headache but nothing more, I honestly forgot about the "challenging" landing coming up. Instead, I was almost grateful for the situation. We were trapped alone together in the sky for hours. We would have something remarkable to share; something to bind us to each other. I seized this realization greedily, and, hoarding it, forgot all about the danger.

"You take the controls," he suddenly called, almost an impish gleam in his eyes.

"What?"

"Take the control stick."

"I—I can't!"

"Why not? You want to learn, don't you?"

Why he assumed this of me, I had no idea, but as soon as he said it I realized he was right. This, at last, was something I could *do*. Right now; before I had a chance to think about it and analyze it until I was no longer even sure what it meant.

"You fly," Charles shouted. "Don't be afraid. You can do it."

So I leaned over, reaching with my left hand. His hand was still on the stick, but I grasped it, just above his, and for a moment both our hands were flying the plane, we were steering our path together. And while we didn't even glance at each other, I felt a charge jolt through me and knew that he felt it, too. His breathing quickened.

Then he let go. And I was flying the plane myself. At first smoothly—I was still thinking of his hand, touching mine, unaware of what I was really doing. Then, however, I was aware—aware that I was actually, really, flying an airplane!—and I overcompensated by gripping the stick tighter, which caused it to jerk right. And so did the plane. Steeply, it began to bank, and as my entire body was blanketed in a cold sweat, my hand shaking, I overcorrected and it banked precipitously left.

Charles didn't exclaim, didn't even suck in his breath. He simply sat with his arms folded across his chest, allowing me to find my own way, somehow confident that I would. And finally, my hands still clammy but my heart now steady, I did. We flew in a straight line, and I felt the plane tug against me, like a horse, and I remembered how sensitive a horse is to his bit, and that's how I finally learned to fly. As if I were holding reins instead of a stick; as if I were riding. Even the little pockets of air that we hit began to feel no more dangerous than jumping a horse over a gate.

I don't know how long I flew; my shoulder began to pinch, however, and Charles flipped a switch on the dashboard, looked at his watch, and tapped his head. "I'll take over now. Landing."

"Oh." After he grasped the stick, I let go. Charles suggested, his voice so reasonable even as he had to shout, that I gather the cushions from the two rear seats and place them on either side of me, which I did.

"I'm going to take us down over there." He gestured to a field with a longer airstrip than the one we had taken off from. "We'll need the extra space."

"All right." I was calm. So was he. The air inside the plane suddenly felt heavy, pressing me into my seat, and our voices sounded deadened to my ears. Still, I was not afraid. I trusted Charles Lindbergh, the man who had conquered the sky, to bring me back safely to earth.

We circled the airstrip a couple of times, lower and lower. Several people ran out of a small shack and a neighboring house to look at us. They waved, and I waved back.

"They're telling us not to land." Charles had a grim smile on his face. "They can see we're missing a wheel."

"They're in for a treat, then!" I continued to wave at the figures, jumping wildly below.

"Brace yourself, and as soon as we stop I want you to unbuckle and exit the plane. If the door won't budge, push the window and crawl out. Then run as far away as you can. Can you do that for me?"

It was that last "for me" that stirred me from my eerie calm. It touched my heart; truly, as if the words wormed themselves into my flesh, between my ribs. I felt adrenaline tingling my every pore, and I nodded, holding on tight to the edges of the seat. As the ground came rushing up at us, I instinctively ducked my head, feeling, not seeing, the plane hit the ground. For a suspended breath, I thought we were fine—but then I felt something break beneath us. "The wheel," I said—or maybe it was Charles. It was the only word either one of us, or both of us, spoke.

And then I was upside down.

The plane had stopped, and I was upside down and then I wasn't; I heard a crash and then a rip, and then I had pushed myself through a window and I was running, just as Charles had told me to do, away from the plane. Which was upside down, the propeller still turning like a child's whirligig.

Finally I stopped running, pain pinching my side, but I knew it was only because I was out of breath. I had done it! I had done what he had asked of me and I was all right, he was all right—

Wasn't he? Where was he? I looked around, panicking; there were people—the same people to whom I had just waved so carelessly—hurrying toward me, farmers with pitchforks just like in a motion picture—but there was no Charles. I shouted his name, heard nothing, and then started to run back to the plane when I felt a hand on my arm, pulling me back.

I spun around, and he was there. Disheveled, a bleeding scratch on his cheek, a huge grin on his face. We grinned stupidly at each other for the longest time, until we were surrounded by people jostling us, asking if we were okay, and Charles was wincing. Only then did I see that he was cradling his left elbow with his right hand.

"Are you hurt?" I asked, wanting to touch him but strangely unable to take a step in his direction.

"I think I bruised it." He shrugged, followed by a grimace. "But it's nothing."

"We should get you to a doctor—" I began, but was interrupted by shouts of, "It's him! It's Charles Lindbergh himself! Lucky Lindy!"

And soon more people were running toward us; from where, I had no idea. They all wanted to touch him, shake him, ask if he was all right. A few men headed toward the plane, but Charles, in a startling, harsh voice, yelled for them not to. A few souls realized that I was there, too, and asked me my name. "Miss

Morrow," I replied, over and over, in a daze. I didn't have a scratch on me, however—my clothing wasn't even torn—and soon enough they turned back to Charles, who was trying to organize some men to help flip the plane back over, once the engine had cooled.

"How will we get home?" I shouted over the din, tugging on the sleeve of his good arm. It would soon be dusk, and I suddenly remembered my brother. Dwight would be worried if I wasn't home for dinner.

"I'll call Harry," Charles shouted back. "He'll come pick us up. I hope that farmhouse has a telephone."

I finally pushed my way through the crowd and sat down on a tree stump, so conveniently placed it was as if someone had cut the tree down just for me. No one followed, and so I felt strangely detached from the entire scene. The plane, still upside down like a turtle on its back, didn't even look familiar anymore. The only thing I did recognize, and couldn't take my eyes off, was the slim, sandy-haired figure that moved to and fro, directing, controlling. And on the occasions when he stopped and looked my way, an anxious expression on his face as if he was afraid of misplacing me, my heart soared, as it had the moment I first took flight.

After a time I began to get sleepy just sitting there, watching. I believe I actually did doze off, until I felt a hand on my shoulder, shaking me awake.

"Miss Morrow? Miss Morrow?"

I opened my eyes, yawned, and looked up to see a homely man about ten years older than Charles. He had the slicked-back hair of a banker but the earnest grin of a fellow aviator.

"Come along with me," he said, and I followed him obediently, because Charles had suddenly appeared and was doing the same. The man ushered us into a shiny black car, introducing himself to me as "Harry Guggenheim."

"Of the mining Guggenheims?" I stifled a yawn.

"Yes, I believe I know your father."

"Oh." Then we drove away, all the farmers and their families waving goodbye as merrily as if we had just dropped in for tea. Charles had fashioned a sling out of a scarf, and didn't appear to be in any pain; in the front passenger seat, he happily filled Harry in on our adventure, while I sat in the back. I caught a glimpse of my face in the window; I was grinning again. Harry Guggenheim saw me looking at my own reflection, and he smiled, as well.

"Very nice to meet you, Miss Morrow," he said, when we pulled up to his estate, where Charles's cream-colored Ford roadster awaited; had it been only this morning when he picked me up in it? "I hope we can meet again, under less exciting circumstances."

"I hope so, too." Charles opened the door for me, and I stepped out.

"Sorry about the plane, Harry," Charles said, although he didn't sound very sorry at all. "I'll make it right."

"Don't worry, old man. I'm just happy you're safe." And the two shook hands with real affection.

Charles and I got into his car in silence, and we drove in silence through the gathering darkness. He turned the headlights on, and drove—somehow he was able to work the gearshift and steer the wheel, both, with only one hand—even more leisurely than he had earlier; suddenly neither of us was in a hurry to reach our destination.

And we talked. For the first time, truly, we had a conversation; it was as if the adrenaline was still rushing through both of us, turning two shy people into chattering magpies.

Charles shared with me some of his hopes for aviation's future; his feelings of obligation to ensure that future, to convince the average American that flying was no more dangerous than riding in an automobile, maybe even less so.

He also discussed some of the flights he was planning; he wanted to map out the shortest routes between not only cities but continents. "Can you imagine flying to Australia in less than a week's time?" he asked, and I could only shake my head in wonder.

"But I do like ocean travel," I confessed. "It's very restful."

"Oh, I do, as well. The best sleep I got after landing in Paris was on the boat coming home. They wouldn't let me fly back, although I wanted to. That was the first time I realized my life was no longer my own."

"I can't imagine how that felt."

"It was quite surprising, of course. I hadn't counted on that aspect; I was concerned with the flight only, for so long. And initially, all I felt was the kindness of many people—my backers, the mechanics who built the plane. But almost as soon as I landed, I began to feel it—the awful realization that I'm never going to be left alone. People always want more from me, and I don't know what I can give them. I already flew across the ocean."

"How did you know you could do it—fly to Paris? When so many others had failed?"

He nodded, so earnest. "I did the calculations. I would never take an unnecessary risk. See, no one else had ever thought of flying alone—it was a two-pilot job, everyone knew that, because of how long it would take. Well, I realized that if I flew alone, I could carry much more fuel and have a better chance, even if I went off course. And I'm the best flyer I know."

His confidence was so sure, yet so understated, that all I could do was marvel at it. Unlike men who needed approval, he didn't speak loudly or use hyperbole. He simply *was*.

"Would you have done it, if you knew what lay ahead—all the attention, the press?"

"Yes. It was that important a thing to do. Still, I wish they would leave me alone."

"Who's 'they'?"

"Oh, the press, the people, old school chums, total strangers. All those people who put my name on everything from jackets to songs to dances."

I colored, grateful for the dusk that shielded me. I had earnestly learned the Lindy Hop at a dance, the fall of my senior year at Smith.

"Even movie men," Charles continued eagerly, and it seemed to me he was almost grateful to have someone to say these things to. "William Randolph Hearst offered me what would have amounted to a million dollars to appear in a movie, which I turned down. He couldn't believe it when I said no—he said everyone has a price. But I don't. And yet he keeps asking—they all keep asking, for so many things."

"You can't live your life for them."

"No, I can only live my life for myself. Yet the ironic thing is I do feel as if I have a responsibility. So many people look up to me, of course."

Startled, I tore my gaze away from the road. Even in the darkness, I tried to study Charles through eyes that were no longer quite as starry. Now his confidence bordered on arrogance; with his humorless mouth, steely eyes, and steady hand on the steering wheel, for the first time I sensed the darker side of accomplishing so much, so young.

"Well, naturally they do now, but you know—'power corrupts, but absolute power corrupts absolutely,' as they say."

"What? What is that?"

"You know, the famous quote by Lord Acton—haven't you

heard—never mind." I faltered, because I saw his features harden. I imagined that since Paris, not many people had dared to contradict or school him.

I couldn't quite forget, however, those long months when he hadn't thought to drop me even a note, so I blurted out, "It's just that I think it might be a dangerous thing to believe, that's all—that everyone looks up to you, even if they do. It's probably not a good idea to believe it too much. It could change a person, you know. Harden him."

"You think that, do you?"

"Yes, I do."

"Do you think I'm hard?"

"No. Not yet, anyway." I refused to worry that I had offended him. He had asked my opinion, and I had given it to him.

Neither of us spoke for a few moments. Then he grunted and nodded once, as if granting me a rare privilege. We drove on in silence.

"I fear I have done all the talking," he finally burst out, and I secretly rejoiced that he had felt the need to break the silence first; I had proven to be his equal, in stubbornness, anyway. Then I almost laughed; compared to most of the boys I knew, he had revealed almost nothing about himself. I'd learned nothing about his family, for instance. Or his childhood—it was as if his life had only begun after Paris. And maybe, with the incessant press coverage and public mania, the newsreels, the parades and honors—it had. The part of his life he was willing—or forced—to share, anyway.

"No need to fear," I assured him. "I've enjoyed it. All of it. This whole day—even with the broken wheel."

"Not many women would say that." He grinned approvingly, and I sat up straight, feeling much taller than my five feet. "Tell me something about yourself, Anne. What do you want to do?"

"That's quite a large question."

"No, it's simple, really. What do you want to *do*? The one thing you can't stop thinking about? For me, it was Paris. On all those long flights delivering the mail, I couldn't stop thinking about it, puzzling it over until I had the answer, and when it came to me, I did it. So what do you want to do?"

See the Pyramids. Make my brother healthy and happy. Marry a hero—so many thoughts to choose from, so many ideas coming to mind, that I had to gather them to me, quickly, before I blurted them all out.

Charles Lindbergh continued to wait patiently, but he expected an answer; I could see it in the upward thrust of his dimpled chin, the level gaze of his eyes. Reliving our day together—trapped in the sky in that hot cylinder with such a man, such a courageous, noble man; feeling, for the first time, a woman tested and not found wanting, a schoolgirl no longer—I was aware of something blossoming within me. So I said the thing I had never allowed myself to say out loud to anyone; not even to myself.

"I would—I would like to write a great book. Just one. I would be satisfied with that. To paint pictures with words, to help people see what I see, through my language—oh, to be able to do that!"

Charles studied me in silence, his face impassive. And the man who had flown across an ocean on the power of his own belief and no one else's told me, "Then you will."

Was it as simple as that? I leaned back in my seat and stared at the road ahead; we were nearing the city now, streetlights were lit, buildings closer and closer together. As simple as stating a goal, then doing it? All my life I had grappled with doubts and fears; I wasn't as pretty and smart as Elisabeth, I wasn't a boy like Dwight, I wasn't witty and fun like Con. I had brilliant, driven parents. Always had I felt eclipsed and, I had to admit, there was a part of me that took comfort in that feeling. For it absolved me of ever having to decide, of ever having to do anything but think, think, *think*, every minute of every day. What I needed was to stop thinking, start planning, or better yet, simply *act*. Just as I had done, so magnificently, today after the plane flipped over.

Here, I understood, was someone who would not allow me to take comfort in inertia. Already, I was different with him. Better. *More*.

At last, we pulled up the circular drive of home. I felt a rush of warmth and belonging—I could have wept at the sight of the familiar green shutters, the fairy-tale façade with trimming rather like a gingerbread house, the wide porch with its brick columns, all the green and pink chintz-covered wicker furniture clustered about in cozy arrangements. Soon we all would be leaving this house for the new one, almost finished in a different part of Englewood. Still, I felt that here, in this snug house, my family was present, waiting for me even though I knew that Dwight was the only one inside. And perhaps this was the reaction I had been waiting for; this sudden, overwhelming sense of *home*.

I turned to Charles, wanting to share this feeling, wanting to wrap my happy home around him as well, for I remembered that he didn't have much of a family; suddenly I couldn't bear the thought of him driving off alone to face the world. "Would you like to—" I began, but then stopped. He was staring at me so intently that I shivered, involuntarily. He was searching me, searching for something important within me; all I could do was stare back and hope, desperately, that he would find what he was looking for.

"There's something else," he said, and he didn't sound as sure of himself as he usually did. "Something unexpected."

"Oh?" I thought back to my behavior earlier; had I embarrassed him somehow?

"You may not be aware—no, of course, you're not. I've been rather on a project lately. A mission, of sorts. To find—to find someone to share my life with." He paused, as if waiting for me to say something. I couldn't; I could only continue to stare at him. So he cleared his throat and went on.

"It's lonely—it's been lonely these past months. It occurred to me that it would be better to have someone to share this— all—with. From the moment that we met in Mexico, I confess I've wondered—I've thought about you. And then today. You handled that very well. Like an aviator."

"Thank you," I replied solemnly, understanding that this was perhaps the highest praise he could offer.

"Also, there's one other thing," he said with an odd, pained smile. "I can't quite get it out of my mind. While we were up there today, for the first time I was afraid. Not for myself—I've never been afraid for myself. I've always known I would be all right. The strange thing is, I was afraid for you. Afraid of you being injured in some way. I must tell you, I've never felt such a thing before. At first, I wasn't sure I liked it, to tell the truth." He laughed—or, rather, tried to; it was more of a gulp. "But now, I believe I did—not that you were in danger, but—it seems I have a strong desire to protect you, and that must mean something. It *must*."

"What must it mean?"

"It must mean that I should ask if you would consider marrying me," he replied softly.

"You must be joking!" I couldn't help it, I did laugh, and then instantly was horrified, for I knew, by a quick flutter of his eyelids that allowed me an unexpected glimpse into his heart, that he was not.

I looked back up at the house, the house of my childhood. The house that had always sheltered me; *too much?* I wondered. I knew nothing of the world, other than what my parents had wanted me to know. I didn't even know everything about my own *family*. I only knew that I had to work hard, study hard, prepare myself—for what? That, they had not bothered to teach me.

But nothing could have prepared me for this moment. Nothing could have prepared me for marriage to a man like Charles Lindbergh; a man so unlike any other man I had ever known, those bankers, lawyers, academics. Here was a man who was good, brave, driven; these were the qualities I knew about him. That there were many more qualities, as yet hidden, occurred to me as well. But they could not be as important as what I did know.

That he was a quiet man, a disciplined man. A man who did not take responsibility lightly. A man who needed a partner, so that he would never have to fly solo across an ocean again.

The most famous man in the world, who saw me standing in the shadows and somehow knew that I was braver than I supposed. Already, I had flown an airplane because he believed that I could. What else might I do?

"I would like to think about it," I said gravely, understanding he would not approve of me answering impulsively. Suddenly, all those months apart made sense. He had been planning, preparing for this moment as rigorously as he had for his flight to Paris. *I would never take an unnecessary risk*, he had told me. I knew that meant with his heart, as well.

Charles nodded, his face inscrutable. He then got out of the car, walked around and opened my door, and escorted me, his good arm through mine, up the stairs and to my parents' front door.

And it was this—this touchingly gallant gesture, this nod to courtship—that ensured the successful outcome of his latest mission, although I did not tell him. Not then; not for a long time after.

He kissed me good night, as chastely as possible; his lips brushed mine but did not linger, although I felt, as his lean body surged briefly toward mine, that he would have liked them to. But it was enough for me. I knew with a certainty this was the beginning of *everything*. Everything I had been waiting for my entire life.

Charles refused my invitation to come inside, citing his injury. I told him, in the gently nagging manner of one who had a right to, that he should see a doctor. He grinned—in the gently mocking manner of one being nagged—and promised that he would.

I watched as he walked down the porch steps and got into his car. I waited until he had driven away before turning to go inside the house of my childhood, feeling as if I were entering it for the very first time. And in a way I was; for the first time I crossed that threshold as an adult.

It was only later—much later, after letters and telegrams and a hurried visit to my parents, and then a carefully worded press release followed by an explosion of astonishment and joy from every newspaper in the land, and learning to disguise myself whenever I left my house, trying to go to sleep at night still seeing the blinding pops of light from flash powder even through tightly shut eyes . . .

After I had to dismiss a servant who sold some of my letters to a reporter, and then realizing that I could never say a word or write down a thought that I did not want the entire world to know, and having to sneak into the city late at night to be fitted for my wedding dress, and even then, seeing my entire trousseau, including garters and negligees, detailed excruciatingly in the front pages of *The New York Times* as well as the Smith alumni newsletter, and then, finally, that tremulous day in the living room of my parents' new house, christened Next Day Hill! After the minister declared us man and wife and I leaned up, my heart swelling so that I was sure everyone could see its outline through my silk bodice, to be kissed by my new husband, only to have my cheek chastely pecked, while all our friends and family applauded . . .

It was only then that I looked back on that wondrous evening. And I saw myself at that threshold watching Lucky Lindy, the Lone Eagle—no, no, my *fiancé*—drive away and marveling that of all the women on earth, he had chosen me. . . .

It was only then. After my life had altered so irrevocably that I would never again be able to recognize it without help—photographs, maps, battered passports, and yellowed newspaper clippings—only then did I realize that not once that evening had either of us mentioned the word *love*.

But we didn't need to, I assured myself. Two hearts, in such sympathy—there was no need for words, sentimental, silly, romantic. Charles was too special for that. And now I, as well, was too special for that.

We were too special for that. For ordinary words, spoken by ordinary couples.

ORTY-SEVEN YEARS LATER, as we fly across the country in first
class, I can't help but think, *He* hates *this*.

Charles has always believed first class is the worst thing that's
happened to aviation, worse than anything that commercial airlines have done—worse than the snappy stewardesses in their
daring skirts; worse than the pilots being hidden away by a curtain or a door; worse than the relentless effort to make passengers
forget that they're flying at all. It's like being trapped in a can, he
always says. Sealed off. Given a drink. Told to relax. People can
pull shades down over the windows, so they don't even have to
see that they're thirty thousand feet up in the air.

I glance at his face; it is without color, translucent. His eyes
are closed. He insisted on sitting up until the other passengers
boarded, even though there's a curtain, thoughtfully provided by
the airline, hiding us all—the doctor, the nurse, our children,
me. Him, on a stretcher balanced across one row of first-class
seats. The IV is attached to his arm—so thin, like a sapling tree
branch. He is dressed in khaki pants and a polo shirt.

Frail as he is, when he was carried on board—the rest of us
surrounding him, our backs to the world, as if to shun the
healthy—he sat up straight and returned the salute of the pilot
and the copilot who stood at the top of the ramp, tears in their
eyes.

Even that effort exhausted him. And now, he sleeps.

I keep opening my purse, looking at the letters. Cruelly, I want to shake them in his face until he opens his eyes; I want to demand that he read them aloud just so I can hear him *tell* me, finally, something that is real and honest and from his heart. Even if the words were not intended for me—and why weren't they? Where is *my* touching letter of farewell? Or is it supposed to be enough—as it was always supposed to be enough—that he had chosen me in the first place; chosen me now, to be at his side?

I snap my purse shut; of course, I can't do that; I can't make him read the letters out loud. Not in front of my children.

So I sit beside him quietly, the loyal wife, as far as anyone can tell; his flying partner once more on this, his final journey. We've reached cruising altitude and the bright, chipper "ding" has sounded, allowing us to move about if we feel like it. Scott is on watch right now; he is across the aisle from his father, studying him, his face a cipher. I have no idea what he is thinking, or remembering; I know only that he, of all my children, has the hardest road to travel to forgiveness.

Jon is staring out the window, and I don't know what he sees. He is a man of few words, even fewer than his father. But unlike his father, Jon is not comfortable in the air. His home is the sea; his passion the creatures within it.

Land flew out earlier, and will meet us in Honolulu; his task is to arrange transportation to the far side of the island, Maui, so that Charles can be close to Hana and the home he built for us there. Good, obedient Land; if his father is air, his brother water, he is just as his name sounds—the earth. *Land*. Solid, a man of the west, a rancher.

The girls are with their families, Reeve in Vermont, Ansy in France. Both have small children and can't join us on this last journey, but they were able to say their goodbyes earlier.

How I love my children! How thankful I am for them, and all

they have given me—joy, frustration, hope; a reason to go on living when I thought I had none. And now grandchildren. But are they enough? Enough to salvage this family when—*if*—I reveal what I know?

I touch my husband, just the gentlest touch, and it's like it was in the beginning, when I could never quite convince myself I had the right. Only now, instead of a young god, he is near death, soon to be gone in body if never in memory, and it's not fair. I wanted to have these last days to remember the best of our life together, the good times, the impossibly sweet times.

Isn't that what you're supposed to remember when a spouse lies dying? Aren't you supposed to forget and, most important, to forgive?

But once again, he has denied me a wifely right. Because of the letters in my purse, I'll never be able to forget all the years missing him, wanting him, wondering why he could be with me for only a few days before starting to pace, to look out windows, to plan to fly away from me once more. My own secret does not seem as enormous now; it cannot compare to the ones he has been keeping from me.

I look at him, lying strangely still, unrecognizably weak, his mouth slightly open, his jaw slack; for the first time not telling any one of us what to do or think or feel.

And I understand that betrayal is more enormous than forgiveness. One more thing Charles has taught me, in a lifetime of lessons and lectures.

CHAPTER 4

C EILING. GAS CAPACITY. WINGSPAN. Crosswinds. Throttle. Lift. Technical terms, words I needed to absorb, definitions I needed to memorize, as part of my new role.

Well-done roast beef. No sauces. Vegetables cooked to the point of desperation. Slices of white bread accompanying every meal. A different list, but no less important. And just as vital to my new role, my new life.

Had I ever been to college? Had I ever had an education? In those first weeks of marriage to the most famous man in the world (so famous that I received tearstained letters from ingénues accusing me of stealing their future husband; so famous that instead of the groom receiving the traditional congratulations, it was *I* who was thumped on the back; so famous that movie stars begged us to honeymoon at their estates and directors wanted to make feature-length movies about our wedding), I couldn't believe that I had. For I had so very much left to *learn.*

I went from knowing nothing about my husband to being expected to know *everything* about him. His likes and dislikes regarding food (all of the above), his wardrobe demands (simply tailored suits in brown tweed, starched white shirts, plain neckties, and always those battered brown boots he had worn since his days flying the airmail, no matter the occasion). I was also expected to know his daily schedule, magically, intuitively; beginning the first full day of our married life.

That first morning, I overslept. Exhausted by all the preparations, the constant strain of keeping the press misdirected—we spent the week before our wedding driving out, in full view and pursuit, to various churches just to throw them off the scent—I overslept.

I was exhausted, as well, by my first night as a wife. His reluctance to kiss me in public notwithstanding, my husband turned out to be a very ardent lover in private. His hands—those strong, elegant hands that had so fascinated me in Mexico City—were insatiably curious as they first discovered, then claimed, every part of my body, awakening me to pleasure and pain, both. But mostly pleasure.

Pleasure, repeated, several times during the night, and so I rose late that first morning. We had decided to honeymoon on a new motorboat, as the entire world would be scanning the clouds for the "blissful, daring newlyweds of the sky." The boat rocked gently, nudging me to wakefulness. I resisted, clinging to sleep. I was dreaming of my sister, of Elisabeth; she was twelve and I was ten, and she had hidden my favorite doll and wouldn't tell me where it was, and she laughed at my tears.

Before I was fully awake, I was angry with her, threatening to tell on her to Mother; as I was pulled further into wakefulness by the warmth of the sun baking our galley bedroom, I remembered. I wasn't ten, and I wasn't angry at my sister, but she *had* been on my mind so much these past few weeks.

First the confusion the day after our accident, when the newspapers reported that Colonel Lindbergh and Miss *Elisabeth* Morrow had narrowly escaped death when their plane lost a wheel on takeoff. "I don't understand," Elisabeth kept saying when she called me at home that next morning; I could hear the rustle of a newspaper in her hand. "Why would they say I was even in New Jersey?"

"It was me," I told her, explaining the situation. "I kept saying I was Miss Morrow. I never gave my first name."

"You?" She kept repeating it, to my irritation. "You? Colonel Lindbergh came calling for *you*? And took *you* up?"

"Yes," I said, over and over—itching to tell her the rest, but knowing I couldn't until Charles had spoken with Mother and Daddy.

And then, when I could tell her the rest, right before Daddy's office put out the tersely worded statement that Colonel Lindbergh would be marrying Miss Anne Morrow, the ambassador's daughter, the papers got it all wrong again. They continued to report that it was Elisabeth, not me, who was "the luckiest young woman in the world today, having been chosen by the gallant Lindy to be his copilot for life." Daddy's office issued an even more tersely worded correction. And finally the newspapers appeared to remember that Ambassador Morrow did have another daughter, after all.

When Elisabeth and I were able to meet, soon after we announced the engagement, I ran to her with apologies already tumbling from my lips. "Oh, Elisabeth, what an awful mix-up in the newspapers! I'm so sorry, it's not fair to you that they would make such a mistake. It makes you look like—like—"

"The jilted lover?" She laughed breezily, tossing her head—but I could see the hurt in her blue eyes.

"No, no, of course not, it's just that—"

"Oh, Anne, I don't care about the press! Honestly, not a whit! It's just—it's just—"

"What? What is it?"

My sister grabbed me by my shoulders, looking fiercely into my eyes as tears filled her own, and whispered, "Oh, but I do so want to be happy for you! I do want to! You must believe me!" Then she ran up to her room and shut the door. And from that moment on there was an awkwardness between us; our roles had changed so significantly, neither one of us knew how to behave. Elisabeth had always been the *one*, the golden child. I had always been content to stand in her shadow.

Overnight, I had turned Elisabeth, the beauty, the prize, into an old maid. A jilted old maid, at that. Even though she never accused me of this, I felt it. There were things on her mind that she wanted to say to me but could not; it was evident every time she changed the subject abruptly or couldn't meet my gaze whenever Charles was in the room.

Still, she had attended me at my wedding, even making sure that Charles's boutonniere was secure, and smiled brilliantly all through the ceremony.

And so my sister, not my husband, was on my mind when I finally awoke that first morning of my married life. Feeling vulnerable, exposed, it took me a moment to realize that I was naked beneath the musty-smelling, scratchy wool blanket. Remembering *why* I was naked, I smiled and reached out to my new husband—only to find an empty pillow.

"Charles?" I searched around the tiny, dank cabin adjacent to an equally tiny, dank galley kitchen—it smelled of fish and kerosene—for something to wear; spying a flannel robe that I didn't recognize, and not even stopping to wonder whose it could be, I wrapped myself in it, pulled on some tennis shoes, and climbed the narrow ladder up to the deck.

My husband was bent over a table, looking nut-brown and extremely handsome in a heavy white fisherman's sweater and a blue nautical cap; as much at home on the water as he was in the air. Even as I marveled at his hands tying slipknots on a thick white rope with the assurance of a seasoned sailor, I blushed; my skin was still tender from the memory of those hands gripping *me*.

"You're up late," he said, his piercing blue gaze sweeping over me, taking me all in; the robe was not cinched tightly around my waist, causing it to gape at the top of my thighs. I clutched the worn fabric, but Charles flushed anyway. Then he smiled.

"I know. I'm sorry." I walked over to him, and for a moment didn't know what to do. Should I kiss him? Hug him? The dusky intimacy of last night seemed to fade in the harsh daylight, and no longer was he my husband, my lover who cried out in the dark, over and over; once again he was Charles Lindbergh, the Lone Eagle.

And I still wasn't accustomed to the notion that I had a right to be by his side.

I decided on a fond pat of his arm; he patted me back on the shoulder, and we both exhaled in relief. I told myself that we wouldn't always be so tentative with each other, and I wanted to tell him this, too, but couldn't find the words. Silence, I was learning—another thing to add to my syllabus!—was the response with which my husband felt most comfortable.

We both turned and surveyed the scenery; we were about a quarter-mile offshore. The dinghy in which we had rowed out to the cruiser was tied up and banging against the side of the boat. The sky was overcast; it was late May, so the air wasn't yet heavy with the humidity of summer storms. There was scarcely any breeze.

"What's our schedule?" I turned back to my husband with a playful smile; it was a honeymoon, after all. There was no schedule to be followed, except for lazy breakfasts, candlelit dinners—

and more nights like the one we had just enjoyed. I'd even brought some of my poems to share with him; I imagined him reading them out loud by candlelight.

"I wanted to shove off at oh-eight-hundred. But you slept in, so now we're behind schedule. There are tins of food down in the galley, so I'd like my breakfast. After you clean up—you must scrub out the head with bleach, of course, every day—I'll lift anchor. I expect to make it to Block Island by twelve-hundred. I thought I spotted a plane earlier, about five miles west, so we shouldn't linger too long."

"But—" My head was dizzy with information; I couldn't quite process it all. "Block Island? What will we do once we're in Block Island? I know of a lovely little restaurant there, we could—"

"No restaurants. We'd be discovered. We need to stop for more supplies, and for fuel."

"But I—I don't really cook, you know. I took a couple of domestic science classes at Smith, but that was ages ago. I'm not sure I know how—"

"Then you'll learn. You'll have to learn, anyway, for when we fly together."

"Oh, well, I thought that we'd—"

"You'll find eggs, a rasher of bacon, and some powdered milk and coffee." Charles nodded back toward the stairs below. "Once we're under way, then I'll get out the books and charts and we'll begin."

"Begin what? What books and charts? Charles, please slow down and be more specific!" My voice began to rise, but I was so bewildered and, yes, disappointed. What happened to my romantic honeymoon?

My husband sighed, and the corner of his mouth twitched.

"You're going to learn to fly, as well as navigate. I'm planning a trip to the Orient to chart the routes for passenger flights. I'll pilot, naturally, but you'll need to know how, as well. You'll serve as navigator."

"I—I, *navigate?*" It was such an awesome word. Magellan navigated. Columbus navigated. Da Gama navigated. How could I do such a thing? "Are you sure?" I asked anxiously, twisting the tie of my robe in knots. "Are you sure you want me?"

"Of course. Who else would I want? Who else would I trust but you, my wife? I would like my eggs now, if you please."

I could only stare at him, overwhelmed by all that was expected of me. Last night, I realized suddenly, had only just been the beginning. Charles Lindbergh had chosen me; that, in itself, had been enormous enough to absorb, and I hadn't quite finished doing so. But now I began to understand what that really meant. I would be not only his wife but his copilot. I would not only make his eggs but steer his course to the Orient.

I started to say, "I'll try," but stopped myself just in time. I understood that "try" would not be an acceptable answer.

Instead I said, "Of course. How do you like them?"

"Over easy."

"Perfect. That's just how I like my own eggs."

I did not like my eggs over easy. But it would be simpler, I knew, to pretend that I did.

Yet another thing I was learning. And so soon.

WE WERE DISCOVERED on Block Island. We went ashore to purchase more supplies, and a man said, "Hey, ain't you that Lindbergh fellow? And his new bride?"

I tensed, ready to flee; to my great surprise, Charles simply scratched his nose and spit—two things I had never seen him do before.

"That Lindbergh fellow? Nah. What would he be doing here? I heard they flew to Maine, that's what I heard."

"Huh. Now that I think of it, you're right. That's what I heard on the radio, too."

Charles turned to me with a wink, and I smothered a smile; I caught his joy, his mischievous delight at his deception as he grabbed my hand, for the first time ever in public. He held it tightly, even while we strolled leisurely through the little fisherman's shack, loading up on eggs, cereal, and a can of coffee. (It had taken me three tries to make an acceptable pot that morning, and even then, all Charles would do was grunt and close his eyes as he drank it.)

I thrilled to be claimed in such a manner; that was the moment I felt well and truly married. Even the night before had not made me feel so possessed. I had surely only imagined Charles's frozen look when I tiptoed up for my wedding kiss; I had misunderstood all those awkward poses for the photographers in the days leading up to our wedding, when Charles had never once touched me, never once smiled down at me, never once behaved in any way like a man in love.

Finally, here, in this rambling shack with buckets of worms in every corner, my husband did reach for me; he held on to me and at last all the tense, public weeks leading up to our wedding vanished, and we recaptured the intimate magic of the night he asked me to marry him. My heart did that crazy, weightless leap, like an airplane catching wing, and I could not stop myself from grinning. I even rubbed my face in the scratchy wool of his sweater, like a cat marking its territory. And I think he was surprised, and touched, when I did.

I never wanted to leave that shack; I didn't want to break the spell of this miraculous, ordinary moment when a man and wife discussed the merits of cornflakes versus shredded wheat. I think I knew, even then, that moments like this between us would be too rare.

Oh, how did I know? Did I smell it, like an animal smells an intruder in the wind? Hear it, like an animal hears danger in a branch snapping? For we were animals, Charles and I, trapped, caught; as soon as we left the shack, still clinging to each other in the haze of our astonishing, teasing intimacy, we were surrounded by people and reporters and photographers.

"It's them!" somebody cried, and we sprang apart, caught—doing what? I didn't know; I felt only the shock of confusion, of guilt, as my heart beat wildly and my knees began to shake.

"Charles! Charles Lindbergh!" "Colonel!" "Anne!" "Mrs. Lindbergh! Annie!" "Look here!" "Look over here!" "How's married life?" "Get any rest last night?" Guffaws, applause, questions, questions, and everywhere, people looking at me, staring at me, gaping at me from my head to my toes, and I blushed, knowing why. I'd heard of old-fashioned shivarees, when relatives and friends spied on newlyweds, rousing them out of their beds, making crude jokes of their intimacy. This was a shivaree, a most public shivaree, and I was mortified by what I knew they were all thinking.

"Charles? Charles?" I spun around, blindly; the flash powder was exploding and I could feel the crowd pressing closer and closer. What would happen when they got to us? Would they chew us up and spit us out, our bones picked clean? What was it Shakespeare had said about "a pound of flesh"? I couldn't control my fears; I was imagining us both trampled on the dock, and I knew I was on the verge of my very first hysterics. I could feel everything moving faster and faster, utterly out of control, and I reached, blindly, for my husband.

"Move, Anne! *Now!*" Charles was pushing me ahead of him, simultaneously trying to shield me from the crowd and using me to clear a path. I twisted around to look back at him, but he hissed, "Go on!" His eyes were wild, but his face was that closed-off mask that I had first glimpsed in Mexico City.

I clutched the soggy bag of groceries to my chest, worried that I might break the eggs. Absurdly, I wondered if my hair was combed and knew that it wasn't; it was streaming down my back, unkempt, like my clothes—a baggy sweater, dungarees, tennis shoes. I would be seen like this in every newspaper in the land. My heart sank. For this, ironically, would be my official wedding portrait. We had taken none at the ceremony, for fear someone would sell them.

So *this* was to be the photographic evidence of my marriage— this mad sprint through a shrieking, clutching gauntlet of reporters, fishermen, businessmen, women, and a startling number of children; people who, for some reason, had run to see us, who felt they had a *right* to see us, on our honeymoon. No one would remember my exquisite pale blue gown of French silk, the bouquet of lilies of the valley picked from the garden at Next Day Hill— all was a dream, a beautiful dream, now. So I ran, my head bowed, tears streaming down my cheeks.

Finally we reached the *Mouette*—the crowd chasing us as if we were fugitives—but discovered any escape was impossible. A mismatched flotilla of vessels—dinghies, canoes, fishing boats— were bobbing in the water just beyond the dock, boxing us in, their passengers standing on the decks and even, in one case, hanging from a mast. Simply to get a look at us.

"What do we do?" I turned around, sniffling, wiping my tears.

"Now I wish we had a plane," Charles growled. "We'll have to wait them out. Surely some policeman will eventually come and make them go away. I'll radio for help once we're inside the boat."

A woman broke through the crowd and ran up to me.

"Charles!" Before I could understand what was happening, she reached out to me; Charles tried to step between us, but not before she had wrapped her arms around me and smothered me in an embrace.

"You dear girl, you! You keep him safe and happy, you hear? And may God bless you with a little Lindy as soon as possible!"

"I—I—" I squirmed out of her arms; she was round and smelled of fresh yeast, and her handbag kept hitting me on the side of the head.

"Please," Charles said, pulling her away from me. "Please, leave us alone, all of you. We appreciate your good wishes, but we'd like to be left alone now."

I stepped onto the slippery deck of the cruiser, miraculously managing to hold on to the groceries while falling hard on my knees. Charles helped me up and followed me down to the galley. He assisted in putting the groceries away, not commenting on my trembling hands, the tears that kept springing to my eyes even though I tried to blink them away.

I waited for him to comfort me, to wrap me in his arms and tell me it would be all right. He didn't; he looked at his watch instead.

"Try to have dinner on the table at eighteen-hundred," he said, ducking his head as he disappeared into our little cabin bedroom, where the ship-to-shore radio was. After a moment I heard his voice, calm, soothing, as he transmitted. Outside, there was still a great scuffle of feet on the dock, muffled, excited voices, but miraculously, no one came aboard the boat. Apparently everyone was content merely to stand on deck and watch and wait.

I twisted my hair into a knot at the back of my neck and

splashed some water on my face. Charles came back into the galley with his arms full of books and charts; he spread them out on the little wobbly table while I cooked, or rather heated a tin of beef stew over the tiny gas burner and opened a loaf of that awful white bread.

"Don't let them get to you, Anne," he said, as he studied a page in one of the books and scribbled something on it. "Don't let them make you cry. Never let them win."

"I didn't know we were at war."

"Well, we are. I have been, ever since Paris. I'm sorry that you have to get caught up in it, too. But I'm also grateful that I no longer have to go through it alone."

"You are?"

"Yes." Then he did look at me, and smiled; it did what all his smiles—so few, I was beginning to understand; so precious—did to me. It made my heart soar, my skin prick with warmth and attention; it dried my tears and gave me courage.

So I served up our dinner in that impossible wobbly galley, illuminated only by one battery-powered lantern hanging from the ceiling, swinging hypnotically, casting long shadows across our faces.

After I cleared up, my husband began to teach me how to fly.

Once, I leaned over to get a better look at a diagram of an engine, and paused, ever so briefly, to rub my face in the sleeve of his sweater. With a soft sigh, he stroked my cheek and hugged me to him before he continued his instruction.

Meanwhile, just outside the boat, strangers kept chanting our names, an eerie incantation that plucked at my nerves.

And I knew that this was the bond we would share, that would bind us together forever. Not the experience of losing a wheel on takeoff. Not the passion of the night before, nor even the vows we had uttered, the promises we had made before our families.

No, it was the experience of being hunted. Of being two animals, prey, trying our best to fight off those who would do us harm, even as they wished us well.

TAILWIND. Vertical stabilizer. Longitudinal axis. Yaw.

Keep moving. Eyes down. Never smile. Never engage.

The list of things I needed to learn grew longer with each passing day. Yet I mastered them all. I had to. Without them, I never would have been able to survive in my new role as the aviator's wife.

CHAPTER 5

THE GREAT AVIATRIX paused in the doorway as she entered the room. She was clad in her usual trousers, shirt, and scarf, despite the fact that this was a formal affair. Her sandy hair cropped short, her body lean and long, her resemblance to my husband was obvious—and obviously calculated.

"It's a wonder she didn't change her name to Charlotte," Carol Guggenheim murmured, as the rest of the room burst into applause. The Great Aviatrix grinned, ducking her head in a bashful way, but I saw the glimmer in her eyes. Unlike my husband, she enjoyed the attention.

"Here she comes," I whispered, as she made a beeline toward us. Charles, Carol, Harry, and I were standing in the middle of the Guggenheims' drawing room at Falaise, their country estate, that enormous Normandy castle I had first glimpsed last summer. The party was for us, to welcome us back from our latest cross-country flight. Only Harry and Carol could persuade Charles to attend such a grand soiree.

"Welcome back, sir." The Great Aviatrix saluted my husband and flashed her toothy grin.

Charles saluted back with a faint smile, then shook her hand. From some corner of the room, a camera flashed, and Carol immediately stepped in front of me, protectively, and frowned; she always reminded me of a young lioness, fiercely guarding her young—in this case, Charles and me. Carol and Harry were always looking out for us, weeding out the climbers, those interested in exploiting us, from those who could genuinely help us or simply be our friends. And their home on the sound, with its acres of land and forest, had become a haven for us from the press; we were welcome anytime, no questions asked.

"Harry, no cameras," Carol hissed, eyeing Charles nervously. My husband did not tense, however; he appeared relaxed, even happy, as he chatted amiably with the Great Aviatrix. This evening, anyway, my husband appeared to have called a truce with the press.

Harry sipped his champagne and shrugged. "Can't frisk everyone, you know. I'll go talk to the fellow." And with his broad shoulders leading the way, he barreled through the crowd of people I barely knew but who had been invited to welcome me—to welcome *us*—back home. My family was nowhere in sight, although they were fond of the Guggenheims; Con, Dwight, Mother, and Daddy were in Mexico, and Elisabeth always had an excuse to stay in Englewood these days with Connie; they were about to open their dream school.

Welcome back, The First Couple of the Air! proclaimed a banner hung across the Guggenheims' mantelpiece. That was who we were now; that was what we did. We flew. No one even bothered to pretend that we were like other newlyweds, who set up housekeeping together, or picked out china patterns, or argued amiably over budgets.

Charles and I spent the first months of our married life in the air, crossing the country, christening every new airfield that popped up like tulips in this new, springlike era of aviation. Everything was possible, the future as vast and endless as the sky itself—as long as planes kept flying.

And so we flew, to ensure that they would. Right after our honeymoon, Charles was named to the board of one of the first passenger airlines—TAT, or Transcontinental Air Transport—and like everything in his life, he took his duties seriously. He wasn't content merely to lend his name for publicity and investors; he insisted on mapping out routes himself, with me in the copilot seat. He even piloted the first official flight. And I was the first official "air hostess."

As newsreel cameras whirred to capture the occasion, a group of movie stars and celebrities, including the governor of California, made their toothy way, travel cases in hand, down a red carpet just outside Los Angeles. Only this was not a movie premiere; they were the passengers on that first flight, and at the end of the carpet Charles and I stood in front of a gleaming Ford Tri-Motor plane. While flash powder blinded us, Mary Pickford flirted shamelessly with my husband, and I smiled gamely, pretending not to mind.

I needn't have worried; Mary Pickford was too chicken to actually fly. She simply christened the plane with a champagne bottle and remained on the ground as Charles made a great show of putting on his flight jacket, and I made a great show of tying a ridiculous apron around my ridiculously flimsy flowered dress, and we followed our "guests" up a short temporary staircase onto the plane. Charles piloted it to the first refueling stop in Arizona, while I fussed over the ten passengers seated in wicker chairs, five on each side of the plane, each with its own window, velvet privacy curtain, reading lamp, cigar lighter, and ashtray. I handed out magazines, helped two male attendants serve catered meals on real china, and poured coffee out of a sterling-silver coffeepot. When we hit our first air pocket, all the passengers turned instinctively to me, terror in their eyes; I smiled reassuringly, and soon they were all behaving like experienced flyers.

We also flew to console, to buck up the country's nerves, when, just two months after the inaugural flight, TAT—now dubbed "The Lindbergh Line"—suffered its first accident. The plane went down near Mount Williams, New Mexico, far from any road or path. Charles decided it was up to him, as the face of the company, to locate the wreckage, so I climbed behind him into the cockpit of a Lockheed Vega and kept my eyes peeled, not sure what I was looking for. My stomach heaved when I found it. The blackened, twisted plane looked broken, like a child's toy carelessly thrown; my fists balled up, hitting my thighs as if to inflict the kind of pain the passengers must have felt. I knew there were no survivors—how could there be when the plane had burst into flames on impact? We flew as close as we could, but it was not close enough to see the bodies, for which I was ever grateful; unballing my fists, I wrote down the coordinates that Charles barked to me, and, dry-eyed, handed them to the search party when we landed, fifty miles away, in a flat patch of desert. As the First Lady of the Air, I murmured empty words of sympathy to the families at the mass memorial a week later, proud that I did not disgrace Charles by surrendering to my emotions and sobbing with them. Two days later, when I climbed once more into a passenger plane—half empty; the public scared easily back then—I did so with a confident grin for the photographers that I could scarcely believe when I saw it in the papers.

But, of course, I *was* confident; Charles was piloting this plane, so I knew nothing would happen. It was those poor people's misfortune to be piloted by someone else; someone *less*.

We also flew to set records, to explore. Not just the world, the skies, but our marriage.

I never saw my husband smile as readily as he did the day I

flew solo for the first time, after months of study and practice flights that had been wedged between our official TAT duties. Taking off was easy; my mind was so full of checklists and procedures that I was too busy to be frightened. It was only once I was up, able to relax after those always tense first moments of takeoff, when I realized that even though I had done this a hundred times before, Charles had always been in the instructor's seat.

Now there was no one in the plane but myself. And the enormity of what I was doing—flying alone, relying solely on my intelligence and skill for what seemed the first time in my life, made my veins suddenly fill with liquid lead, my stomach pitch uncontrollably, and beads of sweat break out on my brow. Terrified I would black out, I willed myself to concentrate on the instruments even though, for a sickening moment, they blurred into one smear of lines and circles and numbers. The wind that I always welcomed was now sinister; despite my study of physics and aerodynamics, it seemed a miracle that it didn't simply fling this insignificant little piece of machinery to the ground. How could I ever have imagined I could do this by myself—keep an airplane aloft?

Then I remembered that Charles was below, watching me, always watching me—testing me, as well. To see if I would measure up to his standards, because after only a few months of marriage, I sensed he wasn't quite convinced. Frankly, neither was I.

But there really wasn't any other option—so I talked myself through the maneuvers; banking to the right, to the left, circling carefully into the easiest landing pattern, keeping my eyes on that strip of land and my hand on the throttle at all times, trying to ignore the slim figure waiting, his hat in his hands, at the far end of the runway. I landed the plane with just a couple of bumps—I jerked the stick, reflexively, upon touchdown. When I closed the throttle completely, causing the propeller to slowly cease its spinning, Charles came running toward me. His face was open and boyish, his eyes snapping.

"Good girl! How do you feel?" He helped me step out onto the wing, where I wavered for a second, the wind finally having its say and nearly knocking me off my feet.

"Wonderful!" And I did, all of a sudden. Because he saw me that way.

"I'm very proud of you."

"I know."

And he swept me up into his arms, right there on the airstrip, heedless of the reporters rushing up to us with their notebooks and their pencils. I had passed my test—not just my solo test but my first test of our marriage. He led, I followed, and that meant I had to keep up with him. Now I had proved that I could.

Sometimes, I admit, I was so terrified I couldn't form the words to tell him—such as the time I allowed my husband to hurl me off the top of a mountain like a slingshot. Perched on the edge of a cliff, held back by a tight, corded, thick rope, I sat in a new sailplane, frozen with fear, my hands gripping the steering stick so tightly it left an imprint, although I could scarcely feel it. My face was paralyzed, yet I knew that somehow I grinned that carefree grin at Charles and the reporters and photographers standing around, then I shut my eyes as the cord was winched back and cut. I tried to remember the hasty instructions Charles had given me—"Aim high to find the best current, and then trust the wind!"—feeling my heart in my throat, certain that I would be smashed up against the side of some mountain.

But I was not! Instead, I did catch a current and finally experienced flight as I'd dreamed it—silent, soaring, like a bird, a majestic creature with proud eyes and little use for others. I shouted my joy, unashamed, for there was no one to hear it, and I glided and swooped for what felt like hours but was really only minutes.

I circled lower and lower and made a somewhat bumpy landing in a field. Several cars came driving up as I climbed out of the plane; a startled man poked his head out of his window.

"Where did you come from?" he asked in astonishment.

"Up there!" I pointed back up at the mountain, and laughed at the look on his face. I had just become the first American woman to fly a glider.

Charles and I both rejoiced in moments like these, and built on them; while I logged ever more solo flights on the way to my pilot's license (which Charles carefully put away with his own, for whatever museum would want them someday), I began to study celestial navigation.

Like all flyers, I preferred to rely on the instrument panel, but Charles insisted on my learning celestial, as well; *he* had, in preparation for his Paris flight. I grew to dislike using the sextant, a heavy, awkward instrument resembling a combination telescope/protractor. It was nearly impossible to use while flying, as the plane was never steady enough for me to confidently fix the horizon. And for the longest time, I could not find Polaris to save my soul.

"Anne, for heaven's sake, it's right there," Charles would hiss out of tight, exasperated lips during a rare evening stroll about Next Day Hill, my mother's grand new house. Odd, that I thought of it as hers, not hers and Daddy's. But Next Day Hill was Mother's dream, a mansion with wings and spectacular entrance halls and even a ballroom. And glorious gardens, through which I loved to walk with my husband, who still didn't quite seem to be my husband. So much of our married life was lived on the public stage, where he summoned such frenzy and deification, I sometimes found myself staring at him just as adoringly as everyone else.

It probably didn't help matters that even though we'd been

married for several months, we still used Next Day Hill as a sort of base between flights. No one appeared to expect us to buy a home of our own. We bought planes, instead; a little Curtiss two-seater for me, a much bigger, specially fitted Lockheed Sirius for our planned trip to the Orient. We were, after all, the First Couple of the *Air.*

"See?" Charles would grab my hand—not romantically, like a lover on a moonlit stroll, but impatiently, like a teacher does a dreamy child's—and point toward the night sky. "Polaris. It's the brightest star in the north."

"No, that's the brightest star." I pointed to another, lower on the horizon. Charles snorted.

"That is not a star, it's a planet. Venus."

"Well, it is the brightest!"

"But it's not a star. Anne, you'd think you'd never studied astronomy before!"

"I haven't! I've studied literature and poetry, and I can tell you who first translated Cervantes. You don't know that, do you?" I knew I was on rocky ground; any mention of Charles's lack of education might cause him to spin on his heel and leave me in the middle of the garden, without even a single word of explanation. Yet something about the way he stared down at me, so endlessly, tirelessly gifted and superior, made my skin itch and my eyes narrow to meet his gaze head-on. "It was Thomas Shelton," I continued recklessly, finally tired of the constant lecturing, teaching, *pushing.*

Why couldn't we have a normal marriage? What other young couple walked in a moonlit garden, fragrant with honeysuckle and newly cut grass, and argued over the definition of stars and planets? Never mind that I had known that I was not marrying any mere man, had never for one instant *wanted* to marry any mere man; at that moment, worn out from weeks spent scrutinized by the public, weary from having strangers knock on hotel doors at odd hours, just to get a glimpse of us, I had had enough.

"It was in 1612," I retorted. "That was the first translation of *Don Quixote* into English."

Charles blinked. "That's admirable, Anne, but I doubt it will come in handy when we're flying across the Bering Sea at night. Now, which one is Polaris again?"

Chastened by his patience, not to mention his practicality, I looked back up at the sky. The stars, which used to be so poetic and inspiring, were now simply more things I had to learn because my husband demanded that I do so. I gazed up at them, not seeing the beauty; I saw potential mistakes instead.

That night, for the first time, I did successfully identify Polaris. It was the one star whose icy gaze reminded me most of my husband's.

THE FESTIVE EVENING at the Guggenheims' was to celebrate our latest aviation triumph, a ten-day flight through the Caribbean with Juan and Betty Trippe for Juan's new airline, Pan American Airways. Afterward, Charles and I flew for days in a little two-seater open-cockpit plane over the Mayan jungle in Mexico; we had been asked to photograph the ruins of Chichén Itzá for the first time from the air, and in doing so we'd discovered other ruins as well.

Aside from the archaeological significance, for me this trip had been noteworthy because finally, after we parted ways with Juan and Betty, we had much-needed time alone; precious time, away from adoring eyes and expectations and ceremony and the hectic bustling of my family. Only when Charles and I were alone—which usually meant aloft in the sky, seeing the world in a way no one else could—did I ever feel as if I was truly his part-ner, and not just an adoring appendage standing slightly off to his side. Seated behind Charles but sometimes taking over for him whenever he grew tired, my hand was sure on the stick as I piloted the Lone Eagle over jungles and mountains.

Two years ago I had been just another Smith coed, unable to make up her mind about anything. Now here I was in the sky, charting new paths, breaking records—pushing myself in ways I never would have without him. How on earth did mere mortals live? Soaring, dipping, waggling the wings of the plane, I felt nothing but pity for the girls I had gone to school with. They had settled down on earth into dull, ordinary lives. They had married dull, ordinary men.

But it was on the ground, camping beneath the Mexican sky, that I began to know my *husband*—not the famous aviator or my schoolgirl crush. He told me stories of camping alone on the banks of the Mississippi River in Minnesota when he was a boy, his father never around to accompany him, for C. A. Lindbergh was a congressman by then, away in Washington most of the time. Although he rarely spoke of his father, I got the sense that there was something missing between them; some break in their relationship. His mother he spoke of with more affection.

"She raised me," Charles said one sultry evening, amid the cackling of macaws, the sudden, surprising scampering of tiny lizards in the underbrush around us—a setting so strange and ex-otic, yet it was merely stage dressing; my attention was firmly fixed, as always, on my astonishing husband. "My mother and my uncle. My father wasn't quite—responsible in that way. And my stepsisters, well—I won't get into it all. Of course, that's one reason why I married you."

"What do you mean?"

"You're from such a fine family, with good blood. No irregularities—our children will be pure."

"Charles! You make me sound like a broodmare! As if that was the only reason you married me!" I laughed, craning my head to look up at him.

He smiled down at me, touched the tip of my wide nose, and said, "If that was the only reason I married you, I would never have been able to get past this."

"Oh!" I brushed his hand away, although I didn't mind his teasing, wrapped as it was in the warm cocoon of our surprising intimacy, so far removed from others. Without our aircraft, we never would have been able to find our way back to civilization, and for the moment, anyway, I didn't want to. "What do you mean, no irregularities? I might have a spooky great-aunt tucked away in an attic, as far as you know."

"Do you?" The smile faded away. He was looking at me in that clinical way he sometimes did—I never failed to feel like a butterfly pinned to a specimen board.

"No, of course not!" For a fleeting moment, Dwight came to mind—over Daddy's protests, Mother had arranged for my brother to leave Amherst for a while, after another "difficult" time, during which he again began to hallucinate. She put him in a rest home in Massachusetts and told my father to stop sending his son letters urging him to take control of his mind, as if it were only that simple.

Charles didn't know anything other than that my brother had simply taken a leave of absence, and for the first time I decided he should not know more than that—not yet, anyway. I had never kept a secret from my husband before and didn't quite understand why I chose to do so now; with a guilty little smile, I stirred uneasily in his arms.

He didn't notice; his thoughts were still with his own father. "You know, he did provide me with the money to attend flight school. And I admired his principles, for he took some difficult stands during the war years. He was against our involvement; because of that, he lost his seat in Congress. But there's really no further need to discuss him, Anne. You know all you need to know. He died a few years before my flight to Paris."

"So he never knew how much you've accomplished."

"It wouldn't have mattered to me," he insisted. "At least Mother has lived to see it all. As I said, she's the one who raised me."

I thought of his mother; Evangeline Lodge Lindbergh was a cold, distant woman with the same startling blue eyes of her son, who had sat with her brother during our wedding, a stony expression on her face. I didn't feel that she disapproved of me, or of our marriage—rather that she simply had her own life, apart from her son's. She seemed so removed always, refusing my repeated invitations to visit with cordial, if impersonal, letters. Yet Charles once told me that she had been quite anxious when he left for Paris, even though she scolded a photographer who asked her to kiss her son goodbye for the camera. "We Lindberghs don't do that," Evangeline had chided the poor man, to Charles's delight.

And she was Charles's caring, nurturing parent! My heart surged toward my husband, wanting to give him everything he had lacked before he met me: love, affection, the warmth and constancy of a family circle. Despite his insistence that his father's approval wouldn't have mattered, I felt his shoulders heave, as if shifting a burden, and I couldn't help but remember Dwight. It seemed to me that sons always needed the approval of their fathers. Much more than daughters.

We stared into the fire, or up at the stars, which, now that I had proved my mastery over them, were given back to me as objects of fascination and wonder once more. I could enjoy their beauty and trust in their discretion as they observed a man and a woman come together as husband and wife.

And this was the greatest gift that aviation could ever give me; not the sense of freedom but the sense of permanence, coupling, of being absolutely worthy, absolutely necessary to the one person in the world who hadn't needed anyone. *Before.*

I even, at his urging, recited a few of my poems. Although I was so far removed from my previous life I couldn't have mapped it even with a sextant, my words came back to me readily; those same words I had always insisted I could not remember. But for my husband and lover, I could. And watching Charles's face as he listened, his brow faintly creased, his eyes soft and thoughtful in the firelight, I heard my words as if for the first time, and believed that there was something in them. Something fine, something incipient; some talent worth pursuing.

He was silent for a long while after I finished; then he nodded once, slowly. "Sometimes," Charles said, his voice ragged with astonishment, "I can't remember what my life was like before I met you."

I was overwhelmed with this unexpected gift. My husband rarely spoke of his emotions or even his moods; I had learned to navigate them by instinct, just as I had learned to navigate his plane. His silences could be frosty, intended to shut me out; I knew this by a certain way he set his mouth, a stubborn tilt of his chin. But more and more in the months since our marriage, I had felt his silences to be welcoming. It was as if he was standing by an open gate, waiting for me to walk through it to join him, allowing me all the time in the world.

"I can't, either," I assured him, touching the cleft in his chin that I so loved. He gently kissed my finger, then pulled me to him until all I could see were his eyes, all I could hear was his heart, which he guarded almost as watchfully as he guarded me. And I knew I never wanted that trip to end. I wanted to keep singing him songs with my poems, like Circe; to remain flying above the rest of the world, untouchable, like Icarus.

But we did have to come back—*down to earth*! Standing in the Guggenheims' drawing room, we were an ordinary, if extraordinarily celebrated, man and wife; intrepid explorers alone in the world no longer. The tinkling of glasses, the throaty laughter of society matrons, the ridiculous questions of those who had never traveled except in first class on a luxury liner—all signaled we were back in civilization; what a deceitful, disappointing word!

The Great Aviatrix—after first making sure the entire room overheard her discussing motors with my husband—finally remembered my presence. Nearly as tall as Charles, she smiled down at me with a patronizing air.

"That's a very pretty frock." Her voice sounded brighter, more musical; more suited to the nursery than to the airfield.

"Thank you."

"Tell me, Anne, have you ever read *A Room of One's Own?*"

I gasped, then laughed out loud. Was she serious? I could see by the earnest look on Amelia Earhart's face that she was.

"Excuse me?" I asked politely.

"Virginia Woolf's latest. You should read it sometime. It was written for someone like you."

"Someone like me? What do you mean?"

"Oh, Anne, you're such a sweet little thing!" Amelia laughed her great honking horse laugh. Next to me, Charles stiffened. He did not like Amelia; he'd said many times that I was twice the pilot she was, although he never criticized her publicly. Now he watched me, seeing if I could pass this latest test.

I hesitated. I could fly a plane, be hurtled off a mountain, navigate by the stars, but I shrank from defending myself. In this crowded room full of people I didn't care for yet didn't want to disappoint, I met the Great Aviatrix's bemused gaze. She had only disdain for me in my flowered frock, silk stockings, and high heels, and suddenly, I understood it. I didn't look like an aviator; I looked like an aviator's wife. His exceedingly *decorative* wife.

Then I felt a fluttering within my belly; something turned over, reminding me, in the most elementary way, that I was earthbound after all.

So it was with pure joy—and even, I admit, a little superiority—that I smiled up at the Great Aviatrix, so earnestly boyish, so fiercely alone.

"Thank you for the suggestion, Amelia. I'm always looking for something new to read, you know. I had no idea you were so well read!"

Carol Guggenheim stifled a laugh, and Charles turned away—but not before I caught the grin on his face.

"Charles, may I talk with you a moment?" I turned away from Amelia, took my husband's arm, and firmly led him to a private alcove, away from the glare of the Great Aviatrix's embarrassed smile. I heard her say something to the room that was received with a burst of laughter, but I didn't care.

"You should have said something more, Anne," Charles began. "You should have really put her in her place. You're a better flyer than she is."

"It's silly, in the grand scheme of things. *She's* silly. I don't care what she thinks of me. There are more important things in the world," I replied lightly, almost flippantly.

And then I placed my hand on my husband's arm and tiptoed up to whisper something in his ear. While the party in our honor continued noisily behind us, I informed him he was soon to be something other than an aviator.

He was soon to be a father, as well.

CHAPTER 6

May 1930

THE SIDEWALKS OF THE LOWER EAST SIDE were chaotic; so noisy, crowded, steamy, and dirty that for a moment I faltered, overwhelmed. Bile rose in my throat, and I wondered if I would faint right in the middle of Houston Street, and if it would be reported in the newspapers if I did, and if so, how would Charles react?

Oh, I thought I was through with morning sickness! After a few deep breaths, however, I realized that I wasn't used to being in New York; that my life was so very different than it was when I used to walk these sidewalks with confidence. Back then, the constant honking of horns, the wailing of children, the hum of perpetual conversation, the ever-present drilling of a jackhammer—all were merely background noise. Just as the roar of an airplane engine was to me now.

I wasn't used to being jostled about by *people;* that was it. Isolated as I was, either in the air with Charles or in the warm cocoon of family at Next Day Hill; protected by chauffeurs or maids or police escorts at public events—I hadn't been out in public in forever. The last time Charles and I had gone out had been months ago, to the theater, to see George S. Kaufman's *June Moon*. I had a false hairpiece with bangs and glasses; he pasted on a fake mustache and wore glasses as well. We looked so silly we giggled like children playing dress-up; still stifling giggles, we'd entered the theater separately and sat a row apart in our own disguises. Yet we'd been discovered anyway, and the play had to be stopped because of the furor in the audience. After police escorted us to our car, I'd been so humiliated, sorry for the actors, that we hadn't ventured out in public since.

So I had forgotten what it was like being simply one in a crowd—how claustrophobic it could sometimes be.

Still, even for one used to the city, taking a stroll in the Lower East Side was an adventure. Farther uptown, Manhattan might be pushing into the future—the nearly completed Chrysler Building stood tall and proud even as the new Empire State Building was rushing to eclipse it—but here it might as well be the turn of the century. Immigrant mothers wore ankle-length black dresses and head coverings; raggedy children played with wooden toys, if they had toys at all; horses still pulled delivery wagons. The stock market crash of last autumn might be starting to affect the other parts of the city—there were reports of breadlines even as far north as Washington Square—but here, it couldn't make any difference at all. These were the tenements, and why Elisabeth and Connie thought they might find students here for their new progressive school was a mystery to me. Although I couldn't help but admire their charitable impulse.

I turned a corner onto Allen Street and walked a few blocks until I came to Delancey. Charles did not know I was out walking alone; he would never have allowed it, and he forbade me to take the train into the city. So I told him I was taking the car. Which, technically, I had; at least until I got to Houston Street. Then I asked Henry, the chauffeur, to let me out.

"I'd like to walk the rest of the way," I explained, as I removed my coat, for it had turned unexpectedly warm in the May sun.

Henry pulled over and carefully put the car in park; despite the fact that he was the only person who drove it, Henry treated the Rolls as if it was on loan to him, as if he didn't quite have a claim to the driver's seat. His whiskered chin was set in a stubborn square, just like a cartoon character. Daddy required all the staff to be clean-shaven, yet for some reason he allowed Henry to be the one exception. "Miss Anne," Henry began, with the familiarity of an uncle, and indeed, that's how I thought of him, "Mr. Charles won't like this. Neither will your parents. I was told to take you directly to the agency. That's where you're supposed to be, not in this—part of town."

"Yes, and I'm telling you to let me out here, because I'd like the exercise. And the air."

"In your condition, Miss Anne, I don't think—"

"In my condition I require exercise."

"You know how people can get, now. You know how Mr. Charles—"

"Yes, Henry, I know. But it's been so long since I was out on my own like this. It'll be an adventure, and our secret. I promise I won't tell a soul! And if there's any trouble, I'll make up some story for Charles. No one will blame you."

"Miss Anne." Henry shook his head, then sighed. He did not know how to treat me now that I was expecting; no one really did. Mother was the only person in the family who didn't look at me as if I was about to break into pieces at any moment. All the men—Charles included—were suddenly very afraid not only for me but *of* me. And while I didn't feel fragile—indeed, now that I was nearing my eighth month, I felt more invincible than I ever had in my life—I was slyly learning to take advantage of their reluctance to contradict me.

"Henry, please. I need to walk for a bit—it'll do me and the baby good. You understand, don't you? That it's for the baby?"

Henry removed his spectacles—a recent necessity, and he was

very embarrassed by it—to give me one last paternal squint. Then he put them back on, sighed again, just in case I hadn't quite registered his disapproval, and opened his door, walking around to open mine. "I'll be in front of Miss Elisabeth's office in exactly one hour."

"Thank you—you're a dear!" I pushed myself up and started to skip down the teeming sidewalk, feeling like a student just released from school—until I felt that wave of nausea, that panicked, crowded feeling. I would have sat down on a stoop had I not been aware that Henry was patiently following me in the Rolls, staring so intently at me he failed to notice the jeers and cries of the neighborhood boys who ran alongside the car, daring to touch its gleaming surface with their grimy hands.

So I walked on, keeping my eyes focused straight ahead, on the backs of people's heads, and soon that closed-in, hot feeling passed and I was able to relax. What was I afraid of? I'd flown through countless storms, never once doubtful of the outcome.

Yet why did I always feel danger lurking around every corner, when my feet were firmly planted on the ground?

I did not meet anyone's gaze, acutely aware that I was not wearing my disguise, and wouldn't allow myself to smile. For whenever I was photographed, that was how I was recognized: by my cheerful, tomboyish grin that never failed to surprise me when I saw it. Never in my life had I felt as carefree as that smile implied.

Someone jostled my elbow, trying to pass; as he did, he stopped and stared right at me. It was a man, unshaven, wearing a torn black overcoat. I heard the sharp intake of breath, the heavy step toward me, and I steeled myself for the moment of recognition, the inevitable "Say, aren't you—you look just like her—is it Mrs. Lindbergh?"

I hurried on, walking quickly but not allowing myself to break into a run, which would only call more attention. And nothing happened. Heart thudding, I slowed, and then I couldn't stop myself from turning and looking back at that man. He was still staring at me, but he did not smile, did not ask for an autograph, did not bless me or wish me well. His face was a blank. Then he spat on the sidewalk, unmistakably in my direction; he scratched his nose, gave me one last bleak stare, and turned and went on his way.

He had recognized me, I was sure of it. Yet the fact that he *hadn't* done anything about it, had simply watched me instead, felt more sinister than if he had shouted my name.

Then I shook my head, laughing at myself. Well, I didn't want anyone to cause a fuss, did I? This was precisely why I needed a good stroll out in the open: to reacquaint myself with life back on the ground—real life, as most people called it.

I also needed, perhaps, to rid myself of some of the darker thoughts that seemed to intrude, much more than they used to, now that I was about to bring another life into the world.

Still, when I reached a narrow brick building with determinedly cheerful yellow chintz curtains hanging in the front window, tender young geraniums in neat pots on the scrubbed stoop, I hurried up the steps, eager to hide within its shelter. Opening the front door, I found myself in a room packed with tired-looking young women and small children. Every head turned toward me as I entered, and I couldn't prevent myself from recoiling and shielding my face with my handbag; it was an instinctive gesture by now, not intended to be rude. Although I knew it appeared that way.

Head still averted, I approached a woman in a starched white nurse's uniform seated at a desk. The nurse looked up, a helpful smile on her face, and immediately recognized me. With a small cry, she jumped up and grabbed my arm, ushering me past all the poor mothers and their children, most of whom were not adequately clothed even for this temperate day. As we hurried past, I felt their weary, resentful gazes taking me in—my fresh flowered dress, silk stockings, polished leather pumps, expensive handbag, immaculate white gloves. I even felt guilty about my scent— Chanel No. 5, a gift from the president of France.

"Mrs. Lindbergh," the nurse whispered, but some of the women heard. I saw them sit up straighter, lean toward me with a frank, curious look. "Miss Morrow is with someone just now, but I know she wouldn't want you to wait out here." And she led me down a short hallway, knocked on a door, opened it, and pushed me inside.

So on edge did I feel that it took me a moment to process what she had said—and so I gave a little start at the sight of Elisabeth perched on the edge of her desk, talking earnestly to a young woman holding a small child on her lap. Both the child and the woman had red, watery eyes; all three looked up as the door closed behind me. Elisabeth smiled, a conspiratorial little smile, which I returned; we had both run away for the day.

My sister had suffered a mild heart attack two months ago. Nothing to be alarmed about, the doctor assured us; just a lingering effect from the rheumatic fever she'd suffered as a child. Elisabeth had always been a bit fragile, although, like Dwight's illness, it was not something we Morrows ever discussed. But like me, she was supposed to be resting at Next Day Hill, not out gallivanting in the city.

Even in all the brand-new spaciousness of my parents' home, however, I couldn't help but feel hemmed in there, suffocated by Mother's boundless energy; her endless committee meetings, her constant urging for me to sit in, take a role, play a part. Charles was so restless now that we were grounded due to my condition that he escaped to the city most days, attending meetings he usually avoided like the plague. And I knew Elisabeth felt the same way, which was why she and Connie Chilton planned this outing in the city. I hadn't told her that I'd planned the same thing, though.

"Anne! What are you doing here? Mother will absolutely kill the two of us when she finds we're gone!"

Connie Chilton rose from her seat behind the desk. "For the record, I had no part in this. Someone has to remain on your mother's good side."

"I arranged to interview for a baby nurse here in the city," I confessed. "I just had to get out. And I couldn't resist seeing what you were up to."

Elisabeth glanced at her slim wristwatch, a frown faintly creasing her smooth, high forehead. She shook her head, her curls—held back by a severe-looking snood—remaining in place. "We're not up to much, I'm afraid." She rose and escorted the woman and her child out. "Thank you so much, and I understand," she told them, and then shut the door with a sigh. She looked at Connie, who shook her head and crossed a name off a list.

"Perhaps we were a bit misguided," Connie said. She didn't appear daunted, however; she grinned so that her freckles danced across her apple cheeks and broad nose.

Connie Chilton was a primitive, earthy force; had it not been for her impeccable upbringing, she would have been viewed with some trepidation by my parents. But her doctor father was a Yale graduate, her mother a Smithie; they had a penthouse in New York and a house in Saratoga. Despite all this, I often thought Connie would have looked much more at home leading a covered wagon across the prairie than she did sitting in a box at the racetrack, sipping champagne.

"We should have known better," Elisabeth admitted. "We

can't expect people from the Lower East Side to be able to bring their children to Englewood for school. Maybe someday we can open a school here. But for now, I suppose we'll have to content ourselves with educating the middle-class children of northern New Jersey." She smiled faintly; she was still so awfully thin, her complexion so waxy, that I worried about her.

I wasn't the only one. Connie firmly bustled my sister into the desk chair, and then she turned around and did the same thing with me, practically pushing me down onto the small sofa. "There! Someone has to look after you two Morrow girls—oh, excuse me, Mrs. *Lindbergh.*"

For some reason, Elisabeth laughed at this, and although I was puzzled, I laughed as well. Despite our shared imprisonment at Next Day Hill, we actually saw each other very little, only at mealtimes. And there was still a strangeness between us; she was polite, always, to Charles, although never completely at ease with him. I so wanted him to know the old Elisabeth—the relaxed, witty creature he first had met. Not this overly courteous, stiff acquaintance she seemed to have become around him. With me she was always careful to show her affection by draping an arm about my shoulders, hugging me before I had a chance to reach out for her, but I felt, sometimes, that it was just that—show. With Charles always looming in the background, we had yet to revert to our old, teasing relationship.

Finally here, away from Englewood, surrounded by grinding poverty, filth, and purpose, I caught a glimpse of the sister I missed. Yet as soon as I sat down and studied my ankles, swollen even from my short walk, I felt that unyielding politeness return.

"Are you well, Anne?" she asked. Connie sat next to me on the worn leather sofa. I wondered how many young mothers, like the one I had just seen, had sat here in the same condition, but in very different circumstances.

"Yes," and I felt guilty even saying it, surrounded by so many reminders of others not so fortunate. I *was;* I was monitored, cared for, saw a doctor every two weeks, had a beautiful nursery already prepared for my child—more blankets, diapers, bonnets, and gowns than he or she would ever use. When I felt ill, I was urged to rest. When I craved the oddest dishes—creamed herring on toast, just last night—they were prepared for me. My child wasn't simply expected; it was *awaited,* like royalty. There was even a column in the *Herald Tribune* devoted to speculation about the sex, name, and astrological significance of the date of the Lindbergh baby's anticipated birth.

"You look it." Connie patted my arm. "Plump and pretty. You'd been looking awfully thin after the wedding." She looked over at my sister for confirmation; Elisabeth nodded vigorously, appeared to want to say something, then shut her mouth.

Connie's eyebrows shot up, and she turned back to me. "Too thin," she insisted. "He pushes you too far."

"*He?*" I asked, knowing perfectly well whom she meant. Connie, unlike Elisabeth, did not conceal her dislike of my husband, who likewise did not conceal his dislike of her. "She's too inquisitive," he once grumbled after an unpleasant dinner during which Connie quizzed him relentlessly about his religious and political beliefs. "Too concerned with other people's business."

"Charles, that's who," Connie told me. "The sainted colonel himself. Dragging you here and there without asking what you want, forcing you into that kind of life. That latest flight—breaking the speed record, and you pregnant and miserable. He didn't even consider your health."

"I wanted to go along," I insisted, although, in truth, I had been violently sick the entire trip. Just a couple of weeks ago, we'd picked up our newest plane, a Lockheed Sirius, in California, and then flown at a high altitude—twenty thousand feet—

across the country in fourteen hours and forty-five minutes, three hours under the previous record. I'd had a pounding headache from the altitude and gas fumes, and was so nauseated I couldn't climb out of my cockpit at first. It was only after Charles hissed that I had to because of all the cameras that I was able to climb, shaky but still grinning that unreal, jaunty grin, out to wave at them all.

But I'd wanted to do it, and was proud of my accomplishments. "I like flying, you know," I insisted with a small laugh, trying to lighten the mood, for I had the oddest feeling that Elisabeth and Connie had been waiting patiently, like two cats, for the right time to pounce on me about this subject. "I enjoy it. I'm *good* at it, too," I couldn't help adding, defensively. "Very good. Even Charles says I'm one of the best pilots he's known."

"And we're proud of you," Connie insisted. "But it's his life, isn't it? Not yours, exactly. When was the last time you did anything on your own, for yourself?"

I frowned; remembering Amelia Earhart's patronizing, *"Have you ever read* A Room of One's Own*?"*

"It's been ages," Connie continued in her forceful way—as if the notion of disagreement was not to be entertained. "And Charles never goes anywhere, does anything, unless it's related to *him*. And he never allows you to, either."

"That's not true, really, it's not." I glanced at Elisabeth, hoping for help. She appeared only too ready to let Connie speak for her. "He—well, he is on so many boards, you know, for aviation, and naturally he wants me to accompany him to all the banquets and dinners. And he's been helping Daddy out with his campaign—and, of course, I should accompany him there, too. Mother does, you know." My father had left his ambassadorship and was preparing to run for the vacant Senate seat in New Jersey. Charles had been extremely supportive, lending his name and flying Daddy about the state for appearances.

Connie snorted. "When was the last time you insisted *he* accompany *you* somewhere? When was the last time you did anything on your own—joined a committee, or a club?"

"Well, today," I retorted gaily. "I came here, didn't I?"

"And it's been ages, Anne. Since before you graduated."

"No—really? It can't be." I couldn't bear Connie's pitying, yet challenging, gaze, so I glanced down at the handbag in my lap and tried to remember. When *was* the last time I had initiated an outing on my own? I used to come to the city at least once a month when I was in school, accompanied by Elizabeth Bacon, seeing shows, shopping, even once patronizing a speakeasy, although the entire time I'd been terrified we'd be raided. And Bacon—why, was it possible that I hadn't seen her since before the wedding? I'd wanted her to be my bridesmaid. But Charles had insisted only family be present, which, of course, I understood; there was just too great a risk of some member of the press getting in. But why hadn't I seen her since? She'd sent a lovely present, I supposed. I honestly couldn't recall; all my wedding presents were still packed away in crates, since we had no home of our own yet in which to display them. Still, that was no logical reason why I hadn't seen her; I had some memory of her phoning, at least a few times, and none of me returning her calls. I was probably too busy studying navigation, or flying, or riding into the city with Charles for one of those innumerable banquets that all blurred together, always ending with the two of us exhausted in the backseat of the car, a loving cup or plaque or diploma of some kind between us, engraved with his name.

His name. Never mine.

I glanced up at the two of them. Elisabeth was studying me,

sympathetically but patiently—as if waiting for me to come up with the correct answer to an unasked question. Well, what did they want me to say? That I had no friends, no life of my own any longer? That I hadn't seen any of my classmates since graduation?

It was true, all of it; Carol Guggenheim was the only woman outside my family to whom I was remotely close, and again, that was because of Charles's friendship with her, first.

I slumped down in my seat. No wonder I had felt such panic earlier, walking alone on the sidewalk. Charles hadn't been there, hadn't arranged it for me, as he arranged everything else. It was an entirely impulsive act; possibly the first one I had taken in almost two years—since I decided to become handmaiden to the most famous man in the world.

"I, that is—I *have* been meaning to do things," I explained lamely. "We've—*I've* just been so busy. And now, with the baby—we're finally getting our own house, you know. We're talking with an architect about a place outside of Princeton, in the country!" I looked up now, hating myself for nodding so eagerly, for seeking their approval so obviously.

And I realized, my face burning with embarrassment and confusion, that all the time that I had been feeling sorry for Elisabeth, she had been pitying me. The rest of the world admired my husband—and admired *me,* for taking care of him, for keeping up with him, and now, more than ever, for providing him with an heir.

That my own family did not admire me for this stunned me.

"A new house? That's wonderful," Elisabeth enthused. "Connie, isn't that wonderful?"

Connie nodded, not nearly so excited. "Yes, it is. It's about time."

"And I can't wait to see the drawings," Elisabeth gushed, her smile fiercely bright. I looked away, then glanced at my wristwatch. I rose in a great huff, which was somewhat marred by the fact that I had to hold on to Connie's shoulder to get my balance.

"It's getting late, and I should be going. I need to interview for a nanny, at some office on Park Avenue. A friend of Mother's recommended a service—they specialize in Irish nursemaids, which Charles—which *I* gather is the thing to do."

"Of course it is. And we must get back to interviewing these poor families, although I don't really think we're going to find anyone willing to travel to Englewood." Elisabeth became animated, as if everything was all right again. "You know, Anne, you really should consider hiring someone from this neighborhood. Don't you think it's a good idea, in these terrible times? Everyone needs work, and Mother's always so snobby about the servants. But you're in a position to do some real good, you know."

"Do you really think Colonel Lindbergh would allow such a thing?" Connie snorted with amusement, almost as if I wasn't there. She was right—Charles never would allow such a thing. But my cheeks blazed with anger at hearing Connie say so in such a derisive way.

"*I* will be making the decisions concerning the household staff," I told them coolly, if not entirely truthfully.

"That's marvelous! Then you'll consider it?" Elisabeth slid her arm about my nonexistent waist. "Anne, dearest, please don't go away feeling as if we were ganging up on you."

"I'm afraid I do feel that." I sniffed, fussing with my gloves.

"I know, and I'm so sorry, dear. It's just that we hardly ever get a chance to talk with you alone. And you know I am very—fond—of Charles, but—well, he's such a *strong* personality, while you're—"

"Weak?" I met my sister's gaze head-on; she was the one who looked away first, her cheeks flushing prettily.

"No, of course not, Anne. Just sweet, and eager to please. What Connie and I are really saying is that you're in such an important position now—*you*, on your own. Think what you could do with it—how much you could help others."

"I had planned on an Irish nursemaid," I repeated weakly—or, rather, *sweetly*.

Connie sat on the sofa, looking at me, her thick eyebrows arched in amusement. At that moment, I despised her solid self-righteousness. I also quaked at the idea of hiring a girl with no training, from a questionable background, to look after my baby.

"I'll consider it," I finally said, desperate to get away, to rush back to my refuge—back to Charles, who would be waiting for me. We always dined together; it was a rule. If one of us had to leave the house, we were always back in time for dinner unless we both went out; he said it was important for a husband and wife to establish this habit early. I agreed, of course. Why *shouldn't* I agree to my husband's desire to spend time with me? It was what I wanted, too.

"Fine, that's all we're asking," Elisabeth said, as she walked me to the door. "I'll see you back at home tonight."

"No hard feelings, now, mind you," Connie added. "You know I think you Morrows are the tops."

"Good. Then take care of Elisabeth, will you? Make sure she gets home in plenty of time to rest." I couldn't help it; I wanted to treat my sister as childishly as she had treated me. Although I was worried about her. She seemed so delicate, so *temporary*, somehow. So wispy that even memory couldn't hold her.

I hurried away from the two of them, standing side by side, framed by the doorway. Rushing down the hall to the reception room, I was truly worried now; I was going to be late for that appointment.

Just outside the window, Henry and the Rolls were waiting to whisk me away in luxury. I wouldn't have to worry about a taxi. I never had to worry about a taxi. Or the subway. Or even dinner—of course, it would be waiting for me when I got home. I never had to worry about anything these days.

Our flying trips, when I had been so strong, so independent— so *vital*—seemed like a dimly recalled dream to me now. Could Charles and I be true partners only when we were in the sky, cut free from everyone else's expectations?

I suddenly stopped in the middle of the crowded, stale room, and I made myself look around, meeting the gaze of every woman there. I needed to look at these women, these normal, earthbound women, with lives so very different from my own. I needed to see what they were like; who I might be if I were one of them. And I needed to see through my own eyes, not Charles's. I was so used to seeing the world from behind him, or beside him; our view was always exactly the same. It was as if there was only one set of goggles between us.

So I took in the old-fashioned dresses, the head coverings, some tattered lace, others simple black. Most had dark eyes, thick hair, sallow skin; there were a few fair Irish-looking faces. But they were all women, tired women; women simply wanting help, wanting more for their children. Just as I would want for mine— with a warm flush of recognition, I felt a kinship with them that I could never feel while flying above them, looking down.

My coaxing smile only made them uneasy; most looked away. The few that did not stared at me with unconcealed resentment flickering in dark, hungry eyes. A couple looked frankly at my stomach; one wagged her head and said something that I couldn't understand—and then she laughed.

"What's *she* doing here?" I heard someone else mutter. "*She's* rich."

"She's Colonel Lindbergh's wife," another whispered. "What's she want?"

"*I* should go visit *her*," a woman said loudly. "I bet they don't have nits in *their* house!"

Several women burst into knowing laughter. I was rigid with mortification. There was no way I could walk outside the door and get into the Rolls now, for everyone would see that it belonged to me, and I was sick with shame for it; shame for who I was. Elisabeth and Connie ridiculed me for being a wife; these women ridiculed me for being rich.

Was it any wonder I stayed safely in my husband's shadow, where, if anyone noticed me, they only admired me for keeping up with him? Was it any wonder I took refuge in the clouds, where I was strong and capable, more myself than I had ever been, could ever be, here on earth?

And what did two spinsters know, anyway? If I were married to a physician, I would be Mrs. Doctor. If I were married to an attorney, I would be Mrs. Lawyer. No married woman had a separate identity, not even my own mother, with all her education and energy. She was the senator's wife, first and foremost. That I was married to an aviator made me different but no less dependent on my husband. That was one thing these women and I knew that my precious sister, with all her education and lofty ideals, did not.

Spurred by this discovery, I spun around and marched back to Elisabeth's office. Without knocking, I opened the door.

"Elisabeth, what you don't understand is——"

I froze, unable to speak; unable to absorb the scene before me.

Elisabeth was sitting in Connie's lap, their arms about each other, their lips—*their lips*—upon each other's. They didn't spring apart—oh, why didn't they spring apart? They remained where they were, only turning their heads to look at me for the longest moment. A moment in which I gasped, my insides lurching and plummeting as if I had just plunged down an elevator shaft. And I felt that I must have; I must have fallen into another world, another reality. This was not my sister. This could not be my sister.

And yet even as we three gazed at one another, and Elisabeth finally slid off Connie's lap, her face scarlet, her body trembling, so many things suddenly made sense. The secret looks they always shared, the insouciance with which Elisabeth had always treated men, as if she had no use for them at all—and now, I saw, she hadn't.

What I had assumed to be her jealousy at my marriage to Charles I now realized was her distaste for him, pure and simple. The strained awkwardness, the brutal shifting of our relationship, was not because I had stolen something from her that she wanted. But this realization was accompanied by a childish sense of disappointment. For deep down, hadn't I enjoyed thinking that I had?

"Anne, please," I heard my sister say, in a voice that sounded a million miles removed. "You mustn't—"

I never heard what I mustn't do; I turned and stumbled blindly through the lobby and out the door. Henry tucked me into the backseat with a rug, as if I was an invalid.

As we drove away, my mind still reeled from the image of the two women so entwined. Elisabeth? Kissing a woman—*Connie?*

No irregularities, Charles had said that night, when we camped out under the stars. *Our children will be pure.* I laid my hand upon my unborn child; it swam within my flesh, restless, innocent—

Pure.

"Are you all right, Miss Anne? You look as if you've seen a ghost!"

I shook my head. "Just drive, please, Henry."

And I knew I could never tell anyone what I had seen. Not even—especially—Charles. Too many people could be hurt. For the sake of my child, my marriage, myself, no one must ever know. For the sake of my sister, most of all.

I had to protect Elisabeth as I had never been able to protect Dwight—but as I would have to protect my child when it was born. And I could. Like a magnet, I felt it pulling my thoughts and fears inward where they could be guarded, this strength, this steel that Charles had seen, that my mother had seen, but that had taken me so long to acknowledge.

And in acknowledging it, an unaccustomed contentment warmed my shaking limbs, calmed my rapid breathing, and I no longer worried about being late to the appointment, or whether or not Charles would be waiting dinner for me, or what those women in the reception room thought of me. None of that mattered, for I felt ready, now; ready for this baby.

Ready for motherhood; the one journey I must take where my husband could not accompany me.

CHAPTER 7

"LOOK AT THE CAMERA! Sweetheart, look at the camera!" I stood behind Charles, beaming at my son. Little Charlie sat in a high chair, waving a spoon, a tiny cake with one candle on the tray in front of him. Daddy and Mother stood behind me; we all waved and cooed and acted much more foolishly than the baby. He simply scowled at us all with comical gravity, his plump fist clutching the silver spoon, until finally he cocked his head as if pondering what strange creatures adults could be.

"Perfect," Charles said, as he clicked the camera. "That's a keeper."

"Should we release it, then?" I walked over to the baby. Now that we had all stopped acting like trained monkeys, he had turned his attention to his cake and was demolishing it with his spoon, cooing and giggling at the mess he made. My heart soared, watching his complete bliss; how marvelous to be utterly content with a spoon and a pile of crumbs! How innocent, how sweet, my baby was! I longed to pick him up and wrap him in my arms as a way to preserve his innocence—to catch it, even, as if it were a giddy virus—but I fought the impulse by picking up a tea towel instead.

The maternal instinct must be smothered; I repeated this phrase to myself a hundred times a day. Charles and I had agreed to raise the baby according to the Watson method, then much in

fashion. It was a strict scientific method—Charles Junior's schedule was planned to the minute, feedings coming precisely the
same time each day, along with nap time, playtime, et cetera.
Nothing was left to chance, and, most important, the child was
encouraged to develop on his own, without the unnecessary, po-
tentially harmful, influence of maternal love and anxiety.

Immediately after his birth, I had been relieved to relinquish
control of my child to this method; I couldn't wait to resume my
life with my husband, just the two of us, my body miraculously
light and easy again, as if it could fly on its own accord. The nurse
I had hired was given precise schedules and charts by which to
run the temporary nursery at Next Day Hill. When we were
home, we saw the baby only a few times a day; he was presented
to us, much like an exotic specimen of flora or fauna to be admired. And when he was placed in my arms, wrapped and pinned
into a neat little bundle, I didn't know what to do. Because I felt
no attachment to the squalling, red-faced creature whose greatest
desire appeared to be a myopic determination to suck his fist.

I knew he was mine; I remembered struggling out of the fog
of ether after he was born, seeing the deep cleft in the chin, exactly like Charles's, and smiling in relief that he did not look like
me; his nose was button-perfect, and his eyes did not slant down-
ward. I felt a bit like a princess, actually, as I fell back against my
pillows with a contented sigh; I had done my job. I had produced
the heir that Charles—the entire world—had so desired. While I
recuperated upstairs, downstairs my parents' doorbell kept ringing for days, as bushels of congratulatory telegrams were delivered, along with flowers and gifts—Louis B. Mayer sent a small
movie camera; Al Jolson offered to come to the house and sing
"Sonny Boy" to him in person; Will Rogers sent him a pony. The
Sunday after his birth, churches all across the land singled out my
child for special prayers; musicians composed lullabies in his

honor; schools were named after him. Some in Congress suggested his birth be declared a national holiday.

And Charles, that day—I'd never before seen him so worried, and then so proud when it was all over. Even more proud than when I first soloed in an airplane. He had held my hand until the pains got too much for me and I was put under—and the memory of him beside me, never wandering off to have a cigar or do any of the distracting things men usually did at a time like that, remained with me, each detail etched in my heart. His worried brow, usually so smooth and implacable; his soothing murmurs, not real words at all, and this from a man who was usually so economic with his speech.

And then his face, when I awoke—his mouth open in astonishment as he held his son, gazing down at him as if he were a miracle, as if he'd never believed this could be the logical result of the previous nine months. Charles's face was stripped of that polite mask he wore so much of the time, naked with hope and wonder.

So it was my husband's behavior, his vulnerability and concern for me, that I most cherished that day—not the miraculous fact of our child. Little wonder, then, that it took me a while to appreciate him.

By now, his first birthday, I had. I had fallen in love with my son in approximately the same time it had taken me to fall in love with his father. Not immediately, but over a series of increasingly precious events. The first time he smiled and we were sure it wasn't gas. The first time he waved when he saw me enter a room. The first time I could brush his curls—reddish blond, just like Charles's. The first time he sat in my lap and peered intently into my face, patting me on the cheeks, studying me almost as clinically as his father sometimes did—as if trying to memorize me.

I had my heart shattered, as well—just like any woman who

falls in love: the first time he said, "Mama," and looked at the nurse instead of me.

"I suppose I should release one of these photos," Charles said now, as he put the lens cap back on our Kodak. "Perhaps it would satisfy those vultures, those newspapermen. At the very least, it would give them something new to write about except breadlines and Hoovervilles."

It was June 1931; the Depression was no longer a nightmarish notion but a grim reality. Yet here in the beckoning warmth of the early summer sun, it was easy to imagine that we were removed, charmed, as if in a fairy tale of our own at Next Day Hill. Mother and Daddy were temporarily home from Washington, where he was now the junior senator from New Jersey. Dwight was doing better, working with a tutor while he continued to stay at a sanitarium in Massachusetts. Con was home from school for the summer.

The gardens seemed to have exploded overnight, struggling early shoots replaced with enormous blossoms and garishly-flowering bushes. The lawn was so green as to look artificial, tidy and manicured, dutifully cared for by an army of gardeners. My baby's birthday cake had been lovingly frosted by the cook. Betty Gow, our new nurse, was hovering in the background in her light denim nurse's dress, a blue sweater around her shoulders, ready to remove the baby, should he begin to fuss.

But there were shadows gathering near the manicured borders of our little world. "If you don't release a photo for his birthday," I told Charles, as the others went inside to get the presents, "the newspapers are sure to start up that nonsense again about the baby being deformed."

"I don't like offering up my son like ransom," Charles muttered, looking about the garden as if, even now, a photographer might be lurking behind a tree. "Why do they care?"

"If we don't give them some information, they print the

most awful things on their own. We didn't release a photograph after he was born, so they retaliated by saying he was—he was a freak."

"You shouldn't care what they print. I've told you so many times." Charles scowled down at me. Against the brilliance of this sky, his eyes did not look quite so blue, although they were clear and steady as always. His brow was still forbidding and noble; unlined, even though he was almost thirty. He looked very much like the earnest young man who landed in Paris, except that his reddish-blond hair was beginning to recede a little. And he had faint crinkles around his eyes.

"I'm his mother. Naturally, I care what is said about my child, Charles. Naturally, I don't want people saying that he's de-formed," I explained, wondering why it was necessary to do so.

Did I look any different to him, after two years of marriage? I was a trifle more plump after the baby, mainly around my hips. I was glad that the fashions had changed, that the slim, boyish fig-ure prized in the twenties was no longer in vogue.

"I know you care." Charles looked bewildered, shaking his head. But his expression changed as he gazed at his son; it soft-ened, then turned impish in a flash; his lips curled up into a grem-lin's grin. Before I could stop him, he had snatched the spoon out of the baby's hands.

The baby reacted by crumbling into a sobbing, cake-covered mess; his eyes scrunched up, his face turned red, and tears streamed down his cheeks, dribbling off his chin.

"Oh, Charles!" I hated it when he did this; when he got in what Betty called, in her Scottish burr, his "awful devilish" mood, teasing and tormenting everyone in his path. It was as if the crude, practical-joke-playing young airmail pilot was trying, with one last, mighty push, to break free before he was forever trapped inside the marble statue my husband was becoming.

"Charles, give it back to him," I pleaded, trying to take the spoon, but he held it high above my head.

"No, we need to teach him that sometimes you don't always get to keep what you want," Charles replied, waving the spoon so that the baby could see.

"He's just a baby!" My heart constricted, then leaped toward my child as if to provide him the comfort my arms could not. I knew that if I took a step toward him, Charles would block my way. I glanced at Betty; she, too, was standing so rigid, yet every muscle seemed to be straining toward the baby. Then she looked right at me, her chin raised, her blue eyes challenging; I was shamed by that look. *I'm only a servant,* it seemed to taunt me. *But you're his wife, the child's mother. You can do something about this.*

But I couldn't; I could only watch helplessly as Charles Junior continued to wail as his arms flailed about, looking for his spoon, for comfort, for something. And Charles Senior watched his son with a maddening smile on his face, and I told myself he really didn't enjoy hurting him so. I told myself this was just his way of toughening up his son, even at such a tender age; that he really felt he was helping him, being a good father; the father he himself wished he'd had.

Tears stung my eyes, and I blinked and blinked, my arms, my chest aching to comfort my child. Just when I thought I couldn't stand it any longer, my mother came hurrying out onto the terrace.

"What on earth?" She ran to her grandson and snatched him up out of his high chair, not caring that the front of her silk dress was instantly covered in a mixture of tears, saliva, and cake crumbs. She soothed and patted, and while Charles narrowed his eyes, he heeded my silent warning as I grabbed his arm. "Why were you all standing around? My poor little man!" She began to walk little Charlie around the terrace, bouncing him up and down in her arms so instinctively that I was jealous; I was even more jealous when he quieted immediately and nestled his head against her shoulder, his face still wet with tears.

But jealousy was overshadowed by frustration; why couldn't *I* simply ignore my husband the way my mother just had?

Because she would soon go back to Washington. And I would remain here with my husband, dependent on him for everything.

"She's spoiling him," Charles growled, throwing the spoon back down on the high-chair tray.

"It's his birthday. He deserves to be spoiled on his birthday." I joined my mother and son at the table, which was soon towering with the birthday presents that Con and Daddy brought out. And I couldn't help but contrast this obvious, ostentatious display of affection for my son with the cruelty—yes, cruelty—just exhibited by Charles. I felt my loyalties torn, not for the first time, between the two; between my child and my husband.

After we helped open all the presents—the baby was more interested in playing with the ribbons than any of his actual gifts—we lingered. It was such a beautiful afternoon that no one in my always bustling family seemed in a hurry. For once, we were all content simply to sit and be.

"Daddy, you're looking a little tired." I turned to my father with a smile. "Are they working you too hard in Washington?"

"Nobody can work a Morrow too hard," he replied. Yet he remained slumped in his chair, unaware that he had crumbs of cake on his necktie.

"Well, just you wait. I'm afraid it's going to get much, much worse." Mother shook her head. Her gray hair, bound simply in a low knot, looked almost white in the sun. She had new lines on her face, too, just like Daddy; lines that were not there before he became senator.

"I know," Daddy predicted, stirring slightly. "Hoover hasn't exhibited any grasp of the situation, I'm sad to say."

"I don't know about that," Charles replied. He turned his gaze elsewhere, to that far-off star on the horizon only he could see. Once I had found this inspiring, a symptom of his courage, his vision. Now I had to admit I sometimes found it aggravating: It was as if those of us nearest to him could never really matter enough.

"Hoover's a good man," my husband continued, squinting into the distance and sighing at what he found there. "It's the system that's broken. Capitalism is inherently flawed. Look at what's happening in Germany. There's an example of something broken, but at least its leaders are looking for solutions. They're not content just to sit back and slap a bandage on a gaping wound, and hope the fat cats get around to doing what's right."

My parents exchanged a look. I knew they didn't want to contradict Charles; no one ever wanted to contradict Charles. When they looked at him, everyone still saw that brave boy of '27—that unique and fearless boy who had captured the world's heart and imagination. The man of '31, however, was harder to love.

"Well, let me tell you, young man," my father began, as I tried to distract him by waving at the baby, who was still in Mother's arms, reaching for a strand of pearls that she deftly pulled away from his chubby hand.

"Dwight, Charles, no politics at the table," my mother murmured, but Daddy couldn't be stopped.

"You want to become a socialist nation?" he continued. "Like Germany? Where there's very little in the way of free press these days?"

"They're not socialist yet, Daddy," Con interrupted, with her sunny, earnest smile. "Hitler didn't quite steal the election from Hindenburg, although he might on the next ballot."

"I doubt the German people will elect Hitler," Charles said with authority. "Although I don't disagree with some of his party's practices, really. At least he has vision."

"I don't know what to think of the situation over there," Daddy said, with a shake of his head. "I don't like either of them. Hindenburg's a holdover from the days of the kaiser."

"Hindenburg's just a puppet. It's immaterial. Germany doesn't matter in the grand scheme of things; it will never recover from Versailles, although if it does, it will be because of a man like Hitler—someone who has energy, anyway. Someone who can engage the people. But the truth is, we have dangers enough here at home."

"Dangers? From without or within?" My father glared at Charles.

"Both," Charles replied mildly.

My father nodded and slumped back down in his chair, breathing heavily. He stirred himself a little, turning to Con. "It's good to see you taking an interest in current events, missy."

"How could I not?" She shrugged. "With a senator for a father?"

"My daughters," Daddy complained. "They run the show, the women in this family. Be glad you've got a son," he said to Charles.

"As do you, dear," Mother said, so mildly that it took a moment for her words to register. Con and I exchanged wary glances, while Daddy merely nodded, and slumped even farther in his chair.

"It's been so long since we were all together as a family," he said wearily. "Anne, just when we get you and Charles to stay put for a while, your sister has to go missing. What's so important in Maine that Elisabeth can't come out here even for her nephew's birthday?"

"She still needs her rest," I reminded him.

"Has she even seen little Charlie since he was born?"

"Oh, Daddy, of course she has," I answered as I felt the tips of my ears burn, and I looked down at my lap. Although, to be truthful, she hadn't seen him very much, so busy was she with her new school—and with avoiding me. Taking trips to Nassau, to Maine, all in the name of recuperation; at least, that's how she put it to the rest of the family.

With me, however, she was more honest. Woundingly so.

I remembered her first visit after the baby was born. I was still in bed, my breasts painfully hot and engorged, my lower body wincingly tender, when Elisabeth swept into my room, an enormous stuffed giraffe in her arms.

"Goodness, look at you!" she exclaimed, while not doing precisely that—looking at me. Her cheeks were scarlet, her eyes so bright I suspected tears. She made a beeline to the changing table, where the temporary nurse was fussing over the baby. Elisabeth gazed at my child in awe for a moment before abruptly turning away and fumbling in her purse—for a cigarette, I suspected—until she seemed to remember where she was, and shut the clasp with an exasperated sigh. She looked about the room as if she'd never seen it before, jumpy, ill at ease; I knew she would vanish again in a moment if I didn't speak first.

"Could you see about some tea?" I asked the nurse, who nodded, returning the baby to his bassinet before she left the room. Then I patted my bed, beckoning to my sister. "Elisabeth, please. Sit for a moment. I'd like to—I'd like to talk to you, like—"

"Like we used to?" Elisabeth smiled ruefully but joined me. As she settled herself carefully at the foot of my bed, I studied her. She was still so thin, pale; almost translucent. I could see the blue veins beneath her porcelain skin. Her blond curls seemed to have lost their luster as well, although it was hard to tell; she had them so tightly encased in a plain brown snood.

"Well, not quite like we used to." I smiled over at the bassinet in front of the window, where my newborn was cooing and sighing.

"No, it will never be like that," Elisabeth admitted, nervously pulling on the tips of her gloves.

"I've been meaning to talk to you—" I began, before Elisabeth held up a hand.

"No, don't do that, Anne. I know you haven't. I haven't, either. We've been like weekend guests in this house, always so terribly polite to one another, but that's all."

"I know," I admitted. "It can't be easy for you, with all this fuss." I gestured around the room at all the flowers, the enormous baskets of fruit and candy sent by congressmen, senators, the president of Smith. Even President Hoover sent a bouquet from the White House.

"Anne, that day—"

"It doesn't matter," I interrupted. My face was glowing with embarrassment; suddenly I saw her again, seated in Connie Chilton's lap, so helplessly compliant.

"Yes, it does. It does matter, and we both know it. The thing is—I'm so *ashamed*, Anne. You don't know how it is—I'm just so ashamed."

I didn't reply; I didn't know how to.

"Connie and I—the way you saw us—it's something I've fought for so long. I don't want to be that way—truly, I don't. I think we can be friends, working next to each other, but then something happens—something comes over me. *She* isn't ashamed, though, and I think that's what makes it worse. It seems I can't please anyone! I can't have a life—the life that you—and now the baby—oh, Anne! I want that, I do! I want a normal life, with a husband and a child, and I don't know how to do it. I just don't! Not with my illness, not with my weakness!" She bit her lip, tears falling down her cheeks before she could brush them away. Still, she wouldn't look at me.

"Elisabeth, I don't understand. Although I *want* to." And it was true; I desperately desired to know what was within my sister's obviously tormented heart. But it was so beyond my understanding, my imagination, even. And my imagination had never failed me before.

"I know you do, Anne. Just know that I love you—truly, I do! And that I'm happy for you. I'll be all right—somehow, sometime. I'll figure this all out. Oh, look at the time!" She consulted her watch and gave a little start. "I need to get down to the school, Connie will be expecting me. She sends her love, too. Anne . . . Anne, please try to understand—for me, it's hard right now, seeing you this way. With the baby, a husband, so happy. I want that so much, and yet—it's just hard. I seem to make a mess of things lately, so many things, and I don't want to do that to you. Please understand if I spend some time away. Please understand if I keep to myself—and for goodness' sake, try to make Mother understand. Will you?"

I nodded, suddenly, terribly, sad. Now that I was a mother, I wanted fully to be a sister again. And a daughter. I felt a powerful need to reestablish ties, to define roles, to understand the mysteries and frustrating intricacies of *family*. I'd hoped, somehow, naively, that the baby would bring Elisabeth back into my life—but now, I knew he would do the opposite. I watched as my sister stood over his bassinet, gazing down at my son while her entire body trembled—with longing, I thought. With absolute, heartbreaking longing.

"Elisabeth?"

"What?" She wouldn't turn around, and all at once I realized how fully our roles were reversed; she looked defeated, small, bending over her nephew.

"You'll be fine——" I sounded exactly like my father, with Dwight, and stopped. "I mean, please know you're welcome here, always. This is your home, too—more than it is mine. And you know that we'll be moving, anyway—it's just, I want my son to have his family, just as we did when we were growing up. I want him to know what family means—I want him to know his aunt Elisabeth."

Her face lit up at that, and then she smiled, rushed over to kiss me, and whispered goodbye.

That was the last time we'd had a real conversation. Almost a year ago, now. While dutifully present at most family gatherings, Elisabeth managed to remove herself from the rest of us, even Mother. And her health was not improving; the doctors warned her that her heart was permanently damaged from her rheumatic fever.

I felt my mother's piercing gaze upon me, but I looked away, smiling at my son. My blissfully innocent infant son, who looked up, recognized me, and beamed. I felt myself being pulled toward him. It was as if there was an invisible thread between his lips and my heart.

"I think we'll be able to leave in a month," my husband said, snapping that thread. My chest tightened; why did he have to bring this up today, of all days—on his son's birthday? On *my* birthday, too—for today was a twin celebration; there would be champagne and cake for me later that evening.

"Oh, Charles, let's not talk about it today." I had to look away from my baby's bright, trusting gaze; I wasn't worthy of it.

It had been four years since Charles's historic flight to Paris. The *Spirit of St. Louis,* now hanging from a rafter in the Smithsonian, looked flimsy and old-fashioned compared to the huge, gleaming new planes and ships. Despite his fame, which seemed only to increase with each passing year, Charles worried that there were few routes left uncharted; few things left for him to conquer. After all, he wasn't even thirty.

So he was planning a bold, dangerous expedition to chart an air route over the Arctic, and then to the Orient. Naturally, I would be his copilot. This was what I had been training for since we were married; I understood that now. Charles had been training me not only to fly and navigate, but also—to leave those I loved, to loosen the ties of my family, to divorce myself from anything and everyone, except him. Including, even, our son.

And I was an excellent student. I always had been; after all, I was a Morrow.

I learned Morse code, so that I could earn my third-class radio operator license. I mastered celestial navigation. I had learned to fly our massive new Sirius seaplane, by far the largest aircraft I had flown.

My heart was proving more difficult to conquer, however. Lately, whenever I had to say goodbye to my baby, I couldn't do so without tears.

"Charles, how long do you think we'll be gone?" Nervously, I began to play with a cloth napkin, embroidered with an *M,* for Morrow. Charles had yet to reveal the true extent of the trip to anyone, least of all me. The Lone Eagle—sometimes I wondered if he would always be that, even with a wife and a child. In so many ways, he still lived his life as that young airmail pilot, alone in his cockpit, planning his future without regard to others' expectations.

"At least six months. I've been thinking that if we get to the Orient safely, we might as well try to circle the rest of the globe. It would be foolish not to continue."

"*What?*" The baby, startled, began to cry again. "Six months? The entire globe? When did you decide all that?"

"Just recently. There's no rational or technical reason why we can't undertake something of this scale. Juan Trippe at Pan Am is salivating at the opportunity."

"You discussed this with Trippe before me? Then let him do it! No rational reason? What about Charlie?" Reaching for my son, I kissed him on his cheek, tasting the salt of his tears. My arms were wrapped fiercely about his squirming body.

"What do you mean? The baby will be adequately cared for by Betty. Isn't that the whole point of having a nurse?" Charles turned to Mother, genuinely puzzled.

"Well, of course, but—this is rather a long time to be away," she replied, even as she looked at me, her eyes wide with sympathy.

"I think it's a bully idea," Con said, her eyes dancing. "What fun! Will you bring me back a kimono?"

"It's a fine, fine thing." Daddy's voice was approving, although he looked wistfully my way, as if already missing me. "You'll do our nation proud."

"Anne." Charles moved his chair closer to mine. "You're overwrought. We've been planning this trip for months."

"I know, but—it's just that I didn't realize we'd be gone quite so long. And, oh, Charles, the baby! He's at an age where he'll—he'll know when I'm gone. He didn't before, he was too small, and so it didn't seem to matter whenever we flew away. But now—" Stifling a sob, I buried my face in my son's soft curls.

"Anne." My husband's voice was low and coaxing, like a well-tuned engine. "Come, now—I don't want you to become a slave to domesticity. We're too fine for that—*you're* too fine. I don't want to lose you to the nursery forever."

"I know, I know, and I don't want to let you down! But we've

never been away from Charlie for more than two weeks before—
and now you're talking about six months!"

"Anne, this is our life—flying. It's what we do. It's why I
married you, because I knew you were meant to be my copilot.
I thought it was what you wanted, too. I thought you liked flying
with me."

"Oh, I do! Of course I do—I love it!" As I met his genuinely
confused gaze, I remembered the trip to Mexico, when we photographed the ruins; the intimacy, the purity of our love, too fine
for words. How could I ever give that up?

"I suppose I *could* fly with someone else." Charles said it
thoughtfully, as if puzzling out a complicated problem. "Of
course, any number of pilots would leap at the chance to accompany me. Wiley Post wired me this morning, in fact."

"No!" It was as if he'd suggested taking a lover; that's how
betrayed I felt. "No, no, of course, you can't fly with anyone else
except me! But Charlie—he needs me, too!"

My husband grabbed my hand and said the one thing that
made sense only when he said it. "*I* need you," he murmured.
"Anne, I need you. You're my crew. You'll always be my crew."
Then he let go of me and settled back in his seat, waiting.

That was it, was all; Charles Lindbergh wouldn't beg, he
wouldn't plead. He had said all he would on the matter, and it was
up to me. Bending my head down to caress my baby's hair, as
golden and silky as corn tassel, with my cheek, I felt my heart
begin to form a fault line, and I knew that it would forever be split
in this way. Charlie needed me—of course he did. He was my
child. He didn't even know how much.

Charles needed me—and, oh, it was a *miracle* that he did!
Once more I felt that giddy disbelief that he had chosen *me*, of all
the people on earth. He'd given me the world and all the sky

above it; he was also capable of taking it all away from me with a single gesture. Who on earth would I be without him?

I knew, with a weary resignation, that whenever he asked, wherever he went, I would follow. Charles was the wind that blew me hither and yon, that lifted me off this earth, kept me aloft, pulled me along like a helpless kite, but also gave me wings with which I could touch the sun.

What chance did a baby have against *him*?

"Of course," I said, still resting my cheek against my son's downy head. "Of course, you're right. We should go as far as possible, and it will be tremendous. You simply took me by surprise, that's all."

To my astonishment, Charles kissed me on the cheek. He never did that in front of anyone—not even my parents. "Good girl," he said softly, and I looked into his approving eyes, and felt everyone else—even the child in my arms—fade away.

Everyone, except for him. I smiled and reached out to touch the cleft in his chin that so enchanted me; the happiest moment of my life had been when I realized our baby had one just like it.

"Excuse me? Mr. Charles?" The head gardener, Johnson, came running around the corner of the house. All the help deferred to Charles now, instead of Daddy; it had happened slowly, but inevitably, and Daddy didn't even seem aware of it.

"Yes, Johnson?"

"It's—it's—" The older man stopped to mop the sweat from his brow with a large, dirt-streaked handkerchief.

"What is it?" Charles's voice sharpened.

"There's an intruder, sir. Some poor woman demanding to see little Charlie. Said she has something she has to tell him on his birthday."

"Oh, not again." I tightened my grip around the baby even as

Betty Gow ran up, as if to do the same. I smiled, touched by the concern in her eyes. "I'm sure there's nothing to worry about," I assured us both.

Betty nodded, unable to prevent herself from holding on to the baby's chubby leg.

"I'll deal with it," Charles said grimly. He patted his breast pocket—I knew there was a pistol in a holder. There was always a pistol in a holder.

The shadows had fully encroached on us now; I shivered, and not entirely from the chill in the air. Without the bright, transporting sun to trick us, it was all too evident that this was no idyllic fairy tale after all.

For we were under siege, pure and simple—and we had been since our son's birth. Since before, even; I'd given birth here at Next Day Hill, my bedroom fitted as an operating theater, because we couldn't risk a hospital; there were too many reports of staff being bribed to allow reporters and photographers into the delivery room.

And now people showed up at our door—they simply showed up, as if we had invited them! As if we would welcome them into our home and say, "Thank you so much for coming!" I hadn't answered the door myself in so long, I wasn't sure I remembered how. We paid private detectives to do so now, and there were police camped out at the end of the drive. Even so, people sometimes got past by climbing over neighbors' fences, or hanging from trees. There were the usual reporters and photographers with no assignment other than to capture a shot of Charles Junior. But there were others; people who, as the Depression wore on and on, had nothing else to do. And no one else to turn to.

One man said that he had to touch the baby in order to be cured of cancer. One woman swore that her own child had been stolen from her at birth, and that she was sure we had done it, and that the baby was hers. Countless clairvoyants insisted on look-ing at Charlie's palm, touching his head, or reading his chart. Most were simply confused people looking to my child for help in some way, although there were others who were less confused.

For mixed in with the thousands of cards and letters congratu-lating us on Charlie's birth were requests for money; letters that told of deprivation, desperation, punctuated with tears. And re-quests were sometimes followed by threats; threats to kidnap my child and hold him for ransom. Although Charles tried to shield me from this knowledge, I was aware that more than one person with a weapon had been apprehended at the end of the drive. As the mood of the country grew darker, the resentment I had first glimpsed in Elisabeth's waiting room had turned on the First Couple of the Air. We were blessed, we were successful; what had been celebrated two years ago was now a source of anger and resentment. The qualities that had brought Charles such acclaim—his stoicism, his dogged pursuit of perfectionism, his ability to float above the ordinary details of mere mortals' lives— were ridiculed and debated now. "What more do they want of me?" Charles had grumbled recently, showing me a headline that asked the sour question, "What Has Lindbergh Done for Us Lately?"

It appeared now they wanted his happiness. Or, barring that—his child.

"I'm sure it's nothing, but take the baby inside, just in case." Charles spoke to me soothingly—exactly as he had when we were in the plane, so long ago, and we lost the wheel on takeoff.

I must have looked more worried than I intended to show, for his features softened. The corners of his eyes crinkled, and he smiled gently, warmly, down at the two of us—his son and his wife. "It will be all right, Anne. Don't worry. You know I will protect you and the baby, always. I'll reason with whoever is here—if we can only keep reasoning with them, surely they'll leave us alone eventually. But you see, now, that this flight couldn't be timed any better? You see how important it is? It will divert attention from the baby, and back to us. We can withstand it. He can't."

"Yes, but—oh, Charles! This is why I'm so afraid to leave him! What if something happens while we're gone? While I'm—you're—not here to protect him?" I nodded at the gun in his pocket.

"We'll hire additional detectives, and the police will step things up. I've already planned it all. We can't live our lives in fear, Anne. You do know that?" He searched my face anxiously, testing me, as always. And for a moment I faltered; my child in my arms, I knew only that he would be safe as long as he remained there.

Then I nodded, even as I couldn't quite stifle a sob, and so I had to lean into Charles's chest to muffle it. I felt his strong arms reach awkwardly around and hug me to him until I dried my eyes and pushed myself away. With a bright, understanding smile—that same carefree grin that I always flashed to the photographers—I shifted the baby in my arms.

My son waved at Charles and said "Bye" so happily that I thought my heart would shatter right then. I followed Mother, Daddy, and Con through the French doors into Daddy's study. Charles strode off, his hand still inside his vest, around the side of the house; Johnson followed a few paces behind. I had to smile at the sight of the gardener wielding a small spade, as if that could help.

Some of the servants crowded into the study with us; Violet Sharpe, one of the housemaids, cried out, "Oh, the poor little thing," and began to weep. Con rolled her eyes and went to comfort her; Violet was always rather excitable.

"Shhh," I whispered to Charlie, still so blissfully unaware in my arms, babbling happy baby nonsense. "It's all right. Daddy will take care of you. Daddy will always take care of you." But I couldn't prevent myself from imagining what might happen when Charles would not be there to take care of him, even with the policemen at the gate.

"Anne, dear?"

I turned; Mother was watching me, her eyes soft with concern.

"I'll stay home with the baby and Betty," she said firmly. "I'll cancel my plans. Will that help, my daughter? Will that make you less fearful?"

I nodded, so grateful I wanted to sing for her, dance for her, do something unexpected and charming and grand. But I had to content myself with a soggy smile over my son's head.

And I thought back to my childhood, to all the times I had missed her, all the times I had wondered why she had to rush out the door, late for an appointment. Nothing to compare to how long I was going to leave my own son, of course. But I had missed my mother, anyway, as all children do.

Now I wondered—had she missed me as well? All those years; had she missed her children, had she been forced into all those activities by her husband, too? Was she now trying to make up for it?

I smiled at my mother with new understanding, grateful to be old enough, finally, to have a second chance, to forgive, to reconnect as women, mothers. I kissed my son on the top of his soft, fragrant head; he smelled like Ivory soap and warm flannel. And I whispered a plea for his forgiveness, too.

For now, I could only look forward to the day when he would be old enough, wise enough, to grant it.

CHAPTER 8

"ANNE, ANNE—JUMP!"

The water, muddy and churning, *vicious*, rushed up at me. We were inside the plane, our trusty steed; one minute we were hovering over the Yangtze River on a rope, ready to be lowered onto the water so we could take off. The next we were listing dangerously to one side, water rushing up to entrap us in the plane, like a tomb. And I thought, more curious than terrified, *Death by drowning. Of all the ways I thought I might die, this was not one of them.*

Then my husband's voice, commanding although not panicked, pierced through my drowsy rumination, and I jumped as he told me to. I jumped, just as I had the day the plane overturned. Survival instinct, my compliant nature; maybe a combination of the two. But I leaped, sprawling, out of the plane and hit the flood-swollen waters of the Yangtze, terrified I would be pulled down by the weight of the parachute on my back, my heavy flying clothes. Already praying because I knew that this time I would not survive. I would never see my baby again.

I swallowed filthy water, retching it up as I somehow, miraculously, bobbed up to the surface. Only to feel myself tugged helplessly down again by my parachute. The water closed over my face and I couldn't breathe. Writhing in panic like an eel, twisting, I managed to shed the parachute and bob back up again, gasping. I thought of all the times I'd been so careful to boil the water before I brushed my teeth or washed my face.

Amid shouts from the men on the boat nearby, I heard Charles call my name.

"Over here!" I waved an arm, and paddled toward him.

Charles was treading water, his hair plastered down, his face splotched with mud. When he saw me, his eyes widened with relief, and he waved back.

"Get away from the plane," he called over the wind, the shouting, the engine of the boat. I nodded and swam away, threading my way through swirling sticks and logs and other debris carried along on this raging river.

Our ship, our beautiful Lockheed Sirius, was on its side, one great pontoon rising up from the water, the other just below. Water was pouring into the cockpit, and I winced at the thought of my radio and transmitter shorting out, ruined forever. This plane had been our home for the last two months, since July 27, 1931.

That was the day the "Flying Lindberghs" were driven to an airfield on the East River just outside of Queens, New York. On a platform that ramped down to the river, our great black-and-orange Sirius perched precariously on two huge pontoons, waiting for us to board. In the pontoons themselves, each item scrupulously weighed, was everything we could possibly need for several months' journey to the Arctic, the Orient, and beyond. Our few items of clothing, extra trousers, shirts, and a flying suit for each of us, as well as warm parkas. There were also tins of food; pots for boiling water; a first-aid kit personally packed for us by the chief of staff at Columbia-Presbyterian Medical Center; letters of introduction signed by President Hoover himself; an anchor, oars, an inflatable boat, extra parachutes, firearms, ammunition, fishing equipment, an extra radio, and blankets. Almost as an afterthought, we both carried brand-new passports.

Surrounded by reporters, photographers, and Movietone men with their whirring cameras, we waited as two mechanics made a final check of the Sirius. Charles was asked by male reporters about the technical difficulties of the challenging flight. I was asked by female reporters how I intended to set up housekeeping in a plane, even as my fingers nervously tapped out practice messages in the Morse code I had been studying for weeks—*Engine failure. Send help. Location unknown.* Not once was I queried about my technical skills, even though I was to be the radio operator on this trip. Waiting for me in my rear compartment was my radio and all its coils and tubes, the receiver perched on a shelf to my right, the transmitter a cold, hard presence at my feet next to the antenna I would slowly crank out of a compartment on the floor whenever I needed to transmit. The huge, noisy dynamotor was behind my seat, where it would occasionally give me a kick, literally, in the pants.

"Mrs. Lindbergh, what clothes are you taking on the trip?" "Are you going to show the new spring fashions to the Japanese?" "Do you think you'll miss your son very much?"

"Yes," I replied, in answer to them all—thanking God that it was time to leave. I waved goodbye with that jaunty grin that I could never recognize when I saw it in photographs. Charles had built a little ladder that enabled me to ascend the enormous pontoons; from there I could then hop up onto the wing, and then into the plane itself. We settled into our respective cockpits, Charles in front, me in back, and then Charles started up the plane. Nosing awkwardly down the ramps, we hit the water with a wallop that splashed waves all over the Movietone men, to my great delight.

Our first attempt to take off was cut short by a boat full of newsreel cameras that veered too close. Our second was successful, although I held my breath as Charles maneuvered our way through a flock of airplanes full of more newsreel cameras, some so close I could see the stripes on the bow ties of the photographers. (Newsreel cameramen, I had discovered, always wore bow ties, for reasons I could never fathom.)

Soon enough, we shook them, and we said goodbye with a jaunty little wiggle of the wings that was Charles's signature. Only then did I see my husband's shoulders relax; he turned to me with a jubilant grin that made me laugh out loud. We were on our way, just the two of us; on our greatest adventure yet, one for the history books. Charles hadn't looked so free, so joyous, in months; since long before our son was born.

We would navigate across Canada, up through Alaska, over the Bering Strait, skirt Siberia, and hip-hop down the islands of Japan to China. Along the way, we would eat raw fish with Eskimos in huts, file into a mess tent with prospectors in Anchorage, sit on the bamboo floors of palaces in Japan to partake of ancient tea ceremonies. Everywhere we landed we were mobbed by the population, even if the population was only ten hardy soldiers on a remote island outpost. In the air, we were partners; I took over flying when Charles was tired, or when he needed to map out our routes. But on land, we were always separated; I was shuttled off to be with the women, where I was expected to be interested only in domestic duties. I lost count of the number of times I was asked how I kept the cockpit tidied.

Charles smarted at these questions on my behalf; I would catch his sympathetic head shake. Yet the only time he ever came to my defense was early in the trip, in Ottawa. Waiting for a banquet in our honor to begin, I found my husband seated on the floor of an anteroom, surrounded by fellow pilots.

Charles was a different person around pilots and mechanics; I had learned this early in our marriage, on our first barnstorming trip west. Suddenly the great aviator I had married became "Slim" to all his old colleagues and mechanics; the ones who had remained where they were, content to fly the mail and do tricks for air shows, when he had set his relentless gaze across an ocean, to Paris. They played jokes on one another, told dirty stories, and allowed me to watch, amused and touched. My husband had been a boy, after all; this was my real glimpse into who he was *before*.

So I smiled when I saw them all huddled on the ground, looking like a gaggle of small boys shooting marbles. They were studying maps, nodding intently as they discussed routes over the Arctic, joshing and teasing one another. But then one pilot suddenly looked up and saw me; he sniffed and grumbled to Charles, "I'd never take my own wife on such a trip."

Charles didn't get angry; instead, he merely shrugged and answered, with a proud glance my way, "You must remember that *she* is *crew*."

My skin flushed with pride, with accomplishment. That was my favorite memory of the entire trip; maybe of our entire marriage. For in that moment, everyone knew with certainty that we were truly partners; I was his equal, the equal of every man in that room.

But then Charles and his friends turned back to the maps, and I found myself surrounded by bright, gilded matrons in evening gowns, their hair elegantly coiffed. I was in a limp frock still wrinkled from being packed in the pontoon, and my hair, newly bobbed, was a mass of unkempt curls about my face. My moment of triumph was over as soon as it had begun, and I retreated back in the uncertain shadows of my life here on earth, neither pilot nor matron.

I knew that I would be looking for that proud glance; that

feeling of belonging, of knowing who I was, that I *mattered*, for the rest of my life.

THERE WERE OTHER less jubilant moments on that trip. Moments when the fog was so thick around us as we flew over the Arctic, we couldn't see where to land. Moments when we almost ran out of fuel, because we had to navigate around capricious storms that caused our plane to buck and heave like a bronco, and I didn't know if we'd land miles beyond civilization and the nearest refueling station or simply fall out of the sky.

Moments when I angrily cursed myself for believing Charles when he said he was the best pilot he knew, that he would always protect me; for believing him when he said we would see the baby again. Moments when, my eyes shut against the fog, the white blindness, the only image I could see was that of my son's face, so clearly I wanted to cry out; the shy, sweet smile, the cleft chin, the round blue eyes always trusting—trusting me to come back to him.

Moments when I feared I wouldn't.

After every storm, every menacing fog, every teeth-jarring landing on a narrow strait, the wings of the plane just barely missing rocks and cliffs, my hands would shake when I undid my harness.

But Charles—Every time! Every single time!—would bound up out of his cockpit, turn around to me with a grin, and exclaim, "Well, that was fun, wasn't it!" And he would insist that we'd never really been in any danger; he would insist it was all in my head, and that I worried too much, and had I remembered to pack the sandwiches for dinner?

What could I do, in those times? What could I do but nod, and marvel, and chide myself for not being as strong as him, after all? For not acting worthy; worthy of his crew?

And so we traveled on, mapping routes, spreading goodwill across the globe, dispatching letters home when possible. We reached China in late September, where our mission became one of mercy. The Yangtze River had flooded so awesomely that tens of thousands of people were displaced, starving, or drowned. I piloted countless hours over its path, as Charles mapped out areas for possible flood relief, and we delivered much-needed medicine to isolated villages. We were about to leave on one last mission when the Sirius overturned in the Yangtze.

Charles and I were rescued by sailors and brought aboard the British aircraft carrier *Hermes,* which had tried to launch us in the first place. Somehow they managed to lift the plane out of the water. But as I watched on deck, wrapped in a musty blanket, I saw that there were huge holes in one of the wings and the fuselage.

"Oh, no," I moaned, sickened by the damage done to our plane; the plane that I had trusted to bring me back to my son, and now I knew that it wouldn't.

"I can fix it," Charles promised, that terrifyingly certain set to his jaw. "We'll have the *Hermes* take us up to Shanghai, where I can probably get the right parts. I won't let this be the end of our trip."

"No, no, of course not," I replied, too quickly. I couldn't prevent my entire body from shuddering with cold and, I suddenly realized—heartbreaking disappointment. He would fix it, of course he would. And we would soon be winging our way across the rest of the globe; winging our way to some fresh danger, some impossible situation that no mere mortal could be expected to survive. How many of them could we cheat? How long before even Lucky Lindy's luck ran out?

I walked away from Charles, my stomach queasy from the water I'd swallowed; I ran my tongue over my teeth and found grit there. I hurried over to the side of the deck and spat frantically over the railing, desperate to get some of the filth out of my mouth; I shivered even though the air was quite warm. Behind me, I heard my husband barking out orders to some of the ship's crew, as they tried to do something to our plane.

So the ship changed course toward Shanghai, where we'd have to stay; how many days I had no idea, but each one a nail in my heart, hammered in by the knowledge that it would be that much longer before I saw my son, held him in my arms, felt his fingers curl warmly around mine.

It was growing dark, and I was still covered in mud; now I was desperate to get to our little shipboard cabin. If only I could shut the door and take a hot shower, wash the filth and despair off me, look at the photographs of little Charlie that, thank God, were still in my stateroom, safe and dry. My legs weak with exhaustion, I was halfway down the deck when an officer came running toward me.

"Mrs. Lindbergh? Mrs. Lindbergh?" He waved a yellow piece of paper. A telegram, I knew in an instant. I froze, unable to take another step. "Dear Mrs. Lindbergh, I'm sorry—"

"What? The baby? Oh, the baby!"

Charles came running up behind me. "Anne. Let me see what this is."

He snatched the telegram out of the man's hands, and read it. As he did, I thought of all the things I would say to him if something had happened to my child. All the blame, all the recrimination; words, sentences—angry, bitter, accusing—flew through my mind and were almost on my lips when I heard my husband say, very gently, "It's your father."

"What—Daddy?"

"Yes. He's—he's dead, Anne. A stroke. This morning, apparently."

"Oh." And I smiled.

Charles looked at me oddly, but then put his arm about my shoulders. He made some kind of apology or statement to the always present newsmen on board the ship, and ushered me quickly down the deck to the telegraph room. He wired my mother to say we would be returning home right away.

Through it all, my husband watched me with grave concern, and I knew he was wondering *when,* not if, I would collapse or give way to my emotions, those emotions he always despised because he did not understand them. But this time, even Charles understood the sadness of losing a parent. Of course, I must be distraught.

How to explain, then, that all I felt was relief? Relief that little Charlie was fine, that we hadn't drowned in the Yangtze after all. Relief that it was only my father.

For I would see my baby. Sooner, much sooner, than I had thought. Because my father had died, I was released from my duty as my husband's crew. At that moment I couldn't feel grief about the reason.

I only knew the pure happiness of one who has been relieved of a great, crushing burden. I could hardly sleep that night, I was so eager for the morning.

We took a ship back to San Francisco, where we borrowed a plane and flew across the country. We did not encounter any storms or mishaps. And three weeks later, when the car finally pulled up to Next Day Hill, I ran ahead of my husband. I brushed past my grieving mother, my stricken sisters, my silent brother; I ran upstairs on feet that fairly flew.

And I grabbed my child out of the arms of his surprised nurse. Dancing around the sunny, light-filled nursery with Charlie in my arms, I whispered that I would never leave him again.

W E HAVE REACHED THIS ISLAND, this place he has chosen as his home, finally, once and for all. The far side of Maui, a
place called Hana; a jungle, really—screeching birds, jumping
fish, the roar of the ocean so loud that it can't be called restful.
These last few years, Charles has turned his back on technology,
the modern age. Instead, he devoted his fierce attention to envi-
ronmental causes—saving rain forests, hugging trees, preserving
indigenous tribes. He fell in love with Hawaii; he even built a
two-room hut, ostensibly for us but really for him. He knew that
I would never consent to live permanently so far from everything
we've known, so far from our children and grandchildren, our
memories—and perhaps that was the point.

Here is where he is preparing himself to die.

The hut is too far from the closest clinic, so we have borrowed
someone else's home, and it grieves me that he will have to die
within a stranger's walls. But he seems content with the arrange-
ment; a hospital bed is in the front room, positioned so that the
ocean, yards away, is in full view. Charles is propped up in it, but
there are no tubes attached to him, no noisy machines, no one
checking his pulse every five minutes; all are banished, at his
command. He has spent these last couple of days calmly making
lists between naps of startlingly deep nature; there has been more
than one moment when I was sure he had slipped away, only to be

startled and relieved to hear him take a wrenching, crackling breath. These lists outline, in his usual exhaustive detail, the steps we are to take as soon as he breathes his last.

Farther from the beach, in another small hut, a man is crafting a long, narrow casket out of native eucalyptus to Charles's specifications. Deep in the jungle, about a mile in from the ocean, two other men are digging a grave. It is on a plot of land big enough to hold two caskets; Charles has already informed me where I am to lie, when my time comes. Far, far away from the world, with only him for company; the precise thing I once longed for; the reason I abandoned my baby forty-three years ago.

Scott, having had a last, healing talk with his father, has left; his wife and child are in France, and he has been away from them long enough. Jon, too, had to return to Seattle to his family. Land remains, drifting in and out as I sit vigil, offering to relieve me. But I say no, rather snappishly. I want him to leave for now. I don't want him to go far; I just want my son away from the house. I *must* talk to Charles, and I'm terrified that time is slipping away alarmingly. With every ragged breath he takes, Charles loses a little ground.

Finally, I instruct Land to visit the grave site to make sure it's progressing. And I wait, and I watch, and at last Charles snorts, and groans, and wakes up with a wrenching start, blinking as if surprised to find himself still living.

"What time is it?" Out of habit, he tries to raise his left arm, but his wrist is far too thin for a watch.

"Two o'clock in the afternoon." I hand him a glass of water to sip. He can't hold it himself, so I do it for him; I want to cry to see him so helpless, so wasted.

But then I remember the letters in my handbag. And I place the glass back down on a small teak table and return to his side, standing over him so that he can see me.

I have no time to reconsider; I plunge into it now, before he slips away again.

"The nurse gave me your letters," I say.

He is tired, and sick, and his eyes look more gray than blue now, almost milky. "What letters?" he asks. And I realize he truly doesn't understand.

"The letters you wrote." I answer with the patience of a teacher, helping him to remember because I desperately need him to remember, so I can have this long-delayed moment of absolute honesty with him. "All three of them. To those women."

"Oh." He blinks as if trying to focus his eyes. Then he turns to gaze at the rolling, crashing waves outside his window.

"The letters to your—lovers, I suppose I should call them? Your mistresses?" I take a tremulous breath; I have been rehearsing this for forty-eight hours straight, even in my sleep. I will not stumble and cry and shout; I've done those things already today, walking along the beach before dawn, the pounding surf the only thing more stupendous than my rage. "Those women you hid away, all these years. Even more thoroughly than you hid me."

"I didn't hide you. I told you that, once."

"I need to know why. I need to know how—how could you do this to me? To your children, especially? How could you hurt us all so?" Despite my vow, I feel the sting of angry tears.

I turn away, and so I can't see his face when he whispers, "I never wanted to hurt you, Anne. But I did, didn't I?"

"Yes, you did!" I wheel around, prepared to continue this, but he interrupts: "No. Not now. But then. Back then, in 'thirty-two. The baby."

The blow, as always, is visceral but not as devastating as it used to be. Time, as everyone told me then, does soften the pain.

"You? What do you mean, *you* hurt me? Charles, no, don't you remember, they found the man who—"

"No. It was me. It was always me."

Every muscle tensed against the onslaught of memory, I wait. Is this it? Is this all?

But he begins to breathe raspily, steadily. And I know that he's fallen back to sleep.

CHAPTER 9

"BETTY, DO YOU THINK we ought to give him a bath to-night?"

"I don't know. He's still sniffling so, Mrs. Lindbergh. I think not."

"You're right, Betty, as usual." I smiled at her, and she blushed, looking, for just a moment, like a young girl. Pretty, with red hair, a quick smile, Betty Gow normally exuded such authority in the nursery that I felt the difference in our ages acutely. I was only twenty-five to her twenty-nine. This always made me feel as if our roles should be reversed; that she should be the mother, and I the nursemaid. She simply knew so much more than did I.

"I suppose just change him and put him in a new sleep shirt?" I winced at the question mark in my voice. "I'll be downstairs, seeing to dinner for the colonel. I'll come up before you put him to bed. I wish we had brought more clothing with us this week-end, though. I'll be happy once we're all moved in." I glanced around the airy nursery, freshly painted and papered; the only room of our new home that was completely furnished. So far we came down only on weekends, without Betty; playing family, I thought of it. Just the three of us, and I cared for the baby myself, almost as if it were a game. Knowing that I couldn't do that much damage, for come Monday, Betty would be there to undo it.

But when Charlie woke up this past Monday sniffling and feverish, I'd decided to stay put until he was better. This morning, Tuesday, I'd rung up Next Day Hill and asked Betty to come out; I wasn't feeling well myself. Taking care of a sick baby full-time was more work than I'd anticipated, and I felt my inexperience keenly. In short, I needed her help, especially since Charles had gone into the city as usual yesterday morning.

"Thank you so much for coming," I told Betty again. "I hope you didn't have any plans tonight?"

"Oh, Red and I were going to see a movie, but I called him and told him I couldn't go, and he could either like it or lump it." She winked at me, so assured; I had never been that assured of a man and even after being married for almost three years, I still wasn't.

Standing there so competent, complete with my baby in her arms, Betty didn't seem like a woman in love, and I fervently hoped she wasn't. Her boyfriend, Red Johnson, was a nice enough man. But I relied too much on Betty; I didn't want her to marry and leave me. *Us.*

"Was he—was he angry?" I hated to pry, but Betty and I had so little to talk about, usually. Other than the baby.

"Oh, he'll get over it," she replied tartly. "He knows our Charlie comes first."

I smiled, even as I was in awe. I was the baby's mother, and I couldn't imagine saying that to Charles.

"Well, that's good," I said, suddenly shy; I'd pried too much. "I'd better go see about dinner."

Betty nodded and brought little Charlie over to me for a quick kiss. His nose was crusty, and he was breathing noisily through his mouth. He didn't act as if he were sick, however; he smiled up at me with a gay little wave before being borne off by Betty to be changed.

FIVE MONTHS HAD PASSED since Daddy died. Five months of sorrow on the surface, but pure contentment underneath as finally, after two years of delays caused by Charles's meddling with first one architect, then another, our home outside of Hopewell, New Jersey—about sixty miles from Manhattan—was almost completed. With no plans for future flights on the horizon, I disregarded, once and for all, Mr. Watson's parenting advice and gave myself over to the pure joy of being with my child. I smothered him with kisses and spent entire afternoons in the nursery, knitting or mending while he played contentedly at my feet, Betty bustling about in the background with her Scottish competence and humor. Spoiling him; I freely admitted it. I had to, while I could, for I was expecting another child. Soon little Charlie would have a sibling to contend with, and my attention would naturally be divided. So I showered him with it now.

Of course I missed my father. But with my own family to care for, I missed him less than I would have before; I understood that, and knew that he would have, too. So while I mourned him; mourned, once and for all, the end of the family I had thought I'd known as a child, I saw it as a natural progression. My father had died, and I was expecting a new life. Wasn't that the way it was supposed to be?

I wanted to worry about Mother, but she wouldn't allow it. She seemed to be doing surprisingly well; she'd packed up the Washington townhouse with no regrets.

"It killed him," she said bluntly, the day she moved back to Next Day Hill for good. "Washington. Politics. He hadn't the heart for it, and he couldn't say no."

"What will you do?" I couldn't imagine my mother's future without my father, so seamlessly had they always worked together for the same common goal—his career. She had so much energy. So much determination. What on earth would she do with it now?

"Don't worry about me," she answered, quite mysteriously. "Worry about your husband instead."

"Charles? Why would I worry about him? Of all the people in the world, Charles doesn't need anyone to worry about him!"

"Things are changing—the world is changing. *You're* changing. Even if you don't know it yet."

"How silly! I'm the same as ever—plain old Anne." I laughed at my own reflection in a mirror, and patted my stomach. I hadn't yet started to show, but soon, I knew, I would be a dumpling once again.

"No, you're not. You're a mother, not just a wife; the second one really makes you understand that. There's a difference—and I'm not entirely sure your husband will ever understand. Mine didn't."

I looked at my mother—my surprisingly wise mother—in astonishment. Why hadn't she been so honest and straightforward when I was growing up? Then, her inner life was hidden not only from the world but from her children. All I ever saw was the perfection of my mother's marriage, the impossibly shiny surface that reflected my own doubts and fears back to me a hundredfold. Daddy alone was allowed to have his faults; he was loved, indulged for them, while my mother stood smilingly, soothingly, supportively by.

Were we women always destined to appear as we were not, as long as we were standing next to our husbands? I'd gone from college to the cockpit without a chance to decide who I was on my own, but so far, I was only grateful to Charles for saving me from that decision, for giving me direction when I had none. Even so, I suspected there were parts of me Charles didn't understand; depths to my character he had no interest in discovering. I wasn't resentful; he was so busy. *I* was so busy. We were young. We still had time to appreciate each other; we still had time to develop the marriage I'd only imagined my parents had had.

"I'm so sorry," I blurted out, before I could stop myself.

"Sorry? Whatever for?"

"Sorry for you, that Daddy died before he had a chance to know you like this—know you for yourself, not just his wife."

"Oh, Anne." Mother smiled, touching my cheek, ever so gently. "Don't feel sorry for me. No one knows the truth behind a marriage except husband and wife. Especially not the children! We knew each other, darling. You can be sure of that. Like I said—don't worry about me. Worry about your own marriage. We're the caretakers, we women. Left on their own, men would let a marriage run itself out, like one of Charles's old rusty airplane engines. It's up to us to keep things going smoothly. And, my dear, life with Charles is never going to be easy. You have much more work ahead of you than I did."

"How do I know I can manage it?"

"Because you can. Because you have to. Because you don't have any other choice; no more choice than any wife. Now, hand me some of those towels to fold, will you?"

We busied ourselves with folding the towels and placing them in a basket, and I wanted to ask my mother, "At what cost? What did it cost you, all these years? What will it cost me?"

But I didn't. She was right. Children didn't need to know everything about their parents' marriage. And my mother, for all her surprising attributes, was no fortune-teller.

"I do hope you won't be lonely if we're not here so much, now that the house is just about done," I said instead.

"That's the way it should be," Mother said briskly. "Two captains of the same ship—it never works. You two need your own household, finally. And I still have Elisabeth and Dwight and Con, you know. My family still needs me, I should hope!"

"I know Elisabeth does."

"Why do you say that?"

"No reason, just, you know—her health."

"Well, doctors don't always know what they're talking about. Elisabeth will be fine. Perfectly fine." Mother smiled, a bit too fiercely, and folded a towel with such vigor, I feared the crease might never come out.

I nodded and patted her hand—and was surprised when she clung to mine longer than was necessary. The shadow of losing her child was in my mother's eyes; so frail, so fragile was Elisabeth these days, she didn't seem a whole person anymore.

"We're not quite out of your life yet," I reminded my mother with a laugh. "We still don't have all the furniture, and it's easier to stay here during the week until we have a full staff. It is so *nice* here!" I admit, I rather thought of Next Day Hill as a luxurious hotel, a place where I could lounge around, have my meals brought to me, not worry about the details. I also knew my son was safest here, with all the guards, the dogs. The police in Englewood were almost our own private security detail. And, flattened with the nausea accompanying my new pregnancy, I enjoyed being cared for and pampered—instead of having to organize and run my own household.

"Well, of course you're always welcome to stay, dear. I love having you! But do think about Charles. I don't think he's quite so content."

"No, you're right." Charles was solicitous of my second pregnancy—although not quite so solicitous as he had been with the first—but it was true that with my father gone, he chafed a bit at what he called the "harem" of Next Day Hill.

"Take care of your marriage, Anne, like I said." She laid the towel down on the stack and rose to go. I had to smile; she looked so Victorian at that moment in her sensible dress, old-fashioned hairstyle, watch pinned to her shirt. "Charles is not like Daddy."

"I know," I assured her with a rueful smile. "That's the one thing you don't need to tell me. I know."

I WAVED GOOD NIGHT to my son and went downstairs to see to my husband's meal, wishing my mother could observe me acting as the lady of the house. Even if it did seem just that—acting. Or playing. It didn't seem real yet, that this house was actually mine, so used was I to the back cockpit of a plane.

But I did love it, our home on four hundred acres atop a rocky mountain outside of Hopewell, New Jersey. The reason we'd chosen this location was precisely because it was so challenging to find. Charles and I still sometimes got lost ourselves, driving out—even though the newspapers had "helpfully" printed a map of the location, complete with the names of the few marked roads. Still, we no longer feared people simply "dropping by," as they did at Next Day Hill; our driveway alone was a mile long. Charles hoped we could give our children a taste of the carefree rural childhood he had known, unencumbered by security details and guards.

I paused for a moment in the entryway of our first real home together. It was a big house, although somehow cozy; a center hall with two perpendicular wings, one for the drawing room and study, the other for the kitchen and dining room. The staircase led up to five bedrooms and a nursery—I blushed when Charles insisted, saying that we would need them for our "dynasty." The nursery was in the room adjacent to ours, although Charles had not liked this. I'd held my ground, and insisted.

Most of the house was papered and painted by now, although

a few bedrooms remained unfinished. Not all the rooms had a full complement of rugs for the stone floors, some of the furniture was still delayed, and we'd hired only two people so far who lived here full-time—Elsie and Ollie Whateley, a middle-aged English couple.

Charles was due back from the city at any moment; while he wanted a chauffeur so that he wouldn't waste even a minute of the day, for the time being, he was driving himself in his old road-ster. We had a new Ford on order, although it hadn't yet been delivered.

"Elsie?" I stepped into the kitchen; it was snug and bright, everything painted white, with the exception of the sunny yellow tiles for the backsplash. Tonight, with the March wind howling outside, it positively glowed with warmth and security.

"Yes, Mrs. Lindbergh?"

"I think we'll eat in the dining room tonight, so can you please light a fire?"

"Yes, ma'am. When will Mr. Charles be back?"

"Any minute, I'd think."

"Oh, no, Mrs. Lindbergh." Ollie popped his head into the kitchen. "Colonel Lindbergh called. He'll be late tonight."

"Well, keep dinner for as long as you can. I'll wait for him."

I started back upstairs, pausing halfway up; I heard thumping against the side of the house. "Ollie?"

"Yes'm?"

"Do you hear that?" Something banged against the house again.

"Oh. Must be a shutter that's not fastened. Or maybe that flagpole bangin'. I'll look at it first thing in the morning."

"Thank you." I continued upstairs to the nursery, papered with blue sailboats, a pattern that Charles had picked out. "What will we do if the next one's a girl?" I'd teased him.

"It won't be," he'd growled, with a proud, masculine swagger, and I'd laughed.

Betty was on the floor, a needle in her mouth, a piece of flannel in her lap.

"The poor lamb spit up on his sleep shirt," she explained, removing the needle. "I was afraid he'd ruin this new one with all that oil on his chest, so I made him an undershirt. I used an old flannel petticoat of mine."

"Very clever." I went over to the baby, who was standing in his crib clad only in his diaper.

"Mama!" Charlie crowed, reaching up to me. Then he coughed, a barking little cough that turned his face red.

"Poor little lamb!" I rummaged around in a cupboard until I found a jar of Vicks VapoRub; I was surprised that we had it, actually. I was forever leaving things behind while we juggled the two households. "Now Mama must rub some on his chest."

"No—no!" He pushed my hand away with surprising strength, and I laughed, holding his sturdy little body down on the changing table and rubbing the greasy, camphor-smelling stuff all over his chest. Betty handed me the new shirt, and I pulled it over his head.

"There. All better."

"Bettah," he agreed, immediately compliant.

"Now we go night-night," I cooed, as I bundled him into his new Dr. Denton sleep suit, gray wool.

"Nigh-nigh," he agreed again, with a crooked, dimpled smile.

I carried him over to his crib, placed against the interior wall so that he had a lovely view out the windows. His room faced east, out of the back of the house, so the sun was the first thing he saw every morning.

"Go right to sleep, baby boy, and Papa will come in and kiss you when he gets home," I promised. Charles sometimes spent more time in the nursery than I did; he delighted in lining up all the baby's wooden soldiers, and then watching as little Charlie knocked them all down with a rubber ball—a military version of bowling. And this man who was so restless that not even the skies seemed big enough for him spent countless hours teaching his son the names of all the animals in his menagerie. The sight of the two heads bent together in such serious contemplation never failed to cause my heart to swell, as if to capture and contain them both.

Part of this paternal interest, though, still took the form of toughening up his son; once, Charles placed the playpen outside and left the baby out there for an hour, all alone. Fighting back tears, I watched the entire time, knowing I couldn't rescue little Charlie as he first played, then tired, then wailed once he realized no one was there. He stumbled around the playpen, clinging to the rails and shaking them in his rage and fear, until finally he collapsed in a corner and fell asleep sucking his thumb for comfort. Only then would Charles let me rush outside and pick him up, tears still wet on his hot cheeks, his sweaty curls plastered to his head.

"It's good for him," my husband insisted, as he followed us upstairs to the nursery. "The sooner he learns to rely on himself, the better. You coddle him too much."

I couldn't speak. He honestly believed what he said. After all, he had been treated much the same way, he assured me—and look what he had accomplished!

How could I answer that? I couldn't. I was sentimental, I was weak—I was a mother. And I no longer wondered why Charles's own mother preferred to live her life away from her son; Evangeline lived in Detroit, and visited us only once a year. When little Charlie was born, she sent him a set of encyclopedias. She, obviously, had not coddled her son—and so she had his admiration, as well as the admiration of an entire country. What she didn't have, as far as I could tell, was anybody's love.

Would my son love me, when he was old enough to know what love meant? I smiled down at him as I covered him up with his quilt; I couldn't resist touching that dimple in his chin. *I* wasn't sure I knew what love meant, even at my age. Except for this—my child snuggling down to sleep, clutching my finger trustfully in one hand. He closed his eyes obediently and let out a soft, contented sigh.

I bent down to kiss his forehead, then carefully pulled my finger out of his moist grasp, and let Betty ease the metal thumb guards over his thumbs; Charles insisted we try to cure him from sucking them in this way. They looked like medieval torture devices to me, but they didn't seem to bother the baby; they clamped to his sleeves, and the metal caps fit neatly over his thumbs. Betty turned off the overhead light, switching on a soft night-light, of which Charles did not approve. But he wasn't home yet; wordlessly, the two of us agreed that it wouldn't do the baby any harm if it was left on until then. There was a chill in the air, so I went to pull the shutters over the windows. But the ones at the corner window were warped. Maybe that's what I'd heard, banging against the house.

Betty came to help, but even the two of us, leaning out the window and tugging with all our might, couldn't shut them, so we left them open and closed the windows. Outside, I could see the low moving clouds, occasionally giving up a glimpse of the moon. We shut the door softly behind us, then paused in the hall. As always, when faced with a Betty who was not busy caring for my child, I didn't quite know what to say to her.

"Well, I'll wait downstairs for the colonel," I said. "If the nursery gets stuffy, open one of the windows halfway."

Betty nodded and retreated to her own room adjacent to the

baby's, while I went downstairs to the study, where Elsie had lit a fire. I sat down at my desk and pulled out my notes. I was trying to shape a narrative out of our trip to the Orient, at Charles's urging.

"You're the writer in the family," he reminded me after we returned, and magazines began to clamor for articles about the trip. "I'm busy, and besides, you need to start writing something more substantial than your endless letters to your family. This is something you should do, Anne."

So, as always when he urged me to do something, I was doing it. Or, rather, attempting to. Hazy with pregnancy, enjoying the cozy domesticity of my child and my husband and my new house, I was not making much progress. I was happy, I admit; happier than I had been for a long time.

I wasn't so sure, however, about Charles.

Lately, he drove into the city more often than he flew, forced to preside over board meetings for TAT and Pan Am, gnashing his teeth as bureaucracy inevitably obliterated the pioneering romance of flight. He was also tinkering with an idea for a mechanized heart; with Elisabeth's illness claiming her more and more each day, my husband had wondered why a damaged heart couldn't simply be replaced, just like a damaged motor. To this end, he was working with a man named Alexis Carrel, a Frenchman, a Nobel Prize winner who, Charles claimed, was a genius. And my husband did not use this word often.

Lucky Lindy. He'd conquered the skies; now he was conquering medicine. Was there nothing Charles Lindbergh couldn't master? I could only sit, one child in my womb, another mainly cared for by a more competent woman than myself, and marvel at him while I tried to stir myself to some kind of creativity, to master the written word, as my husband expected me to. And failing, failing, failing; more often than not, I found myself napping instead of writing, or reading, or simply walking outside, content to breathe deeply, admire my sturdy footprints in the muddy ground, and simply—be. Happy. Settled. Content. New words for me to ponder and explore, even as I knew that my husband derided such unimposing vocabulary.

Certainly, despite his accomplishments, his busy schedule, Charles was never content. The other morning, I happened to glimpse him as he left for work; he stood in front of the long mirror in the hallway of Next Day Hill, a slim, tense figure in his tweed suit. He stared at himself for the longest time, as if he didn't quite recognize the ordinary businessman, carrying a briefcase instead of a parachute, staring back. And I felt uneasy watching him leave, wondering, for the first time, if today was the day he would decide to jump into a plane and fly away from me for good.

Sitting at my desk, I must have dozed off once again. I found myself startling to wakefulness by the sound of a car in the drive. Our terrier, Wahgoosh, who was snoring softly at my feet, did not move, however.

"That must be Charles," I said, even before I was fully awake, to no one in particular. I shook my head, pinched my cheeks, and picked up my pen, trying to look alert and busy.

But Charles did not walk inside the house, so I must have heard something else, not a car. That wind, perhaps.

It was another twenty or so minutes before Charles finally arrived home. I heard him come into the kitchen from the garage; Betty and Elsie both said hello to him. I looked at the clock; it was nearly eight-thirty.

"Was the drive terrible?" I asked Charles, as he came into the living room.

"Not too bad. I'll have to get used to it. An hour and a half, just about. Have you gotten a lot done today?"

I hastily turned over my pages, so he couldn't see how little

I'd accomplished. "A fair bit. The baby took a lot of my time, you know, until Betty came out." Charles had been in the city for two days, working with Carrel; I hadn't seen him since Sunday.

"How is he?"

"Better." I followed Charles up the stairs to our bedroom, where he quickly washed up for dinner. Then we ate together in the dining room, chilly even with the gaily dancing fire. After dinner, I fought back my encroaching drowsiness as we sat, talking over our day; normally I cherished this ritual. But tonight, as I attempted to follow his discussion of his work on the mechanical heart, I couldn't prevent my eyelids from drooping. Finally, with an understanding smile, Charles suggested I go to bed.

"I'm afraid I should," I admitted, and we both went upstairs; Charles had a quick bath and then went downstairs to his study to work. I settled into a nice long bath with a book, trying to warm my chilly bones. Even with the most modern of furnaces, this house was drafty.

Wrapping myself up in a warm robe, I emerged from the bathroom with flushed skin, damp hair, so ready for bed I could already feel myself surrendering to the feathery, bottomless mattress. Just as I was turning down my covers, Betty burst into the room without knocking; she was breathless, as if she'd been running.

"Do you have the baby, Mrs. Lindbergh?"

"No. Maybe the colonel has him?" Without replying, she had wheeled and was out of the room and down the stairs. After a moment, during which I could only stand, strangely rooted to the floor as if my legs had forgotten how to move, Betty and Charles came running to me.

"Do you have the baby, Charles?" I asked, still puzzled. Why were we looking for little Charlie, at ten o'clock at night?

My husband pivoted and sprinted toward the nursery. I followed, and for a second I held my breath, remembering that the night-light was still on. But then I saw that *all* the lights were on; my baby's room was filled with cheerful light that revealed an open window, a curtain flailing about in the wind—and an empty crib.

"Mr. Lindbergh, you're not playing one of your jokes, are you?" Betty was wringing her hands.

Charles didn't answer; with a grim look, he ran back to our bedroom.

"I came in to check on him like I always do, and it was cold," Betty babbled. "So cold! I went to the crib, but he wasn't there, and then I switched on the light and saw that the window was open. Where is he? Oh, where is he?"

Seeing her wild eyes, I began to tremble. Then Charles came back, a rifle in his hand—and my knees buckled. My baby was not where I had left him. For the first time in his life, I did not know where he was.

"Charlie, Charlie, where are you?" I shouted it, running to and fro, picking up the oddest things—a handkerchief, a book— as if he could somehow be hiding beneath them.

I tore through the upstairs, dimly aware that Charles and Betty, and now Ollie and Elsie, were doing the same thing; we were all running from room to room, meeting and bumping in the hall, and for a moment I had the strangest urge to laugh, for we resembled nothing more than characters in a Marx Brothers movie.

Then we swarmed downstairs, peeking under tables, inside cupboards, even looking up the chimney.

We moved upstairs again, to the nursery, where suddenly we all stopped just inside the door, simply staring, and I finally registered the open window, and what it could mean. And I saw, for the first time, the envelope—a small white envelope, the kind I might use for an invitation to lunch, or a thank-you note—on the windowsill.

"Charles!"

In a flash he was by my side; he saw what I was pointing to, and his jaw set in an awful way. He started to the sill, but then, with a visible effort, stopped himself.

"Call the police," he barked, and Ollie dashed downstairs.

"The police? Open the envelope! See what it says, Charles—if it says where the baby is!" Oh, how could he not be ripping it open? I lunged past him to do it myself, but he grabbed me by both arms and held me back.

"No! Anne, no! We can't—we have to wait for the police. This is—this is evidence. They have experts who can examine it for signs, even for fingerprints. We can't touch it until they get here."

"Evidence?" A horrible realization was trying to worm its way into my heart, my brain, although I fought against it, fought for one last precious moment of innocence. Reluctantly, I turned to face my husband; behind him I saw the small, sobbing outline of Betty; the plump, uncomprehending face of Elsie. I forced myself to meet Charles's gaze; I found no shelter from my growing knowledge in his eyes—muddy with doubt and fear for the first time in our life together.

"Anne, they have taken our baby," my husband told me, and I felt his grip on my shoulders, ready to catch me as I fell.

But I did not fall. I only nodded, and felt a coldness in my heart and an emptiness in my chest where my child's head normally fit cozily, helplessly. Oh, so helplessly—Charlie was just a baby, he needed me, surely he was crying for me right now—

I ran to the open window, leaning out into the black, cold night with the wind howling, no stars, no moon, no comfort anywhere for my baby—

I called for him, over and over, until my throat felt like sand-paper, until my eyes were raw with tears, lashed by the cold wind.

And when I finally stopped, collapsing back into my husband's arms, the only sound I heard was the thumping of that shutter, banging relentlessly against the house in reply.

EVERY LIGHT WAS ON; the radio was blaring in the kitchen; the phone never stopped ringing; strange men trooped mud all over my new house. I sat on a chair in the upstairs hallway. No one paid any attention to me as they all followed my husband from room to room, the tail to his comet.

When they emerged from the nursery, one man had the envelope in his cotton-gloved hand; he pinched it between thumb and forefinger as if it were a foul-smelling rodent. They all trooped into the kitchen; I heard a murmur, then a shout, then a murmur again.

Meanwhile more police, carrying flashlights, stormed inside the house, their muddy footprints smearing the others on my new carpets.

No one asked me about the events leading up to this; no one inquired of me if I had any idea what might have happened. As soon as the doorbell rang and the first police officer showed up, Charles was the one to whom they turned. And I willed myself to stay still, out of the way; these men had a job to do, and it was to find my baby. If I interfered, they might not be able to do that job.

So I sat on the chair, my hands clenched in my lap, my jaw so tense my teeth ached.

"Mrs. Lindbergh." I looked up; Elsie was there. "Drink this tea. It'll make you feel better."

I shook my head. Why should I feel better? Why should I have any comfort, when my son was—

"You need to keep up your strength. Not only for the baby missing, but for the one you're expecting."

And for the first time, I remembered. I was carrying a child. I must keep him or her safe, for Charlie.

I pushed Elsie away, bolted out of my chair, and ran downstairs, grabbing a mackintosh from the hall closet. Pausing in the kitchen doorway, I saw a contingent of official-looking men huddled around the table. Most wore muddy brown police uniforms covered in trench coats. Charles was at the head of the table.

"Charles, I'm—"

All faces turned my way; all registered surprise at my presence.

"I thought I'd go outside and help—"

"Anne, come here." It was a command, and so I obeyed; I walked to my husband, who gave his seat to me.

"Anne, the expert has brushed the envelope—"

"Brushed?"

"Examined it, collected evidence, but there was no fingerprint. We've just opened it—it's a ransom note."

I nodded. By now it had thoroughly registered that my child had not simply wandered off, or been misplaced like a pair of spectacles. Something far more terrible had happened. It was confirmed, and now we needed to meet whatever demands they had and get him back. And it all seemed so logical; a kind of blanketing calm came over me for the first time since Betty had burst into my bedroom—how long ago? I glanced at the clock on the stove. It was ten past midnight. Only about two hours ago. A lifetime ago.

Someone—the expert?—pushed a small white piece of paper toward me. I was afraid to touch it, afraid somehow to contaminate it so it couldn't be used. Leaning forward, I read—

Dear Sir!

Have 50,000$ redy 25000$ in 20$ bills 15000$ in 10$ bills and 10000$ in 5$ bills. After 2–4 days we will inform you were to deliver the Mony. We warn you for making anyding public or for notify the Police. The child is in gut care. Indication for all letters are singnature and 3 holds.

Where there should have been a signature were two blue circles. They were joined together by a solid red mark, punched with three square holes.

"Charles! We told the police!" I jumped up, shaking with anger. "How could you? You see? What he says?" Why I assumed the kidnapper was male, I don't know, except that I couldn't imagine a woman stealing another woman's child.

"Anne, of course we had to involve the police. The fingerprints, for example—they're dusting the nursery now, so they can compare any strange fingerprints against ours."

"But—the note says!"

"Anne." And Charles gave me a look; a stern look I knew too well; the impatient look of the schoolteacher trying to teach me celestial navigation.

"Yes. Yes, of course. So, we'll give him the money. Then we'll get the baby back." I sat down again.

There were glances over my head as if I couldn't possibly understand. I intercepted one—from a man who was bigger, better dressed than the others. Not in a uniform but a tailored suit; still, he wore a shiny badge on his lapel and carried a gun in a holster across his barrel chest. His gaze, unlike the others', was not furtive; it was steady, pitying, and therefore terrifying.

"It's not usually so simple," this man said, not bothering to elaborate. Then he tipped his head toward me. "Colonel H. Norman Schwarzkopf, ma'am. Superintendent of the New Jersey State Police."

There was something solidly steady about this stranger; he reminded me of a huge tree with deep, unfathomable roots, and his face was as craggy as bark, although he had a rather dashing salt-and-pepper mustache. His eyes were deep-set but alert, and he had a bulbous nose just like W. C. Fields. I found myself looking to him as the others began to discuss the note and all its implications.

"The thing to do is to search the perimeter again as soon as the sun comes up," my husband said excitedly. "I should answer all calls—can you set up a switchboard in the garage, Colonel? We need some kind of headquarters, base of operations, like an airfield."

No one contradicted him; everyone nodded eagerly. I looked around the table; all these policemen, Colonel Schwarzkopf included, were looking to Charles for answers. Shouldn't it be the other way around?

"Airfield?" I couldn't help myself. Charles cleared his throat and continued—ignoring me without even a look.

"We must not release this note to anyone—I know newspapers. They will try to infiltrate the household, so we must be vigilant. But that sign—the two circles with the holes. That's the key. It's how we'll authenticate any communication from the kidnappers."

"Exactly," Colonel Schwarzkopf said with a nod.

"Colonel, you will be in charge of your men. I'll monitor everything from the house, including all communication, incoming and outgoing. Anne"—Charles finally favored me with a look—"you write up some kind of list of things the baby would need—his diet, his schedule—in case the kidnappers ask how to care for him."

They all agreed with everything he said; every plan, every list—my husband was a great one with lists—every rule he laid down: If anyone called or showed up with information, Charles himself was to see that person, no matter what. All interviews with persons of interest were to be conducted in his presence. No lead was to be considered too small or too inconsequential. Every tip would be followed up on.

I was to stay upstairs, out of the way, and rest, and think positive thoughts—he actually said this, in front of everyone. "Anne, I know you. I know you worry, I know you fear. But you can't, do you hear me? For the baby's sake, you can't give in to such emotions."

"But, Charles—" I tried to push through the icy waters that were slowly swirling over me. "What do you know about—"

I stopped. I couldn't. I couldn't contradict him, I couldn't question him—I saw it in the adoring eyes of every man in that room. Charles was a legend; I was the child's hysterical mother. It was written on every face.

Charles, however, was not only the child's father but the greatest hero of our age. He was also eager, energized, in a way he hadn't been in such a long time—not since our flight to the Orient. He was champing at the bit to get on with it—to command this mission, the most significant mission in a life full of significant missions. If anyone was going to bring our son home, there was no doubt in anyone's mind that it would be him. He was Colonel Lindbergh. The Lone Eagle. Lucky Lindy.

My heart plummeted; already I felt that my child was being forgotten in the eagerness to find, once more, in Charles Lindbergh the hero everyone needed in these dark, desperate times.

No longer the boy who had crossed an ocean, now he was the man who would single-handedly rescue his son from evil kidnappers in the midst of a Depression.

"Anne." Charles helped me up from my chair and bent down to my level. Now his eyes were clear and resolute—just as they had been the day I met him, and recognized him as the most perfect, capable man alive. His voice did not waver. Despite my inner turmoil, I drew strength from him, as I always had.

"Anne, they have taken our baby. But you have to trust me. I will bring him home to you."

"Yes," I said, marveling to hear my voice clear and strong—as strong as his. "Yes," I repeated. "I know you will."

It was a sacred, intimate moment, as if we were repeating our marriage vows. Only this time I wasn't pledging my troth; I was pledging my baby's life. We stood together, as close as we'd been since the trip to the Orient. And I gave my child over to my husband in front of these muddy state troopers, in this house so blazing with light it must be visible from five thousand feet up, in this darkness that whirled around outside, howling to come in once more, just as it had done already this endless day. Two hours—one lifetime—ago.

If I let the swirling blackness inside again, even masquerading as doubt, it would never leave; it would poison the two of us forever. At that moment, I was frantic to believe that we hadn't already been ruined beyond recognition. So I nodded as Charles told me—so boyishly earnest, so heartbreakingly sure—that he would bring our son back home. And that there was absolutely no reason for me to worry.

I *believed* him, just as I always had, just as I always wanted to. Of course, I believed him; I was his crew. He was mine.

In that terrible hour, long past dusk, dawn an unimaginable miracle away, what other choice did I have?

CHAPTER 10

THE BABY WAS CRYING. I stirred in my sleep, an automatic reflex; kicking away the covers, I rolled over, eyes still shut but breath held, hoping he would stop. Of course, he didn't. Now he was crying out, calling my name—my real name, how odd! Not Mama, but Anne. "Anne—Anne—"

I was crying, too. I was calling out his name, calling "Charles, Charles!" I had never called him Charles before; it was always Charlie, or Little Lamb, or Baby Boy. The poor thing! He didn't really know his name. So how would he come, if I kept calling it? Now I was running; it was dark and something kept hitting against the house, the wind howling about, filling my ears with its primal moan. I called, "Charles, Charles!" and I realized he wouldn't know it was me, I realized he wouldn't understand his own name, if he could even hear it in the storm. But I kept calling.

"Anne! Anne!" But why didn't he call me Mama? How did he know *my* name? Was he already lost from me? Had a lifetime passed, and he was grown up now and I didn't recognize him anymore? Him, this stranger shaking me, calling out my name?

"Anne!"

"Charles!"

My eyes flew open; it took me a moment to realize I was in bed. My husband was holding me by the shoulders, and I was struggling against him, because I had to go to the nursery—Charlie was crying. That was what had awakened me. Charlie's cry.

"Is he up already?" I asked, bewildered. Why was Charles still wearing the clothes he'd worn yesterday?

"Anne."

"Did Betty feed him?" I yawned, rubbing my eyes—astonished to feel tears on my cheeks. I looked at my wet fingers, and knew that even as I did so, I was still crying.

And then I remembered.

"Oh. Oh!" And the grief was real and raw, as if all that had happened the night before was happening all over again. I struggled to get up, to run to his room, but Charles pinned me down.

"Stop it! Let go of me!" I was shouting, and he looked uneasily toward the closed bedroom door, as if someone was standing just outside. "I mean it—let me go!" I actually kicked at my husband, allowing myself a tiny burst of triumph. It felt good, even for so childish a moment, to lash out at someone.

"Anne, hush. I woke you because there's someone I want you to see."

I stopped squirming instantly. I held myself perfectly still, allowing his words to penetrate first my mind, then my heart. Then I laughed, pure joy bubbling out of me; it *had* been a dream, after all!

"The baby? You found the baby? Oh, where is he?" I threw my arms about him. His body remained rigid; he plucked my arms from around his neck.

"No, no. Not the baby." His eyes narrowed, as if I had somehow challenged his authority—no, his *competence*. "Pull yourself together, Anne. There's a man outside I thought you should see—or, rather, he wanted to see you. He might have some information."

"Oh." I nodded, looking away; I couldn't let him see my disappointment. "What time is it?"

"Eight o'clock."

"You look terrible. Did you sleep at all?"

"No. We've been searching outside—although we couldn't keep the reporters out, not at first, so quite a lot of evidence might be trampled over."

"Did you find anything?"

"A ladder. Broken in pieces."

I nodded, not really understanding. What did the pieces of a ladder mean?

"And some footprints, men's footprints, on the ground beneath the—his—window. The press, of course, is having a field day. You'd better—well, I don't know. You'll find out anyway. If you want to read the newspapers, they're in the kitchen. I would advise you not to. But get dressed now, please, for this gentleman."

Charles joined whoever it was in the hall while I went through the motions; I splashed water on my face, ran a comb through my hair, and pulled on a housedress, only to find that I couldn't get it all the way over my hips. I had to wear an ugly yellow-and-black checked maternity dress that I'd somehow thought to pack instead. The first one I'd worn for this pregnancy; I couldn't help reflecting on the irony—that the new life I was carrying was making itself visible on this, of all days.

Then I opened my bedroom door and stepped into the hall, wholly unprepared for the chaos outside. Men were running in and out of my son's nursery. Even more were tramping mud all over the front hall carpets. There were tables set up in the hallway downstairs. As I hung over the upstairs railing and peered down through the open front door—shivering in the frigid air; had it stood open all night long?—I could see a small army of cars parked haphazardly, as if all had been driven in a great hurry and then urgently abandoned on the drive.

"Mrs. Lindbergh?"

I turned; a small man in a navy blue suit, his thin red hair plastered flat on his head, his eyes small and nervous, stood before me, holding his hat in his hands. He was barely taller than I was; next to my husband, he looked like a paper doll. He resembled an illustration in one of Charlie's nursery books—a particularly sinister image of the Pied Piper of Hamelin with long, sharp, ratlike features. The only thing missing was the flute.

"Yes?"

"This is the man I was telling you about," Charles exclaimed, unable to keep the eagerness out of his voice. "Please, come into the bedroom."

He ushered this man—this stranger!—into our bedroom. Our house was being turned into a headquarters for evil, just as Charles had said—but couldn't I keep one room untouched? Unsullied by the dirt and filth that had blown in through that open nursery window?

"Please," I said, turning my nose up, folding the corners of my mouth primly. I gestured for the man to sit on a footstool, while Charles and I sat, side by side, on our bed.

"Mrs. Lindbergh, I thank you from the bottom of my heart for seeing me. But I have information that I am certain you will want to hear." The little man now crumpled his felt hat in his excitement; there was a gleam in his eyes that almost made his thin, watery face beautiful.

My heart began to pound, and I reached for Charles's hand. "Yes?"

"Your child, he is safe."

"How? How do you know?" Charles asked, gripping my hand tightly.

"He is safe because he is away from here." The man rose and began to pace before us. "You do not know God, you worship at the feet of false idols. Man was not meant to fly, not meant to have wings. For God created him in His image, not the birds'. Your child has been taken from you as punishment. Whoever has him must have seen this, must have known this, and I feel it is my duty to make you aware of your sin, and to urge you to repent of your evil ways. If you do, surely God will see fit to return your child to you, but until then—"

Charles gripped the man by the arm; I thought he was going to throw him out the window. Instead he lifted him up, carried him—feet dangling—across the room, and shoved him out the door, shouting, "Get this idiot out of here!" before slamming the door shut.

I was trembling, sick; my skin was clammy, and I felt my stomach churn—or was it the baby kicking? Desperately, I wanted only to lie down and close my eyes—after first scrubbing every inch of this room, to rid it of that horrible stranger's presence.

"That was a mistake," Charles said, and I had an absurd urge to laugh. It was such an understatement. "I shouldn't have brought him up to you, Anne—it was my fault. I feel, however, that we must take every person seriously. We can't possibly know at this point who might or might not have information. That said, I should have interrogated him further. But he did insist—he insisted on seeing you, not me. I thought—well, I thought. I was wrong. Forgive me."

"Oh, Charles, I don't blame you!" Why was he being so distant and formal?

"No, Anne. I am responsible for that. I am responsible for you, especially now, in your condition. I can protect you, at least—" He turned away, and cleared his throat several times before walking to the window.

"Charles—" I moved toward him, aching to reassure him somehow, to remind him he was not alone in this. But before I could take another step, he turned to face me. "I arranged for your mother to come," he said briskly. "I thought it best that she be here."

"Oh." I, too, was lost; lost once again in my own terror as I looked out the window and saw strange men tramping over some bulbs I had planted last fall. Tulips, I remembered. Dutch tulips, white. Charlie had helped me; he had carried the knobby tubers in a basket before dumping them all out and arranging them in little patterns, gurgling happily, calling them "bubs."

"Have you heard from Elisabeth?" I asked Charles, dabbing at the tears on my cheek before turning around. "Dwight? Con?"

"The police have been alerted, and they're safe," he replied, and somehow we faced each other while never once meeting each other's gaze.

"The police are talking to them?"

"I allowed it; I thought they might be of help. Anne, Colonel Schwarzkopf would like to talk to you when you're ready. He would like to talk to the servants, as well. Betty, in particular."

Betty! "How is she?" I asked, stricken with guilt—I'd forgotten all about her. I hadn't seen her since last night—since she had run to her room, sobbing, after Charles called the police. She loved little Charlie so—oh, how could I have neglected her? She must be as frantic as I was. I must go to her at once.

"Of course, it's absurd," Charles continued, as if he hadn't heard my question. "The staff, naturally, is above suspicion. I told Schwarzkopf that. He agrees but still needs to ask basic questions in order to establish some kind of timeline—I'll be present, regardless. But I refuse to let him administer a polygraph test on any of them, or the family. That would be unnecessary. And the press might get wind of it, and inflate it, as usual."

"Good," I quietly agreed.

"I'll send some breakfast up," Charles said. "Try not to wear yourself out. The important thing is to remain hopeful. For the baby's sake."

"I know," I said, and once more, I longed to reassure him, to be the strong one, for once. But I felt that if I were suddenly to move, to make any unexpected, careless gesture, I would fly apart. Molecules and cells and bones would fragment, splintering all about the room—Humpty Dumpty, indeed.

Oh, why could I not stop recalling nursery rhymes and fairy tales this morning? Everything reminded me of my child. Everything good, and everything bad.

Charles stood for a moment, his back to me. Then his shoulders finally squared, his head snapped up, and he strode out of the room without another word—that famous Lindbergh discipline on full display once more. My husband, the father of my child, vanished before my eyes. Now he was the hero we all needed; that *he* needed, most of all. It was as if I was seeing him again for the first time, in a newsreel.

All the king's horses and all the king's men, I sang to myself, walking slowly back to my bed, carrying my hope and terror both, one fragile, the other already so stolidly familiar I couldn't remember life before it, within my heart. Within my womb, as well; next to my unborn child, who would have to make room for them now, and for the rest of his life.

Could they put the Lindberghs together again?

WAITING. WAITING. WAITING.

That was all I could do. That was all that was expected of me.

The next day, we received a postcard postmarked from Newark, addressed to *Chas. Linberg, Princeton, N.J.* The scrawled message read, *Baby safe, instructions later, act accordingly.* It did not have the same three-hole signature as the initial letter, but the handwriting was similar enough for the police to take it seriously. *Baby safe*—I repeated the words to myself, my mantra, as another day passed with no further communication from the kidnappers. Although it brought masses of communication from everyone else in the world—phone calls, telegrams, letters. The Boy Scouts of America were on full alert, every member pledging to scour roads and paths across the country in search of my child. Women's institutes and other organizations, too, volunteered; they went door to door, looking for him.

President Hoover—who had just lost reelection—offered the services of a new United States Bureau of Investigation, headed by a man named J. Edgar Hoover. Colonel Schwarzkopf turned him down, which I thought wise (even though Mr. Hoover insisted on setting up some kind of headquarters in town, where he gave interviews to anyone who would listen). But I couldn't imagine how more well-intentioned men, milling about my house, knocking things over and looking grim, could help the situation.

The National Guard was called out. Our child's photograph—the one that Charles had taken on his first birthday—appeared on the front page every single day, and every newspaper vowed to keep it there until he was found. Charlie was on the cover of *Time* magazine. Fliers were plastered on every telephone post in New York, New Jersey, and Connecticut. Roadblocks were set up across three states as well. Anyone who looked remotely suspicious—although that description seemed to change by the minute—was pulled over, their vehicles searched.

For the second time in five years, the name Charles Lindbergh was on everybody's lips. For the second time in five years, everyone prayed for him, as special church services were called throughout the land.

The same radio commentators who had broken the miraculous news of Charles's 1927 landing now broke in every ten minutes with an urgent bulletin about the kidnapping of his son. No reporters were allowed on our property after that first horrific morning, but that didn't stop them from writing as if they were. Every day, I insisted on reading what I had worn on my walk the day before (dresses I had never owned in my life), what I had thought, what I had eaten, if I had napped. I read columns and columns of purple prose praising my "Madonna-like patience" as I "awaited the safe return of my little Eaglet."

Was I patient? I suppose I appeared that way, compliant in my stone jail, leaving only for short walks in the gray March weather, always shielded by a respectfully silent contingent of police. It was numbness, though, more than patience. I could not believe that this circus—people were selling photographs of my child as if they were souvenirs, right at the end of our driveway!—had anything to do with my precious baby. Or my husband. Or my life. So I removed myself, mentally. To participate fully would have endangered the child I was carrying—of that, I had no doubt. And I couldn't bear to lose both of my children; I couldn't bear to do that to Charles.

Who was trying, so valiantly, to remain in control of a situation that grew more fantastic and bizarre with every telegram, phone call, letter. Mediums offered to come hold séances, in order to determine if the baby was "in the spirit world." Crazed zealots wanted to cast off the evil spirits in our home; one even managed to get past the security, and painted a strange symbol with a bucket of pig's blood on our front door before she was taken away.

The most bewildering were the offers from other mothers to give me their children. How could any mother be willing to part with her child voluntarily? And the notion that my son could simply be replaced by another—I shook with rage at the thought. Yet we received dozens of such letters and telegrams.

Charles was trying to oversee everything; trying, in vain, to shelter me from the worst of it, constantly reassuring me that it was only a matter of time before he returned Charlie to me. He barely ate, fitfully slept. He spent most nights seated upright in a chair in our bedroom, watching me, as if he was terrified I might disappear, too. But when I was awake, he could hardly look me in the eye.

To Colonel Schwarzkopf, to the hordes of policemen, detectives, working on the case—to the world at large, holding its suspended breath—he remained the calm, cool aviator in total control. He allowed Schwarzkopf and his men to sort through the thousands of letters delivered three times a day by a special mail truck, to follow up the vaguest of anonymous tips, to continue to tramp about our property in search of clues. But he made it clear that he, and he alone, would communicate with the kidnappers, and I heard Colonel Schwarzkopf express his first doubts about Charles's leadership the next night in the kitchen, when I padded downstairs to get a glass of warm milk.

"You can't be serious?" I heard the colonel ask in his blunt way; I stopped just outside the doorway. "You're really going it alone? Colonel Lindbergh, you have the entire police force of New Jersey and New York at your disposal."

"I am perfectly serious. They need to trust me. That's the only way we'll get him home, don't you see? Once I can establish that trust, I do not intend to betray it. I will make a statement declaring that no police will ever be involved in our communication, and that I alone will meet with them, no questions asked."

"You're a man of honor, aren't you, Colonel?"

"Of course."

"Well, whoever took your baby isn't." Schwarzkopf slammed outside, so furious that he didn't see me standing in the hallway. Through a window, I watched as he kicked a stone, drew a deep breath, then took a cigarette out of his pocket and lit it, angry face raised to the moon.

Peering around the corner, I saw Charles slump down in his chair, hiding his face within his hands. I knew I mustn't go to him; I couldn't let him know I had seen him like this. He needed me to be hopeful; I needed him to be strong. These were the roles we had assigned each other.

But for the first time, I understood that they were just that—roles.

MOTHER ARRIVED ON SATURDAY; by then, my baby had slept somewhere else for four nights. Was he crying out for me? Or was he, so used to me being gone as I flew away with his father, already trusting his kidnappers? Could he be bestowing on them one of his sweet, serious smiles? My heart could not withstand such questions—but still they came, as relentless as that shutter that still beat itself against the house.

"I don't know what to say to you!" Mother blurted the moment she saw me. "I have no idea what you're going through. I can't even imagine."

So I found myself comforting her instead; I had just led her to the study when Charles burst into the room.

"Anne! Come. There's another note."

My heart started to thunder; I leaped to my feet and followed Charles into the kitchen. There, once again, an army of men stood round our table, gaping at a thin white note as if it might jump up and bite them.

We have warned you not to make anyding Public also no-tify the Police.

I felt sick; I closed my eyes, but not in time to stifle an image of my child lying cold and still, sacrificed because we had done what any parents would do under the circumstances. But then I heard Charles, reading the rest of the letter out loud, say, *"Don't be afraid about the baby,"* and my nausea disappeared. I opened my eyes and saw for myself the three-hole signature, just like the original.

"He says don't be afraid!"

"Yes, he does. He also says he increased the ransom to seventy thousand." Colonel Schwarzkopf picked up the note.

"But that's wonderful, right? It means the baby is unharmed!" I scanned his face, desperate for confirmation.

"Yes, of course, it's a positive thing," Charles said, with such authority it banished the tiny, imperceptible fear worrying my heart. "Colonel, where was the letter postmarked?"

"Brooklyn. We've already brushed it for fingerprints, but there's nothing to pull. It was in the mail, and probably touched by a hundred hands along the way. I suggest, then, that we post lookouts at every mailbox in the borough."

"No." Charles shook his head. "That will scare them off."

"Colonel, we can do it in such a way no one would notice—"

"No." Charles's voice rose; it silenced Colonel Schwarzkopf. "I said no police. Didn't you read the letter? I think we need to contact Spitale and Bitz."

"I urge you to reconsider—"

"Spitale and Bitz," my husband repeated, his voice a low growl.

Schwarzkopf pulled at his lower lip, glaring at my husband. Charles glared back.

"As you wish, Colonel Lindbergh," Schwarzkopf muttered; he then looked at his men, nodded, and strode out of the kitchen. One by one, his men followed him—each mumbling, "Ma'am," to me as they left.

Don't be afraid about the baby. I knew that I would repeat that phrase, over and over, through this endless day.

"Charles, who are Spitale and Bitz?" They sounded like a vaudeville act to me. I sat down at the empty table. My kitchen was no longer a warm, inviting place; there were cigarette butts in saucers, stacks of empty coffee cups on the counter in an assortment of mismatched china patterns. Elsie must have had to send away for extras. Newspapers were piled in corners: "Lindbergh Baby Kidnapped!" "Little Lindy Vanishes!" "The Crime of the Century—Will Lucky Lindy's Baby Ever Be Found?"

"Who are they? Why is the colonel so upset?" I asked my husband again.

"Anne, I ask you to trust me. These men have never been involved in a case like this. They may be well intentioned, but I don't want this bungled. Do you?" Charles met my gaze warily. We were both on an uncharted trip to a land we never even saw as we flew so high, untouchable—or so we had once believed. And just as he had needed me to navigate his path before, he needed my trust now; without it, he might never find his way back to himself, the man who had never been lost, not even while crossing an ocean alone.

"So what do you plan next? What is your—*our*—next move?"

"Harry Guggenheim has been helping me come up with the money. I'll have to wire him about this new sum. Anne, that is all I'm going to discuss with you at the moment. I don't want you to know more."

"Why? What possibly can be worse than what I already know?"

"There are some rather—unsavory characters that I'm dealing with. But they can be very helpful, even if I detest having them touch my son—even if I would prefer not to associate with their kind."

"Kind? What do you mean?"

"Mobsters, Anne. Men like—Al Capone offered his services. There, now you know. And some New York men. They offered to act as go-betweens, instead of the police, and I believe that's the best course. I prefer not to tell you more. You mustn't worry. Your job is to remain hopeful."

"You keep telling me this, but I do worry!" I was shaking with fury. "Of course I do—and so do you! But you won't tell me, you won't talk to me, and I don't understand why. Charles, I was your crew! I was baptized in the Yangtze and let you push me off the top of a mountain in a glider—but now you think I'm too *weak* to understand or help? Too frail? Charlie is my son, too!" I pushed myself away from the table in disgust. "How can you imagine that I'd care whom you deal with? Deal with the devil himself if you have to! But stop thinking you can protect me from this. You can't protect any of us anymore, so stop trying to."

Charles winced, but I didn't care.

"Don't you see?" I asked hoarsely. "It's already happened. Now we need to get him back. They'll have to give him back to us, once we pay. Won't they?"

"Of course they will." Charles picked up the note and studied it again. "It's simply a matter of communication and trust. Spitale—one of the New York men—is certain he knows who is responsible. I'll respond through him—I'll give him this letter as proof, and my reply. I don't know why the colonel wants to make it into something else—like an army invasion! Does he really think he can post men all over Brooklyn and no one will notice?"

"You're going to give this—character—this letter? The actual letter? But—that identifying mark, should you let anyone else see it?"

"Anne, as I said, it's a matter of trust. I may not like these men, but there is a certain honor among thieves."

"What does Colonel Schwarzkopf think about this? Are you going to tell him you're releasing the letter?"

Charles's face flushed. "I'm in charge, Anne. I've told you."

"And I'm your wife, and Charlie's mother. I'm telling you to run this by Colonel Schwarzkopf."

Charles didn't reply. His fury was different than mine; it was coiled, so tightly wound you might miss it until it sprang out, cutting deeply. I didn't often see it. But I sensed it now, and while once it might have terrified me, today I had no fear to spare for my husband. Only for my son.

When finally Charles spoke, his words were measured, precise. "Anne, I believe I'll include the baby's diet with our response. Would you write it out now?"

"Yes, of course."

I got to my feet, then I paused behind his chair. Leaning over, I kissed Charles on the cheek. He didn't respond. As I pulled away, hurt, he put his hand on my cheek for a moment, drawing me close before releasing me.

Then he returned to his study of the note, as if he might see something in those crudely written letters that the rest of us could not.

I started up the stairs; Colonel Schwarzkopf was seated on the landing, his head in his hands. He looked up. And suddenly I knew what I must do.

"Colonel! You can't stop him!" The colonel rose in alarm. "Listen to me. You can't stop Charles in this. He must do this his way—he always has, and it's always been the right way before. That's what he can't understand now—that he's wrong, that this is too big for him. But please, I beg of you. Do whatever you have to do."

"Behind his back?"

"If possible, yes, but Colonel, I am serious. I'll answer to Charles. I'm not afraid, like the rest of you."

"Are you saying——"

"Colonel, listen carefully. I'm saying my husband has no idea how to proceed, but he will never admit that. So I'm admitting it for him. I'm saying that I authorize you to do whatever you have to do. Interview the servants. Post men at mailboxes. He wants to release the latest letter to those New York men, and I believe that's a terrible mistake. Just——do whatever you have to do to bring my boy back home."

The colonel stared at me. Then he cocked his huge head—like a bulldog's, square and jowly—toward Betty's closed door at the end of the hall. Her light was on; it spilled out from beneath the door. When had I last seen her? I couldn't remember. "Can I question Miss Gow again? Colonel Lindbergh said——"

"Ask her anything," I instructed Colonel Schwarzkopf. "Give her the polygraph. Betty loves the baby, but maybe someone near her doesn't. Ask her about Red. Then talk to Elsie and Ollie. Ask them anything. Anything you need to. All of the servants. Here and at Next Day Hill. Start with Violet Sharpe—she's the one I spoke with on the phone that day. She knew we would be staying here."

He studied me skeptically, perhaps looking for the hysterical mother. Then, to my surprise, he cupped his big hands around mine and said, "Thank you, Mrs. Lindbergh. I know this wasn't easy for you."

I let my breath out in a surprised laugh. *Oh, men!* How little they knew, after all. "No, Colonel, you're wrong. This is my child we're talking about. It was very easy."

ONE WEEK PASSED. Eight days. Ten. Fourteen.

Two weeks since that terrible night. Two weeks with only one additional communication, increasing the ransom amount again.

The house had taken on a rhythm now, a busy, purposeful hum, although it was not even close to being back to normal; I couldn't remember what normal felt like. The switchboard was still in the garage, ringing with tips and cranks and people hoping to hear my voice, or Charles's. Our lawn was churned to mud. Colonel Schwarzkopf still showed up every morning, his men still camped out in droves, and I never knew at what hour I might be asked to leave my bedroom for yet another conference between detectives or policemen. Politicians drove up our drive simply to have their photographs taken on a broken ladder they'd found lying outside my child's empty nursery.

Only the baby's room remained untouched, after that first frenzied night of searching. A fine layer of dust had settled on every surface, undisturbed save for whenever I went inside. I did so once a day, at the time he would normally be put to bed. It was habit, it was routine—and I would not relinquish it. If I did, I was terrified that I'd never get a chance to resume it.

Surprisingly, I did not mind the chaos. The constant activity meant hope—all these people were working to bring my Charlie home because they believed there was a chance.

As the days dragged on, my surroundings grew more bizarre; cloistered in my new home, I was aware that, at the end of my driveway, people sold photographs of my missing son as souvenirs. Planes flew low overhead, full of eager onlookers. Sightseeing tours launched from a nearby airfield.

But nothing could have prepared me for the headline I saw one frigid afternoon, when a few late-season snowflakes fell halfheartedly outside my window. "Spurned Sister Suspected in Lindbergh Baby's Disappearance. Why Hasn't Miss Morrow Been to Comfort Mrs. Lindbergh?" And next to it was a jarring photograph of Elisabeth taken years ago; uncharacteristically, she was not smiling. Instead, the ink so smudged and dark, she looked almost malignant.

Oh, Elisabeth! How had she been dragged into my nightmare? All of a sudden the months fell away; I forgot the awkwardness between us, forgot how sick and frail she had been lately. I remembered, instead, the sister who had always been there to laugh with me, coax me, pull me into the bright sunlight constantly surrounding her, even when I insisted I was happier in the shadows. *She* was the one who urged me to try to stand up to Mother when I wanted to go to Vassar instead of Smith. *She* was the one who insisted, when I was ten and wanted to put lemon juice on my hair so that it would look more like hers, that brown hair was prettier than blond.

She was the one who was supposed to marry the hero, not me. I needed to tell her that I understood why she hadn't, now.

I started toward the telephone in the front hall, but when confronted with its black, solid efficiency, I wavered; I couldn't pick up the receiver. Fortunately, my mother chose that moment to bustle around a corner with a pile of blankets in her arms.

"Mother, I was thinking. Could you—do you think Elisabeth could come down? Is she strong enough for all this, do you think?"

"You saw the newspaper." It wasn't a question, and I realized I still was gripping it in my hand.

"Yes. But that's not the reason, truly. I miss her, and I want her here with me. I need her."

Mother put the blankets on a bench and sank down next to them. She rubbed her eyes until they were red, and the lines

around them carved themselves even deeper into her skin. I realized suddenly how selfish I had been. So many people's lives, not
just mine—all tainted forever. Like the ripples on a pond when
you toss a pebble in; the aftershocks kept moving farther and farther away from the center.

"Anne, I know something happened between you two. I've
never asked what it is."

I couldn't reply. What on earth could I tell her?

"So I think you should call her yourself. Don't you?"

"Oh, Mother, I——" But even as I protested, Mother had dialed
the number and handed me the telephone receiver. "Next Day
Hill," a wary voice answered. Violet Sharpe's.

"This is Anne——"

"Oh, mercy!" And with a strangled sob, she put me through
to Elisabeth's bedroom.

"Anne? Is there any news?" Elisabeth's voice was panicked.

"No—no, nothing. I only wanted to—I want to ask you to
come out here. To stay for a while. To stay with me, I mean. For
a while."

"Oh, Anne! My poor darling! Of course. I'll come at once."

"You don't mind? After all this——"

"Anne, stop it."

"I've missed you."

"I've missed you, too, dearest. I'll be there as soon as I can."

"Thank you," I whispered, as if Mother could hear, in those
two words, the reason why we'd been estranged.

"Shhh," my sister murmured into my ear. "Shhh. Now go lie
down, Anne."

"Stop telling me what to do," I protested, just as stubbornly as
when I was ten and she was twelve.

"Never!" As she hung up, she was laughing. And the years
and distance between us disappeared.

Mother took the telephone and placed it back in the wall nook. "Sweetheart, you must get some rest. You look dreadful. Where's Charles gone off to?"

I shook my head and rubbed the small of my back. "He wouldn't tell me. He takes phone calls at all hours, he meets late at night with men he won't let me see. He's—he's having a difficult time."

Colonel Schwarzkopf, while still respectful, careful never to contradict Charles in public or in the press, no longer asked Charles for permission to proceed. The colonel conducted rigorous interviews with our household staff every day, and he no longer hid them from Charles. He seemed particularly interested in the staff of Next Day Hill; he was paying special attention to Violet Sharpe. Mother was very upset at the questioning; she felt protective of Violet, as the girl was so excitable and simple. I liked Violet; despite her occasional hysterics, she had always been sweet and loyal, given to happy tears whenever she received a present or a bonus or even an unexpected day off.

But I couldn't forget that she was the one who had answered the phone when I called to have Betty come down to us that fateful Tuesday. Violet was the most logical person to have alerted someone to our change in plans. Charles was furious at having his authority and his judgment questioned. He never knew that I was the one responsible for it. I wouldn't have denied it if he'd asked, but he never did. Perhaps he didn't want to know.

His fury couldn't disguise his despair, however. I pretended I didn't see the smudge of exhaustion under his eyes, the way his clothes hung off him now, the exhausted blinking that overcame him at times.

This morning, Charles had mumbled something about a new lead before rushing off to meet another stranger. I nodded trustfully and, as I had every day since my child had gone missing, told my husband that I believed in him. Then I went into the cold, empty nursery and stared out the window as Charles started up the car and roared down the drive, all the policemen standing respectfully at attention.

At times like that, I missed believing in my husband almost more than I missed my child.

"You go upstairs," Mother insisted again, taking the newspaper with that awful headline out of my hand. "Rest. Take care of that baby you're carrying."

I nodded. I was so weary of people telling me what to do. Yet I went upstairs, intending not to rest but to write. In these last weeks, I'd started writing poetry again. Dark poems, hopeless poems. Poems of loss and despair; sonnets of impending grief I prayed I would one day find and laugh at for their absurdity.

"Mrs. Lindbergh?"

I looked up, startled; Betty was standing outside my open door. Still in a denim nurse's dress, a white apron around her waist. But I looked at her now through new eyes; our roles were finally as they should be. I was the mother. My loss, my grief, was so much more monumental than hers, and I felt, finally, older. Ancient, actually; every day my child was missing seemed to add years to my life so that I was surprised, when I saw my reflection, that I was not stoop-shouldered and arthritic. Surprised to find my hair still dark brown, and not turned white overnight.

Betty, on the other hand, seemed much younger; uncertain, finally, for the first time I'd known her. Uncertain of her role in a childless home; uncertain of her grief; how much to show, how much to hide. Uncertain of our loyalty, Charles's and mine. And although I did not blame her, I could not look at her without anger and recrimination.

She had held him, been privileged to care for him, far more often than I had. For so much of his life, I'd been gone, and I resented her bitterly for it. But I was most angry at myself. For following Charles whenever he snapped his fingers at me; for abandoning my son, over and over and over.

"Mrs. Lindbergh, I must talk to you," Betty whispered, shutting the door behind her. I motioned to a chair just by the window, and I took the one opposite. The woods that surrounded our house were still stripped, naked; spring seemed an eternity away. And I hoped it would remain so; I couldn't bear to see the world come back to life if my child wasn't with me to share it.

"What is it, Betty?"

She moved her chair closer to me and took my hand; startled, I drew back. She'd never touched me before; she, who had showered my baby with kisses and hugs, had never even shaken my hand.

"Please, please, forgive me, Mrs. Lindbergh!"

"Forgive you? Forgive you for what?"

"For not checking in on him enough that night. For not making sure the shutters closed. For—"

"For telling Red that we'd be here? For telling someone else?"

"No! No, I don't think—you don't believe Red is involved, do you? Or anyone else at Next Day Hill? Mrs. Lindbergh, of all people, you don't believe—why, the colonel doesn't believe any of us is involved! How can you?"

"Because I'm Charlie's mother! Because I don't know what to believe anymore! No one knew we stayed here at the house that night except you, and Elsie and Ollie, and the people at Next Day Hill. No one else knew! If anyone had been planning this, they would never have planned it for a Tuesday night, because we'd never been here on a Tuesday before!" Unleashing all my darkest suspicions, I lunged toward Betty. "But *you* knew. *You* told Red. Who else did you tell? Who?" Now I was shaking her, and she was crying, "No one, no one!" over and over again, but still I shook her, demanding an answer.

"Anne!"

Betty and I jumped apart; she whirled away from me, weeping; I spun toward the window as Charles charged into the room, a package in his hands.

"Anne!"

Still breathing raggedly, I clenched my fists, which still itched to lash out at someone—my fury, smothered for so long, was blazing. My husband ran toward me.

"Anne, you remember James Condon?"

"Ma'am," Mr. Condon said with an absurd bow. "Mrs. Lindbergh, it is my privilege to greet you again."

"Yes," I said, as I retreated a few steps, my mind whirling, still reworking the conversation with Betty while now forced to absorb a stranger in my bedroom. And then I glared at Charles. What else was he going to put me through? How many crackpots was he going to bring me?

Last week, he'd presented to me a psychic, a woman clad in perfumed scarves and cheap jewelry, who grabbed my palm with her dirty hand and told me that it foretold a great joy sometime soon. The week before, he'd introduced me to a medium who proposed holding a séance in the baby's room.

Condon was just the latest in a series of shysters and charlatans, an obsequious person who had gallantly (his own word) volunteered to serve as go-between between "the hero of our age" and the "odious kidnappers." Last week Charles had brought him here to meet me, even allowed him to sleep in the nursery and take one of the baby's toys with him, in case he had a chance to meet with the kidnappers in person.

"Anne, you remember, I told you this morning about a new

lead. Condon here put an ad in the paper, and what do you think? They contacted him! He met with them!"

"It is my patriotic duty, madam." Another bow. "I am just a citizen, a private citizen. The kidnappers, however, must feel my sincerity, for they did indeed meet with me."

"Anne, sit down," Charles said breathlessly. I'd never seen him so excited; his eyes were wide, his face flushed. "This is it, the break we've been looking for. The kidnappers did not want to speak with the mob, but for some reason they do want to communicate with this man."

"How do we know it's them? After—after your contact sold the ransom note?" Just as Schwarzkopf had feared, Charles's underworld contact had sold the ransom note with the authentic signature to the newspapers. Now we received notes by the bushel with that odd three-hole signature. It was impossible to know which were real and which were not.

"Because there's something else," Charles said quietly. He placed the brown package in my lap, then reverently unwrapped it, revealing a piece of gray wool fabric. A gray Dr. Denton wool sleep suit. Size two.

I lifted the fabric to my face; eyes squeezed tight, I inhaled it, wanting desperately to smell the innocence of my child, the downy hair, the apple scent of his shampoo, the grease of the Vicks I rubbed on his chest that night. I so wanted to smell these things that for a moment I did—and then I knew it was only the desire of memory. This fabric did not smell like any of those things; it actually had very little scent at all. Only a faint whiff of damp, as if it had been freshly laundered.

But it had been so long; two weeks now. If Charlie had been disguised somehow, in different clothing, then they might have laundered his sleep suit—

I handed the fabric back to Charles and looked at Betty, hard.

"Is this his suit? What do you think? I need you to tell me the truth, Betty. Always."

"I think it is! I really do, Mrs. Lindbergh! I think I recognize it!" Betty's cheeks were scarlet as she reached out a tentative hand to stroke the fabric.

"Then it is it! We are on the right trail, at last!" Charles strode about, energized, nearly knocking over a lamp on the table. He crossed the room in one giant stride.

"Anne, this is it," he said to me—only to me; it was as if there was no one present but us, now. He knelt, and smoothed the fabric in my lap, speaking softly, urgently. "Betty recognized this right away. And you did, too—I saw it in your face. I know you want to be absolutely sure, Anne. I know what a strain this has all been, and how confused you must be—and how hard it must be, now, to hope, after everything. But Condon here spoke with the man who gave us this. He said this had been planned for a year, that the baby was in good health, was being taken care of on a boat by two women. Two women! Think of that! He seemed very sure of himself, and he had this." Charles grasped my hands tightly, as if he could transfer all his confidence to me.

I shook my head, still hesitant to believe. He was right. I *was* afraid to hope. Even though that's all I had been told to do— the only job entrusted to me—deep in my heart, I hadn't. But now—oh, Charles was so sure of himself! Finally, after weeks of dashing about, playing a desperate game of cloak and dagger, he looked like the old Charles. The clear-eyed boy. The best pilot he knew; the best there ever was.

"Will you—if Colonel Schwarzkopf can verify this—" I took the fabric once more, slowly claiming it, allowing its worn folds to soften my heart. Charles paled at my mention of Colonel Schwarzkopf, but I didn't care. As much as I wanted to believe him, I needed to hear Colonel Schwarzkopf's opinion even more.

My heart beat fast, my face flushed, as if he'd discovered me in an indiscretion—but I did not flinch from his gaze.

"I understand. This has been such a strain. I understand." And with those words, Charles allowed me to question his methods for the first time.

"It *has* been such a strain. For both of us. But if Colonel Schwarzkopf agrees, well, then—" I nodded, coaxing myself into giving in, finally, to the luxury of hope. "I do think this is the baby's, it really does seem like it. I do! So—now what? We know they have him. Do we just give them the money, then? Is that how it's done? And then we'll get him back?" My heart began to beat faster and faster with every word until I jumped out of the chair and grasped Mr. Condon's hand. "Oh, thank you—bless you!" And I could have kissed him, right then, but I didn't. The odd little man did bow, once more, and wiped a tear from his eye.

My own eyes were dry, and I felt a sudden surge of energy, of optimism, race through my veins. For the first time in weeks, I was hungry. Ravenous! The child within me kicked, as if to remind me how starved he was, too, and I laughed out loud.

"We have so much to do," I told my husband, who nodded indulgently as time sped up, calendar pages fell away, and I began to recognize the world again. "The house is a wreck! I don't want him to come home and see it like this, do you?" Charles shook his head, but I hardly even paused to register it. I continued to pace about, my mind full of plans—blissful, ordinary plans, plans that other families were making, too, right at this very moment! "We'll have to get him some spring clothes, you know. We haven't had a chance to buy anything new. Do you think he's grown very much? Babies do grow so fast at this age. Charles, Charles, do you think Charlie will remember us?"

"Of course, Anne," my husband murmured, and suddenly I was aware that everyone in the room was staring at me as if they'd never seen me before. And I suppose they hadn't; they hadn't seen this happy, hopeful creature at all. Until now.

"I'm sorry, I rather lost my head," I said sheepishly, but no one seemed to mind. "Please, go on and do what you have to do. Please—go!" I took Charles's arm and propelled him out the door—to his great surprise, and to everyone else's. "Go talk to Colonel Schwarzkopf—show him the fabric, and then arrange it all! This is what we've been waiting for, isn't it? Go!"

Laughing, Charles allowed me to push him down the hall. Condon followed—again with an elaborate bow. Betty grabbed my hand, and the two of us embraced. Forgotten was the anger, the suspicion, the recrimination; now we were united in joy. Then she left, as well.

I went to my desk and began to make a list of everything we would need for the baby's homecoming. Charles had taught me so well! I had not been such a great list maker before we met; now, I found, I could make them easily. All because of my husband— one more miracle he had wrought!

But before I began, I found myself writing one word. Just this one word, the word I had not allowed myself to write, to speak, until now—

Hope!

CHAPTER 11

I

T WAS MID-MAY. More than two months since my child was taken.

The house was so quiet now. The switchboard was still operative, but we received only a hundred calls per day. Police and other strangers no longer camped out in the house; Elsie had had all the rugs cleaned, the floors polished, the camp beds removed.

I was terrified by the silence, the orderliness. All those people had been working to bring my baby home because they thought there was a chance. It was impossible not to recognize the more sedate atmosphere as resignation.

Colonel Schwarzkopf still maintained an office in the house, working independently of Charles, although Charles had listened to him in one matter; he had paid the ransom to Condon's man in marked gold certificates, so they could be traced.

But the colonel no longer believed my baby was alive. He hadn't told me, and he certainly hadn't told Charles, but I knew it, even as I didn't quite register it. It was like a particularly difficult math equation from school: I could recognize the symbols and letters. But what they represented simply would not penetrate my understanding.

Over the last month, the investigation had taken a grotesque turn. Without Colonel Schwarzkopf's knowledge, the state police sent a man to inspect the incinerator in our basement. He had insisted that Charles and I accompany him. Eyes flickering suspiciously over us both as we stood beside the glowing furnace, he sifted through the ashes with a shovel. "Searching for fragments of bone," he informed us icily. I recoiled, falling against my stony husband; neither of us spoke a word for hours after the man— reluctantly—left, empty-handed but still glaring our way, accusing us of the unthinkable.

Another time, I heard a repeated thumping outside; looking out the dining room window, I saw several broken ladders on the ground, and an intact one leaning against the house, beneath the nursery window. A policeman was halfway down it, about five feet off the ground, carrying a flour sack the size of an eighteen-month-old child. With an ominous groan, the ladder split exactly where the original broken ladder had split; in three pieces. The policeman clung to one side of the ladder, held firmly by his compatriots on the ground.

But the sack tumbled to the ground with a sickening thud, hitting the stone façade of the house on its way down as the men whooped with accomplishment—"It's broken like that every time, just like the ladder we found! That sack weighs what the kid weighed, right?"

I crumpled to the floor, hitting my chest with my fists, shaking from the force of the unleashed scream that echoed furiously within.

Spring had persisted in arriving, cruelly unaware of our desolation. On the walks I took about the house, accompanied by Elisabeth, I looked for meaning in everything. So did she.

"Look, Anne, look at the new leaves! The tulips are coming up," she said one afternoon, when the sun was healing and the wind was coaxing.

"But they're coming up wrong. All bent over."

"Only because all the policemen stepped on them," she chided. "They'll be all right next year."

"Next year." I shook my head, unable to comprehend it. "Where will we all be next year?"

"Charlie will be almost three, and the new baby will be crawling around!" Elisabeth laughed. "Can you imagine what a mess these flowers will be then?"

I forced a smile, trying to picture it. But the new baby looked like Charlie in my mind. And Charlie at three—to my horror, I couldn't see his face; the toddler in my imagination had his back to me, running away. Never coming back.

"Oh!" I couldn't help it; I stopped in my tracks, terrified to go any farther.

"What? Anne, are you ill?"

"No, it's just—silly. But for a minute I couldn't see it. I couldn't see *him*. Charlie. Oh, Elisabeth, what if—?"

Unlike my husband, unlike my mother, both of whom were relentless in their refusal to allow me dark thoughts—my sister allowed me this question.

"I don't know, Anne. I don't know. Somehow, you'll go on, though. You'll have to. But you won't be alone. You'll have Charles, and Mother, and Con and Dwight. You'll have me."

"I know." And I grasped her hand; her frail hand, the skin so thin I could feel her pulse. I prayed for her, right then; I needed God to spare her, because if she left me, there would be no one to talk to. How foolish we'd both been, before!

"I have a secret to tell you," she confided, as we began to stroll once more. "I've fallen in love. With Aubrey. Aubrey Morgan, you know him. We're going to live in Wales, at his estate. After our—marriage." She said it shyly, as if it were a wish that would vanish when spoken.

"Elisabeth, are you sure? I mean, what about Connie? And

it's not easy, you know. Marriage. Even if you're—uniquely suited—to it, like—"

"Like you?"

"I believe you did call me out on that once, if you recall. Although I think you used the word 'sweet.'" I raised an eyebrow, and she grinned. "You know, I always thought when we were young that you would be the one to marry, but now—I suppose I've grown to think of you as above it, somehow. Are you really sure?"

"Yes, Anne. Yes, this is what I want. That struggle, with Connie—I'm not strong enough for it, and so I released it. It's simpler this way. And Aubrey is a kind man. He wants to make life easy for me. Not harder, like with Connie. But easier."

I glanced up at Elisabeth's face; she looked radiant. Like a bride already.

"Then I'm so happy," I assured her. "Does Mother know?"

"No. We—we've thought it best to wait until—until Charlie is back."

"Do you love Aubrey?" It was ridiculous to ask if he loved her; of course he did. Everyone loved Elisabeth.

"Yes. Oh, Anne—yes! He's always fussing over me, saying I have to listen to my doctors. But what do they know? They want me to live like an invalid, but I won't do it. I've waited too long for this—this contentment."

I squeezed her hand, and didn't lecture that I, too, wanted her to listen to the doctors. Or that contentment can be a prelude to tragedy. She allowed me my despair; I had to allow her happiness. So we continued to walk, arms linked; lost in our own, very different, thoughts.

Perhaps because of Elisabeth and her perfect understanding, I had begun to write in my diary again. Finally, something unspooled within me and I had to release it on the page and I didn't care what my husband said about it. When I married Charles, he had asked me to give my diary up, for fear someone would steal it and sell it to the newspapers. And I'd agreed.

How laughable now, to remember a time when my thoughts were considered something to be guarded as closely as my child! Now, sitting prisoner in this unfinished building, I looked forward to taking up my pen once more. I could rage, cry, pray with it, as I could not allow myself to do in real life. Sometimes I was terrified by the emotions I released, for Charles did not escape my rage. Those pages I burned, a good little acolyte. The rest I kept hidden, not ever wanting to read them again but not wanting to destroy them, either. They represented something to me; some small triumph, some battle won.

"Have you seen Colonel Schwarzkopf today?" I asked Mother the evening of May 12. I was in my room, writing in my diary; she brought me some tea.

"He got a phone call about half an hour ago and went out."

"Maybe it was Charles?" I looked up.

My mother smiled her sad smile and shook her head. "I don't think so, dear."

I nodded, but I wasn't really disappointed. I was too full of disappointments to register any more. Every note that appeared in the paper from Condon, begging for further instruction from the kidnappers now that the ransom had been paid. Every week that went by without a reply. Every crackpot who said he had some new information. Every wild-goose chase that Charles followed, with that same determined, grim set to his jaw, the heartbreakingly resolute way he put his hat on as he left—a sharp bend to his elbow, a resigned pat on the top of his head, almost for good luck, I thought.

He had been gone for several days now, piloting his plane off Cape May, searching for a boat that yet another man—this one named Curtis—with a craving for publicity had tipped him to. Why it was always a boat, I had no idea. But maybe, just maybe, this time—

"Has Charles called at all today?" I asked, but this time I did not look at my poor mother's face. She was kindness and patience and suffering and despair; she—along with Elisabeth— was everything to me these days. Everything my husband could not allow himself to be; not until he brought little Charlie back home.

"No, dearest," my mother said with a sigh. Then she bent to kiss my cheek, and left me alone.

Taking the teacup, I picked up a book; a book I had been reading before: *The Good Earth*. I'd had to stop reading after O-Lan killed her daughter because of the famine. Now I wondered if I'd ever be able to finish it. I dropped it to the floor and grabbed something else, something mindless, frivolous. *The Inimitable Jeeves*.

Stretching out on the bed, I tried to read. But after only a few minutes my eyes fluttered. Sleep was a refuge. Hours could pass and I wouldn't have to know, wouldn't have to feel. So I let the book fall off my lap, and I buried my head in the pillow, shutting out the world with eyes squeezed tight. But before I could fully surrender myself to unconsciousness, there was a knock on my door.

"Charles?" I sat up clumsily, guiltily; he did not like me to nap so often. "Charles? Is it you?"

The door opened, but Charles wasn't there.

Mother was in the doorway, and behind her stood Colonel Schwarzkopf. I didn't even glance at Mother's face—I looked right past her, my gaze drawn to the colonel. And I knew, before I could even catch my breath and prepare myself; before he said a word. With shaking hands, I grabbed a pillow and pressed it to my chest, as if it could shield me from what he had to say.

"Mrs. Lindbergh," he began, in a voice thick with unaccustomed emotion. "Mrs. Lindbergh, I am so sorry to have to tell you this."

"Anne, Anne," Mother whispered, and she began to cry. I began to tremble, violently.

"A body was found this morning," the colonel continued. "By a driver. A truck driver," he corrected himself, as if this detail was important. "Five miles away. The decompo—the body of an infant. Deceased. Approximately eighteen months of age—"

"Anne, the baby. The baby—he's with Daddy now." My mother wept, and it was as if the two voices, one so clinical, the other so sympathetic, were a fugue, weaving in and out of my understanding; tearing apart my heart.

"Oh—oh!" I looked to each of them for confirmation. It was there, in Colonel Schwarzkopf's suddenly glistening eyes, his jaw working back and forth; in Mother's terribly aged face, sadness pulling every feature down like a giant hand had erased everything good that had ever happened to her.

My heart—it disappeared. Disappeared with my child; I knew I'd never know either of them again. I was simply an empty vessel, a shell, and my spirit was floating away from it. From somewhere near the ceiling, I saw myself sitting on that bed, my mother's arms around me—

And then, still floating, drifting above—but not quite flying—I saw the empty crib. The empty room. My empty arms. And my heart reminded me angrily, vengefully, that it would not disappear so easily as my child; it shattered, piercing my soul, the shards then splintering into diamonds with sharp, unpolished edges. "I knew," I heard myself say, gasping for air, for reason. "I think I knew from the beginning—"

He was gone. My golden child, my sweet, serious little man. Gone. No more on this earth, no more in my life. Taken.

Taken. Taken. Taken. *Dashed.*

"How—how did he—?" I was having trouble breathing. I fought to stay conscious—I fought to hurt, to feel. I had to do it, for my child. It was the only thing I could do for him now—or ever. *Forever.* It yawned ahead of me, a great abyss of darkness and sadness and I knew, in that moment, that forever I would be searching for him. Forever I would see an empty crib, an empty place at the table, an empty date on the calendar that should mark a birthday, a graduation, a wedding.

I will love you forever and ever, I used to sing to the babe in my arms—oh, he was so little! So dear! Forever had seemed like a gift then. Now it was a prison sentence.

"A blow to the head," Colonel Schwarzkopf replied, that gruff voice incredibly gentle, although he still stood just inside the door, as if afraid his presence could do more harm than his words already had.

"Oh!" And as he said it, I felt it—that blow. To my heart. I cried out, reeling from it, just as my boy must have. But unlike him, mercifully, I knew I would have to relive this blow, over and over, every day, for the rest of my life.

"We think he died instantly, Mrs. Lindbergh. Almost immediately, in fact—the night of the kidnapping. For the body was—it had been there awhile."

"How, then—how do you know it was him?"

"Dental records, physical resemblance, his hair, for instance—also, some fabric; it appears to match the sleep shirt that Betty made that night. In fact—Betty helped identify the body."

"Oh, no!" Even in my grief, I felt for her, such a young girl having to perform such a horrible task.

"Your husband is on his way to the coroner's to do the same. We need a family member, you see."

"Charles! Oh, how did you—where was he?"

"We contacted him on the radio—he was on a boat, waiting for some word from that Curtis fellow. He's on his way now. These people played him for a fool, Mrs. Lindbergh."

"Oh, Colonel, you can't tell him that. You can't ever tell him that!" It would kill Charles to think that someone had been laughing at him all along, playing him, as the colonel said, for a fool. He was pride—all pride. His reputation meant so much to him. He couldn't—

No! I would not think of Charles now. My thoughts belonged, finally, to my baby. Suddenly I saw him. I saw him lying in the leaves, alone, cold and still, without me. Had he really died right away? Or had he suffered? Had he called for me—his face, tear-streaked, appeared before me, the blue eyes so innocent, the cleft chin quivering, and I couldn't bear it any longer; I heard a high-pitched wail, a howl of grief, and I knew it was me. I didn't want Charles, I didn't want Colonel Schwarzkopf or Mother or air or water or life—all I wanted was my baby. I *needed* him as he must have needed me; I ached for him against my chest, in my arms; I reached and reached, blindly, clutching nothing but air—empty, useless air.

At some point Colonel Schwarzkopf left me. Much later, my mother crept out, and I heard her sobbing in the hall outside my bedroom. Then I fell asleep—or collapsed; all I remember was blackness, heat, my clothes sticking to me, my hair plastered in strings down my neck, my breath sour against my fist, which I still held to my mouth as if this was a sorrow that could be stifled.

When I awoke, I was already sobbing. This time, I had no blissful moment of forgetting; I remembered in an instant what had happened. My baby was dead. My ribs ached, as if from a terrible palsy. My throat felt raw; I didn't think I could ever open my eyes again, they were so red and swollen.

I heard a cough, a stir. Too shattered to lift my head, I opened my eyes, and what I saw was my husband, slumped in a chair next to my bed. His clothes rumpled, his face unshaven, his hair uncombed. I wondered if this was how he looked when he landed in Paris, after being awake for more than thirty-six hours straight.

I didn't want him to be here. I didn't want to deal with him, to be strong so as not to displease him, to think hopeful thoughts—to look for Polaris instead of the brightest planet. I hated him, and I wanted to have one thing—my grief—all to myself.

"Anne." He rubbed his eyes wearily. I was aware that it was dark outside my window, even though the curtains had been tightly drawn. It was nighttime. How long had I slept?

Still I lay, my head, my entire aching body, pressed so deeply into the mattress by the terrible weight of all that I now knew.

"You're awake," Charles said. His voice was hoarse and flat. "Anne, they—I decided to have the body—the baby—the body cremated."

His body—gone? I couldn't hold Charlie one last time, couldn't say goodbye?

"How dare you?" Rage—finally, blissfully, rage. It pushed me up, clenched my hands, blessed me with speech. "How dare you? Why? Why didn't you ask me what *I* wanted? He's my baby! Mine!"

Charles looked away. "They took photographs of him, Anne. The press. Before I got there, they broke in and someone took a photograph of his body. There wasn't—he wasn't—our baby, not as we want to remember him. I couldn't let that happen again. Do you understand me? I had to prevent that from happening—they can't take him away from us like that. They have no right."

I tasted horror and revulsion as they rose up in my throat, and I thought I was going to be sick. I shut my eyes against the spinning room.

Charles brought me a glass of water, placed it carefully on the bedside table, then took his seat once more. He did not reach out to me, and I did not reach out to him.

Sometime later, I fell asleep again; it was a fitful sleep from which, occasionally, I found myself swimming up, as if I were afraid to drown in it, before deciding it didn't matter.

And all the while, my husband sat watching me. Once, I heard him whisper, "I thought I could bring him back home. I thought—I *knew*—I would bring the baby back to you."

I did not know to whom he was talking, whom he was trying to convince; himself, or me.

IT IS A TERRIBLE THING when you can't see your dead child. When you can't touch him, play with his hair, put his favorite toy in his sleeping arms and whisper goodbye.

You are doomed, then, forever to look for him. Because you can't help but think, in unguarded moments when you release the tight grip of your own hands upon your sanity, *I don't know for sure that he is dead. I don't know, because I didn't see him.* And so you look for him wherever you go. On the subway. In crowds. At playgrounds.

Inescapably, time passes. And you know that while you still search for the sunny toddler, the golden-haired angel, if he really was alive he would be five. Then ten. And now—

An adult.

Men write to me, still, and tell me they're my son. The Lindbergh baby, they write, as if there was only the one. Grown men who have lived their entire lives tell me they miss me, and wonder how I could have given them up. They assure me it was all a mistake, a hoax, a practical joke gone wrong. That they have waited all their lives for me to find them.

For a long time, I wanted to see these people. Almost immediately after Charles took off alone one cruelly sunny May afternoon, flying over Long Island Sound, near where we first honeymooned, to scatter our child's ashes, we started receiving letters, phone calls, unexpected knocks on the door. And I wanted to meet them all, each and every one. Even when Mother, when Elisabeth, told me I couldn't put myself through the strain, that these were sick people, bad people who wanted more of us than we had already given. Even when Charles forbade it, threatening to lock me in my room while he went downstairs and kicked more than one adult grasping the hand of our "son" off the front steps with his own well-placed boot.

There was always a sliver of my best, most optimistic self that wondered, *What if Charles was wrong, that day in the morgue? What if the dental records were wrong? What if my baby is still alive?*

I never did meet them; I never let these people into my house. I never answered any of the letters. Although I read them all.

I resigned myself to looking for that face that I clearly recalled—until the day when I couldn't. It happened so suddenly. His dear little face was before my eyes even as I opened them in the morning—and then it was gone. Vanished, just as the thief who had stolen him intended. From that moment on, I could recall only him frozen in one of the photographs we had, usually that one taken on his first birthday. The one that we had released to the public, that had ended up on the "missing" posters that once dotted an entire nation, uniting them in prayer and then—in grief.

The nation didn't move on, for a long time. It didn't allow us to move on, either. Anniversaries came and went. Laws were enacted to protect children; laws with my son's name on them. There was a trial. A sensational, horrible trial—the Trial of the Century, the newspapers called it; and the souvenir salesmen proclaimed it; and the celebrities who attended, just for fun, trumpeted it. I testified one day, and I saw tears in every person's eyes. Except for the man who was on trial for murdering my son; the man who was finally discovered because he spent the money that Colonel Schwarzkopf had insisted be marked. It turned out that at least one of the crackpots who led my husband on a merry chase, even as our child lay lifeless in a half-dug grave in the woods, was involved, after all.

Him I couldn't look at, not after my first glance at his flat, expressionless face. So I never knew if he wept for me or not.

That man burned. Some people said he was the wrong man, or at the very least, not the only man. But just as the nation needed a hero, it needed a villain even more, and this man looked it, with his guttural accent, poor immigrant ways, one eye that drooped menacingly. If others were involved—and there were whispers, rumors, although Charles would not allow them inside our house—this man alone was electrocuted; an eye for an eye. Retribution. I could not feel it.

I was beyond feeling; even the pain of childbirth couldn't penetrate my shell. I had a baby, a new baby; a different baby. We named him Jon, after no one in particular; after himself, the one who had to come after.

As soon as possible; as soon as my body healed itself, I agreed to fly with Charles again. I even urged it, to his surprise and, I think, gratitude. Up in the sky, just the two of us, untouchable, just like *before*—only then could I feel. Secure in the knowledge that Charles couldn't hear me from his seat in front, I wept in the back.

Through all my tears, through all my pain, I never saw signs of his, even as I was always looking for it. That first night, I couldn't reach out to him, and I didn't want him to reach out to me. But later, I did. Sorrow was even bigger than the sky we had shared, but hadn't we charted that, once? We needed to chart our path together through this new, infinite journey.

On one of our rare aimless flights with no real mission—other than to give us both an excuse to be alone, together, in the air—we landed on an island off the coast of Maine. It was late fall, and Jon was just a couple of months old, well protected by Mother, detectives, and two ferociously trained guard dogs in the nursery at Next Day Hill. Already it was cold, the ocean steel gray. Beneath the huge wing of the Sirius, now repaired, Charles and I huddled together on a blanket, teeth chattering as we tried to sip soup out of a thermos.

"Charles, do you remember when we took Charlie up for the first time? That afternoon at the Guggenheims' when Carol had a bad cold?" I smiled, remembering; Charlie had cried at first because of the pressure in his ears, but then he'd settled down on my lap and clapped his hands.

"I wonder if we should replace the cockpit window?" Charles poured his soup on the ground and screwed on the thermos lid until it cracked. "We've put so many miles on this plane, and then there's the European mapping flight coming up."

"If you think so, but—do you remember how Charlie clapped his hands when we landed and said, ''Gen! 'Gen!' and you thought he was saying 'engine,' but I told you he was saying 'Again'?"

"I'll telegraph out to Lockheed. While I'm at it, I might as well check on your transmitter. I thought you said one of the tubes was giving you trouble?"

"All right, yes. Go ahead. But, Charles, don't you remember—?"

"Yes." He shoved the thermos into my hand, then walked away so that I couldn't see his face. I saw only his tall, unyielding figure in his brown flight suit, boldly etched against the gray sky and the gray water. The wind blew his reddish-gold hair—so like Charlie's, less like Jon's, which was a bit darker—until it stood straight up on top of his head.

"Of course I remember. How can you think I don't?" I heard him ask above the rushing surf, the call of the seagulls.

"But you never talk about him. I think we should. Sometimes it feels as if I'm the only one who lost anything—"

"No, Anne. We need to forget. All of it. Now, we ought to be getting back."

Stunned, I watched as Charles Lindbergh walked back to his plane with a sure stride, a resolute set to his jaw, just like in all the newsreels. And I watched myself climb in behind him—just like in the newsreels, too.

Just like before, I sat behind my husband on that flight, and all the rest; charting our course, relaying our position to whomever was listening. Imagining little pinpoints of grief tracked by latitude and longitude.

But as time went on, and even with my sextant I still couldn't locate *his* grief, I knew this would poison me against him. It would poison *us*—the Lucky Lindberghs, the First Couple of the Air. And I needed the notion of *us* too much. It was all I had left. I couldn't let go of that, too.

So I had to believe, was *desperate* to believe, that whenever we flew over a certain part of the sound, he looked down at the waves as I did and felt a stab of pain so jagged his vision blurred. And in that tortured moment he remembered a golden-haired boy with a crooked, shy smile.

I convinced myself that the noise of the engine muffled the sound of my husband's tears for his lost child; that in the air, soaring, winging; in the skies, where we had always shared the same view, navigated the same course, and where Charles was always so much *more*—

My husband found a way to mourn our son.

WATCH OVER HIM as he sleeps in this stuffy hut on a lonely beach, just as he watched over me that terrible night, so long ago. Despite my anger, I pull his blanket up to his chin, surprised to find a hidden well of tenderness inside me, still, for this man and what we've been through together.

It is an unexpected, welcome gift, this quiet, peaceful moment, and I decide to let him sleep for a while longer before my betrayal comes roaring back, as inevitable as the waves crashing against the rocks outside.

It's been forty-two years, I think, watching over my dying husband.

And still we can't quite comprehend all we lost on that terrible March night.

CHAPTER 12

"HEIL HITLER!"

The crowd, as one, raised their arms and shouted it. Stirring uneasily in my seat, I wasn't sure what to do. Should I join in? I was grateful for the bouquet in my arms; bending my head down, I sniffed at the white, starlike flowers—*edelweiss,* I had been told by the young girl who had presented them to me with a grave curtsy.

I glanced at Charles; he sat next to me, erect as always; never did he wonder what to do, how to act. He was simply himself, immune to persuasion, and once more I had to admire him, even in this throng of spectators. Even with Chancellor Hitler himself standing on a platform just a few rows below us. The red flags with the swastika, that black mark that looked like propeller blades bent backward, hung behind him, before him, over him; they hung from every balcony and banister in the enormous *Olympiastadion.* The white Olympics flag, with its intertwining rings, was also in evidence, but not in nearly the numbers as the flag of the Nazi party.

Our hosts for the day, Herr Göring and his wife, were seated next to us in a private box; Truman and Kay Smith, the American military attaché and his wife, were with us as well. We'd been in

Berlin for more than a week, and today, our last day, happened to coincide with the opening of the 1936 Summer Olympics. Charles had hoped we would be able to speak with Chancellor Hitler himself, but it seemed now that we had to be content with merely sitting near him.

The sheer spectacle of the opening ceremony, of course, would have prevented any meaningful conversation; the fevered crowd, the endless salutes, the songs; I was hoarse from shouting. And I did not speak German well; I found the language harsh and guttural, my ear simply couldn't find it pleasing, and so my brain refused to try to make sense of it. I'd relied on Kay to translate during our stay.

"Is it not a fine day, Herr Colonel? Is Berlin not a fine city? I trust you have found it so—but of course, you are famous for finding cities, are you not?" Laughing at his own joke, Herr Göring slapped his thigh. He spoke excellent English, although he did so with a thick accent. It was rather a surprise, coming from a man who looked so much like a pig farmer from a children's book; he was huge, portly, with a shiny, jowly peasant's face.

Charles smiled politely. "Yes, yes," he shouted over more cheers from the crowd as another country's athletes marched into the stadium. "Berlin is quite impressive. We have very much enjoyed our stay."

"We are so proud that you inspected our *Luftwaffe*—what you in America would call an air force. As you are a military man yourself, we value your insight."

"Naturally, I was honored. Although as a military man, I cannot offer any specific insight, you understand. Even if the United States and Germany are allies."

"Of course. We are simply happy that you have visited at last.

France and England cannot have you all to themselves!" And Göring laughed again—it was more like a donkey bray. He was very jovial, very eager to please. Although not very polished; I wondered how he had risen to such a position—minister of the *Luftwaffe*—in Chancellor Hitler's government.

His wife smiled indulgently at him; she was a pure Brunehilde, a daughter of Norse gods. Fleshy, rosy-cheeked, with blond hair in a braid atop her head, nearly as tall as her husband. I'd found her very cold, however, to me.

There was another roar from the crowd.

"Oh, look! It's the United States team!" Sitting up straight, I was proud to see the rows of American athletes, all in white, as they marched by the stand. Proud to see that unlike the other countries, they did not dip their flag in front of the chancellor's box, even if this drew a shocked murmur from the crowd.

"Charles, didn't they look fine?" I called over to my husband.

Charles merely nodded, giving no indication he was proud of his country, nor that he even missed it.

I noticed a group of young boys approaching Chancellor Hitler's box. They were clad in the black shorts and brown shirts of the Hitler Youth organization, but their faces were so young. This group must have been about five or six. Feeling that familiar tug on my heart, I smiled as the smallest bowed, so solemnly.

After more than four years, I still couldn't look at a little boy without thinking of him.

My husband did not notice them; he was absorbed in his single-minded way with the ceremony unfolding before us. He seemed so relaxed, happy, even; the way he'd been all week. He had responded to Germany by going back in time, I thought; he'd reacted to the polite yet adoring crowds with a gleam in his eye, a surprised, shyly pleased gleam. The same gleam I had first noticed in the newsreels I'd seen of him, after he landed in Paris.

Back when his face was open, boyish; back when he did not know the dark side of fame.

Back when I was just a girl in a movie theater, marveling at the hero on the screen.

Stifling a sigh, I turned back to the crowd, many of whom were smiling and waving our way, occasionally tossing bouquets up at us. I wondered who they saw when they looked at me. The ambassador's daughter? The aviator's wife?

Or the lost boy's mother?

Minister Göring finally seemed to register my presence; he had not spoken one word to me until now. He had not seemed to notice me much this entire visit; his attention was riveted on Charles, always. Even a man as important as Herr Göring behaved like an adoring acolyte around my husband.

"You like Germany as well, Frau Lindbergh? You see how beloved we are by all the world! Of course, as an author, you might wish to write about us!"

"You are an author?" his wife inquired, with a smirk to her rosy lips. "You?"

"Mrs. Lindbergh is a famous author." Kay Smith leaped to my defense. Despite her tiny size—she was even smaller than I was—she possessed fierce confidence, hyperarticulate certainty in her own beliefs. I was happy to let her speak for me; I admired and liked her tremendously, even after such a short acquaintance.

"Oh. Famous?" Frau Göring purred. "I apologize. I did not know."

"Not really," I corrected her. "I've written some articles, and a book about our flight to the Orient."

"Which became a best seller," Charles interjected, looking at me sternly.

I nodded but felt my face flush, and I buried it in the cool flowers in my hand; I wished I could claim my achievements with the pride of accomplishment, but I simply couldn't. Everything I did now seemed shaded by a ghost or a shadow: the baby's, or Charles's.

At Charles's relentless urging—why had I ever confided my hopes to this man who did not believe in hopes, only action?—I had finally attempted to write. I tried to recapture my passion for language, for playing with words almost as if they were flowers to be constantly rearranged into beautiful bouquets. I tried to remember that once I had had dreams of my own; good dreams, not nightmares of empty cribs and open windows. It wasn't easy; my youthful poems and attempts seemed silly to me now. Reality had so intruded in my life that flowery verse seemed fanciful, foolish, even.

But Charles insisted that I do something with my life other than mourn our son; he insisted it would be good for me. I also suspected he thought it would be good for him; another trophy in the closet—an accomplished wife. First my pilot's license; now a best seller. It was expected of me.

I obeyed him, as always. My lone defiance of his authority was like a scar on our marriage, but it was a scar I thought only I could see. And I was eager to keep it that way.

Working for months on an account of our trip to the Orient, in the end I still wasn't satisfied with it; I had found it impossible to capture the innocence of that time before my baby's death. It had done modestly well, and Charles was proud of it, although I couldn't help but think that most people bought it out of morbid curiosity. The bereaved mother's little book—could you read her tragedy between the lines? I'd imagined people paging feverishly through it, eager to find evidence of a splotched tear, a blurry word, a barely suppressed sob.

"Germany is a country of poets and authors, of course," Herr Göring continued. "Goethe, Schiller."

"Thomas Mann," I added eagerly. "*The Magic Mountain* is one of my favorite books."

Kay inhaled sharply.

"Ah." Göring stared at me for a long moment, the genial farmer's smile still on his face, even as his eyes glittered with some strange warning. "Mann. Yes. But what a pity he married a Jew."

My smile faded. "Surely that has nothing to do with his books and stories? They're great literature."

"They are Jewish propaganda, deranged, and dangerous to the state. Mann is an exile. He is forbidden to return to Germany, as I'm sure you're aware."

I was not. I sat blinking at this fat man in a Nazi uniform, smiling dangerously in the bright sun, and I felt like a newborn chick just breaking out of her shell, trying to adjust her eyes to the confusing, blinding assault of *life*. Instinctively, I shrank back against the cold, hard stadium bench, touching Charles's arm.

"What?" He didn't stop looking at the ceremonies, going on below.

"Nothing," Herr Göring said smoothly. "Frau Lindbergh, are you cold? You look pale."

"No." Turning back to the smiling faces, the waving flags, I shrugged off the cool shadow I felt fall on me just then. I let go of Charles and tried to lose myself in the frenzied gaiety of the moment, the proud parade of nations filling the stadium grass, the flags waving, the Germans in the stands cheering lustily, calling out "*Sieg Heil!*" with military regularity. Everyone looked well fed, clean, and happy. Everyone looked tall, fair. So like my husband, I realized with a start; usually he stood out with his clean Nordic good looks, especially next to my small, dark self. Not here, though; with his Swedish heritage etched in every lean line of his body, every golden follicle of his hair, he would have blended into the crowd of Germans gaily waving those strange Nazi flags.

No wonder he seemed so at home.

HOME. It was a word I no longer recognized.

Four years had passed. Four years, several houses, airplanes, countries, oceans, a passing array of acquaintances, none of whom was allowed to get too close—all were now between us and that gray, weeping spring. At times I felt it had been a lifetime ago; other times, usually as soon as I opened my eyes on a particularly gloomy morning, it was as if it had all happened yesterday.

To Charles, the events of '32 were firmly in the past, never to be spoken of again. That's how he always referred to the kidnapping: "the events of '32." As if it were merely a page in a history book, and I supposed by now it probably was. Under the entry "Lindbergh, Charles." After the paragraph about his historic flight, there it would be: *the events of 1932, which culminated in the death of his son and namesake, Charles Lindbergh Junior, twenty months of age.*

One day, about a year after the baby was found dead, Charles came across me sobbing behind a tree outside Next Day Hill, missing my son so much I could feel it in every breath. I crept off like this every day, thinking he didn't know. Yet suddenly he was there, looking down at me with one corner of his lip curled up in distaste. And he tore into me as if he had been hoping for this moment for months; he berated me, calling me weak, less; irretrievably broken.

I am! I wanted to shout. *I am broken! Because he's gone!*

"What a terrible waste of time this is," he continued, in that detached, superior tone of his. "Think of all you could be doing.

Instead you're still giving in to sorrow, letting it consume you, change you. What happened to that book about our trip? You wanted to write a great book, didn't you? What have you done in the last few years, Anne? What?"

I followed you wherever you went. I brought life into this world. And then I saw it stolen from me. My tears wouldn't stop; I kept weeping, my head bowed down with every scathing word, every woundingly honest phrase heaped upon it. He was right. I was unable to see past my own personal sorrow. I could never have accomplished what he had accomplished. I would have been too afraid, would have let others sway me as I was letting others sway me now—see how Elisabeth still coddled me, telling me I needed time to heal, to grieve?

I despised myself for letting him talk to me like this, and I never would have, before the baby was taken from me. All the fury I had felt during the ordeal, when I had no problem acting on my own—it was gone, obliterated as thoroughly as my baby's body had been.

Charles never would have talked to me like this before, either. We were both changed, but at the time I couldn't see what tragedy had done to him. All I knew was that it had wounded me so that always, I felt as if I was walking about on shattered limbs, held together by only the very wispiest of threads, too fragile to stand up to him.

But I dried my tears, and assured him I would not cry in front of him again. Then I went upstairs to our bedroom and found a suitcase—a blue suitcase, I recall—and methodically, as if I were packing for one of our flights, I began to fill it. First my lingerie, then a few day dresses, a nice suit, three nightgowns. I could send for everything else later; later when I had found an apartment in the city big enough for Jon and myself; big enough for my grief. But too small for Charles.

I would leave him. If fury had deserted me, calm rationality had taken its place. I would leave this cold man, this stranger who mocked my grief. I would start over with Jon, and maybe the two of us would have a chance. I would have a chance to mourn Charlie, which was my only chance to heal, I knew. And Jon would have a chance to live a life not darkened by his father's shadow. I would find us a place near Central Park, so Jon could have somewhere to play. I would arrange everything myself, for I was a woman who had navigated by the stars; surely I could learn to navigate the subway. I would find just the right school for Jon, I would look up old friends, like Bacon, or make new ones. Friends who would want to know me, Anne; just Anne. I would cry whenever I wanted to. And laugh, as well.

I changed my clothes, put on a pair of black suede pumps that always made me feel taller than I was, and walked out the bedroom door, down the stairs, toward the front door. I would phone Mother later, from the city, and tell her when to bring Jon to me.

"Anne?"

I stopped, my heart racing, my face already hot with guilt. Then I turned around. Charles was before me, a pad of paper and pencils in his hand.

"What are you doing?" He looked at the suitcase.

"I'm—I'm going to visit Con, in the city. Just for the weekend."

"Oh. I suppose that's a good idea, to—get away for a little while." But he frowned, not really understanding.

"Yes, I think so. Would you tell Mother I'll phone her later?"

"Yes. Now, Anne, when you get back, I have a suggestion." He held out the paper and pencils, like an offering. "I think you need to start over. I mean the book about our flight to the Orient—start that over again." He smiled, a coaxing, almost bashful smile I hadn't seen in years. "I can't do justice to it, and it should be written about. You're the only one who can do it. You're the writer in the family, Anne. Not I."

Unable to meet his gaze, I looked out a window. Mother was pushing Jon in his pram, up and down a garden path. Even from this distance, I could see Jon's expansive Viking forehead, his blond hair; just a shade darker than his father's.

"I'll think about it," I told Charles.

"Good. Have a nice weekend."

"I will." Turning to leave, I felt a hand upon my arm; Charles bent down to give me an unexpected peck on the cheek before taking my suitcase and following me down to the car. As I was driven away, I turned back; Charles was still standing with the paper and pencils in his hands, watching me. He didn't wave. Neither did I.

I was back on Monday morning, exhausted from two nights spent tossing and turning and not sleeping in Con's guest room, the bed too big for just me. I was back, despite my certainty that never again would I be able to talk about our shared tragedy with my husband, and my uncertainty about what that would mean in the long run. I was back, knowing that I would never be able to look at my son without thinking of his father.

I was back, because of a pad of paper and some pencils.

I knew that Charles thought he was being supportive in his own way, providing me a path out of my maze of grief, and I was touched by that. It was the most he could do for me, and that had to be enough, for now. But it was never over for me; I never quite found my way out. Sorrow was my constant companion, even though I no longer wept. It was the shadow that followed me on sunny days, the weight pressing down upon my spirits on cloudy ones.

I had even seen it, trailing after me while I walked down the gangplank the day we first arrived in England, almost a year ago, now. Jon was only three years old; Charles carried him in his arms while I pushed his pram toward the waiting reporters and photographers. My grief wasn't the only thing chasing us down that narrow path; frustration, disgust, and horror pushed us across an ocean as well.

Two months before we left America, an intruder had been caught outside Jon's nursery window, ladder in hand.

Two months before *that*, I had been besieged when, on a whim, I dashed, unaccompanied, into Macy's after a doctor's appointment. Silly, but I'd had a notion that a new hat might perk up my spirits. Just as I reached for a red felt model with a feather, I found myself surrounded by a crowd of shoppers, all staring intently at me, waiting for me to do something—break down, I supposed. Some began to murmur sympathy, others started squealing my name, and even in my fear—for they surged forward, trapping me against the glass counter—I envied them. Passionately. For these *were* women for whom a new hat—or the sight of a stranger whose face they recognized from the newspaper—might bring happiness. And as the police came to my rescue just as my coat was torn by grasping, seeking hands, I knew that I would never again be that kind of woman.

The breaking point, though, occurred on a parkway just outside of Manhattan. Charles was driving Jon and me back from a pediatrician's appointment in the city. Suddenly a car pulled up behind us, too close. And then another pulled alongside, before swerving in front of us. Cursing, Charles had no choice but to veer off the road. Our car hit a tree with enough force that I bit my tongue, tasting blood along with fear. The child on my lap was unhurt; Jon started to cry only when I hugged him to my chest, trying to protect him from the men surrounding our car.

With a mad cry, Charles leaped out, swinging at them, and at that moment a flashing light went off just outside my window.

Photographers, I realized, bending my head down over my child, and my relief that they weren't kidnappers was swiftly eclipsed by my outrage at their reckless tactics. Charles shouted at them, asking them if they had no shame, no decency, but all he received in reply were more flashes, strident questions about how we were handling our grief, how we were raising our second child in the shadow of his brother's death.

All I could do was remain where I was, my arms so fiercely wrapped around Jon that they would have had to rip them off to get at him, while Charles warned that anyone who tried to get in the car would be shot, no questions asked. At one point our gazes locked through the car window, grimly acknowledging the truth; once again, it was the two of us against the world. If grief couldn't bind us, self-preservation would.

That night, we surrendered. We packed our bags and left in the dead of night for the Guggenheims'. There, we holed up, deep in the bowels of their enormous estate, deciding what to do next. Harry and Carol were sympathy itself, welcoming a squalling baby into their orderly world without a raised eyebrow or shrug. Carol delighted in pushing Jon about her manicured lawns in his pram, walking with me for hours without speaking, her undemanding companionship a balm to my soul.

Despite the Guggenheims' endless kindness, we knew we couldn't stay there forever. Finally we decided to sell the house in Hopewell to the state for a pittance. After that May we had tried, halfheartedly, to reclaim it as a home, but there were too many ghosts.

We kissed the Guggenheims and my mother and Con goodbye; we gave Dwight control of our financial interests in the United States. And we booked passage on a freighter bound for England, the sole paying passengers. The night before we sailed, Charles wrote a letter to *The New York Times* explaining why we were leaving the country for which he had done so much. In measured words nevertheless tinged with anger, he decried the lack of morals, the depravity he saw becoming part of the character of every American. He blamed the press—and those behind it—for our son's death. He expressed the desire to return to the nation that he loved, but only at such a time when he could once again call himself a proud citizen of a good and useful society.

Now we were renting an estate just outside of London, Long Barn, where it seemed, finally, that we had found peace. Charles could walk the sooty streets of London, only occasionally garnering a startled look. No strangers ever showed themselves at our door; the village constables made it their business to know every car, every bicycle, within miles. I could put the baby to sleep upstairs with the two nannies and three guard dogs, and only feel the need to go up and check on him four times a night, instead of forty.

Best of all, Charles and I took long walks outside in the garden at night, just like we had when we were first married, when he tried to teach me the stars. He didn't try to teach me anything now, and I was no longer quite so willing to learn. We walked in silence, mostly; afraid, or unable, to share our thoughts but finding a measure of unity simply in breathing the same air, admiring the same moon.

We were always at our best, together, when we were looking at the sky.

His days were still filled with scientific endeavors—working with aviation experts to improve fuel efficiency and range, as well as his continuing work with Alexis Carrel, who followed us across the ocean with his wife, living on a small island in Brittany. And one day I read an article in a magazine about a man named Goddard, who was working on something called a rocket; I showed it to Charles, who was now corresponding with him and helping him find funding.

Eventually the world found him, even in our farmhouse in the English countryside. Invitations blew across the channel from the various governments of Europe to inspect their new commercial airliners and airports, just as he had done in the United States. When he started to accept them again, I dusted off my goggles with a resigned sigh. It is difficult to explain how I could leave Jon behind, after all that had happened, to be cared for by strangers in a strange country. It was fear, I suppose—that powerful emotion that Charles so disdained but which I could not resist. Fear pulled me toward my child, and pushed me away from him, too; fear of getting too attached, of having to lose him. Just as I had lost the brother he would never know.

Fear that, having hidden us away so neatly, Charles might forget to come back.

So, him in the front seat, me in the rear, we flew to every European capital, inspected every airplane factory, every new airport. We even charted a few passenger routes, although more and more, these were already established. The age of the aviator/explorer was over, and nothing was more evident of that than the increasing number of military planes we saw on our tours.

And no country had as many as we'd seen at the Staaker airfield outside of Berlin this week; I wondered if Charles had been as stunned by the display as I had.

"THIS IS AN EXTRAORDINARY OPPORTUNITY," Truman Smith had said when we first arrived in Berlin, inhaling a cigarette greedily. He snapped the lid on his silver lighter with an expert flourish, and put it in his breast pocket. He was the very image of a military man; it was difficult to imagine Truman out of uniform, and indeed, I never saw him in street clothes. His figure was tailor-made for dress uniform; tall, broad shoulders, slender waist.

"What is?" Kay and I were returning from a quick tour of their apartment, where we were staying. It was on a clean, neat street, just as all the streets in Berlin seemed to be; I'd never seen a city that appeared to be so *scrubbed.*

"Göring's invitation to the colonel, to inspect the *Luftwaffe*. Astounding, really. We may not get another like it." Minister Göring had met us when we landed and assured us the government was eager to grant us our every wish, even though this was not an official diplomatic visit. He'd even invited Charles to tour their military aircraft facilities, the notion of which seemed to intrigue Truman.

"I'm here at the invitation of Lufthansa, not the Nazi government," Charles reminded him. His lanky body was folded up so that he could perch on a satin-covered gilt chair; Kay had exquisite, if not entirely practical, taste in decorating.

"Yes, but, Colonel, the Nazi government has not been forthcoming about its military development to anyone. Obviously they're building it up, but we've been unable to ascertain anything concrete. This might be a wonderful opportunity to learn more."

"I'm here as a civilian," Charles insisted. "I'm no politician, and I'm not on any kind of military mission."

"Times are changing. Quickly—more quickly than perhaps you two are aware." Truman smiled sympathetically at both of us, and I understood what he meant. On our recent trips to the various European capitals I'd felt it, too—that for the last few years Charles and I had been so absorbed with our own lives, so locked together in a protective shell of our own making, the world had passed us by. Changes were occurring, swiftly, even violently. Royalty was out; dictators were in. Mussolini and his Black Shirts controlled Italy—and now Ethiopia, as well. Stalin was making noises about the spread of Communism. Living in Europe, it was impossible not to hear sabers rattling on all sides.

"Colonel, you are in an enviable position. You have no political standing, yet you are a world figure. Everyone still respects your accomplishments, and wonders what you'll do next. That's a wonderful passport, you know. You are invited everywhere— even to Russia, I understand?"

"Yes, we are invited to tour their airports," Charles said mildly, still pretending not to be interested. But he sat up straighter and stopped drumming his fingers on the armrest.

"You are being given an unprecedented opportunity here, be-cause of who you are. I assure you, Hitler wouldn't do this for anyone else. And you can be of great service to your country by helping me prepare a report about Germany's airpower."

"Wouldn't that be a bit duplicitous? Almost spying?"

"No—they don't expect you *not* to report back. In fact, I imagine that's part of their plan, to show their hand to America and make them take notice. This government—well, I'll just say that nothing goes on that isn't absolutely anticipated beforehand. Did you notice there was no press when you landed?"

Charles and I exchanged glances; it was the first thing we had noticed.

"Hitler controls the press," Kay remarked, as she poured her-self a cocktail from a silver shaker. She reminded me of my mother, with her large, owl-like gray eyes; watching, always watching, even as she purred silkily and smoothed over argu-ments. The difference was that Kay was much more glamorous, with fashionably waved auburn hair and a moss-green bias-cut Vionnet gown, daringly low in the back. Charles would never have allowed me to dress like that. I couldn't help but feel frumpy next to her, in my modestly cut blue velvet gown bought from a sensible dressmaker on Regent Street. "Hitler forbade the press to cover your visit."

"Oh, how heavenly!" I exclaimed. Kay's eyebrow shot up.

"Surely you're not saying that Hitler's stifling of the independent press is a good thing?"

"Oh, no—no, of course not. It's just—it will be very restful not to have to contend with the press for a change." Again, Charles and I exchanged a look. We could not explain what the press had done to us; no one who hadn't lived through what we had could ever understand our feeling. The American press had stolen our little boy; it was as simple as that. Printing maps to our house, reporting on our every move—and then, ultimately, taking photographs of his mangled body in the morgue. We had been violated in every sense of the word.

"I'm still not quite comfortable with what you propose, Truman," Charles protested—rather feebly, I felt, knowing how unmistakably he could make his thoughts known when he wanted to. "What would Lufthansa say?"

"They'll say what Hitler wants them to say," Kay replied wryly.

Truman cleared his throat, then pointedly turned to address me, not my husband. "I understand the air force has been experimenting with new engines. The most powerful engines yet, or so it's rumored."

I stifled a smile.

"Really?" Charles now stood, going over to pour himself a cocktail—something so stunning that I almost gasped. I rarely saw him drink, only wine at dinner, sometimes brandy with Harry Guggenheim. "I wonder—I would love to see a Messerschmitt firsthand."

"I'm sure that could be arranged," Truman replied, stifling a smile of his own. "The Stuka has been improved as well, I hear."

Charles sipped his drink—dry martinis that Kay had prepared with quantities of gin and hardly a splash of vermouth; his cheeks flushed slightly red, and he grinned. "All right, then. If you insist, I will take up Herr Göring's offer and help you with your report. Of course, I must comment only on the scientific aspects. Not the political ones."

"Of course," Truman agreed smoothly. "No one expects you to understand the political situation—after all, you're an aviator, not a statesman. Far from it."

I stiffened, my stomach tightening as I watched my husband. He was staring at Truman, his jaw set, the corner of his mouth curled up arrogantly. Then he took another hefty swig of his martini and set the glass down so forcefully, I was surprised it didn't break.

You did not tell Charles Lindbergh what he was or was not. After all, everyone had told him he was only a mail pilot, not an explorer capable of a trans-Atlantic flight; I sometimes wondered if he'd have bothered to take on the Paris flight, if so many people hadn't assured him it was impossible.

Even with the study windows closed, as Kay began to fill in the sudden silence with harmless gossip, I felt a shift in the very air, the currents. Experienced copilot that I was, I didn't even need to look at my husband to know that I was being pulled toward a different—and dangerous—course.

THE GERMANY THAT WE saw in those days leading up to the Olympics, as we toured factories and airfields and museums and schools, was a balm on our battered souls. True to his word, Chancellor Hitler kept the press at bay; we were able to relax, talk, see, listen, and not be afraid that our every word would be misinterpreted or used against us. There was a purpose, a drive, to the German people that was lacking everywhere else we'd been, both abroad and in the United States; the Depression hadn't broken down its citizenry, as it had elsewhere. We didn't see a single breadline or soup kitchen. No protests; no workers milling about buildings with signs or placards; no strident, blaring headlines tearing down one political party or another. No boarded-up storefronts, no farms with foreclosure signs in front, no children playing in alleys with sticks and stones because that's all they had.

Indeed, all the people we encountered fairly glowed with good health—plump and rosy cheeks, white teeth, shining hair. Precious little girls in dirndl skirts, contented matrons with well-fed babies in their arms. The Hitler Youth—the young men in brown uniforms—patrolled the streets like well-mannered Boy Scouts, picking up litter, carrying shopping baskets for the elderly. I toured nursery schools—*kindergartens*—where the children held hands and sang songs praising Chancellor Hitler. "Herr Hitler loves children," one teacher explained to me. "Healthy children are the future. He encourages those of pure race to have families."

"Pure race?"

"Those who are not genetically sick. Or genetically inferior."

I nodded, and was reminded of something Charles had said once, about our children being pure. But what did "genetically inferior" mean? I had my suspicions and was about to ask, but then I was whisked away to my car, and taken to lunch at a biergarten.

Charles and I were seldom together during the day; he toured military and airplane factories, while I toured schools and museums. But something happened between us at night; something that hadn't happened between us in a very long time.

Passion. Passion was rekindled in Germany, of all places. Charles was rejuvenated, pulsing with hope and optimism in a way he hadn't been since before 1932. All the wandering, the tinkering, the move to Europe—none of it had satisfied him. I could see that now. Once again, he could barely wait for me to remove my silk stockings at night, to step out of my slip. With hungry hands, seeking lips, he filled me with his hope and optimism, as well. Our bodies hummed and throbbed, electric; I felt light, ethereal, a wisp of smoke that only his hands could catch.

"We should move here," Charles said, the evening before we were to leave. "Make our home here—maybe not in Berlin but somewhere in Germany. Munich, perhaps. It's prettier, they say, in the mountains."

"Really?" I pushed myself up on my elbow; we were in bed, the sheets tangled around us. My mouth felt deliciously bruised and ripe.

"Anne, there's no other country in Europe right now that can be compared to Germany. Hitler has pushed his nation into the modern age—think of it, compared to England! England, with its ancient empire and outdated navy—how absurd! It's all about airpower now, and Germany is clearly in the lead, not that I believe Hitler has ideas of war. In fact, I sincerely hope he does not. But this is a technological country, not merely an ideological one. Ideas—what are they unless they're backed up by technology? That's the wave of the future."

"We'd be left in peace," I mused, reflecting on the freedom of these last few days, when I never had to wonder if some photographer was hanging around, waiting to catch me doing something awkward or—heaven forbid, for then they'd make up some ridiculous caption!—ordinary. I couldn't imagine being chased down roads by anyone here; I could even allow myself to picture putting my child to bed at night with open windows, so that he might breathe the fragrant night air. "Think of it, Charles! I'm sure we could have a lovely little house right in the center of town—we wouldn't have to be on any remote island or isolated farmhouse. I could go to the theater! Opera! Shopping!" Saying the words out loud, I realized how much I had missed doing these things—missed culture, art, *people*. It was as if some deadening, numbing medication was wearing off; I hungered for all the things I had been denied. All the lovely, silly, soul-preserving things that other people did without thinking; popping into a shop without calling ahead and having to slip through the back door after-hours. Attending the symphony without wearing a disguise. Meeting friends for lunch in restaurants. Pushing my baby in a pram out in the open, watching him play with other children in a public park.

"And no one would bother us—Chancellor Hitler could see to that," I continued, playing with the fine blond hairs on Charles's forearms, watching his face fight the urge to give in to ticklish laughter. "Imagine having a public official on our side, protecting us! But, Charles, it's such a step—we don't really know the language, of course. We haven't seen everything—only what the chancellor has wanted us to see. You know that." For even in my excitement, I couldn't ignore the feeling that I'd had all week— the suspicion that the Germany being shown to us was like one of the little villages we'd seen in our flights to South America, particularly in the Andes. On certain cloudy days, you could walk the pleasant, ordinary streets and never see the mountains, but still you knew they were always looming, barely kept at bay by the swirling gray mists on all sides. I had the same sense here; that there was something hidden, something suppressed—yet always close at hand.

"I suppose so," he admitted, leaning back with his arms behind his head. His chest was so lean, yet muscular; there wasn't an ounce of fat on him still, nearly ten years after his flight to Paris. He was so obviously no longer a boy, yet he did sometimes still have boyish ideas—I understood this about him but could never let him know. His view of the world tended to be more simplistic than mine; this was what frustrated him about me, and me about him. He always saw the clearest, straightest path to any solution, and was mystified when others could not. Politicians, for example; he had no patience for the murky ways of compromise, of weighing issues, of giving some importance, dismissing others. There was only good and bad, right and wrong, to Charles Lindbergh.

"But we're here, Anne," he mused, looking up at the ceiling, covered with gilt panels. "We know what we see. It angers me to think how the newspapers in America and England depict Hitler—as a clown, a buffoon. It's the Jewish influence, of course. They hate him for the Nuremberg Laws. And while I may wish that Hitler wasn't quite so strident, I can't fault his logic, because obviously, it works. Germany is a remarkable nation, strong, forward-looking. Hitler is simply thinking about what's best for his country, and he has the courage to do it. Unlike these other so-called leaders."

"You sound very political," I teased, leaning my head against that lovely chest. "Very statesman-like."

"I have been reluctant to assume that mantle, but as Truman said, the times are changing. Look at the war in Spain—that's an air war, the first real one. Countries with airpower, like Germany, like the United States, need to be very careful, for in the future civilians will be casualties. Perhaps I can be a voice of reason. And really, Germany isn't a natural enemy; the northern races should never fight each other. The Asiatic nations, like the Soviet Union—that's the true enemy, not Hitler. But people like Chamberlain and Roosevelt don't realize it. They're grumbling about

Hitler because the Jews are pushing them, making more out of the situation here than there is—and what a tragic mistake that will be."

At this new mention of the Jews, I disentangled myself from his arms. And a question I had wanted to ask him for years could no longer go unasked.

"Charles, what about Harry Guggenheim? You know he's Jewish, yet he's been such a great friend to you—and me. Sheltering us, after the baby, after all the chaos. All the money he's helped you find for funding, not to mention—well, back in 'thirty-two. The guidance, the support. What about him?"

"The individual Jew, I have no problem with. Harry has been a good friend, and I won't deny it. It's the overall influence, particularly on the press and the government. Roosevelt is surrounded by Jews, and one of these days, I'm afraid he's going to listen to them. And that will be tragic, and one reason is that no country can stand up to Germany in terms of air superiority. That is one thing I've learned this week that Roosevelt has not."

"Then, I suppose you need to speak out," I said slowly—reluctantly, wondering how we could reconcile this development with the dream of living, forgotten, in Germany. I had seen how politics practically killed my father. And I feared the singular glare of the political spotlight; it was much more unforgiving than even the one we had been under. "I suppose that's the right thing to do."

"Of course it is. As Truman said, I'm in a unique position. I have a responsibility to the world now."

He said it so matter-of-factly. I remembered that drive back through the city the night he proposed, when I had first heard him talk in this manner—this calm recognition of the unique position he was in, and the responsibilities that came with it. I had chided him on it, but I could afford to then. I was young. Untethered. My entire life ahead of me.

I couldn't afford to now. I was too dependent on him, too wrapped up in his life, too marked by it. And at thirty, I could no longer imagine what lay ahead of me, because of the tragedy of all that was behind. So I didn't speak out; I didn't question him. Not then, not later. I sat by and watched the untouched boy of '27 become someone else; *something* else.

And I allowed him to turn me into someone else, as well. Someone who could sit, beaming, just a few rows up from Adolf Hitler while he received the straight-armed salute of the Nazi Party. Someone who could eagerly look forward to the next time we visited Germany, in 1937, and again in 1938, when we actually started looking at houses, even after the Anschluss and Czechoslovakia. Even after I understood that Thomas Mann's wife was not the only Jew who was not welcome in Germany.

Someone who could smile and nod when Minister Göring presented Charles with the Order of the German Eagle, on behalf of the Nazi Party and Herr Hitler himself.

Yet for all my smiling and nodding, my eyes were shut; shut deliberately to a truth I didn't want to see because it interfered with my dream of an untroubled life with my children; a stable life, for if Charles was content, maybe he wouldn't keep asking me to fly off with him. With every leave-taking, now that Jon was growing into his own little, absorbing person—so different from Charlie, and now I could rejoice in it—more and more of my heart was left behind.

Were we to live in Germany, one of Hitler's aides promised us at a private meeting, Charles could have his pick of jobs with the *Luftwaffe*. We would have complete shelter from the press, and government guards posted around our house at no cost to us. Jon could attend school, just like any other child.

However. I wasn't so changed, so dazzled by promises and dreams of a real home, a real *family,* that I couldn't hide a grimace after Charles placed the heavy iron cross in my lap. He scarcely looked at it, so used was he to medals and awards.

But I did; I fingered the cold, raised Nazi insignia on the medal. And I whispered, more to myself than to him, "The Albatross."

CHAPTER 13

April 1939

"MAMA! Are we going to live in America now?"

"Yes, darling."

"With Grandma Bee?"

"Yes, of course."

"And Uncle Dwight and Aunt Con?"

"Yes."

"Will Father be there, too?"

"Of course he will! He's already there, you know that!"

"Will you have to fly away with him again?"

I looked up from my desk, where I was reading over the letter from Charles that I'd just received, full of clippings of various houses we might rent. I also had the latest shipping schedules, although they seemed to change by the minute as the world turned upside down around us. Seated on the floor, playing with some wooden toys that had not yet been packed, Jon looked up at me so wistfully. His reddish hair needed cutting; I reached down and brushed wispy bangs out of his eyes.

"I hope not."

"Me, too. Land cries when you go away. I don't. Not anymore."

"Oh, my boy! Why didn't you tell me?"

"Because Father doesn't like it when I cry. Land's still just a baby, though."

"Come here!" I opened my arms wide, and he ran to them; I hugged him so tight, his face was red when finally I let him go. "I don't mind if you cry. I cry, too, sometimes. I *hate* leaving you. I think about you all the time when I'm gone!"

"You do? Then why do you always go when Father asks?"

Because if I don't go with him, I'm afraid he'll never come back— the answer was so ready, it took me by surprise and I almost blurted it out loud. "Because—because that's what married people do. They do what each other asks. Most of the time." I gave him a sloppy kiss as he returned to his toys. "But I think that now Father is going to be so busy that we won't have time for any trips. Let's both hope, very hard, for that, all right? So no more crying! And Grandma Bee is so happy we're coming home!"

"Will Violet be there? And Betty Gow?"

"Where did you— How did you hear of those names?" I asked him, shocked.

Charles had forbidden me ever to speak of the events of '32 to our surviving children. He had decided they did not need to know what had happened to the brother they would never meet. As far as Jon knew, he was our firstborn. As far as he knew, there'd never been a Betty, or an Elsie, or an Ollie. Or a Violet.

"I heard someone talk about her," Jon replied, even as he was terribly absorbed in rolling his wooden truck, so that it made little tracks in the pile, across the carpet.

"Who?" Who would talk about this in front of my son? I wanted to shake some sense into such an idiot.

"Germaine and Alfred."

"Oh." Our Parisian couple. Who, I decided in that instant, would not be accompanying us to America.

"Betty. That's like Grandma's name," my son continued in

his measured way. Jon was patient, obedient, utterly unlike any other six-year-old; I often wondered if he had absorbed all the terror and drama surrounding me, while in the womb. And so knew that he must make up for it, once born.

Land—my little Land, my Coronation baby, as he was born in London the day King George VI was crowned—was playing less obediently on the other side of the room, systematically destroying a plant, leaf by leaf. I was too stunned to stop him.

"What did—what did they say about Violet?" I tried to keep my voice casual but it did waver; I could not think of her without wanting to cry—guilty tears, more than anything. While I had disciplined myself not to weep for my child, I was not able to do so for the others whose lives were also cut short that terrible May. That so many were wrecked, ruined—tragedy following tragedy, innocents destroyed because Charles and I flew too high, too close to the sun—was truly more than I could bear.

"Germaine said Violet killed herself. Mama, how can someone do that? Is it true?" Now Jon did stop playing; he looked up at me with eyes so pure and innocent, I flinched; I did not want to be the one to introduce these awful notions.

"Someone can do that, yes, but it's a terrible, terrible thing, darling. A weak thing. Now, let's not talk about this—it's not very nice. Someday, maybe, you can ask me again. But let's not talk about it now, especially not in front of Father when we see him again. He has a lot on his mind, these days. Promise?"

Jon smiled; there was nothing he liked better than having to promise. He squared his little shoulders, adjusting them to take on this newest responsibility. When he was satisfied he was fully prepared, he nodded.

"Promise, Mama!"

WE WERE NOT MOVING to Germany, after all. Not after the evening of November 9, 1938. *Kristallnacht.* The Night of Broken Glass.

The night that even Charles couldn't justify; the night that the German authorities destroyed any remaining Jewish businesses and all the synagogues, killed an unknown number of Jews, and imprisoned an even greater number in enforced labor camps. It was a night of such brutal violence that Charles was appalled.

"I don't understand why Hitler had to resort to this. It's unnecessary. Beneath him," he muttered, reading the English newspapers; at the time, we were in Iliac, our home near Alexis Carrel and his wife in Brittany. We had no electricity there, we had to use a gas-powered generator and a radio telephone. We were almost a nation unto ourselves. So isolated were we, I couldn't quiet the suspicion that Charles wouldn't stop moving until he had hidden the boys and me completely from the world. Which was why I had clung to the idea of Germany, where even Charles believed we could live a normal life; not the life of fugitives.

Until Kristallnacht.

"We can't move there now, Charles. We simply can't." I was disgusted by the images reported; the beaten and bloodied men in the street, the women and children cowering, the senseless destruction. The shards of glass, the *Kristall,* gleaming ominously, like dangerous teeth, on the pavement.

"No, I don't see how. If there's going to be more violence— and I can't deny that there might be—it's not the place for us. But where is? These are important times. We need to be more available than we are here, at least during the winter. If there is war, and I'm afraid that despite Chamberlain, there are people in the British government intent upon it, England is not the place to be. Maybe France?"

"Why not—America? Back home?" I looked at him, not hiding the hope in my eyes. The truth was, even in the excitement of planning our home in Berlin, the promises I held out for myself, like little presents to be opened at a later time—promises of shopping and theater and a real social life, unencumbered by the press—I missed my country. I missed New Jersey, primeval and green in the summer, a Currier and Ives painting in the winter. I missed hearing English sloppily spoken, at least according to my veddy, veddy proper British acquaintances.

I missed my family, in particular—what little of it I had left; I still felt guilty for leaving Mother. No amount of letters crossing the fathomless ocean between us could ever make up for the remorse of running away when she needed me most.

"I don't think so," Charles said grimly, turning the British edition of *The New York Times* toward me. On the front page was a photograph of Charles with the German Iron Cross about his neck. The headline below it said "Hitler Annexes Lindbergh."

"Joe Kennedy telegraphed me last night, Anne. Do you know what he wanted? He wanted me to return the medal."

"The ambassador asked that? Do you think it's his wish, or someone else's?" While the new ambassador to Great Britain, Joseph Kennedy, was known to be a loose cannon, this sounded more like President Roosevelt.

"I don't know. I don't think I will, though. Why? It was presented to me on behalf of a government, thanking me for my pioneering flight. If I return it, I might as well return all the other medals on behalf of all the other governments in the world. It's not political, it wasn't given to me in that spirit, and I don't see why anyone would think it is." Charles frowned, narrowing his gaze, while his fingers drummed edgily on the stack of newspapers beside him.

I agreed with him. But I also knew better. In these days, everything was political; everything was full of significance.

So we packed up again in December 1938 and moved to a little apartment in Paris, right across from the Bois de Boulogne so that Jon could have somewhere to play, and events appeared to calm down. The Munich Pact was still fresh in everyone's minds; Chamberlain's little white piece of paper signaling "peace in our time" stopped the ditch-digging, the sandbag piling that had been occurring on both sides of the channel. And we enjoyed the early months of 1939 in Paris; I bought my first Chanel dress, I took the children to museums, and we even dined with the Duke and Duchess of Windsor. Like everyone else, I had been captivated by their romance, and was eager to meet the woman who prompted a king to give up his throne.

She was steel encased in the finest Chanel had to offer; so thin yet with large, masculine hands, a wide, snapping mouth. He had tiny eyes, was more feminine than she was with his slight frame and soft, dainty hands, and was the most boring man I had ever met. Charles yawned openly in his face during an earnest monologue about whether or not white shoes for men were de rigueur for summer.

As for my increasingly political husband, he continued to shuttle between Paris and London, giving his advice concerning their military air fleets. He even went, secretly, back to Berlin; France enlisted Charles's aid in persuading Germany to sell them some planes in order to shore up their nonexistent air force. Charles, doubtful, did use his influence, to no avail.

Yet our lingering presence on the continent, our now highly publicized and scrutinized past visits to Germany, were cause for much discussion back in America. At least, according to the worried letters, full of newspaper clippings, I received from my family.

One night, Charles and I went out for a romantic dinner at La Tour d'Argent. Just as the third course arrived, we heard an overdressed American couple at the table next to us say, too loudly, "I guess America's not *good* enough for them! So what if their baby was kidnapped—we've all had hard times, but none of us ran away from them."

I froze, my fork halfway to my mouth. I looked at Charles, who raised an eyebrow, forbidding me to react in any way. I continued to eat, as I heard the woman say, "I guess sauerkraut's more to their taste, not apple pie."

"Sauerkraut and iron crosses," her husband agreed.

The pressed duck was tasteless in my mouth; the wine turned to vinegar. Charles was right. If this was what was waiting for us in America, we could not return.

Charles, however, was smacking his lips with gusto, tearing into his duck as if he hadn't eaten in days. His eyes gleamed with purpose. I knew he had just recognized his latest mission.

Two days later, he was on the phone to Cunard, arranging our tickets home.

AND SO WE RETURNED, leaving a continent about to be torn apart by war for the safer shores of America, or so we thought. Charles went first, to report directly to Washington about all he had seen—and to caution them as well. He firmly believed that Germany would easily overtake Poland; he thought England and France were foolish to declare war outright, and had even written a secret paper to Chamberlain and to Daladier urging them not to. I wished he hadn't done that; he was already being maligned as an appeaser, even a spy, in some quarters.

But Charles, single-minded as always, did not appear to notice. After he reported to Washington, he looked for suitable homes near Mother but delayed taking one until I got there. It was a good thing that he did, for none of the clippings he had sent me mentioned schools, and when I chastised him for this, he was honestly perplexed. It had not yet registered with him that our children were growing up, needing schooling and friends and doctors and all the other things children required. Beyond the fact of their births, that primal inclination to protect them from harm, he did not seem much interested in parenting. I wondered if it was because of what happened to little Charlie; if he couldn't see the point of getting too involved, only to have them taken from us. Or if he simply couldn't understand the needs of a child beyond the age of twenty months, the age of his firstborn, forever. I understood this, had feared it in myself when Jon was first born, but found my heart miraculously expanding along with our children as they grew. I rejoiced that I was able to love and care and worry just like any other mother.

Yet other mothers did not pin whistles to their children's pajamas so that they could call for help in the middle of the night.

In April 1939, I trudged down the gangplank of the *Champlain,* clutching Land with one hand, Jon with the other. Dozens of police escorted the children and me to a waiting car amid the usual blinding torrent of cameras, which terrified the boys, who had never before faced such an onslaught. Land turned his face to me and wailed, while Jon held tightly to my hand, his face pale and grave.

"Mrs. Lindbergh! Mrs. Lindbergh! Are you glad to be back? Where is the colonel?" I shook my head at the usual questions, but then froze when confronted by new ones.

"What do you think of the Nazi Party? Did your husband really meet secretly with Hitler? Is it true that he was offered a commission in the Luftwaffe?"

I started to get in the car but turned around, unable to keep quiet.

"My husband has been recalled to active duty as a colonel in the Army Air Corps. He's unable to meet me because of his work."

Then I ducked inside the car, my heart pulsing daringly; I knew I shouldn't have answered them. Charles had forbidden me to do so; he felt it best that he always be the one to speak for us in public, and normally I was only too happy to let him. He wasn't here, however, and I heard the hostility behind those questions, and felt that I had to defend him—even though I knew he would not see it that way. But I was proud of the work he was doing now; because of his knowledge of the European situation, the military had him flying all over the country, inspecting air bases, suggesting which factories could be modified to turn out the type of planes necessary to make America the leading air power in the world.

I was proud of it, and wanted to tell the world about it—for I didn't know how long it would last. Already, I could see that Charles was on a collision course, torn between his sense of purpose and his sense of duty. They were very different things; I saw that clearly. I wasn't sure that he did, however.

"You spoke very well, Mama." Jon patted my hand. "They were such nasty men."

"I did? Well, thank you, darling."

"Are we home now?"

I looked out the car window; we were still surrounded by strangers peering into the windows, trying to catch a glimpse of my children, flashbulbs popping, blinding us. I hugged them both to me, and sighed.

"Yes, we are, darlings. We're home."

AS WE DROVE OUT of the city, across the bridge into New Jersey, my stomach fluttered. And with every mile we drove toward Next Day Hill, my head began to throb, my skin to feel clammy.

"What's wrong, Mama?" Jon asked.

"Nothing," I said, trying to smile. My son frowned, knowing that I had lied to him.

Now that we were almost there, I was dreading coming home. Being away for three years had kept the ghosts at bay, but now I was about to encounter them in their own setting. For it was at Next Day Hill that Violet Sharpe—poor, excitable Violet Sharpe, barely older than myself—had taken her life a few weeks after the baby's body was found. After being summoned for yet another round of questioning about her involvement in the kidnapping, she had swallowed a glass of chlorine cyanide.

I was horrified and sickened at the news. And racked with guilt. I should have known; I should have realized that Violet didn't have a Charles to bully strength into her, to force her to look ahead, to forbid her to dwell in the past. She didn't have anything in her life but my mother's protection and shelter, but even my mother couldn't protect her from Colonel Schwarzkopf's ugly interrogations; interrogations instigated, originally, by me.

I made myself look at her body, even though Charles flat out forbade me to. I couldn't explain to him why I needed to see her, register the thin, worried face, the sad little ribbon tied in her hair, her mouth blistered and stained from the poison. The whites of her eyes, still visible beneath half-closed lids, staring at me accusingly.

When I saw Violet's broken body, as twisted as the wreckage of the plane I had once located in the mountains of New Mexico, I wept. How could I have ever believed this fragile girl was involved? No matter that I was desperate, insane with fear for my child; I should never have told Colonel Schwarzkopf to question her or any of the servants. Who was I to play God?

Too late did I believe in her innocence. Only days after her suicide, the police determined that the only thing poor Violet was guilty of was being foolish. She had been involved with a married butler in my mother's household. Her frantic tears, her inability to stick to a story about her activity that awful night; it was all a cover-up for trysts with her lover.

So Violet would not be at Next Day Hill to welcome us home. So many of the servants, familiar faces to me since childhood, were gone now, chased from the house by the police, or retired, grown old in my absence. Even Ollie Whateley had passed away.

And Betty Gow. She would be absent as well. I don't remember if any of us actually spoke of it, but somehow, in those weeks after Charlie's body was found, it was agreed that Betty had to leave the household. I knew she would never love the new baby in the same way; she knew it as well.

Violet, Betty. And Elisabeth, my sister. She, too, was gone. There were still times I found myself picking up the telephone to call her, before remembering.

She'd looked so vibrant on her wedding day in December 1932. Jon was just a cooing baby in my mother's arms as I stood with my sister in the same room I had been married in. It was a rare moment of celebration for my entire family; we all spoke and wrote about it for weeks after, reliving the beauty, the poignancy. The relief that Elisabeth seemed well, loved, cared for. Although I never saw her look as happy, as joyful, with Aubrey as she used to, when she was laughing and scheming with Connie.

Elisabeth's goodbye kiss was a promise to me; a promise that despite her marriage, I would never be alone. I would always have someone willing to listen, not judge; sympathize, not urge me to action. And I would do the same for her.

Two years later—almost to the day—she was dead. The harsh Welsh climate was too much for her; doctors ordered her to sunny California. Aubrey whisked her away, but she died of pneumonia, Mother and Aubrey by her side.

I would never stop missing her.

So lost in my thoughts, I didn't realize that we were home until we were turning into the private drive of Next Day Hill. There was a new man on duty, but he recognized us and pressed the lever for the gate to open. As the gates closed, two black cars that had been following us—reporters and photographers, I realized—parked outside. I sighed. Now we were well and truly home.

"Mama, is this where Grandma lives?" Jon was climbing over me, eager to get out. "Can you please move?" He gave me a playful shove, so I did. I pushed myself out of the car; Land and Jon scrambled after me. We walked up the steps, the boys scampering ahead.

The door swung open; my mother appeared. Before I could blurt out my apologies for leaving her all these years, and for bringing photographers back to her home, she had me in her arms. "Welcome home, my daughter," she sang out. "Anne, Jon! And you must be Land!" She released me, reaching for the boys. "I haven't seen you since you were a baby, when I visited you in England. Do you remember me?"

"No."

My mother laughed. She threw back her head and laughed. This was no sad old lady, as I'd imagined her; no Miss Havisham surrounded only by memories, grieving her life away. No. My mother looked ten years younger than she had when I'd last seen her; she was trim, stylish in her own club lady way, although her hair was still corralled in that severe Edwardian manner. But she was electric with energy and drive; it was I who felt old and feeble, exhausted by travel, overwhelmed by being back in my native land.

"You look terrible, dear," she confirmed my assessment, shaking her head at me. "You'll have your old suite again, of course, and the boys can go up in the nursery. There's room for your nurse—where is she?"

"She had to come on the next boat; there were things she had to arrange before sailing."

"Of course, of course. I can't imagine the chaos over there! Charles is here already; he drove straight through from Washington overnight. He's upstairs, sound asleep."

"He is?" I was stunned; I hadn't expected to see him so soon, and, ridiculously, I longed to powder my nose and put on a fresh frock before I saw him.

Mother must have sensed my bridal jitteriness, because she suggested I have a glass of brandy first. So I followed as she marched down the hall into what used to be Daddy's office, but which was now redecorated. No—reborn.

Flowers bloomed in vases; the stuffy leather furniture was replaced with comfortable chintz. There was a Picasso on the wall, which worked surprisingly well with the cabbage roses of the fabric. Where Daddy's enormous banker's desk had been was now a delicate French writing desk. It was piled with papers.

"I thought you'd be surprised." Mother's eyes twinkled.

"Surprised? I'm lost. Is this the house of the very proper ambassador's wife?"

"No, it's the house of the very busy former suffragette." She laughed, and the boys laughed with her. She bent down to hug each of them. "Oh, I won't be able to get enough of these two! Do you want some cookies? Milk?" She looked at me, and I nodded.

"Get those children some cookies, would you, dear?" She turned to a young woman who appeared out of nowhere. The girl nodded and ushered the boys toward the kitchen.

"Who was that?" I couldn't seem to move my legs, couldn't

sit down—even after my mother gestured to a comfortable arm-chair.

"Oh, that's Marie. She's part of my staff."

"You have a staff?"

"Of course! One needs a staff when one is about to become acting president of Smith College."

"What? Mother—when? *How?*"

"Naturally, the world situation is making the search for a new president more difficult, so I was asked to step in during the in-terim. The college has so many ties, you know, overseas. We can-not turn our backs on our friends, and I'm going to see to it that we don't."

"Mother, it's just me you're talking to—you don't have to make a political statement!"

"Oh, goodness! Did I? I'm sorry, I suppose I'm practicing!" My mother laughed, and I laughed along with her. I was so happy for her, so happy she was busy and engaged and not grieving, as I had imagined. I shouldn't have, I realized; when had she ever stopped long enough to give in to an emotion?

But she seemed so different now. She reminded me of Charles, that was it; they both had that purposeful gleam in their eye, a secret, a goal, that only they could recognize.

"What do you think of Aubrey and Con?" I asked, abruptly changing the subject to one that had been festering in my mind for a while now. Elisabeth's widower had married her youngest sister in 1937.

"I think it's wonderful. Aubrey was lost, the poor man. Wid-owers always have to remarry, have you ever noticed that? Women are fine on their own, but men . . . anyway, Con will keep him on his toes. She needed a project like him."

"And what about love?"

"Oh, they love each other, Anne! I'm not sure that's the most important thing in their case, however. Not like with you and Charles. If you didn't have love, I'd worry more about the two of you. But Con and Aubrey, they'll be fine."

"Thank you. I think." I sipped my brandy and, despite my resentment at her breezy attitude, knew she was right. "But Elisabeth—isn't it disloyal, somehow?"

"Elisabeth is gone, dear. The living have to live."

"But it's as if she never married him at all—it feels as if they're erasing her, somehow."

"I don't think that's true, dear. Not for them."

I shook my head. Mother reminded me of Charles in other ways as well. I was the caretaker, I realized; the caretaker of the dead and of their memory. If no one wanted to think about Elisabeth, then I would. If Charles didn't want to remember Charlie, then I would have to remember him for the both of us. I admired both my mother and my husband for their energy, their dogged focus on the future.

I also, for the first time, pitied them. For despite the pain of loss, as time went on, the memory of those I'd loved warmed my heart more than grieved it.

"I'm glad you're so happy for them," I told my mother. "And I'm very glad about your appointment, Madame President! Now, where are you keeping my husband?"

"Upstairs. Dinner is at eight, as usual. I'll have something sent up for the boys; I've already prepared the staff. Now I must run off to a meeting."

"Of course you must." I embraced her, delighted and proud, even as I felt myself unable to keep up with her any more than I was able to keep up with Charles. The world was falling to pieces around us, and all I wanted was to find somewhere to hide myself and my children from the wreckage. While my husband and my mother came running out, arms open wide, to make something good from it. Something worthwhile.

The only problem was, I knew that their definitions of "worthwhile" were dramatically different.

"I MIGHT HAVE KNOWN," Charles said that evening. "Your mother. What did she say, about not turning her back on those overseas again?"

"Just that. Nothing more."

"Nothing more? She said it to spite me. She's never forgiven me for taking you away to Europe."

"That isn't Mother," I said crossly as we dressed for dinner, turning away from each other, oddly shy—or uncomfortable, I wasn't quite sure which—in our state of undress, after the weeks apart. He was in his boxers, pulling up his dress socks over his lean shins and snapping them into their garters. I was in an ugly, utilitarian slip, and I felt that way—ugly, utilitarian. After three pregnancies, my figure was losing its elasticity. I had a definite pooch to my stomach now, and my breasts sagged, even as we both hoped for more children.

For some reason, our reunion had not gone well. Almost from the first hello, we had snapped at each other. "Your little speech to the reporters was unnecessary, Anne," he had said after he pecked me on the cheek.

"You might have remembered to send two cars to pick us up, as we had to leave the trunks behind," I had retorted.

I wondered if that was how it was going to be, now that we were back in the United States, back among so many others who had claims on us; so many issues suddenly crying out for attention. One thing I had learned—among all the lessons he had set out to teach me, and others he had imparted unconsciously—was that we were at our very best, as a couple, when alone.

"Mother's not petty like that." I chose an outdated brown evening dress I had left behind, years ago, as my trunks had not yet been unpacked; even before I put it on, I felt dowdy. I turned around so Charles could zip me up. "She's like you, actually. You both believe you're absolutely right about everything." I was surprised by the bitterness in my voice. Still, I made no effort to hide it. "You forget how active she was in the fight for women's votes, back when I was a child. And she and Daddy—well, they were both Wilsonians, and passionate about the League of Nations. She hasn't changed."

"She knows perfectly well how I feel about the situation."

"She's not married to you, you know. She's her own person."

"What does that mean?" He turned to me, eyes narrowing.

"Nothing." I turned away and started rummaging in my travel case for some earrings.

"Well, she's agitating for war, don't think otherwise. And now she'll have the whole of Smith College behind her. She's beating the drums, just like Roosevelt." He sneered that last word; *Roosevelt* had become a bitter taste in his mouth.

"Well, you yourself said it's inevitable."

"It's inevitable in Europe. But not here—unless people like your mother scare the American public into thinking that it is."

"She's not scaring anyone—for heaven's sake, she's done nothing yet! She doesn't even take office until next term."

"She'll probably join one of those Jewish refugee societies next," Charles said, as he tied his tie with vengeance.

"So what if she does? You yourself said how awful it was that England was having to deal with so many refugees."

"That doesn't mean I think they should wash up here instead. You think we should allow more Jews into America? To influence the press? The government? The movie industry—for God's sake, they're all Jews there, every one of them, running all those studios, brainwashing the American public. Any minute now they'll start making movies portraying Hitler as a clown, or worse. Yet not one of them has been to Germany recently. Not one of them has seen anything firsthand, like we have. Do you honestly think we should send our young men—our sons—to fight because of *them?*"

"I don't—no, I guess, not when you put it that way—I don't think that; I don't think we should send young men off to fight. But, Charles, Mother believes in what she's doing. Just as you do. Don't you see how I admire you both for being so passionate?"

"What do *you* believe?" Again, his eyes narrowed challengingly. For the first time, my husband asked me this question. Until now, he had always assumed I believed what he did. And I had assumed that, too. Wasn't that one of the reasons I had married him—because I wanted to be just like him? Heroic and grand and good?

But now I wasn't sure what "good" meant. Too many participants in this increasingly terrible situation claimed to have goodness on their side.

Anne Morrow—the Smith College graduate daughter of Ambassador and Mrs. Morrow, both advocates for the League of Nations—would answer, "I'm with Mother. The Jews need to be saved. Hitler is a dangerous man." But I would say these things because they told me to, or hoped, by their example, that I would come to believe them on my own.

But I was no longer Anne Morrow; I was Anne Morrow *Lindbergh*, the wife of a legend who was an admirer of Hitler—and an increasingly vocal proponent for keeping America out of any European war.

Fleetingly, guiltily, I envied my mother; old enough to have outlived her parents, a widow without a husband to think of. What if, like her, I had the time to think for myself? To have the honest courage of my own convictions, and not the false courage of borrowed ones? My marriage would be different, that much I knew.

But would it be better?

I shook my head, tempted by the notion but not blinded by it. My duty now was to my sons, whose needs I had neglected for their father's for far too long. I had to settle Jon into school, find a doctor because Land was prone to ear infections, and move us all into a house. I had also just come out of years of purgatory, purgatory I had wandered with only my husband for companionship and security. Once, I had thought I could leave him, but it had only been Jon and me. Now, with two sons and hopefully another child on the way (for I suspected I might be pregnant, although it was too soon to be certain), I couldn't risk pushing Charles away from me. "I'm on your side, of course. I mean— I'm on our side," I continued, sitting on the edge of the bed so that I could slip my feet into a pair of evening shoes. "It's *our* side. I'm with you. Of course, I don't think we should go to war. Not over Germany, anyway; not over the Jewish influence."

"Good girl." Charles smiled, that rare, prized personal smile, relaxed, so that all his teeth showed. And I smiled back, waiting for that familiar, belonging glow to fill me up, make me better, *stronger;* as good as him.

But I waited in vain. For the only thing that filled me up was a shameful weariness, an enveloping languor that made me wonder how on earth I was going to make it through dinner, let alone the next few weeks, seated between my husband and my mother. Forced to decide, once and for all, who I was now: the ambassador's daughter?

Or the aviator's wife?

CHAPTER 14

May 1941

WE DROVE THROUGH A TUNNEL, so dark I felt like a ghost, my skin a pale wisp of smoke. I moved closer to Charles, who patted my shoulder absently as he smoothed the papers on his lap. And then we were born into the light; dazzling, blinding, relentless light. A roar greeted the sight of our car; a wild, frightening roar. The driver steered the car down a narrow path, lined on all sides by waving, shouting throngs fielding, like weapons, signs bearing my husband's name. Then we stopped, and Charles emerged from the car first. His appearance whipped the crowd into an even greater frenzy; the cheers were so unhinged I heard violence simmering just beneath the surface of approval. I was afraid to step out of the car; afraid of what could happen tonight. It seemed that anything was possible these days; anger was so prevalent, rippling like waves over our country. Outside Madison Square Garden, the anger had been directed toward us. Cries of "Nazi! Fascist!" had greeted our arrival. Rocks had been thrown at the armored car.

There was anger inside the Garden as well, but Charles was not the source of it. Rather, he was the white knight leading this seething crowd toward their common enemy—President Roosevelt. The guards were having a difficult time holding back the swarming crowds; my limbs felt like lead, my chest as if I'd swallowed a block of ice, as I finally slid out of the car.

"Lindbergh! Lindbergh for President!" roared the crowd. Flashbulbs popped, more blinding than ever in my life; I had to shield my eyes from the relentless glare. My ears rang from the noise of the crowd, all around me, above me, as well—I felt like we were truly in a fishbowl. And I couldn't help but think of what good targets we would be, were someone to aim a rifle at us.

Somehow I followed Charles down a red carpet to the podium, where others were already seated—Father Coughlin himself, the leader of the Christian Front; Norman Thomas, the leader of the American Socialist Party; Kathleen Norris, a popular writer; Robert R. McCormick, the publisher of the *Chicago Tribune*. We took our seats, "The Star-Spangled Banner" was sung, and one by one the others spoke. Brief, heartfelt speeches on the necessity of staying out of the European war, and of building up America's defenses instead of building up England's. I did not pay them any mind; I was concentrating on Charles. He looked relaxed; his limbs loose, his hands still, even as his jaw was set in that familiar angle of determination, and those blue eyes were more focused and intent than I had ever seen them. I was glad he did not turn his gaze upon me, for I felt it might burn a pinpoint hole, just like a magnifying glass would, through my skin.

Finally Charles rose, and every voice in the cavernous arena fought to shout the loudest. "Lindbergh for President!" "Lindbergh for President!"—the chant started in some far-off corner, building and building until my face throbbed from the intensity of it.

Charles did not acknowledge the chant; he simply stood tall, full of purpose and right, and in that moment I knew I was seeing my husband finally make the transition from boy hero to monument. He was giant, he was granite; he was supported by the stone foundation of his convictions. And despite my fears and misgivings concerning the entire situation, my heart thrilled at the sight of him; no one but him could have rallied such a mismatched group of people. Communists, Socialists, anti-government radicals, pacifists; left on their own, they would simply have languished and died.

But Charles had rallied them all; he had taken up the mantle of leadership as easily as he had slipped into his first leather flight jacket. *America First,* that was his cry. America First—Lindbergh would keep us out of war.

"My fellow citizens," Charles began, and then waited for the crowd to settle down. "We are assembled here tonight because we believe in an independent destiny for America." A frenzy of foot stamping, hand clapping, cheering filled the hall. Charles stood humbly, accepting it, before he continued with his speech; his plea for America to stay out of the war now raging all across Europe.

"We deplore the fact that the German people cannot vote on the policies of their government, that Hitler led his nation into war without asking their consent. But have we been given the opportunity to vote on the policy *our* government has followed? No, we have been led toward war against the opposition of four-fifths of our people. We had no more chance to vote on the issue of peace and war last November than if we had been a totalitarian state ourselves." Charles didn't mention Roosevelt by name, but he didn't have to. And only I heard the sadness behind the bitterness in his voice.

What many people forgot was that my husband was, first and foremost, a military man. His training had been invaluable. He believed, passionately, in the future of a military air force, and in his allegiance to his commander in chief.

But when his commander in chief publicly likened him to an appeaser, a Copperhead, he could no longer remain loyal. Most fatally, President Roosevelt had questioned the Lone Eagle's courage. "That young man would have wanted Washington himself to quit, given the odds," the president had recently told a newspaper reporter. " 'We can't possibly win' is no reason for an American not to stand up against aggression."

So Charles had resigned his military commission only a couple of weeks ago; it had troubled him greatly, but ultimately he could think of no other option. And he turned his considerable powers of concentration and charm to the aid of the America First Committee, flying all over the country, making speeches like this on its behalf. With me, naturally, by his side.

I sat there. I sat there, listening intently to his words, increasingly sure, always measured, never giving in to the frenzy that inevitably greeted him. I was ever mindful of the cameras, for I was suddenly a politician's wife.

I see myself now, from a distance, sitting there, a grim smile on my face, so different from that jaunty, carefree grin of the daring aviatrix I once had been. A young woman, yes—barely in her thirties, her mind almost always on her children at home. But that was no excuse.

A mother who had lost her firstborn in the most horrific, public manner, and whose vision was still often clouded with the residue of tears. But that was no excuse.

An eager young wife who had been shaped, just like every other eager young wife of my generation, by her husband, but I was a wife who had *wanted* to be shaped, had willingly put herself in his hands and demanded he make her over in his superior image.

But that was no excuse.

Just as I ran out of people and events and coincidences to blame for my son's death, I have run out of excuses for sitting there and publicly endorsing my husband's views. Even if, inside, I questioned, even if I wondered, worried, saw the inevitable outcome long before he did and despised myself for not doing enough to prevent it; despised *him* even more for not being able to see it, too—

I did it. I sat there and nodded and clapped.

And I've regretted it every day of my life since.

Charles looked out at the crowds, more and more frenzied as time went on, and spoke straight from his heart. Recognizing this, I questioned *my* morals, not his. At least, I knew—and I also understood that this knowledge would have to remain foremost in my mind and heart, if we were going to survive the next few years—that he spoke only what he truly believed.

I, however, did not.

That night, after we left Madison Square Garden for the refuge of our Manhattan hotel room, having fielded phone calls from the press, supporters—Frank Lloyd Wright sent a telegram congratulating Charles on his fine speech; William Randolph Hearst invited us to a weekend at his castle, San Simeon; Henry Ford offered him a job for life—Charles was the one who slept the peaceful slumber of those whose hearts and minds are untroubled.

I did not find such peace that night, and I knew I wouldn't the next night, either.

Nor had I, for many, many endless nights before, and I could not blame only my husband for that.

WHEN WE FIRST RETURNED from Europe, Charles had been able to keep his political thoughts separate from his military duties, and in the beginning, the press backed down, as if to let him prove his patriotism. But after Great Britain and France declared war,

Charles could not remain silent. After the Battle of Britain, he began to write articles and give speeches cautioning against any rush to take sides; at first, he was given as much airtime as he wanted by the various networks. After all, in this time of crisis, America wanted to hear from its hero.

But as time went on, he more than cautioned; he became an outspoken critic of the administration. Soon he had become the de facto spokesman for America First—that ragtag group of individuals bent on keeping America out of the war for a number of reasons that didn't really matter, at least not then, because a significant number of Americans agreed with them. The war in Europe was not our business.

But most of our friends and family, East Coast elites—and many, like my brother-in-law, Aubrey, with family overseas—were appalled; they sniffed, long before it was verbalized, the unspoken anti-Semitism of my husband's cause. Initially, I was exempt from this; my friends sometimes asked me, point-blank, how I could betray my father's legacy, but they did so with the indulgent disbelief you would give a child having his first tantrum.

In late 1940, however—finally pregnant again, after years of trying—I did my best to alienate them for myself.

"Anne," Charles said one autumn evening, "I need you."

Those words. They would never fail to sway me. They were uttered so seldom, and I couldn't resist responding to them in a physical way—my body flushing, as if from desire; my nipples even tingling, my pulse racing, reaching.

We were seated in the den of our rented home in Lloyd Neck, Long Island; the boys were in bed. The radio was tuned to *Amos 'n' Andy*, a show that Charles loved for its childish humor—he would laugh, slapping his knee, whenever the Kingfish would exclaim "Holy mackerel!" at Andy's latest misadventure. To all appearances, we were just any American family, and in our hearts, that's how we saw ourselves. No one else did, however, and I was increasingly lonely and scared, wondering when—if—this madness would stop, when would Charles cease cultivating controversy, when would we once again be the First Couple of the Air, adored, admired. The only thing that would stop it, I knew, was war—and lately, I had almost been longing for it. And then chiding myself for thinking such a thing.

Charles turned the sound down on the radio and came over to the sofa, where I was seated, lazily paging through *Life* magazine, even though I had to be careful. These days there were too many articles vilifying Charles glaring at me, accusingly, from the pages of every newspaper and magazine. Most, as Charles was quick to point out, were owned by Jewish publishers.

"You know how I've always felt that you're the writer in the family," he continued—and he put his arm about my shoulder.

"I am?" I asked mildly—although I was pleased beyond reason to hear him say so.

"Yes, you are, and don't be coy; it doesn't suit you, Anne. What I need now is for you to turn the tables on the press. I was thinking that it would be powerful if you wrote an article about our position. Clarifying it, really, for naturally the press keeps getting it wrong, simplifying the reasons to further their own views. But you were in Germany. You saw what the future can be—and you saw what democracy did to us, to our baby. This ridiculous march to wage war against a power that is greater than us—maybe even *better* than us—I need you to write about it. From *our* point of view."

Those shared goggles! My heart ached at the memory of how we used to fly together; after coming home to America, I had gotten my wish, we had settled down—or I had, anyway. The last time Charles had asked me to fly with him, I had refused.

"What do you mean, you want to stay home?" he'd asked, incredulous.

"The children need me. I'm their mother."

"You're my wife."

"Yes. And I love being with you! And we will take many trips together. Just not this one. Land has a cold."

Charles had looked down at me, a perplexed purse to his lips, a disapproving furrow to his brow. Then he went off to make preparations for his trip—to San Francisco, I believe it was. Watching him make his preflight checklist, pack his old calfskin travel bag that he'd had since we were married—he never let me pack for him; he said women didn't know how to pack things efficiently—I sensed the passing of an era, not just in our marriage but in the world at large. Aviation was no longer romantic, hopeful, bringing countries and peoples together; it was about to tear the world apart.

Tucking Jon and Land into bed at night, I rejoiced that I would be able to do so the next night, and the next, and the next; that they would no longer greet me warily after a long trip, as if they weren't quite certain they should get attached. But sometimes, I remembered—and longed for—the time when it was just the two of us, above. Not Charles, flying solo. Not Anne, worried about the children. But Charles and Anne; a glorious creature, mythic.

Adored.

I continued to page through the magazine, not seeing, not reading. The glossy pages were slippery in my fingers. I felt my husband's need—his surprisingly desperate, and desperately cloaked, need—pulling me toward him, irresistibly as always.

But for the first time ever, I was suspicious of it.

"Why me? Why can't you write it? You've written other articles; you've written your own speeches. You know how difficult this would make things between Mother and me—not to mention Aubrey! Mother has been awfully good about not criticizing you publicly. Do you want me to break her heart?"

Charles didn't answer, not at first. He leaned forward, his elbows on his knees, his chin resting in his hands. He stared at something, something I couldn't see, something I could never see. I always had assumed it was too brilliant and fine for my eyes. Now I wondered if it was really there at all.

"I don't mean to sound vulgar," he said finally. "But—so far no one has dared to attack *you*. You're—you're always going to be the baby's bereaved mother, and so above reproach. Which is why you are in the perfect position, really. If you give our cause *your* voice, your name, you will elevate it. Even more—than I can . . ."

I knew this last wounded him, for his voice trailed off. Yet I flinched, and my heart—my poor, put-upon heart that was still stretched and patched beyond reason—stiffened against this latest indignity. The baby's death was terrible, but it was sacred; it was mine. Not Charles's. I'd always felt that; I'd always hugged it to me, selfishly unwilling to share it with him. Or with the world. How many times had I been asked to write about it? To give the "bereaved young mother's" side of the story? Never, I'd said. And Charles had supported me.

Now he was asking me to trade on it. And for what? Europe was in flames, Stalin was now allied with Great Britain, and I knew the sentiment in our country—in the heartland that had, at first, agreed with Charles—was slowly turning; there was a sense that our involvement in the war was not just inevitable, but righteous.

Still, I didn't respond, and Charles did not press me. I knew he would not; he never did. He stated—or much less frequently, *asked,* just once. And then withdrew, as if it was beneath him to repeat himself.

"Anne, please," he said, his voice suddenly a whisper. "Please. I would very much appreciate it if you would do this for me. I can't do it for myself."

My hands—my heart—fluttered, then were stunned into absolute stillness. Only once had I heard my husband ask like this. And that was for the safe return of our son.

I heard myself say, "Yes. Yes, I will do this for you," before I could fully comprehend the consequences.

Charles nodded. He did not thank me. He did not ask what he could do for me. He simply went back to his chair by the radio and turned the knob up. The accents of Amos and Andy, thick as molasses, exaggerated as the funny papers, filled the suddenly oppressive air of our den.

I picked up the copy of *Life*, and began paging through it once more. An old photograph of Charles, young, grinning, just landed in Paris, caught my eye. Beneath the photograph it said, "Lucky Lindy—No Longer Can We Count on Him to Know Right from Left. Or Wrong. Where Did Our Hero Go?"

The country missed him. I missed him.

My husband, sitting upright in his chair—for he never slumped—chuckling at the radio, missed the hero, as well. With his lean, bronzed body, high forehead, chiseled jaw, he did not look ordinary; he never could. But he did look lost, somehow; smaller. For so long he had stood tall against the endless horizons of our country's possibility; now they threatened to engulf him. More than anyone else, Charles Lindbergh missed the hero he had once been; the boy who only needed himself and his machine, beloved by all the world simply for doing what he knew was right, and for doing it better than any man alive.

It was not that easy anymore. And for the first time I felt him passing over the controls of our marriage to me, trusting *me* to steer us both out of this storm, acknowledging that at least for now, he did not know how.

I had been a passenger in our life together for far too long. And so it was because of this—my desire to restore my husband back to himself, to his countrymen, and, yes, to me—that I sat down at my desk the next day and began to write. Still a devoted diarist, I remained unable to understand my thoughts and emotions until I could write them down, play with them, move them about on the page.

Now, I prayed, I could do the same with our lives, although even then, I suspected that there was no page big enough, no ink powerful enough. But I tried; I had to. My husband, the hero of all heroes, amen, had asked me to.

But the words did not come easily. And when they did, they looked wrong on the page.

"AMBASSADOR MORROW WOULD WEEP"

"BOTH LINDBERGHS SHOULD BE BEHIND BARS"

"TREASONOUS TRACT TARNISHES TRAGIC TIARA"

"MRS. LINDBERGH'S MOTHER DENOUNCES DAUGHTER"

I was not surprised by the reaction. And my mother did not denounce me.

She did, however, burst into tears when she first read my little book, a pamphlet, really, called *Wave of the Future*. Con told me this, later, after she refused to take the money I earned from it for Bundles for Britain. And I couldn't blame her. I tried to have it both ways, fooling myself into believing I could please both my family and my husband. Of course, I ended up pleasing no one. Least of all myself.

I wrote of the past, and the future; of democracy and its legacy of chaos, of turmoil, of leaders elected promising one thing and delivering another. I compared the democratic leaders to the modern dictator, so unlike Napoleon, Nero, the czars. The modern dictator, I wrote in words suggested to me by my husband, recognized the world was changing, and that a new order was being established, based on new economic principles, new social forces.

I decried the treatment of the Jews in Germany, neatly failing to mention my husband's views about the Jews in America. I said I could not be loyal to the Nazi government as it existed now, but that beneath its tainted flag had been something good, something optimistic, before it got derailed.

I explained how people who loved this country—people like my husband—spoke out against the futility of fighting this future precisely because of their patriotism; how they wanted America first to be healed, to be protected, to be set on its own glorious path to the future. Not destroyed by a war that was probably unwinnable—or by coming to the aid of an empire long past its usefulness.

I signed my name to all of this. I posed for a photograph at my desk, looking pensive. My husband embraced me and assured me I had done the right thing not only for my country but for myself. This would be the beginning of a true literary career, he enthused, just a tad too eager. Hadn't I always wanted to write a great book? I was well on my way now.

He was wrong, of course. Although he never admitted it. But reaction against my essay—more than five thousand words, reproduced as a slim volume, most of which ended up in bonfires—was most strong in the very literary community to which I had always aspired. The dreamy young men of my youth were now editors and publishers and critics. More than one wrote to me personally, asking how someone as bright as myself could be poisoned so thoroughly by someone as evil as my husband.

Smith College also wrote, asking me to please stop saying that I was a graduate.

Slings and arrows—bullets and grenades. I felt attacked from all sides; I did not completely understand what I had done, only why I had done it, and that reason did not seem enough in the sobering aftermath of publication. I was shaken, battered, and acutely—surprisingly—resentful. At first, I found refuge in my newborn daughter, delighting in her perfection, hiding from the world in my childbed. But for a week, I found myself unable to say more than "Good morning" and "Good evening" to an annoyingly affectionate Charles, who, for the first time in our marriage, began his day by asking what he could do for me.

The conversations I had with myself, however, were endless—and even less satisfying.

So by 1941, both Lindberghs were hated equally and once, I would have rejoiced in that; that my own actions were finally considered as significant as my husband's. Our unlisted telephone rang and rang, and every time I picked it up I heard hatred. Often inarticulate hatred; spewing and venom, not real words. But hatred doesn't require a common language to be understood.

Jon came home from school with a quivering chin, wondering why his father was a traitor. Land came home from school with a black eye, defending his traitor father. The new baby, Anne Junior, called Ansy, was the only innocent in our household; now almost a year, her happy gurglings and funny talk were a balm upon my soul. I loved to pick her up and hold her, walking from room to room, as if she were my talisman against evil.

In September 1941, just a couple of months after the frightening rally at Madison Square Garden, Charles gave another speech, this one in Des Moines, Iowa; a speech that I warned him not to give. A speech I knew would be the one he would be remembered for, despite the hundreds he had given since that night he landed alone in Paris, the world at his feet.

The sinking of the *Greer* had just occurred; the sentiment of the country was even more resigned to war. Many of those who had initially supported Charles had turned on him; the crowds were smaller, composed equally of those for and those against him. It was a desperate time, a time when the country seemed to be dancing on the edge, knowing that soon, too soon, we would all be hurtled into the abyss. Dresses were gayer that season, more garish, more colorful than I could remember; songs were faster; people laughed louder, as if to cover up the booms of the war guns across the ocean. Charles knew that he had to make his most exhaustive, reasoned case to date; he must leave no question unasked, however painful.

He began the speech by listing the three groups he believed were agitating for war: the British, for obvious survival reasons; the Roosevelt administration, which desired to use war to increase its power.

"It is not difficult to understand why Jewish people desire the overthrow of Nazi Germany," he continued, moving on to the third group, and I felt my stomach tighten, my breath sour. Sitting in the tiny living room of a rented home on Martha's Vineyard—we had to leave Long Island when we could no longer walk along the beach without having invectives hurled our way—I listened to my husband on the radio, his voice tinny but sure, confident.

Speaking up at last, I had begged him to rewrite his speech. "This is going too far. You're going to come off as anti-Semitic. And you're not." *Are you?* I'd wanted to ask, but could not.

"Nonsense."

"Charles, just by mentioning the Jews, you will color yourself the same as Hitler and the Nazis. You don't understand what's happening now. People will accuse you of Jew-baiting. Listen to me! For once, listen to what I'm saying—you do not know what you're about to do."

He shook his head. So caught up was he in this mission, he no longer needed any crew. He was flying solo again, right into the cyclone of history.

"The greatest danger to this country lies in their large ownership and influence in our motion pictures, our press, our radio, and our government," he continued to broadcast, talking about the Jews. "We cannot allow the natural passions and prejudices of other peoples to lead our country to destruction."

Other peoples. The Jews—to my husband, they were other people. Not like him. Even if that was not what he intended, it was what would be inferred, and now it was too late. He had said it. Immediately I thought of Harry Guggenheim. Such a dear man; such a good friend.

He'd stopped returning our phone calls a year ago.

I switched the radio off, too sickened to listen to more. I jumped up, desperate to know where the children were; I felt I must gather them close to me and keep them safe. After I made sure that the boys were playing quietly in their room and Ansy was gurgling in her crib, I locked the doors and shut the windows. Whether it was to keep evil inside or out, I could not have decided at that moment.

And if evil was in the shape of a tall, clear-eyed man with stern lips and an unshakable sense of his own right, I could not have decided that, either.

THE PUBLIC OUTRAGE after Des Moines was so vehement that America First almost disbanded. Ultimately, it didn't matter that they decided to carry on, broken and battered. Soon an event occurred that was larger even than my husband; the headlines, for the first time, more hysterical than they had been announcing his landing in Paris, or the kidnapping of our son.

Pearl Harbor. The bombs dropped—that afternoon, as we huddled by the radio, Charles could only repeat his astonishment that the Japanese had aircraft capable of such long range—and the world changed. America First disbanded after Charles issued a statement urging all Americans to unite, regardless of past differences; he grandly acknowledged that our country had been attacked and naturally we must now fight back. All of us.

Then he telephoned the White House, eager to report for duty; even admitting to the secretary with whom he spoke that his recent political stand might cause complications—such a bitter pill for him to swallow, but he did it manfully, as he did everything else. *However,* he continued, he hoped the president would agree that differences must be set aside for the good of the country.

While he was waiting for an answer, Charles was asked, offhand, by a reporter about the disbanding of America First. He said, truthfully, that he was saddened for his country. "It was unfortunate," he added, that the white race was currently divided in this war, when the true enemy was the "Asiatic influence." His wish was that somehow Germany could have been appeased, and allied with us against Japan, China, and Russia. He closed by restating his desire to fight for his country, no matter what. "I'm an American first," he said, and I winced.

Soon after this, he heard from the Pentagon. His request to be reinstated was denied. For the duration, former colonel Charles Lindbergh's services were not required.

Devastated, and so honestly surprised I almost cried, Charles then turned to all the commercial airlines he had helped form, almost from the dust of the fields that, with his name attached, they had been able to turn into giant, gleaming airports and factories now busy with war work. He returned home from several meetings enthusiastic and optimistic. But when the phone did not ring for him the next day, and the day after that, and the day after that, he sank into a despair I had never before witnessed, not even when the baby was taken.

"I don't understand," he muttered, sitting erect in his chair, even then. "I have more knowledge of the German air force than anyone. I traveled around our airfields when I first came back, helping them to modernize, teaching them fighting tactics I learned in Germany. And one would hope that now, more than ever, differing opinions about the world would be welcomed, for only the best research comes from a result of all different points of view."

My heart broke for him, seeing what no one else did—the naive farm boy instead of the hero. Statue that he was, monument to his own beliefs, he was no match for wily politicians. Washington wasn't interested in what he knew; it was interested in how he was perceived by a public that would probably have to elect a president in the middle of a war.

But I did not have time to soothe him, for overnight I was forced to deal with ration books and gas cards and rubber drives. The girl I had in every other day to help clean left to work in a factory. The cook—for I had never learned to make more than scrambled eggs and grilled cheese sandwiches—did the same. With a copy of *Betty Crocker* in one hand and my ration book in the other, I tried to find some way of feeding a family of five. Six, soon, for I was expecting once more; Charles's vision of a dynasty seemed to be coming true, at least. I was providing him with his own brood of blond-haired, straight-teethed children, none of whom looked at all like me except for Ansy, who inherited my unfortunate nose (which looked much less unfortunate on a rosy-cheeked face framed with white-blond curls).

I had no time to go on walks with him, as he suggested coaxingly, almost flirtatiously, for the first time in ages—since before we'd come back to America. It pained me to have to say no to him. But there was always a meal to prepare; it astonished me how frequently my children required nourishment, now that I was the one to provide it.

And there was no time to sit in the den with him at night and listen as he read from drafts of speeches he wrote but had no opportunity to give, for there was always a child to cajole into bed, a glass of water to fetch, the last bit of a story to read. If I had a minute to myself, I was darning clothes and letting hems out, for everyone was predicting a clothing shortage.

"I despise seeing you like this," he said one day, and he sounded sincere, which only made me angry, busy as I was—and as he was not. "I despise seeing you waste your potential, no better than any other housewife, worrying over casseroles and coupons. What about us, Anne? What about *you*—your writing? Whatever happened to that?"

"Well, I'm not enjoying it much myself, but I don't see any alternative," I snapped, and went back to the preserves boiling on the stove, studying them closely, wondering why on earth they wouldn't *jell*. Shaking his head sorrowfully, Charles left me to the stove—and the pile of dirty dishes that I couldn't help but notice he had not offered to help wash.

So I was grateful—almost to the point of hysterical laughter— the day I picked up the phone and heard a wheezy voice say, "Henry Ford here. Is Colonel Lindbergh home?"

If there was one man capable of defying Roosevelt and giving my husband a job, it was Henry Ford. Despite Ford's own isolationist—and more obviously anti-Semitic—background, the government needed him. Or, rather—it needed his factories. Detroit was being turned into a wartime machine, and Ford was calling to ask Charles to help oversee the aviation operations, which would be responsible for building bombers, B-24s.

Charles left the next morning, a blustery March day, and

drove straight through to Detroit on a special gas card issued to him by Ford; essential war work, it declared. I rose at dawn to see him off, and I admit I felt relief at seeing him go, despite all the work ahead of me—closing up this house, packing, finding another in Detroit, moving the household, finding a new doctor for me, one for the children, dentists for us all, schools. . . .

But mostly, I felt relief. Not only at being parted—there was some of that, I had to admit; his presence in the house had been oppressive these last few weeks, an annoying, spiteful shadow nipping at my heels wherever I went. But mainly, I rejoiced at the knowledge that for once, we were like everyone else. Not heroes, deified; not demons, vilified.

Just a man and wife saying goodbye because of the war, unsure when we'd see each other again, because housing was difficult to find in Detroit—and Charles made it clear to Mr. Ford that we were to be given no special favors. We would exchange letters, call occasionally when we could get a long distance line. I would take photographs of the children so that he did not miss anything. I would encourage them to write to Daddy, and help them sign their names in cursive, even though they did not yet know how.

As I waved goodbye to Charles, I had tears in my eyes. Tears of pure, soul-cleansing joy, for I felt an honest happiness in sending my husband off to war—as if this one small sacrifice could somehow make up for all the wrong I had done, in both our names. Yet at the same time, I also felt the lightness of anticipation, believing that somehow, the worst was behind us. And that from now on, Charles and I had only good times to look forward to together. Strange, I know, to think that; to feel relief, not sadness; happiness, not horror.

Especially against the backdrop of a world split asunder by war.

CHAPTER 15

"MOMS?"

I looked up, startled. I was writing a letter to Charles, using the thin, small V-Mail sheet I abhorred; I always ran out of room before I ran out of things to say. Jon was standing in front of me, just home from school. He was neat and tidy as always; Land was the one who always had a slingshot in his pocket, a half-eaten apple in his hand. The only sign that Jon was a normal eleven-year-old was his new vocabulary of slang that he sometimes tried out. "Hi-de-ho" for "hello," "creep" for his brother, "Moms" for me. Although his father was never "Pops"; even to his children, there was something about Charles Augustus Lindbergh that did not lend itself to slang.

"Yes, dear?"

"The teacher was telling us about Father's flight to Paris today. It's in our history books, you know." He blushed; so scarlet you could see a rosy glow beneath his fine reddish hair. So this was why he had been uncommonly quiet in the car on the way home. "It was kind of embarrassing, because everyone looked at me. Even Polly Sanders."

I stifled a smile; Polly Sanders had hit him in the school yard yesterday. A declaration of love if ever there was one.

"But then the teacher started talking about a kidnapping. She

said that Father's first baby was stolen and died. Charles Lindbergh Junior. And when I told her she was wrong, that I was the
oldest, she got real quiet, then she shut the book and told me to go
home and ask you about it."

"Oh." Without thinking, I tore up the letter I was writing to
Charles. Writing to him was my lifeline, as it was his; I often felt
we were courting again through V-Mail, sharing our fears, our
hopes—everything that we hadn't been able to tell each other in
person. Forced to live apart now, after so long huddled together
against various storms, the war had given us a chance to tell each
other who we were again. To reinvent ourselves, even. On the
page, I sounded strong and resourceful.

He sounded reflective and kind.

Even though I missed him so much that I had taken to sleeping on the chaise in my bedroom just so I didn't have to see his
pillow every night, I was suddenly, violently furious with my
husband. Why was he not here to address this? After all, it was a
situation of his own making; *Charles* had decided that we would
never display our lost baby's pictures, never tell his siblings about
his existence. "I don't want any reminders," he had declared, a
lifetime ago, when we were packing up the house in Hopewell.
And that was it. I gathered all the baby's photos into one shoe box
that I still kept beneath my bed. Now and then, when I was alone,
I sat cross-legged on the floor and spread them all out before me,
a jigsaw puzzle that would never be complete.

Baby. I sighed. Of course, he would not be a baby now. He
would be two years older than Jon. A teenager.

"So, I'm asking you," Jon said, ever patient—although I
could see that he was shaken. He had a difficult time looking at
me directly, and his hands, in his trouser pockets, were balled into
fists. "Did I have—have a big brother, I guess? And he died?"

"Yes." I pushed myself away from the desk and went to my bed; I patted the coverlet, and Jon sat down next to me.

As I sorted through my tumbled emotions—anger at Charles; the tender sadness that any mention of "the events of '32" still invoked; frustration at the teacher, for having introduced the subject in the first place—I glanced about the bedroom. It was a woman's bedroom, not a man's, with dainty lace curtains, dresses in the closet, lipstick on the vanity. No tie rack, no shaving kit, very few suits, and those in the back of the closet. I wondered how many other wives lived in such a bedroom; how many other wives had subtly, over the last couple of years of war, remodeled their homes, their lives, around someone's absence.

Most, probably. I was not remarkable enough to be the only one.

Our house here in Bloomfield Hills had not been exactly to either of our tastes, but given the housing shortage, we leaped at it. Four bedrooms, three acres, only $300 a month in rent. It was decorated in an ornate, fussy style that I longed to change but couldn't; our landlady, who was living with her sister for the duration, had a habit of popping over unannounced, just to make sure we hadn't touched anything. The boys shared one room, Anne had another, and the new baby had a separate nursery; and then the master bedroom, in which I slept alone. For Charles was now, finally, at the front.

During the past two years he had worked tirelessly for Henry Ford, insisting on being paid only what he would have earned in the army. He had made himself into something of a human laboratory rat. Volunteering for everything, Charles tested high-altitude chambers, oxygen-deprivation chambers, sound chambers; he usually came home at night slightly ill, or with his ears ringing, but always with a satisfied smile. And as the war marched on, and so did time, and memories, he crossed the country, testing bombers for other companies as well—North American Aviation, Curtiss-Wright, Douglas: all companies that had turned down his services after Pearl Harbor. Finally, he convinced Lockheed to send him into the Pacific theater, where he used his experience to teach pilots how to fly at high altitudes in the P-38. Officially, he was not allowed into combat, which should have quelled my worries. But I knew my husband too well; I also knew how other pilots idolized him. Whenever we flew commercial—even during the worst of the America First ordeal—Charles was treated like a hero. The pilots, grinning like schoolboys, always came back to shake his hand, stuttering that it was a privilege to fly him, of all people.

I could not imagine Charles Lindbergh failing to talk a mere military pilot into allowing him to tag along on a combat mission.

Despite my fears, I rejoiced that we were now, truly, like every other wartime family. I worried, and waited for infrequent letters, and managed everything on my own—secretly sure that my husband was having the time of his life, while I was not.

"This—the kidnapping—was mentioned in your history book, then?" Oh, how right I had been, all those years ago! Our personal tragedy was history now in every school textbook. Neither of us had thought of *that* when we sent our children off to be educated.

"Yes," Jon answered, settling beside me on the bed. "There was a picture, too, of the man they said did it."

"God." I shuddered, remembering Bruno Richard Hauptmann's blank, expressionless face when I testified while everyone else in the room was weeping.

"Why didn't you ever tell me about it? I might have been able to help!"

"Oh, sweetheart!" I wanted to laugh and cry both; how innocent, how sturdy he was—truly the man of the house, like so many little boys during wartime! "You weren't even born yet. There was nothing you could have done. There was nothing anyone could have done—not even Father, although you must believe me. He tried. He tried so very hard to find our baby, to bring him back to me. Charles Junior. That's what we named him. Charles Junior. Charlie."

"Like Anne? Anne Junior?"

"That's right." And I remembered my horror when Charles named her after me; he insisted, saying it was tradition. I'd felt it was inviting tragedy into our lives once more. But over time, this feeling had faded. Anne was a healthy three-and-a-half-year-old now, always chasing after her big brothers—and nearly always catching up. She was also a dutiful older sister to Scott, born in August 1942.

"What was he like? Charles Junior?"

"Oh, well—he was a baby, of course. Not even two, so we didn't really get a chance to—to know him." My voice caught on the jagged edges of my heart that had never healed, and I had to take a deep breath. "But he looked an awful lot like Father. More than you, even." I smiled at my son, already tall and lean for his age, hair the same reddish-gold as Charles's. But his forehead wasn't quite as high as the baby's had been, and his eyes were a darker blue.

"Did you like him?"

"Of course, Jon. Of course. We loved him. Just as much as we love you."

"Then you must have been very sad."

"Yes, I was. Very sad."

"Did you cry?"

"Yes, I did cry. Sometimes—sometimes, I still do. Not very often, though."

"When you go outside by yourself at night? When you say you're locking up the garage? I know you don't really do that, because I always lock it after dinner. I've never missed a time."

I laid my cheek against my son's head and sighed. "Yes, that's when. But not for long."

"Did Father ever cry?"

It was a blow—a punch in the stomach, this question. I inhaled sharply, and Jon looked at me in alarm. Biting my lip, I turned away from his innocent, searching gaze.

What responsibility did I have to my children, regarding their father? He had been gone for several months, a long time in the lives of those so young. And even before he left for the Pacific, he was an infrequent guest in his own house with all the flying he had to do for his work.

The children knew that he was famous, of course; his Paris flight was part of our family lore. Other families told a story about the time Father ran away to join the circus only to come home a week later, hungry and penitent; our family told the story about the time Father flew to Paris by himself, only to come home the most famous man in the world.

Charles, of course, embodied the role of hero; a strict, somehow aloof parental presence, expecting his offspring to be miniature versions of his own ideal of himself. And I was left to try to make up for all the warmth and understanding he didn't display; to make up for his absence, his focus, always, on something bigger, something more important, than his family.

Now it was up to me to tell my son about his father, and I wasn't sure how truthful I should be. Should I tell him how he had berated me for my tears, so long ago? Should I reveal how he had laughed and clapped when the man found guilty was electrocuted, while I excused myself and quietly vomited in the bathroom?

Should I share with my son his father's coldness, how he sometimes turned away from me at night if I had dared to question his judgment during the day?

Should I tell him his father was anti-Semitic?

But there were so many other things to tell as well—how comforting he could be, simply because of who he was, the bravest man in the world. How charming, when he forgot to be the hero, and remembered how to smile, truly smile, so the ice in his eyes melted into cloudless sky. How boyishly happy he was tinkering with anything mechanical, every limb loose, grease streaking his clothes. I'd long ago learned that those were the times I should ask him for something; the times he had a wrench or a hammer in his hand; the times when he was just a boy with a fascination for all things mechanical, and a curiosity that could not be sated.

Should I reveal how utterly helpless I was on those nights when he turned to me first, or those rare days when he reached for me, just to hold my hand for no reason at all?

No, I did not have to tell him, I decided. Not yet. There would be time enough for the children to learn who he was, firsthand, after the war; there would be time enough for them to decide who their father was, or was not.

"No, Father didn't cry," I told Jon, even as I pulled him close to me in a hug. "But he was sad. Very sad. He loved the baby, just as he loves you."

"Have you ever seen Father cry?"

"No, I haven't, but I never saw my own father cry, either." Which was the truth; the difference was I somehow always knew my father was capable of it.

"I haven't, either. I just can't imagine it, can you? Father, crying?" And Jon laughed, shaking his head, as if he'd just been told a whopper of a lie. "Father simply isn't the type!"

"No, he isn't," I agreed, then let him go with a sloppy kiss.

Jon wiped it off, very manfully, but with a sympathetic smile for me. Then he trotted over to the bedroom door, ready to go do his homework. I never had to remind him.

"Make sure Land does his reading," I called after him. *Land,* I did have to remind, for he was apt to be sitting on a stair step somewhere, fighting Nazis with just a stick, or wiping out Japs with the help of an old piece of wire and his imagination.

"I will. Moms, you know what?" Jon paused, his hand on the doorknob.

"What?"

"I can't wait until Father comes home, so I can figure out exactly what type he is!"

I exhaled—as if I'd been holding my breath this entire time—and laughed.

"Good luck with that, dear."

And then I waved him away, waiting until he had closed the door behind him to whisper, as I walked back to my desk to start another letter to my husband of fifteen years, "When you do find out what type he is, will you let me know? For I'm still not quite sure, myself."

SIX MONTHS AFTER HE LEFT, in September 1944, Charles came home.

We had moved once more, back to the east coast, Connecticut. I had never felt as if we belonged in the Midwest; everything was on such an expansive scale there—the sky, the land, the lakes, the people—that it frightened me. I was glad to be closer to home, back in the world I had grown up in, even as I scolded myself for not being able to appreciate the experience we had been given in Detroit.

But we had hardly settled in our new home, a rental once more—in fact, the children were still staying at Next Day Hill while I dealt with furniture and utilities and the chaos of unpacking—when I got the telegram from Charles saying that he was back in the States, safe and sound. In a comical dance of anticipation and dread—I couldn't wait to sleep next to him again; would he approve of the way I arranged the living room furniture; would he find me changed, older—I rushed to get the house in order.

Two days later I heard the taxi pull up outside; I was running through the dining room with a table lamp in my hand. I froze, and stared as a tall brown figure came up the sidewalk, sure and confident, as if he had walked those steps every day. And then he was inside—not even a tentative knock on the door, he just came inside, already king of the castle, calling, "Anne? Anne?"

And I was in his arms, he was picking me up and swinging me, burying his head in my hair. I thought I had never seen him before; I was knocked over, as I had been the very first day we met, by the startling clarity of his eyes, that suddenly bashful, boyish grin. But he was so tan! So handsome! Bronzed by the sun, lean, a few more crinkles edging his eyes, a few less sandy brown hairs on his head.

"Oh, I missed you," he whispered, and my heart couldn't contain my joy; it overflowed, and my eyes brimmed over with tears.

"I look a fright," I sniffed, pushing myself away from him, suddenly shy; I cupped my hand over my nose, my horrid, horrid nose; I was sure it was red as a clown's.

"You look beautiful." And he wouldn't let me go; he pulled me back, claiming me and even though there was no one else to see, I glowed with pride and belonging. And love.

We had one beautiful, sacred night together, before the children arrived.

At first they were shy around him, asking polite questions like: "Did you have a very long journey?" "Was the train crowded?"

But then Land asked, his eyes wide and hopeful, "Did you kill any Japs?" And the ice was broken; Charles laughed, a deep belly laugh, and ruffled Land's hair, assuring him that he had. Then Charles picked up Scott and tossed him up to the ceiling—and my heart froze, overwhelmed with a memory. A memory of Charles doing the same thing to little Charlie, who had always called, "'Gen!"

"'Gen!" Scott shrieked the same thing, and if I shut my eyes, I wouldn't have been able to tell their voices apart, the one a ghost, the other a squirming, crowing reality in his father's arms.

"Now, Charles, be careful—"

"Women!" Charles rolled his eyes, and Jon and Land laughed delightedly. Ansy, still bashful, stuck her finger in her mouth and clung to my skirt. "Let's say we take this outside, okay, fellows?" And Charles sat Scott carefully on the floor before grabbing Land and Jon, tucking each beneath his strong arms. He rushed outside, the boys screaming with joy, and he tumbled around on the ground with them, a pack of young wolves.

"He's so *big*!" Ansy exclaimed. "Father is so big!"

I laughed, and kissed the top of her head. "I suppose he is. It will take some getting used to, won't it? For all of us?" I had never seen this Charles; this relaxed, embracing father, roughhousing with his boys. The war must have changed him.

With a contented smile, and slightly loose limbs after a satisfying night of reconciliation, I moved around the house, pausing now and then in my tidying up to look out the window at my husband and sons. Ansy played quietly in a corner of the living room with her dolls. Scott cooed happily in his playpen, piling up blocks and knocking them down.

And I thought, *Yes. He's home now, and we will be a family. A real family, for the first time since—*

Since our firstborn was taken.

Finally at rest, his part in the war over, with growing children to keep him moored, Charles would be home for dinner every night now. He would teach the children things only a father can teach—how to play catch, how to make a radio out of crystal and wire. At night, he and I would talk about our days, just like we used to when we were first married. And we would share our thoughts, equally—for the war had changed me as well, although Charles did not yet know it.

I had run the household. I had rotated the tires, kept the accounts, learned to make a meal out of a can of chipped beef, an egg, and stale bread. When there was a strange noise in the middle of the night, *I* had investigated it. I had cared for four children and not lost a one—I chuckled at this, and was surprised, and pleased, at myself for being able to make such a joke.

I had accomplished this. All of it. I had steered my family through the war, and now it was over. It was all over—the kidnapping, the exile, the clumsy, stridently wrong years before the war, and then, the war itself—we were headed for better times. For the first time in years, I felt strong and confident, unafraid of the future. Charles's equal, not his crew.

With a happy little sigh, I continued my work. His regulation duffel bag was still in the hallway where he had dumped it last night, so I lugged it downstairs to the washer and dryer. Pulling out his dirty socks, his ragged T-shirts—even his old travel bag, which he'd somehow wedged in next to a bedroll—I came across a heavy vest, like an umpire's. A flak jacket.

"Did you kill any Japs?" Land had demanded.

"Of course," Charles had answered. And it finally hit me. He had been in danger. I'd known it, of course, but somehow hadn't been able to imagine it. The heavy, sweat-stained flak jacket made it real, and I began to shake. Then laugh. Because he had been returned to me. My husband, my Charles; the one loss I knew from which I could never recover. I had been spared that loss, after all.

I hugged the jacket—the untouched jacket, not a scratch, not a dent, was in it—to my heart. And I sang a prayer of thanksgiving, while my children and my husband played happily outside.

GENTLY I SHAKE his arm, but he doesn't awake. Holding my breath, I shake him harder; he's so frail, and I don't want to do anything to hasten the end. But I have to have the answers I seek. I have to at least *try.*

"Charles," I whisper, bending close to his ear. "Charles!"

He opens his eyes with a gasp, and again I sense that he's surprised to find himself here on earth. Was he dreaming of the sky? I don't know what his concept of heaven is, but I suspect it's not the same as mine.

"Charles, I can't wait any longer. I need to know. I need to know why. I *deserve* to know why we weren't enough for you. Me, your children, the home I made for you, for us all. But you had to have these other women, too! *Why?*"

"You weren't supposed to find out," he finally says, licking his lips, gesturing for more water, which I bring him. There's a film over one of his eyes, clouding the blue.

"Of course I wasn't supposed to find out! But a nurse—a very kind, decent girl—felt differently, and she gave them to me, because she admired my book."

"That book."

"Yes, *that* book. My book." Suddenly I crave a cigarette, so viscerally that I almost clap my hands as if to summon a genie to provide it. I rarely smoke, but I need something to do with my hands, and I desire something bad, something terrible and filthy, in my lungs just now. Something to mask the stench of death and betrayal that has filled this small, humid hut on the edge of the world.

"I wrote a book," Charles says, and he sounds drowsy, amused, his eyes half closed, and I'm afraid he's drifting off again and as terrible, as horrible as it is, I won't let him. I won't let him slip peacefully away and die an untroubled death. Once, that was all I wished for him.

Now I deny it. Because it is in my power to do so. Drunk with that power, I am demanding his explanation, his attention. At last.

I shake him by his shoulders—his pitifully thin, shrunken shoulders—and ruthlessly ask, "Why? Why weren't we enough? Why wasn't *I* ever enough for you?"

He blinks again, and looks straight into my eyes, my heart, and says, "Anne, I never meant to hurt you."

I laugh. I laugh because finally, Charles Lindbergh is like any man. Any stupid, flesh-and-blood, egotistical man. He is no better than any of them, even if it took him almost to his last breath to reveal this to me, and it fills me with triumph and joy.

Which are followed, dizzyingly, by disappointment and despair.

CHAPTER 16

"OTHER!"

"What is it, Reeve?"

"You tell Father he must stay home. You go find him and bring him back and tell him he must stay this time!" She stamped her foot, shook her blond ringlets, and thrust her jaw out in perfect imitation of her father.

"I'm afraid I can't do that, dear. You tell him next time he comes home, all right?"

"All right. But when *is* he coming home?"

"I don't know." I pushed myself up off the kitchen floor; the drain was leaking beneath the sink again. Dropping the wrench down on the table, for a moment I couldn't help but think, *I have a trust fund. I could just go off and take the children to a nice hotel in the city, where we could have room service and go shopping, and see plays. Why am I on my hands and knees in a drafty old house in Connecticut, miles away from civilization?*

Too busy to answer my own question, I washed my hands, checked beneath the sink to make sure it wasn't leaking any-more—it was—and shooed Reeve out of the kitchen.

"Go tell your sister to please turn down her record player!" I was weary of hearing "Tennessee Waltz" played over and over, which was a shame, as I thought it was a very pretty song. The first hundred times I heard it, anyway.

The phone rang in the front hall; I waited for the stampede of feet to run to it, the cries of, "I'll get it!" But for once, no one did; the phone kept ringing, so I headed for it, picking my way over the piles of skates and cleats and Ansy's field hockey stick that had all been tossed just inside the entryway in the usual after-school rush.

"Hello?"

"What took you so long?" Charles asked on the other end, clearly irritated. "It rang for nearly a minute."

"No, not quite an entire minute. Where are you?"

"Washington, of course. Strategic Air Command work. I thought I told you."

"No, you didn't."

"Is everything all right there?"

"Yes, of course."

"No emergencies this week?"

"Not yet, anyway." Although with four school-aged children, I knew it was only a matter of time.

"Good. Have you taken an inventory lately? We're due for one."

"I'll do it this weekend." Charles frequently required an inventory of all our household items—blankets, pots and pans, dishes, silverware, even shampoo bottles. It was a holdover from when we flew to the Orient—actually, probably from when he planned his flight to Paris; everything had to be accounted for and discarded if it served no useful purpose. Charles saw no reason why a home couldn't be packed as efficiently as an airplane; he himself still traveled with only his small, battered bag, the one he'd used since we were married.

"Fine. The children are well?"

"Yes. Would you like to talk to them?" Although even as I said it, I hoped he would not. For one of them would likely say something to displease him, and I would be the one to bear the brunt of it.

"No, I don't have time. I just wanted to check in and make sure everything was running according to plan."

According to your plan, I thought grimly. *Not mine.*

"When will you be home? Reeve was asking just a moment ago."

"I don't know. After these conferences, Pan Am wants me to attend their annual shareholders' meeting. Then I think I'll be back, and I have a special project I'd like you to work on."

"Oh, Charles." My heart sank; the last time he had dangled a "special project" in front of me, like some kind of reward for being, I don't know, as stupidly loyal as a puppy, I ended up helping him catalog all the trees on our property. Five acres of heavily wooded property.

"I promise, it's not like last time," he added, as if he could see my face. "Are you sure everything is all right there?"

"Yes, I'm sure. Now, go to your meeting. I need to start supper."

"No steak, I hope. Not on a weekday. Roast, I would think, would be the proper meal."

"It's chicken pot pie, for your information. Now, goodbye!" And I hung up the phone, cherishing my little triumph. Then I slumped against the wall, disgusted. Chicken pot pie instead of pot roast! How ridiculous.

If I'd really desired a victory, I would have told him that no, everything was not fine. The sink is clogged, Land got a C in English, Jon's graduation is coming up and he keeps asking me if you're going to be home for it, I'm tired, irritable, and even though I don't have a second to myself I'm so bored I feel like jumping into the ocean just outside this godforsaken piece of land you picked out for us and lured me to with the promise that these would be our golden years.

Oh, I had been so ecstatic when Charles first showed me this house! It was in 1946, a few months after my sixth child, Reeve, was born. After several months away in Europe, where he had gone on behalf of the government to study Nazi Germany's captured rocket program, he was finally home for good. We left the children with Mother and drove out with a picnic lunch to this wooded place on the eastern tip of Connecticut.

Spreading the blanket on a cliff overlooking the ocean, the rambling farmhouse behind us, we sat and discussed our plans, just like every young family was doing. Although we weren't quite as young as some: Charles was forty-four; I, just forty.

Charles was still working in an unofficial military capacity, as an advisor to the Army Air Corps, which was concentrating mainly on high altitude jets now, and Charles was an expert on high-altitude flying. Pan Am also hired him to be a consultant as they began to expand their overseas routes. His postwar schedule was rapidly filling up; already I suspected he wouldn't be home as much as I had hoped.

Still, that day, it seemed as if we had found a permanent home of our own—no more moving every two years, not with a brood of school-aged children. Finally, I thought, we had found our way back to the family we set out to be, *before* "the events of '32."

"See that spot of land?" Charles pointed to a far-off dip in the ground, surrounded by young birch trees. "That's where I'll build you a little house. A little writing house. That's where you're going to write your book, Anne. The one I know you can write."

"Really?" I turned to him; he was reclining on the ground, propping up his head with his hand. He grinned, and the confidence he always radiated fell, like a precious ray of sun, upon me. My face flushed, and I almost felt a pencil between my fingers, saw the sheaves of paper spread out on a desk. It would face east, I thought, so I could write in the morning—always my favorite time to gather my thoughts. I would rise early, before the children got up, before they pulled at me, tugged at me, stretched me thin as taffy, as children had a way of doing.

"Remember, how you said you wanted to write one great book? The war got in the way of that, didn't it?"

I nodded. I had published, after *Wave of the Future*, a fictional account of one of our flights, called *Steep Ascent*. But I wasn't happy with it, and I suspected I never would be as long as I kept writing our past. I needed to find something bigger, something worthwhile—but all the moves, the children; so many pregnancies; all kept muddying my mind, claiming my energy.

"Well," Charles continued, "now you can do it. Here, in this house, we will raise our family, and I'll go off to work and you'll go off to write, and we'll make history again, the two of us. We should be able to hire some decent help, now that the war's over. The schools are good here in Darien—I knew you'd want to know that, so I checked. What do you think? We can fix up the house—I've already talked to a contractor."

"What do I think?" I beamed up at him, thanking God for the miracle of this man who had made it home from the war, back to me—me, of all people! "I think it's perfect!" I touched that deep cleft in his chin, kissed it before he could pull away, then pushed myself up and hiked over to that spot where my writing house would be. Charles remained where he was, staring out at the ocean that threw itself up thunderously on the rocks, far below. Halfway to the birch trees, I turned around to look at him, and my heart skipped a beat; he was so gorgeous, still. I remembered how, on our long flights, seated behind him just like a girl in school seated behind her secret crush, I used to memorize everything about the back of Charles's head, his neck, his shoulders. Cramped as I got sitting in my crowded cockpit, there were moments I was overwhelmed with physical longing for my husband. It might be brought on simply by the way he cocked his head first left, then right, to relieve some tension. When he did so, the muscles of his neck would lengthen and tighten; this glimpse of his bronzed, taut flesh, tinged with reddish-blond hairs—the only glimpse I would have of his flesh for hours on end—would cause a sudden stirring of longing in my belly and between my legs, my breasts tingling as if brushed with tiny, electric feathers.

I felt that way still, when I looked at him; electric, young. Supple and pliant and girlish.

And this—this unexpected generosity, as he remembered my dream after all this time. A cabin, all to myself! We deserved this. We deserved this place, this peace. We'd live the rest of our lives here, together; we'd walk together through the birch grove, and lie together on the cold ground, finding a way to keep warm. Together.

Soon, though, I was reminded that we weren't as young—or, rather, *I* wasn't as young—as I'd imagined. I became pregnant again, to my dismay—a dismay I tried to conceal from Charles and from myself. But for the first time I was afraid; I had been relieved when my doctor warned me not to have any more children after Reeve. This time, I was afraid for my physical well-being, as well as my creative; I felt, somehow, that if I had this child I would never write again, cabin or no cabin. My thoughts always seemed to fling themselves in every direction, farther and farther afield with each child. I would never be able to corral them now.

And it was not an easy pregnancy; I developed gallstones and was advised to have an abortion, which I could not bring myself to do. But nature delivered me from the purgatory of indecision and pain, and I miscarried. Soon after, I underwent the necessary gallbladder surgery.

But I underwent it alone. Charles, who had been present for the birth of each of our children, was strangely absent at the death of my childbearing years.

Our new family doctor, Dana Atchley, a gentle, slightly soft-looking man with thinning gray hair and the warmest, most understanding eyes I had ever seen, was kindness itself. I was in the hospital in Manhattan for two weeks, and found myself dissolving into tears whenever I turned my head, which throbbed and ached almost as much as the incision beneath my belly. But I did my best to dry those tears whenever Dr. Atchley checked in on me, and put on a brave, cheerful face, as Charles urged me to do by telephone, every day. I don't think I fooled the doctor, for he sometimes paused on his busy rounds to sit next to me for long minutes at a time. Often he turned my radio on, and we listened to classical music together, not saying a word, before he got up to resume his rounds. And I would resume my bewildered contemplation of my husband—or, rather, his absence.

For so long it had been just the two of us, together against all foes—wind, weather, the press, the kidnappers, the swirling darkness of world war. Now I was sick, ailing; facing an abyss of confusion and finality that I simply couldn't comprehend and I needed him, needed his forbidding strength, his ruthless, forward-looking vision. Without them, all I could do was lie in my hospital bed for two weeks, waiting pathetically for him. Wondering why he couldn't take the train into the city; wondering why, even with me in the hospital, he'd accepted an invitation to fly to Switzerland and give a speech, leaving the children in the care of secretaries. Leaving me to heal on my own.

Looking back, I see that was the beginning. I would spend the rest of my life waiting for him, wondering *why*. Until it was too late.

Even after I recovered from the surgery, Charles did not reach for me as he once had. It wasn't as if he was afraid to hurt me; that, I would have understood. Instead, it was as if he had decided he had no more use for my body, as it was of no more use to him. No more children, no more little Lindberghs; his dynasty was complete—what physical need did he have for me now?

I didn't have much desire at first, either. But gradually it returned, and I was able to coax him, occasionally, into making love, but he always seemed to be holding back. No longer could he lose himself in my arms; no longer could he expose himself so nakedly, crying out into my breasts. We had always had that between us; our bodies could speak when our hearts could not. Now, that was one more thing I had lost.

Was that why he began to withdraw from the children, too? Did he lump us all together as something finished? All I know is that he began to fly farther and farther away from us all, rarely asking me to accompany him; only occasionally remembering to come back.

To be sure, his presence was always felt even when he was away. He had made out a personalized schedule for each child to follow, starting from the hour they were to awake to the number of snacks they were permitted throughout the day, including chores—and the precise way each was to be performed. (The trash could not simply be emptied into a bin and then taken to the garbage dump; it must be sorted through first to make sure nothing of value had been accidentally thrown away.)

Mandatory reading lists were drawn up for each child, according to whatever flaw in his or her character Charles felt was prominent. Jon was given books to read that praised humility,

Land ones that encouraged focus; Scott was deluged with books that spoke of the virtues of discipline. Ansy had to read about little girls who got into trouble because of their tempers. And Reeve, even before she started kindergarten, had to sit down for an hour a day and page through picture books about baby animals who came to a sad end because they were too curious.

Nor was I exempt; far from it. I had to account for every expenditure, even down to the shoelaces for each pair of tennis shoes and the box of toothpicks in the junk drawer. Naturally, I was expected somehow to intuit the exact hour of his homecoming, even when he failed to tell me; if he walked in the door and I wasn't there to take his hat and coat, he would berate me for ten minutes before finally remembering to kiss me on the cheek.

Still, when Charles was gone, the house was noisy, relaxed; Ansy played her records or practiced her flute all day, the boys ran in and out in various sports uniforms; Reeve scampered about, clutching after her siblings, demanding that they include her in their activities. Dinnertime was like a zoo, as I simply sat and let them chatter to one another, knowing that I'd inadvertently hear the important things. This way, I learned that Jon was going to ask Sarah Price to prom; that Land had blown an axle on the Studebaker and had to borrow money from Grandma to get it fixed; that Scott was keeping a toad in his sock drawer; that Ansy's best friend had told the rest of the cheerleading squad that she had halitosis; that Reeve was not going to get married, ever, because boys, especially boys like her brothers, were horrid.

Usually Reeve would end dinner by saying she missed Daddy, and they would all turn to the empty place at the head of the table, wistful expressions on their young faces—before pushing back their chairs and getting on with the evening, chattering and busy once more.

They may have missed him—I may have missed him. But

when he *was* home, the air in the house was so impenetrable with tension I sometimes retreated to my cabin to breathe freely, and cry.

The evening after he returned from the Pacific, we had all sat in the kitchen, the children staring at him like he was a mythical creature who had somehow turned up in the middle of the sub-urbs, while Charles declared, jovially, "It's a good thing I'm back, Anne, to whip these youngsters into shape." I had laughed, the children had laughed; we were just so happy to have him home. But soon, "It's a good thing I'm back, Anne, to whip these youngsters into shape" became a war cry; it set my teeth on edge, and caused the children to pale. I couldn't bear to witness how he treated them; scolding Land for his C in English until the poor boy broke down—a thirteen-year-old, sobbing like a baby. Or following each child around for a day, making sure that his schedule was being followed exactly, watching so intently that overnight, Ansy developed a nervous tic, her eyes blinking un-controllably at times—just like Charles's had, back when the baby was taken, and my heart caught on the unexpectedly jagged edge of this realization.

Once, Charles went into Jon's closet and threw every single item of clothing on the floor, simply because one sweater had been hung up and stretched out at the neck.

The children loved him, cautiously, respectfully—or loved the *idea* of him, anyway. Growing up a Lindbergh meant they had assumptions made of them wherever they went, and one of those assumptions was that they were brave, daring, and capable of great things. They each saw these characteristics in their fa-ther, of course, and admired him for them. And there were good times; odd, though, as the years went on, the details of these lost their sharpness, so that they became impressionistic paintings compared to the unmistakably photographic images of the bad.

But Charles organized outdoor games on a scale I never could: scavenger hunts and relay races and football, which he and the boys enjoyed with almost too much enthusiasm. Charles allowed his sons to tackle him with as much force as they had in them; force that grew in intensity as the resentments piled up. But Charles never complained, not even when Scott accidentally cracked one of his ribs.

He also encouraged Ansy's love of writing, just as he always encouraged mine, even going so far as to print up her short stories and binding them so that they looked like real books. And he delighted in Reeve's sense of humor, egging her on mischievously, playing silly jokes on her and allowing her to play them on him.

Of course he worried about their physical safety, teaching each basic self-defense when they were old enough to learn, drilling into them the importance of never talking to strangers or getting into other people's cars, training a succession of guard dogs to watch over them when they were very young.

Still, we all found it easier to love and admire him when he was gone. The first day or so after Charles left again we all would continue to walk tentatively, weigh our words cautiously, looking over shoulders in case he was still there. Then, there would be a collective sigh; the air would be light and breathable, and gradually we would remember how to be ourselves again.

Until the next time he came home.

"Jon! Land! Come pick up this mess." Still standing next to the telephone, I stared, horrified, at the collection of shoes and equipment in the hall. How had I let this happen? While I knew, rationally, that Charles was days away from coming home, I panicked as if he were about to walk in the front door. "Come down here this instant and pick this up! Both of you!"

Then I ran back to the kitchen, remembering the leaky drain. I'd never hear the end of it if he came home before it was fixed.

"MAY I COME IN?"

I glanced up; Charles was standing in the door of my writing retreat. Hastily I shut the book I was reading and thrust it beneath some papers, just as I had so often done as a schoolgirl. I picked up a pencil and began to scribble something on a piece of paper. "Of course, you can come in," I replied, turning that brazen grin on him, just as I used to on the photographers.

"I'm not disturbing you?"

"No, not at all." But I couldn't bring myself to meet his gaze; I couldn't let him see how miserably guilty I was. For he had built me a lovely little house out of his own belief in my ability to write, and so far I had done nothing in it but daydream, write in my diary, cry, and read novels. Trashy novels, at that; for some reason, the dense, poetry-filled literature I had loved for so long—Cervantes, Joyce, Proust—muddied my head, these days. I wondered if I had lost brain cells as well as hormones. I buried myself in popular fiction instead; the book I had hidden from Charles was Kathleen Winsor's latest. Although I didn't think it nearly so juicy as *Forever Amber.*

"Do you like the cabin?" Charles had to bend in order to get through the door; he had designed it, with considerable thoughtfulness, for my much smaller frame. So the windows were lower, the roof cozy. He could stand, just barely, once he got inside; the top of his head, now almost completely gray, with just flecks of reddish gold, was only an inch from the ceiling.

"Yes, I do. Thank you so much." Unlike some of Charles's gifts—like the motorcycle he had expected me to learn to ride, forgetting that I had a balance problem that made it impossible for me even to ride a bicycle—so far the cabin had remained a symbol of his thoughtfulness; any sense of failure to make good use of it was only on my end, not his. While he urged, he did not criticize, as he might once have—and perhaps I'd been too reliant on his criticism, after all? For left to myself, I couldn't make any progress. Despite the peacefulness of the setting, the waiting sense of calm, almost as if the very beams, made from ancient pine trees, were content to bide their time until I was ready, I felt guilty every time I entered. I had done nothing worthy of such a gift other than sign permission slips and write out grocery lists. And read trashy novels.

"I wanted to talk to you about that special project. The one I spoke to you about when I called last week." Charles pulled up a chair; in his hands were three thick notebooks. "I've been work-ing on something, as you know, for quite a while. It's a narrative, an account of my flight to Paris." He colored a little, and looked nervously out the window—but he laid the notebooks gently in my lap.

"But—you wrote an account back in 'twenty-seven, didn't you?"

"Oh, that." Charles snorted, leaning back in his chair until it creaked dangerously. "I would prefer to forget all about that. A publisher paid me a small fortune to spend a weekend in a hotel scribbling something down that they then had a real writer trans-late. I was so green, I didn't know any better. This was right after I returned to America. So many people wanted me to do this, go there, speak here, put my name to that, and I hadn't yet learned to say no. But that account is not right. It's not—true. Only now can I look back and see that young man, see what the odds truly were, the dangers, and the importance of it all. I've been working on this for a long time, since before the war, when we were in England."

"You've been writing since England?" I couldn't help it; I felt a punch to the gut, as if I'd been betrayed, somehow. How had *he* found the time, amid all his flying, the politics of America First, the work on the profusion pump, the war? When I, merely bearing and raising children, found it so difficult to focus on writing about anything other than the insipid details of my day?

Fresh evidence, once more, that I was less than him.

Swallowing my wounded pride, I managed not to hurl the notebooks to the floor. "So, what do you want me to do?" I asked instead, opening one of them; Charles's handwriting filled each page, and there were notes and scribbles in all the margins, little arrows inserted into the text.

"Be my crew again," he said simply. "You're the writer in the family." I winced at this, but I don't think he saw. "*North to the Orient,* the letters you wrote during the war—there was poetry in them, just like in everything you write. I don't mean that I want you to rewrite anything, but rather, just help me shape it, I suppose—steer me away from merely citing facts and figures. I want this to be a real book, not just a dashed-off account like the other was. And you're the only person I trust to help me make it that."

I was silent, paging through the notebooks, not really seeing them at all except as evidence of his accomplishment, of the different expectations of men and women. *Why* hadn't I found the time to write my great book? Because he had stuck me out here in Connecticut to watch over his children while he flew all over the world, busy with his work—rehabilitating his image, I understood with breathtaking clarity, remembering all the photo opportunities he had allowed while he worked for the Strategic Air Command, the unexpected interviews he had granted the press recently. And now, his memoirs. Why now, all of a sudden?

Because in two years, it would be the twenty-fifth anniversary of his flight to Paris. Charles Lindbergh was no fool.

As I studied my husband, leaning forward in his chair, his hands nervously gripping his knees, a pleading softness in his eyes I hadn't seen in so long, I felt myself as helpless as always in his presence. There were nights when I dreamed of our early pioneering flights, the closeness, the reliance on each other, only to wake up in my empty bed so lonely I hugged his untouched pillow to my chest, just to have something to hold on to. There were nights when the fury of abandonment surged so forcefully through me I couldn't sleep, let alone dream, and I paced the terrace instead, a wild-haired creature, smoking a cigarette precisely because he wasn't there to disapprove, even though normally I had no taste for it.

But seeing his need for me, a miracle, a mirage I was afraid might disappear once I stepped outside of this enchanted cabin, I had no choice but to acquiesce. Or so I told myself; I was, after all, the aviator's wife. I had made that decision, once and for all, back before the war.

"What kind of schedule do you have in mind?" I knew, of course, that he would have one. His face cleared; he grinned and squeezed my hand in approval.

"Good girl. Well, I thought that you can go over what I have so far—it's merely a draft, of course—and then make some notes. I'll go over what you've noted and incorporate it, and then—so on. There are a couple of publishers interested; I put out some feelers. I wasn't completely sure that anyone would want to publish this after—well, my reputation, in some circles. There are certain—there are some Jews in the publishing world, you know." He frowned, and picked up a pencil off my desk, twirling it around in his long, tapered fingers. "I do feel as if—as if things got a bit out of hand. I truly believed what I said at the time, however, and what else could I do but speak what I felt was the truth? But people change. I've changed. I'm not sure, though, that the public will necessarily believe that I have. I can only hope this might help."

His brow was furrowed, his path obviously not as clear as it had always been. He was thinking only of himself, and his own reputation; he had never once bothered to think about mine, even after he saw the damage done by my essay.

But the truth was the world did not wait breathlessly for *my* apology. I had been welcomed back into my old circles with a pat on the head and a whispered understanding that I had merely been Charles's puppet in that "unfortunate business." Who would believe a mere wife could ever act on her own?

Anger, anger, anger. I was enormous with it these days; constantly stifling one grievance only to feel another pop up in its place. My skin felt twitchy, trying to contain them all. Sadness, I had known; terror, anxiety, occasionally joy. But anger was novel, it was frightening. It could also be, I was only beginning to suspect, exhilarating.

I swallowed this latest grievance and placed the notebooks on my desk, piling them up so that their black spines lined up, like a stack of dominoes. "All right. When would you like my notes?"

"I have to leave tomorrow for Germany, to Berlin, for Pan Am. I'll be back in a month."

"A month? You'll be gone an entire month?" My heart sank even as I silently cursed him for doing something so unexpected as to make me miss him again.

"Yes. That should give you plenty of time, I trust?"

"I should think so. Jon can drive the girls to piano lessons, and if Land doesn't make the baseball team this spring, then I don't have to—"

"Anne." Charles held his hand up. "Stop. I don't want to hear all that. You'll manage it all, you always do."

I waved his hand away, my skin twitchy once more. "It's not as easy as you think it is, Charles. But you don't know, because you're never here. You just assume I can manage, when really you have no idea—"

"If I assume so it's because you always do, which should be taken as a compliment. And I'm here now, Anne," he said mildly. And I understood that this was supposed to be enough.

But was it?

I wanted it to be. Didn't I? I wasn't sure anymore, but I was afraid to break this spell, this rare moment of the two of us spinning in the same orbit, sharing the same view once again. So I made myself believe that it was. With a wave, I managed that forced, fake grin again as he left my cabin; then I opened the first page of the first notebook.

And I began to read.

OH, WHY COULDN'T I have known this boy! This brave boy of '27, this pure, simple, unspoiled boy? When I met him, he was already on the other side of the ocean; already guarded, aware of his place in the history books.

Somehow, Charles had found a way to throw off the layers of expectation and disappointment that the years, the world, had thrust upon him, and to reclaim the heart and the voice of that boy he once had been. I didn't know how he had done it. I knew that I could never again recapture my own innocence, my belief in the goodness, the rightness, of things. The baby's kidnapping had forever changed me, and finally I understood that was why I had such difficulty writing *my* book. Because I still wasn't sure who that young girl, grinning like crazy in all those photographs prior to "the events of '32" had turned into. And I could never quite grasp her; she kept grinning, capering just beyond the picture frame of memory whenever I tried.

But in his recounting of the singular event of his lifetime, Charles Lindbergh had found a way to go back, almost like a hero in an H. G. Wells novel. He had time traveled, truly and honestly, almost twenty-five years in the past.

Writing with a simplicity that was almost poetry—and befitting the farm boy he had been, not the tarnished god he had become—he wrote of the dangers facing him as he prepared for his historic flight, the difficulty finding backers, the ridicule he found at every turn as more experienced men than he laughed at the notion of a fair-haired boy taking home the greatest prize aviation had to offer. He described the hours spent flying the mail route over a country that was no more, a country of barns and dusty roads and a few telephone poles, people running out of houses at the strange sight of his biplane in the air, only a few hundred feet up. The hours he spent going over the practicalities of such a flight, the lists he made on the back of receipts and maps.

And then the flight itself—Charles had built a masterpiece of suspense, the reader perched on his shoulder, holding his breath even though, of course, the outcome was assured. And the landing, when it came—the explosion of joy, yet always this young boy standing in the midst, perplexed, still so focused on his flight that he wanted to stay with his plane, and had to be forcibly removed from it by the mayor of Paris.

His brilliance was in ending the narrative there, in that moment—the moment before he understood that the world was now forever in his cockpit. The moment before he started to suspect that there were punishments for those who dared to dream so big, to fly so high.

I was stunned by his draft; stunned, and envious. Yet it was still unpolished; there were gaps in the narrative, particularly before the flight began, and I had ideas of how to fill them.

And so we began to work together, for the first time in years, even if we were seldom in the same space. He would be gone, I would read what he had left behind and make notes, filling in gaps; he would return, taking my notes with him when he left, and work while he traveled. He would deliver his next draft to me, and so forth, like a duet; we were writing in tandem, just as we had flown, so long ago.

I saw his heart on the page, and wondered if he knew he had left it there. The plane—the *Spirit of St. Louis*—was his true mistress. He spoke of it almost sadly, with the regret of a long-lost lover, and I had to correct that, for it was the one part of his narrative that did not feel immediate. But he had trusted this machine in a way he had never trusted anything, or anyone, ever again. Including, I knew, me.

I wondered why this memoir was written so much more clearly, straightforwardly, than anything else he had written, including his speeches before the war. And I had to conclude that it was because he was writing about a machine. But the others were about ideas, and people—and Charles had always had trouble understanding *them*.

The time we worked together on what would be called, simply, *The Spirit of St. Louis;* the notes that flew back and forth, the evenings, toward the end, when we huddled together in my cabin, leaving the children to take care of themselves—it was the best time in our marriage since our early flights. He allowed himself to be guided. I allowed myself to hope, once more, that we could share space on this earth, share goals, share happiness—and also tenderness, vulnerability.

He dedicated the book to me. *"To A.M.L.—Who will never know how much of this book she has written."*

My heart soared, just like the stars on the cover, when I read these words. Rarely did Charles ever speak of me in print, and when he did, it was almost always in answer to an interviewer's question as to why he married me. Charles usually replied that it was important to choose a spouse of good stock. Like a brood-mare.

I was always furious, even though he insisted he meant it as a joke.

But this—this was truly the first time he allowed the world to see that I mattered to him. And that meant something to me; it meant more than it should have, more than it would have had he been a mere man. But he was *Charles Lindbergh*, still and always—and I felt like an old biplane that had been left to rust in a barn; once useful—once the newest of technologies!—but forgotten as of late. Neglected.

But now that biplane had been remembered, dusted off, shined and tuned up. Old-fashioned, yes—but still able to brush the clouds.

The book sold a million copies in the first year; Hollywood bought the rights, and later, a too-old Jimmy Stewart played Charles in the movie. (We took Reeve to a showing of it at Radio City Music Hall; halfway through, she turned to me with big eyes and whispered, "He makes it, doesn't he?") *Life* magazine visited our home, photographing the two of us, side by side on the sofa, reading the book; *Mrs. Lindbergh, ever devoted, approves of her husband's newest endeavor,* the caption read. The success of the book opened the floodgates to a deluge of awards and accolades; America, it seemed, needed heroes more than it needed villains, and was willing to let bygones be bygones. President Eisenhower presented Charles with a medal for his war work. Once again, almost every town had a Charles Lindbergh Elementary School;

many had changed their names during the war, only to revert back to them now.

I beamed for the photographers beside Charles when he was notified he had been awarded the Pulitzer Prize for biography/ autobiography.

My beam diminished, however, when he neglected to thank me, thanking the Wright Brothers, instead.

It vanished completely when he was given a contract for another book, sight unseen.

JEALOUSY IS A TERRIBLE THING. It keeps you up at night, it demands tremendous energy in order to remain alive, and so you have to want to feed it, nurture it—and by so wanting, you have to acknowledge that you are a bitter, petty person. It changes you. It changes the way you view the world; minor irritations become major catastrophes; celebrations become trials.

I was proud of Charles. He had done this—it was his story to tell and he had told it, brilliantly. No matter how much I had worked on it, it was, at its essence, *his.*

And I hid in the shadows once more, only this time I paced, finding no comfort in my invisibility. Wondering what was wrong with me, wondering what was keeping me there; keeping me from writing *my* story. Wondering if I'd ever have a story worth telling that was my own, and not merely reflected or borrowed from *him;* a story that had nothing to do with our flights or his politics.

You're the writer in the family, Charles always said, and he'd even built me a cabin to prove it, when there was no real evidence of my ability other than long ago dreams, my classical education. And I had always clung to that, grateful that there was something that he felt I could do better than him. I could no longer cling to that fiction. *He* was the writer in the family, now.

So bitter was the constant taste of failure in my mouth, so narrow my vision, I fled. To a place that had always restored me to my best self.

I fled to Florida, to Captiva Island; a healing, nourishing wilderness that Charles and I had discovered before the war, when our friend Jim Newton urged us to come explore this untouched island off the Gulf Coast of Florida. I'd gone there several times since, sometimes with Charles, sometimes with my sister Con.

Now I went there alone. I had to find my own courage, and stop borrowing his. I had to find my own voice, and stop echoing his. I had to find my own story. And tell it. And if I failed doing so, I still would be stronger for the attempt than if I continued to sit beside Charles on the dais.

I packed my bags, bought paper and pencils, kissed the children, and let Charles drive me to the train station.

He sent me on my way with a handshake; the only sign of parting he could allow himself in public. But he told me, earnestly, that I was doing the right thing. He said it in the exact same way he had once told me that I could learn to fly a plane, master Morse code, figure out the stars.

And some of my jealousy melted away right then, because I knew he meant it. He had always been certain I could do more than I thought I could do. He had always pushed me to try, even if sometimes he confused bullying with encouragement.

I thanked him, then boarded the train with a jaunty wave. I was off to Florida, to a ramshackle beach cottage. I did not know when I would return. I only knew that somehow, for both our sakes, for the sake of our children, as well—

I needed to return with my own story to tell.

CHAPTER 17

O NE DAY, WHEN SHE WAS ABOUT TEN, Ansy came into the kitchen with an envelope in her hand.

It was one of those days when every appliance in the house decided to go on strike—the sink was backed up (again); the washing machine wasn't draining right; the toaster was mysteriously burning one side of the toast and leaving the other limp and white. Even one of the clocks was acting up, the chime suddenly tinny and flat.

So I was bustling about, calling repairmen, mopping up suds and water, and stopping in front of the clock every fifteen minutes, as if I could fix it with the power of my gaze. I was wearing a housedress, an apron, bobby socks, and saddle shoes. I hadn't had time to go to the hairdresser in weeks. I had taken to simply shampooing my hair and gathering it in a net, so that I resembled a truck stop waitress.

"Mother, is this you?" Ansy asked, thrusting the envelope out to me. On the outside was written *Anne Lindbergh*.

"Of course it is," I answered, irritated. "You're a big girl. You can read."

"So this is yours, too?" She pulled out a small yellowing card and began to read. *"This certifies that Anne Lindbergh has success-*

*fully completed all tasks necessary to pilot an aircraft for personal
use.*"

"Where did you find that?" I put down the bucket I was carrying, heavy with sopping wet towels. I reached for the card, and
saw that it was my pilot's license. "I thought your father had put
it away somewhere."

"Oh, he did," Ansy answered brightly. "In a file cabinet."

"You know you're not to look through his things. Anne, if he
found out he'd—"

"Don't worry. I'm very careful not to leave any evidence behind, like fingerprints. See?" She held up her hands; she wore
white cotton gloves, usually reserved for church.

I had to smile; my golden-braided daughter—the spitting
image of Heidi—was going through a Nancy Drew phase. "Oh,
I see. Well, please put it back and don't go through his things
again. Please. You know how he is."

"I know. But, Mother, really, this is you?" And she laughed.

"Yes, really, it is. Why are you laughing?"

"Well, because—I mean, really! You, a pilot, just like Father?"

"No, not just like Father, because he's—well, he's Father. But
after we were married, yes, I learned to fly. Oh, you know all
that—the trips we made to the Orient, and so on!"

"No. No, Mother, I don't." Ansy's eyes grew wide, and she
stopped laughing. "You never told me."

"Well, you probably learned about them at school, anyway—
didn't you? When you learned about Father?"

"No, the books only talk about him."

"Well, I was a pilot, too, and we made some very important flights together. I also happened to be the first licensed
female glider pilot in the United States." I pursed my mouth in
that prickly way I had; not sure with whom I was angrier, the

historians—or myself, for never sharing this part of me with my children.

"It's just so strange, to think of you like that," Ansy continued, laughing merrily. "I mean—look at you! You're, well—you're Mother. Father's the pilot, the hero. You take care of us, and the house, but to think of you up in the air, in your own little airplane!"

"I had one—my own little airplane. A little Curtiss. Your father bought it for me, although mostly we flew together in his plane, which was bigger. Mine was just a one-seater. We left it here when we moved to Europe." I sat down on the metal kitchen chair, remembering. "Out at the Guggenheims'. I suppose it's still there. When we moved back, somehow, I just never used it. I had the boys then, and soon you came along. And then the war, and Scott, and Reeve, and—well."

"When's the last time you flew like that?" Ansy sat upon the floor, cross-legged, in that fluid, boneless way of the young, and looked up to me.

"I don't recall. I really don't. Your father rarely flies like that anymore, either—it's all commercial airliners now, for the most part. Although I suppose he does some, for the Air Force, for testing, and you know—sometimes he takes you children up. But it's not like it used to be, back then, when we were the first. We flew all over the country, mapping out the routes that the commercial airliners all take. And we thought nothing of jumping into our plane to fly down to Washington, or up to New England—the way people jump into their cars today. It was what we did. We flew."

"Yes, but I mean—when did *you* last fly, alone?"

"Oh, goodness. I don't know—probably sometime in England, I suppose. I think I did fly solo, once or twice, while we were there. England is beautiful from the air." I remembered how green, mossy green and rolling, the land was; how sweet the neat little cottages were, the astonishing length of the hedgerows, seeming to cover the entire island in an orderly, if slightly serpentine, pattern.

"Do you think you could do it today? Do you think you'd remember?"

"I don't know. I suppose it would depend on the plane." *Could I?* I shut my eyes, remembering the preflight checklist, recalling the pull of the stick against my hand as I eased the plane gently into the air; the little Curtiss was very sensitive, I remembered. Not like the big plane, the Sirius. It had been an instinct, at one time—the ability to feel the craft, understand its tendency to bank right or left, to know how to navigate the currents.

These days, my instincts were centered around whether or not we had enough milk to last the week; how to light the pilot light beneath the boiler in the basement without risking an explosion; prioritizing the various broken hearts and wild crushes inevitable in a house full of teenagers.

"I doubt it," I admitted to my daughter, still seated, uncharacteristically eager to listen to me. Of all my children, my namesake was the one who knew, unerringly, which of my buttons to push. "And with the new radar—we didn't have that, you see, when I was flying. Nor control towers. And of course, there weren't all these planes in the sky, these big passenger planes. It was a simpler time."

"But it must have been scarier, too. You were pretty brave then, I bet."

"You don't think I'm brave now?" I narrowed my eyes at Ansy, who laughed again.

"Mother! You scream whenever you see a mouse!" Still laughing, she pushed herself up from the linoleum and took the pilot's license back, carefully inserting it into the envelope. "It's still pretty strange, though. I mean, it must have been so long ago. Because you're just a mom now, and that's all I can imagine you as. That's all."

She left, whistling blithely—unaware of the impact of her words.

But I never forgot them. To my children, I was just Mom. That was all. And before that, I had been Charles's wife, the bereaved mother of the slain child. That was all.

But before that, I had been a pilot. An adventurer. I had broken records—but I had forgotten about them. I had steered aircraft—but I didn't think I would know how to, anymore. I had soared across the sky, every bit as daring as Lucky Lindy himself, the one person in the world who could keep up with him.

Yet motherhood had brought me down to earth with a thud, and kept me there with tentacles made of diapers and tears and lullabies and phone calls and car pools and the sticky residue of hair spray and Barbasol all over the bathroom counter. Would I ever be able to soar again? Would I ever have the courage?

Did any woman?

Or did we exist only as others saw us? My daughter's unabashed mirth as she tried to imagine me an aviatrix, winging alone above the earth—I never forgot it. And as I spent long afternoons walking along the snow-white beach of Captiva Island, picking up shells just to put them in my pockets, for I was a person who liked to have the feel of something substantial in her pockets, this was the story I remembered. I saw myself through her eyes, I saw myself through Charles's eyes, always; I never looked into a mirror and saw myself through my own.

So I did, one evening after a couple of glasses of Dubonnet. I went into the tiny bathroom, and peered into the lopsided mirror above the vanity, and saw myself—a woman. With graying hair, cut for convenience because I had no time for primping. Brown eyes that slanted down at the edges, ever watchful, ever cautious, trying to anticipate my husband's demands. Olive skin, a bit wrinkled now, even leathery in places, no matter how much Pond's cold cream I slathered on, because of all those years flying in open cockpits so close to the sun. A slightly prim, pursed mouth, as if always holding something back, keeping something in; grief, I knew. Anger, I very much suspected. But perhaps joy, as well?

Who was this woman before me, her face imprinted with the expectations of others?

I was Mom. I was Wife. I was Tragedy. I was Pilot. They all were me, and I, them. That was a fate we could not escape, we women; we would always be called upon by others in a way men simply never were. But weren't we always, first and foremost—woman? Wasn't there strength in that, victory, clarity—in all the stages of a woman's life?

The Shells. That was the first title I imagined for a series of essays, the ideas of which I had had, in the back of my mind, for a few years now. I had played with the idea of comparing the stages of a woman's life with different shells; the Moon shell, the Double Sunrise, the Argonauta, a few others. Each perfect, each different, each serving a singular purpose; individually tempting but as a collection, something like a perfect banquet.

Or a perfect life. A woman's life, always changing, accommodating, then shedding, old duties for new; one person's expectations for another until finally, victoriously, emerging stronger. Complete.

I didn't finish the book on that vacation; it took me several trips to Captiva during the early 1950s to work it all out, and many months wrestling with it in my writing cabin.

Every time I sat down to write, I closed my eyes and said a prayer before beginning. And I didn't stop until I was done reassembling myself, piece by piece, on the page—jewels and shells and buttons and Cracker Jack prizes; medals and ribbons and Communion wafers. Swallowed tears that emerged now, twenty years later, as the palest, most translucent of pebbles—I held them up, and could see the beauty of the sun shining through the delicate layers, grateful for them, at last.

I worked with the myopic concentration of an artisan; I would not be hurried, I resisted Charles's suggestion that I set a schedule, a certain amount of words every day, as he had done. I took my own time, found my own way, lingering over words, searching for imagery. I rebuilt myself as a woman wise, understanding, at peace; I rebuilt myself on the page, praying that I could rebuild myself in life as well. Knowing that if I did, it would be the most courageous thing I had ever done. For I knew my husband too well; I knew that he wanted me to succeed, to be strong and brave, only in the abstract.

In practicality, he needed me to remain weak. Content to look at the world through his goggles, not my own.

Right before Mother died, in 1954, I spent an afternoon with her. She had suffered a stroke that robbed her of her speech and memory, but a few days before the end, she exhibited signs of a miraculous recovery. In her suddenly searching brown eyes, I could see her clear mind once more, and I was so eager to say something to her that I blurted out, "You're my hero."

"Anne?" She turned to me with a crooked smile; only one side of her face had movement.

"I said you're my hero. You are. Because of how strong you've been since Daddy and Elisabeth died, how you reinvented yourself."

Mother shook her head impatiently. "You need to . . . stop looking for heroes, Anne." Her speech was slow, slurred, but understandable. "Only the weak need . . . heroes . . . and heroes need . . . those around them to remain weak. You're . . . not weak."

I remembered those words. I knew they were true, all of them. True about me, and true about Charles. I brought them out, every now and then, as I kept working—on both the manuscript and myself. And, perhaps on my definition of my marriage. No, my *prayer* for my marriage; a marriage of two equals. With separate—but equally valid—views of the world; shared goggles no more, but looking at the same scenery, at the same time.

All the while I worked, I raised my children until one day, to my utter surprise, they were both finished. And I emerged from my cabin with a book; my book. My *Gift from the Sea*.

I couldn't wait to share it with the world. But most of all—

I couldn't wait to share it with my husband.

Now the surf is raging outside; I rush to shut the doors and windows to muffle it. Then I turn back to his bed.

"I don't understand!" I pound the mattress, forcing him to stay awake, stay *here*. "The house in Darien was your idea. The children—*our* children! Why could they never keep your attention except to be criticized? You wounded them then, and you're wounding them now. Forget about me. What about Jon? Land? Scott? The girls? Did you ever stop to think how they will react to this?"

"It has nothing to do with you, or them. You—you are my family. Our children are my heirs. The other women, I won't say they meant nothing. But they aren't you."

"How old? How old are they?"

"I don't know. Young. They are young—or they were, when we first met."

"Younger than me?"

"Yes."

"Is that why you chose them? Because they're young—because they're German?" I want to laugh; but it's far too tragic. After all these years, it still comes back to this? A man who has spent over thirty years trying to change the notion that he's a Nazi—having a secret German love nest? "Your own master race—I should have known! Was I not pure enough? Our children not good enough for you?"

"Anne, you're hysterical." Charles coughs, his entire body racked with the effort, and I hand him the water before the nurse stationed in the next room can hear. He sips, his Adam's apple, so prominent now, sliding up and down, and when he waves his hand, I take the water away. "A man can still spread his seed, no matter his age. That's all I did. I followed my instincts."

"That's such a typically male thing to say."

"Are you telling me you were happy all those years? Are you telling me you never desired companionship when I was gone?"

Now he looks like the old Charles, the healthy, untouchable Charles; his gaze is clear and precise as it pierces right through me.

"I never wanted you to leave in the first place," I reply truthfully, not flinching from his gaze, even as I ponder my own secret.

And wonder, for the first time, if he's ever guessed it.

CHAPTER 18

I T'S THE QUIET THAT YOU NOTICE, first, when the children begin to leave.

And not just the practical fact that the record player is unplugged, the radio turned off. Not simply the lack of some instrument being practiced behind a closed door. Not merely the silent phone, the absence of stampeding feet up and down stairs, the slamming of doors, the constant rush of water in the bathroom.

It's more than that—and less than that, too. It's a hum, a vibration that leaves when they leave. For all of a sudden the very air in the house is slower, duller; gentler against your eardrum.

First Jon left, to go to Stanford in 1950. Dutiful as ever, he came home every vacation, anxious to see the wreckage his siblings had done in his absence and to put it right again. But he also married young, in 1954. He did not come home so much after that.

Land followed him west to Stanford two years later. Our last son, Scott, burst out of the house like a caged animal released; he started at Amherst in 1959, but it was soon apparent he was the one who would have to learn life's lessons the hard way.

Scott rarely came home for the holidays, and I never even looked for him to. His teenage years had been typical—had his last name not been Lindbergh. But Charles simply could not understand the fluctuating grades, the late-night pranks, the minor brushes with authority. He could not understand the lack of focus, the inability to see past tomorrow. Whenever the two of them were together, it was explosive; the girls tiptoed about, trying not to get hit by the debris.

I, however, did not tiptoe.

"You can't talk to him that way," I shouted at Charles, my hands balled into fists, my heart wrecked with pain for my son, who had just been called a lazy idiot by his father. "Words like that can never be forgotten! He'll carry that with him his entire life!"

Charles remained maddeningly calm. "Of course you'd defend him. He's just like you. Your whole family, you Morrows— all so stubborn and perverse. Had I only known—"

"What? Known what?"

"The things you didn't tell me when we were courting. Dwight and his problems. Elisabeth."

"Elisabeth? What about Elisabeth?"

"Her weak heart. Her emotional state."

"Because she felt? Because she loved? Oh, don't make this about my family. We're talking about *your* son."

"It's only that it's no surprise to me he's such a mess, given his genetic history. Still, I'm determined to make him into a real Lindbergh."

"And what does that mean? Someone who has *no* feeling?"

"It means I have to be tough on him, just like my father was tough on me. You're his mother, and you coddle him. Well, your work is done now. I'm his father."

"Did your father toughen you up by making you feel worthless and, and—less? Was he that cruel, as cruel as you are? Tell me. I want to know, because you never tell me anything. You go off and leave me here to raise your children, and you tell me nothing about your life. I don't know anything about your childhood. I don't know what you did yesterday. I don't know what you're going to do tomorrow. I'm your wife—talk to me! We used to, don't you remember? Don't you remember talking over things, when you'd come home from working in the city with Carrel? Don't you remember our conversations on our flights, how much we shared? What happened to that? I miss it, I miss it so much that—"

"You're hysterical, Anne." Still he remained unperturbed, giving outward evidence, once more, of his superiority; he actually picked up a magazine, settled into a chair, and began to read. As if I were simply an annoying fly, buzzing around his head.

I yanked the magazine out of his hands.

"No, I'm finally pushing back," I hissed. "You told me to go find my voice—well, I did. I'm using it now, or can you not hear me, up on that pedestal of yours?"

He didn't respond; we glared at each other for what seemed like the entire length of our marriage, right there—spreading, like a noxious stain, between us, pushing us farther and farther apart. Once, we'd shared the same tiny cockpit for days on end, and he didn't mind. He'd made room for me, even though it meant he had to sit cramped, his long legs twisted and bent. He never once complained.

Now it seemed as if he had to keep entire continents between us. And I had no idea what had changed; I only knew I was the only one of us who seemed to care.

Charles finally rose from his chair, still deliberate, untouchable, and went outside to the garage, where I knew he would remain all night. Lately, when he was home, that's where he spent most of his time, working on some engine or another—something orderly, mechanical, full of gadgets and gears and springs and not emotions; something he could understand.

I crumpled the magazine and threw it away, although I didn't follow him. I nursed my hurt and honed it, just as I had as a child when my father called me "the disciplined one." I carried my grievance about until I couldn't even feel its weight; it felt as much a part of me as the old dirndl skirt I wore when I tramped about outside. I forgot what it was like to be near my husband and not seethe or grind my teeth, even as I couldn't help but weep each time he left, wishing he'd ask me, just once, to come with him.

But I suffered the most for my children, especially Scott. He withdrew even from me; during family celebrations he was there, but he wasn't, sitting, watching; brooding so, you could almost see the tension radiating from him in cartoonish waves.

When he left for school, I knew it would be a very long time before I saw him again. And I knew it was my fault, as well as Charles's. Had I known more about my husband's childhood— still cloaked in mystery, he never would tell me more than he had early in our marriage—would I have been able to protect my own children from his demons? Had I found my voice earlier, would I have been able to ask the right questions, speak up for them, too?

It was too late now. We were all shattered into pieces, pierced by that unflinching steel gaze that judged us all and found us lacking. I could only hope my children would one day be able to reassemble themselves, as I had only begun to do, into the people they wanted to be. And not the people *he* wanted them to be.

The girls were easier, although I despaired to see my own compliant nature so obvious in my daughters, especially Ansy.

She had wanted to go to Paris, to the Sorbonne, but Charles wouldn't hear of it. So she made do at Radcliffe, pointedly, but sweetly, not choosing Smith. She struggled so much to separate herself from me, but it was never a violent wrenching. It was gentler, more persistent; like the endless slapping of waves against a rock, wearing it down over time.

Reeve, the easiest (and most spoiled, we all knew it, were all responsible for it, even Charles), followed her sister to Radcliffe. But even before she left for school, she was never home; the most social of my children, she was always vacationing with friends, sleeping over, going to parties.

And I was alone. For the first time since before I married Charles. I'd thought marriage would mean I'd never be lonely. Now I knew: Marriage breeds its own special brand of loneliness, and it's far more cruel. You miss more, because you've known more.

The calendar—once so full of dates and appointments and concerts and practices—was increasingly just row after row of empty white squares. One morning I picked up a pencil to write something in—a trip to the grocery store, maybe, so it didn't look so dauntingly vacant, but then dropped it. Charles was away, as usual, and I had no idea when he would be back. The older boys were gone by then, Scott was at camp, Anne was spending the summer with her aunt Con, Reeve was vacationing with a friend. Determined not to feel sorry for myself, I decided to go for a walk. I left the tidy, orderly house—strange, how every sink and appliance decided to behave beautifully now that I had little use for them—and marched toward my cabin, far down the hill, in that little dip of land.

But I paused in the middle of the yard and looked around. It was June, and I wore a blouse, dungarees, loafers. The saltwater spray from the ocean far below occasionally flew up and got caught by the wind, misting me gently. The leaves were full, canopies of green splintered with golden rays of sun. A couple of rusty bicycles leaned against a shed, my garden beckoned, a hammock, strewn with paperback novels, half-eaten apples, waved gently between two trees.

This had been—still was—a good home in which to raise children, I decided, and allowed myself the warmth of satisfaction. I had raised these children, these two adults, three adolescents who never failed to astonish me with their opinions, their fully formed personalities, their rebellions large and small. There had been a time when I thought I could never love a child again; there had been a time when I couldn't imagine how to raise one past the age of twenty months. Always, I had an image of a child, and a birthday cake with one candle, and then—someone whisking it away, out of my arms, and having to start all over again.

But I had done it. I had seen them through teething and toddling and adolescence; heartache, tears, stupid jokes and silly laughter. Here, in this strip of land where Charles had hidden us away, only occasionally remembering to come and find us, I had raised a family. Me. By myself.

I knew, finally, that Charles would never really come back to me here. Especially now that the din and racket of children were dwindling, not explosive enough to find its way up to the stratosphere, where he, and only he, resided. He was back to where he had started; the Lone Eagle, jettisoning anything that might weigh him down. Even me.

So I began to build a life for myself. It wasn't easy. I felt guilty—I, who had written a book that urged women to do just this! I, who had sounded so strong on the page; at times I couldn't recognize my own words, because I was still so often afraid in my life. Afraid to anger my husband. Afraid to disappoint him.

Afraid to recognize that he had disappointed me.

My guilt at my success, my need to be his "good girl," combined with my anger at no longer being invited to share his world, no longer being quite so necessary to my children; for a time I found solace in psychoanalysis with the doctor who was treating Dwight.

Charles punished me by moving his belongings out of our bedroom before flying off again, leaving me behind.

But the analysis helped; gradually I was able to release my anger, my grievances, setting them free in the wind that blew up from the sea outside my door. I also released any notions of us settling down in our golden years, or flying together once more, just the two of us.

The next time he remembered to come home, he sat across from me at the dinner table, empty chairs on either side. When he asked me what was for dessert, I told him instead that I wanted to sell the place.

"It's too big for me, alone."

"You're not alone." He actually looked surprised.

"Charles!" I had to laugh. Where did he think the children were? Hiding somewhere in the attic? "Of course I'm alone, more and more. Oh, yes, technically we have three teenagers still at home, but they're never here. The older boys are gone for good now."

"They'll be home for holidays."

"Yes, for a little while, but do I stay here, shut away from everything, until then? Just waiting for them—and for you?"

He pursed his lips. "Anne, you know I have work to do."

"I know you say that, and I know you're gone all the time. I wish I knew what you did and where you went, but you never tell me." I wasn't goading him or accusing him, I was simply stating a fact.

"Of course I do."

"No, you don't. You say you have a meeting, or a conference, or a route to inspect. That's all. You don't give me your itinerary, you don't tell me when you'll be home; I have no way of contacting you except through Pan Am. But you expect me to be here, waiting for you, anyway."

"Did your psychiatrist tell you to say that?"

"No, and don't even try to pretend you know what a psychiatrist does. This is me talking. Anne. Your wife."

He continued to eat, and I had to wonder if he'd heard; he was growing deaf, after all those years of sitting in noisy airplanes. He had always looked down on those—like me—who put cotton in their ears. "It diminishes the experience," he'd snort. But he was too proud now to admit he'd been wrong.

"You don't know what it means to me, to know that you're here," he said after a moment, his voice soft and unexpectedly appealing, and I knew that he had heard me, after all. He came around the table and pulled out the chair next to me, taking my hand in his, and I couldn't prevent a gasp at the touch of flesh against my own. It had been so long since he had touched me; I hadn't realized how long. Days, weeks, months; endless, yearning Arabian nights. It had been ages since *anyone* had touched me; I didn't even get the halfhearted hugs of teenagers anymore.

"It's precisely because you're here," Charles continued, murmuring, low and throaty like a perfectly tuned engine, "and that you've *always* been here, running things, keeping us all going—that I can do the work I need to. I couldn't accomplish half so much without you, Anne. I thought you knew that. You're my crew."

Damn him! I retrieved my hand, pushed myself away from the table and stomped into the kitchen, where I stared out the window. Oh, he knew exactly what to say, and when to say it. Just when I wanted, *needed*, to believe that he didn't understand the workings of my heart so I could take it back for good—he proved, once more, that he could master anything.

I picked up a chocolate layer cake, store bought, even though

I knew he didn't like that. But I was used to simple eating these days; poached eggs, toast, soup. With so little to do, I no longer employed a full-time cook. Then I strode back to the dinner table; he had returned to his seat at the head. I plopped the cake in front of him. Charles frowned, but sliced into it, anyway.

"What are we going to do, Charles?" I took my seat again, and carefully folded my napkin, placing it next to my coffee cup. "Realistically. Logistically—that, I know you understand. I don't want to stay here alone. If you want me to remain at your beck and call, waiting for you occasionally to remember me, I can very well do that somewhere else."

"Anne, you're being ridiculous. I fly—I work. That's what I do."

"That's what I used to do, too," I reminded him. But what did I do now? I waited, fretted, longed, simmered. Meanwhile, I received letters from women envying me my perfect marriage— the one I had conjured up in the pages of my book. My prayer, which was, as yet, unanswered. Perhaps because I had wasted too many years praying to the wrong deity.

"It's different now." Charles was warming up to one of his favorite themes: the Dangers of the Modern World. "The world is changing—too fast, I think. Someday, I'll want to step back and simplify. I need to know that this place will be here, then. I need—" His voice faltered, and he took a sip of milk to disguise it. "I need to know where you are," he continued, pushing at his cake with his fork. "I just need to know where you are, and I like to know that you are here, safe, where I put you. I would think that you, of all people, would understand that."

I opened my mouth, but my heart was suddenly in my throat, preventing speech. I slumped back in my seat, stunned.

I'd never told him about having to explain to our children, one by one, about their murdered brother, after they first found out about him in school. I'd never told him about the box of pictures I still kept beneath my bed.

But my husband had not moved on as thoroughly as he had tried to convince us both he had. And I hurt for him, just as I had hurt for my children at his hands; for the first time, I saw myself in the stronger role. Anger and resentment aside, I had healed; I shared my grief with others who wrote me to share theirs—countless women over the years, seeking my counsel. And I had loved our surviving children, fully participated in their lives, risking my heart over and over again for them.

But Charles—

The distance he put between himself and us; the pushing, the cajoling—was it his way of protecting himself? For so long I had wanted to believe that our baby's death had not sundered us; I had thought it had drawn us together, made us rely upon each other, only. But now, I saw with eyes as clear as my husband's, that it hadn't.

I couldn't help him now, not even if he'd asked me to, which he never would. Once, maybe; once upon a long time ago. But not now.

Sipping my coffee, I chose my next words very carefully.

"We don't have to sell," I said. "I have money, of course, from Mother and Daddy. We can keep this place until Reeve has graduated, at least, and then—for the future, for holidays. I might like to rent an apartment in the city, though. I would like to be closer to people, to the theater, shopping—things like that."

"What on earth would you want to be closer to all that for?" He was genuinely surprised. He laid his fork down, peering at me as if he'd never seen me before—and I was reminded of how he used to look at me, back when we were courting. Clinically, scientifically; as if he needed to try to figure out the inner workings of my brain.

I smiled at the memory, and his face flushed red as he looked away again, caught. "Charles, I am fifty years old. I was a city girl when you met me, remember? I have never lived in a home of my own choosing. You've always chosen. *Your* life, *your* fame, have always dictated where I live. I do think it's time that I get to live for myself, don't you? Choose my own friends, at least?"

"You've read your own book, haven't you?" He frowned, but I caught the admiring little gleam in his eyes, and now it was my turn to blush.

To his credit, Charles had been nothing but proud—if slightly puzzled—by the success of *Gift from the Sea*. He'd even consented to pose for a pictorial for *Time* magazine when it came out. I'd only had to remind him once how I'd done the same thing for *his* book.

"Perhaps," I admitted. "I am serious, though."

"I know you are. I've never known you not to be that. Well, I suppose that sounds like a reasonable plan. Are you sure this is what you want?"

"Yes, this is what I want."

He stared at me, hard; I stared back. Once, a lifetime ago, our gazes had met and it was immediately electric, powerful—so powerful that it frightened us both. There were times, even now, when our eyes would meet and I would feel a thrill jolt through me, shocking my entire being into overdrive.

But this gaze was not like that; it was an assessment. An acknowledgment that I was taking a step that neither of us had ever thought I would, but that he had been pushing me toward, unconsciously, for years now. He'd trained me, he'd taught me—too well, I could almost hear him thinking.

Finally, I *was* strong. I was able. Able to separate my life from his; able to separate myself, from him. Like all surgical procedures, it would not be without pain and regret.

We continued to eat without talking. Silence, after all, had been the thing that brought us together, all those years ago; he'd said he'd never met a girl so comfortable not talking, as I was.

But now that I had found my voice, I wanted to use it; I had the feeling that once I started talking, I might never shut up. And to that end, I wanted to find someone who wanted to listen to me as much as I wanted to talk to him.

And I knew, sadly, finally, that that someone was never going to be my husband.

CHAPTER 19

1958

'D LEFT IT IN A STACK of mail on the table in the entryway. Later, I had to wonder if I'd done it on purpose, but then, that's where I always left the mail. I'd glanced at the envelope, saw my name in the familiar handwriting, *Anne Lindbergh,* and smiled, then left it there—a treat for later, I supposed I thought. After Ansy and I returned from the city.

My daughter was about to leave for Radcliffe and she needed a new wardrobe. Of my two daughters, she was the one who was the most feminine; she was tiny and blond, with eyes that looked mischievous because of the way they turned up at the ends. But she was not mischievous; she was the most solemn of my children, even more solemn than Jon.

She was also the one who hated being a Lindbergh the most; the one who sobbed when a reporter wrote a story about her classroom picnic when she was ten, simply because she was Charles Lindbergh's daughter. The one who, when she was a teenager, cut off her long blond braids because a newspaper article mentioned them. And because her name happened to be Anne Lindbergh, she got double the dose of unwanted, reflected glory; every Mother's Day, some magazine wanted to interview the two of us, the "two Annes."

I wondered if that was why, when she got over her adolescent embarrassment, she made herself so determinedly fashionable, so delightedly girlish. Those were two traits I had never possessed, and these were ways she could establish her own identity, separate from mine.

That afternoon we'd burst into the house, bags hanging from our arms, and went our separate ways until dinner; she, to try on everything all over again; me, to collapse for half an hour. Shopping was exhausting; I was too much my own mother's daughter. I preferred to order five of the same kind of dress or sweater or skirt in different colors, and be done with it. But Ansy had tried on every outfit she saw, even if she had no intention of buying it, just for fun.

I removed my hat, my gloves—my daughter had pronounced them so "terribly dowdy, Mother." It was true that I hadn't bought a new hat in years, although some of the ones I'd seen today—smaller, with darling wisps of veils, little in the way of flowers or feathers—had looked very tempting. Maybe I'd buy one next time I was in the city; next week he and I were going to the theater, then dinner after—

I remembered my letter; my reward. A sly, womanly smile nudged my lips—I caught a glimpse of myself in the mirror, and I was startled by how *ripe* I looked, how my eyes sparkled, my skin seemed to glow. I ran back to the entry table, but the letter was not there—although all my other mail was, bills, a few letters from friends and readers—all addressed to "Mrs. Charles Lindbergh."

"Now, where on earth?" I muttered, turning around to go back to my bedroom.

But suddenly Anne was standing before me, her face red—a piece of paper in her hand.

"What are you—oh." It was the letter. I stared thoughtfully

at her for a long moment. Then I said, "I don't believe that was meant for you."

"I—it said 'Anne Lindbergh,' and I thought it meant me, so—"

"So you opened it." I continued to gaze at my daughter, whose face reflected an avalanche of emotions, one tumbling right after the other—guilt, horror, anger, disbelief.

While I was icy calm. Not one bit ashamed—and this did not altogether surprise me. Once, long ago—before I became the aviator's wife—hadn't I wanted to be an old lady with a mysterious smile, remembering the scandalous affairs of her youth? It was that girl, that passionate young girl, to whom the letter was addressed.

And it was that girl who stood erect, chin lifted, eyes gleaming with pride and triumph, when confronted with indisputable evidence of her passion. Evidence in the hands of her own daughter.

"Mother, are you—are you in *love*? With Dr. Atchley?"

"Yes," I said, then held my hand out. Ansy, her own hand trembling, placed the letter in my palm. "Now, have you tried your clothes on? Are you sure everything fits?"

"Yes," she whispered. Then we retreated to our separate rooms. And, both excellent pupils of the best teacher in the world—

We never discussed the matter again.

AFTER THAT DINNER WITH CHARLES, I made my peace with the house in Darien. Once, I thought I had to leave him in order to be free; now, I realized, I only had to stay. So I started to invite friends out to spend the weekends. Male friends, mostly. I didn't think it was a conscious decision, not at first, but soon, to my delight, I had acquired a coterie of admirers; men whom I had known, always, but never seen, dazzled as I was by the shining light of my hero husband.

Now, breaking free from his spell—the spell I had helped him cast—I looked beyond and saw these men, and summoned them. Enthroned upon my cushioned chair like the Queen of Sheba, no longer in the shadow of anyone—not my sister, not my husband—I thrilled to the sensation of being beguiled, instead of beguiling. I nodded thoughtfully, I smiled mysteriously. My laughter purred, my voice acquired a honeyed huskiness.

For the first time in my life, I purchased silk lingerie, luxuriating in the rich sensation against my skin as I reclined, a cocktail in my hand; giddily imagining the astonishment, the tortured gasps, if I allowed it to be discovered.

Corliss Lamont, who had carried a torch for me since we were children, came when I beckoned, eagerly reciting eccentric poetry while I did my best to keep a straight face. But I flushed when he gazed at me in his eager, puppy-dog-like way. So I asked him to recite more.

Alan Valentine, an academic, former president of the University of Rochester; he found his way to my terrace, where we would sip drinks and discuss politics and literature and, oh, just about anything we wanted; there were no subjects off-limits and my skin tingled when he grasped my hand to make a point, or brushed the hair out of my eyes if I argued too excitedly.

And Dana Atchley. He, too, came to my terrace—*come into my parlor, said the spider!* I was the spider, casting an enchanting web about these men who seemed to think I needed rescuing. Maybe they were right. Although I never allowed more than worshipful gazes, passionate letters. I enjoyed playing, teasing— *imagining*, just as I used to when I was a young girl. I also enjoyed praying at night for forgiveness, secure in the knowledge I'd not really done anything in need of forgiving.

Until Dana. My dearest Dana.

When did it start with Dana? Emotionally, with my operation, I suppose; the one to remove my gallbladder. Right before I went under the anesthesia, alone, vulnerable, sure that I was about to die, I reached for his hand because my husband wasn't there. "Call me Anne," I whispered, convinced that he was the last person who would ever say my name. "Please?"

"All right. Anne." And he grabbed my hand, instinctively knowing I needed to feel someone warm and alive and reassuring. His eyes—behind his thick glasses—were the kindest I had ever seen, the most sympathetic. They did not judge; they did not challenge. They simply saw. And found beauty in everything; even a frightened housewife with unkempt hair and a sheet for a dress.

Up until that point, we had been "Mrs. Lindbergh" and "Dr. Atchley." Afterward, we were "Anne" and "Dana." After my regular appointments, we found ourselves lingering for hours in his office at Columbia-Presbyterian, talking about everything. Once, I even scolded him for spending time with me instead of his wife. "Don't do this," I cautioned him, after we'd exclaimed at the lateness of the hour. "Go home to her. Don't make your work your life."

"I'd hardly call this work, Anne." He smiled. But then he removed his glasses and rubbed the bridge of his nose. "It's hell at home. You don't know."

Oh, we discussed—everything! Everything our hearts were weary of containing. My writing, his patients, the world, our children. It didn't seem wrong to discuss our children with each other, at least not then. We were friends, we assured each other solemnly. Friends who corresponded almost on a daily basis, sending letters back and forth. His "blue pills," he called mine, for I wrote on a light blue stationery.

As friends do, we even sometimes vacationed together with our spouses; Charles liked and admired him, although neither of us really cared much for his wife. The children all knew and loved him as the family doctor. And we might have gone on that way; he might have remained one of my small coterie of chaste admirers, those men who knew that they could never really compete with Lucky Lindy, but enjoyed sipping cocktails on his terrace with his neglected, charming wife and wondering, "what if?"

But there came a time when I wanted more; my skin longed to be caressed by something warmer than silk lingerie. I wanted, I desired, I sought—so I took. I took more than I thought I was allowed, for the first time in my life; no longer the disciplined little girl my father admired, or the obedient wife my husband trained. I stepped through the looking glass to find the passionate woman who had been waiting for me, all these years.

Buoyed by the slightly tipsy flattery of a few middle-aged men as unhappy in their marriages as I was in mine, one day I took the train into New York and checked in at the Plaza. I came to the city frequently, of course, but it seemed that always I was either accompanied by a child or lunching with Con at the Cosmopolitan Club.

For the first time, however, I truly felt on my own, an adult, with adult decisions to make. My heart beat fast, as if on a grand adventure. *Silly,* I scolded myself; *you've visited here a thousand times before.* But not since I was a girl, coming in on the weekend from Smith with my college friends, had I felt so defiantly independent. I was going to rent an apartment, and even though Charles knew and approved, still I felt reckless and daring. And I had the entire city from which to choose! I threw myself into apartment hunting as I'd never thrown myself into house hunting before, when Charles had made most of the decisions.

This time, I was in charge, and I loved it. I loved every minute of it—the running up and down stairs with the tireless apartment agent, the nights spent going over brochures, the excitement of putting a bid in and having it accepted; a two-bedroom apartment with a dollhouse kitchen on the Upper West Side, just a block away from Central Park. Then the decorating—the picking out of curtains, wallpaper, furniture—this last, in Charles's opinion, a luxury since we had more than enough surplus furniture in Connecticut. Why didn't I just take some?

Why, indeed? Because I wanted a fresh start. I didn't tell him that, however; I explained that with the cost of shipping it wouldn't be that much less than buying new. Then I assured him I was keeping track of every expense in my accounting book. That seemed to mollify him.

Soon all was ready, and the first person I wanted to show it to was Charles. I felt, surprisingly, like a bride waiting to be carried over the threshold. It astonished me that still, after all that had happened, he was the first person I wanted to share everything with; good and bad. Somehow, a thing never seemed real until he saw it or experienced it, too—and then told me how to think about it.

But he didn't come when I invited him. He had some Pan Am conference in Germany. He would visit soon, though, he promised. Meanwhile, would I remember to clean out the utility room, as the last time he was home he had noticed some old boxes of soap on a shelf in the corner?

No. No, I would not.

So I spent the first evening in my apartment alone, curled up on my new sofa nursing a solitary glass of wine as I gazed out over the city: the lights, the traffic, the bustle, the verve. All day I had felt queasy, a bit drowsy and thick as a terrible feeling crept over me; the feeling that I'd made a foolish, irreversible mistake. What right did I have, to strike out on my own at my age? What was I thinking? To live for oneself is a terrifying prospect; there is comfort in martyrdom, and for years, my hair shirt had been more comfortable than the silk brassiere I was currently wearing.

Then I heard voices outside my door, disappearing down the hall toward the elevator; the voices of people going out for the evening. All of a sudden I couldn't—*wouldn't*—sit there feeling sorry for myself. So I picked up the phone and—knowing full well what would transpire next—I called Dana.

He came over, and we sat in the growing shadows of evening, neither one of us turning on the lamp; content to have the lights from the city illuminate us as we bent our heads together, for the first time finding ourselves without words, only glances and touches.

Did I feel guilt? Shame? Regret?

Of course I did. I was married; he was married. We both had children that we vowed never to hurt; I couldn't even bear to have pictures of mine in my apartment, after that night.

Oh, but I was *ready*. After a lifetime of being with a man who did not want to hear me speak unless I was mimicking his own views or assuring him he was right, I was ready. More than that, I was desperate to share the parts of me that Charles never wanted to know were there. The *weak* parts: that was how he viewed them and it took me a very long time not to view sympathy, grief, doubt, the ability to be moved to tears by love and happiness and sadness and music—as weak, despicable traits.

Dana taught me that the ability to grieve deeply also meant that a person had the capacity to love deeply, laugh deeply, *live* deeply—and that this was a capacity to be cherished. And that was, finally, why I loved him—because he never complained when I had a headache or changed my mind about something. He never shut down when I revealed my fears, my worries. He never tried to make me feel less, weaker, than he was—because he shared his own emotions with me, as well.

This honesty—this total freedom; it was as if I'd been living in one of those oxygen-deprived chambers that Charles used to test in the war. Until finally, I passed out. And when I awoke, it was to flowers and music and warm brown eyes—and all the air, all the space in the world; not just what was visible in the sky. I believed then that I could never get enough of it.

We were discreet, and it helped that I'd made few adult friends since my marriage. It also helped that the children were far too absorbed in their own lives to imagine I had one of my own.

Dana and I began to gather around us a small circle of his trusted friends, those who understood the nature of his marriage. Although most were astonished to discover the nature of *mine*. And I found, to my surprise and delight, that I was something of a literary star; I became a sought-after guest now suddenly available for dinner parties.

Of course, I knew my publisher was pleased with *Gift from the Sea*. It was continuing to go into extra printings, in both hardcover and paperback. I received lovely, warm letters from women all over the world. They wrote thanking me, asking me how I knew what they had been going through, assuring me that I was a friend for life.

Tucked away in Connecticut, I had not had a chance to taste the literary life—the life I had imagined back at Smith, when I had fancied myself, perhaps, a second Edna St. Vincent Millay or a member of the Algonquin Round Table. So it was with some disbelief, but mainly pure joy, that I found myself invited to speak at banquets and fund-raisers, or to give readings at libraries or wonderfully dusty little bookshops in the Village. I was asked not because I was Mrs. Charles Lindbergh, the aviator's wife; I was asked because I was Anne Morrow Lindbergh, the latest literary sensation.

I rejoiced in every minute of it. And only occasionally did I wish that Charles was there to witness my triumph.

Dana rarely attended these events as my escort—I had other married male friends who were happy to step in—but he was always there as part of our circle of friends, and when the evening was over we'd all go back to my apartment, where Dana would sit in a special chair near the fireplace, and I would sit in my special chair opposite, and we all would talk and laugh and play games through the night. My intellect, my wit—I'd forgotten I'd even possessed them, and they were dull and neglected, to be sure. But in the company of others who prized thought over action, laughter over brooding, they blossomed and sharpened. My tongue fairly tripped with sparkling phrases, insightful comments. Once, I looked in a mirror in the middle of a game of charades; I was smiling that carefree grin, the one that used to look so unfamiliar in photographs. I laughed; finally, the face I presented to the public was the one I wore in private. Charles had done the same thing, only he had become a stone monument over time. I had become a real person. A *happy* person.

Sometimes, Dana would be the last of our friends to depart, and it would not be until after breakfast the next morning.

"You have no idea how beautiful you are," he breathed into my ear the first time we made love. I was terrified and transported, both; to be touched by another man's hands, not Charles's? To be looked at, examined, all my flaws—my too-round breasts, heavy with age; my pouchy stomach, after six pregnancies; my thighs, though lean, now dimpled with cellulite. And my scars— but of course he knew *those* better than anyone, more intimately than Charles, even, and it was that moment, when he ran his fore-finger gently, teasingly, along the scar from my gallbladder op-eration, so close, so dangerously close, to the most tender part of me—

That was the moment I was transported. I stopped comparing him to Charles physically, because he could never compare, and it wasn't fair to him, or to me. I simply gave myself up to his lov-ing, insistent examination of my entire body, and, frighteningly voracious, found myself unable to stop examining his. And it was the differences that excited me; different hands probing, different lips bruising, different sounds, different smells, different meth-ods—

My body had been yearning for a change as desperately as my heart had. For I responded with a passion that first surprised, then enflamed Dana; that night, two middle-aged people who had each, in their own way, thought themselves beyond the pleasures of the flesh discovered that they weren't, after all.

That night, I slept in his arms. I had never slept in a man's arms before. This was not something that my husband ever al-lowed me, not even early in our marriage.

I discovered that there is no pleasure sweeter than timing your breath to match another's until you both rose and fell at the same pace, drifting, drifting along together—finding peace, everlast-ing.

The only sadness I allowed myself was the realization that it had taken me over fifty years to find this out. And when at last I did, it wasn't with my husband.

CHARLES NEVER SUSPECTED—at least, that was what I told my-self. How could he? He continued to drop in and out of my life like an annoying mosquito, on his way to Washington or from the

West Coast or across to Europe—Pan Am business kept him going to Germany quite a lot—or, more puzzling, to places like the Philippines, the Galapagos Islands, the Australian outback. Occasionally he summoned me, declaring it was time we had a vacation together, and I went, keeping up, grinning for the occasional photographers—fewer and fewer as the years went on; acting the role of the aviator's wife once more. Counting the days until I could shrug it off and return to what was now my real life with Dana.

Occasionally the children accompanied us on one of Charles's enforced family outings. These always happened to be in some Godforsaken jungle or rain forest where we had to sleep in tents and use outhouses, and follow him on endless hikes through humidity and bugs as big as pigeons.

"It's good to explore worlds different from our own," he declared, even as sweat soaked through his khaki shirt and he slapped at mosquitoes. "Isn't this wonderful, for us all to get away like this? This is how people should live!"

One by one, the children married—I almost thought out of desperation, so they would have a good reason to excuse themselves from these miserable "vacations." Charles and I showed up at weddings, playing the role of proud parents; he was more and more uncomfortable with any kind of spotlight, barely concealing a scowl when people fawned over him, even if those people were his new in-laws. I found myself soothing ruffled feathers as expertly as my mother once had.

Civilization, Charles said, with a disgusted grunt, wanting no more of it. Once he had pored over scientific manuals; now he read Thoreau. If he hadn't been Charles Lindbergh, most would have called him an eccentric old coot.

I had always issued a standing invitation for him to stay with me in the apartment, just as he had asked, but he only took me up on it once, in the late fifties. His flight overseas had been delayed and so, for once, we both found ourselves in the city. Absurdly, I was beside myself with excitement; he had never before seen it and, fool that I was, I still craved his approval in some stubborn, uncooperative—and childish—part of my heart. So I bustled about, feeling like a little girl playing house, ordering in a lovely dinner, arranging flowers, inviting some of my most trusted friends, those who would be least likely to irritate Charles.

With only a shiver of shame—and anticipation—I included Dana.

Charles sat, stonily silent, throughout the evening as we all talked about music and theater and harmless gossip. Even after I deftly steered the conversation to airplanes and science—Sputnik had just been launched, using the same rocket science Charles had championed with Robert Goddard—he barely contributed, his answers only a mumble, and he rubbed his eyes tiredly, like a small child forced to stay up past his bedtime.

My friends flashed me sad, sympathetic smiles behind his back. Dana was unusually tight-lipped, and unusually gallant, in the face of Charles's sullen presence; he kept rising whenever I ran to the kitchen to refill drinks, and offered repeatedly to help me find things I had misplaced, like the corkscrew, or the box of matches I used to light the fire.

"Didn't you put them in the coffee table drawer?" Dana asked, before clamping his mouth shut and turning white.

Charles, however, did not appear to have heard, and I realized that I could have embraced Dana right in front of him, torn off his clothes and had him right on the living room carpet, and Charles would not have noticed. Charles Lindbergh could never see himself as a cuckold, and I should have been relieved.

I was not. Shaking with barely suppressed rage, I didn't even bother to frown at Dana, whose eyes were dark with guilt and fear.

Finally everyone left, far earlier than planned. My friends— all except Dana—kissed me on the cheek as they went out the door. After they were gone, Charles finally came to life; leaping off the sofa, he sneered down at me.

"What a lot of orchids you've collected, Anne! What a bunch of nothings! Not a person of substance in the bunch, not even Dr. Atchley. I used to think he, at least, was someone sensible. But to hear him go on and on about the theater, of all things!"

"I enjoy spending time with them," I murmured, still livid. Charles had embarrassed me, he'd not even noticed my lover sitting next to him; he'd not said one nice thing about my apartment since arriving. I concentrated on extinguishing candles, gathering up glasses, as outwardly serene as Mamie Eisenhower herself. "They're really quite interesting if you would only give them a chance. But of course, you wouldn't."

"You've changed, Anne. I'm not sure I know you anymore."

"Well, you read my book, didn't you?" I laughed acidly. "That was rather the point."

Charles snorted. "I don't know why you've surrounded yourself with a bunch of New York society types," he continued as he followed me around, watching me intently, frowning if I clanged a glass or dropped cigarette ash, but pointedly not offering to help. "Haven't I always told you you're too fine for that? Too special?"

"Is that why you want me to live stuck out in the middle of nowhere? Is that why you only see me five times a year?" I asked, still smiling, determined not to let him see he had any effect on me. "What do you think I do for the rest of the time, Charles? Sit and wait for you to remember where you've stowed me away?"

Charles did not answer me that. And after I had turned out the last light, I led him down the hall to the bedrooms, although I hesitated in the door of mine. Now that he was here, finally here, I did not want him in my bed. *Our* bed.

"I'll bunk in there." Charles pointed to the guest room; he'd already thrown his old gray travel bag on the bed, his sole piece of luggage. "If you don't mind. I need a good night's sleep, as I'm leaving for Brussels early in the morning."

"No, not at all. Well, good night. There's an extra towel in the guest bathroom." Flush with relief now that I knew he would not intrude any further, I leaned up to him. With a grunt, he kissed me on the cheek; he gave no sign that he had missed my body any more than I had missed his. We both retreated inside our separate bedrooms, and shut the door at the same time.

Charles was gone the next morning before I was up. He had stripped the sheets off his bed and folded them up neatly, like a good houseguest.

AFTER ANNE JUNIOR DISCOVERED the letter from Dana, things were different between us. We went through the next few days as planned, getting her ready for college; I kept a serene smile on my face and would have answered any question she asked. But she asked none.

It wasn't until a couple of years later, when she finally persuaded her father to let her study in Paris—something he had resisted for reasons he did not care to share with anyone—that she acknowledged it.

I took her to Idlewild, and together we wrestled her three mammoth suitcases into the terminal where they were checked. Her hat bag and makeup case would accompany her in her coach seat; Charles forbade any Lindbergh to travel first class. He always sat in the very back of a plane, himself.

My daughter would not meet my gaze when I kissed her good-bye in the terminal; she had not met my gaze once since she found that letter. So I turned to go with a heart as heavy and cumbersome as the luggage she was carrying.

Abruptly, I felt a tug at my sleeve; Ansy embraced me from behind, with more than a trace of desperation, and whispered into my ear, "I understand, Mother. You know, I really do."

When I turned around, the only thing I saw was her white hatbox slipping through the crowd, and then she was absorbed into the line of other passengers waiting to board a Pan Am Stratocruiser to Paris. A Lindbergh bound for Paris—I couldn't help but smile.

There were tears in my eyes as I watched the plane take off; tears of happiness and of relief. I felt as if my own daughter had given me absolution.

I prayed for her, on her way to the rest of her life, to the other side of the ocean her father had crossed so long ago. I prayed for us all. And I couldn't help but hope that her journey would be less eventful than his—and mine—had been.

CHAPTER 20

1968

RECLUSE THOUGH HE WAS fast becoming, there was one invitation that Charles Lindbergh could not turn down. When asked to attend the launch of *Apollo XI,* my husband accepted, although he refused to appear on television, even when Walter Cronkite personally asked him to.

Instead, we breakfasted with the crew the day before. The launch facility in Florida was a stunning compound, with men driving around on golf carts wearing headphones, huge hangars where the crew had worked in the flight simulators, computers everywhere.

Neil Armstrong, Buzz Aldrin, and Michael Collins would soon be flying to the moon. But only one man's entrance prompted an earthquake of excitement and salutes. Powerful, intelligent men with crew cuts and thick black glasses all jostled, like little boys, to have their photographs taken with him. For once, Charles Lindbergh acquiesced with gracious humility.

Despite his stooped shoulders, his white hair, the deep lines around his eyes, to them he was still Lucky Lindy, 'the Lone Eagle. The man who had, one long ago day in May, made this incredible journey possible. I was not the only one in the room moved to tears, thinking about it.

Astronauts are manly; they are the closest thing we now have to what Charles was then; true explorers, just like Cortez and Columbus. Still, after Charles, right before we left, placed his hand upon Neil Armstrong's shoulder and said, "Son, I'm proud of you," the young astronaut's voice wavered a bit when he answered, "Thank you, sir.

"You were the first," Neil continued after a moment. "We only follow in your footsteps."

The room broke into applause, and Charles took a step back as if surprised, bumping into me. He turned and only then appeared to remember that I was there; he was, I thought, grateful for my presence so that he could simply be one of a couple, an old man and his wife.

We didn't speak as we were driven back to our hotel. For once in his life, I believe, Charles Lindbergh was overwhelmed by his legacy.

After the successful return of the crew, we were invited to the White House officially to welcome them home. Richard and Pat Nixon insisted that we stay in the Lincoln Bedroom, and after the formal dinner, I convinced Charles to remain for the dancing in the East Room, where Count Basie and his orchestra played until the wee hours. The magnificent surroundings, the champagne—my new satin gown—all went rather to my head. I found myself dancing the Monkey with Buzz Aldrin, who was surprisingly light on his feet. Jumping around to the music, embracing that once-familiar release from myself that I had always experienced on the dance floor, I caught a glimpse of Charles. He was standing on the sidelines, uncomfortable as ever, looking at me. Simply looking at me. Without a frown or a disapproving glare.

This time, though, I did not stop dancing, embarrassed. I smiled back, then coaxed Spiro Agnew into trying the Twist. Which he did, to the amusement of all.

That night, as we climbed into the enormous canopied bed,

big enough so that we didn't have to touch in our sleep, Charles cleared his throat.

"You looked very happy tonight."

"It was fun, wasn't it? All that dancing?"

"I don't like this sort of thing."

"I know you don't."

"Where did you learn those new dances?"

I was silent; Dana and I had gone to the Peppermint Lounge once, right before it closed, just to see what it was like. Utterly silly after a couple of martinis, we had watched the young people doing all the latest dances, before getting up to try one or two, ourselves.

"Oh, on television, I suppose," I finally answered.

"Television." Charles snorted. He, of course, never watched.

He cleared his throat again. Lying on his back, his arms crossed behind his head, he continued. "It did occur to me, however, tonight—watching you dance, if that's what they call it these days—that if I hadn't married you, this is the kind of life you would have had. You were an ambassador's daughter, after all."

"That's true," I said, sleepily. Rather tipsily, to tell the truth; my fancy hairdo—Reeve had insisted on taking me to her own hairdresser for the occasion—had escaped its prison of hairpins and Aquanet, and was leaning to the side of my head as I lay down.

"It occurred to me that you might have missed that kind of life. Do you? Do you ever wish you hadn't married me?"

"That's a ridiculous question."

"No." Now he turned over on his side, away from me so I could only imagine the look on his face. "It's not a ridiculous question, at all."

I rolled back over, staring up at the canopy, and didn't answer, not for a long time, and eventually I heard him snoring. But I did not fall asleep so easily; I lay awake, blinking in the dark, surrounded by imposing portraits of Abraham Lincoln, wishing that I had had the courage to ask Charles the same question.

The next day, we left to go our separate ways. He was preparing to return to the Philippines, to a remote island where he was spending more and more time trying to understand nature as well as he had once understood technology. I thought I might go back to Darien, or maybe Switzerland, to a little chalet he had built for me, a present intended to entrap, not liberate. It was just one more place to squirrel me away from the part of life he did not understand—which was most of it.

But before we went to the airport, he asked, so politely, which was unlike him, if I might like to stop by the Smithsonian Institution. I agreed, and he thanked me, again, courteously, and I was reminded of how he had been when we first met; how formal, how old-fashioned. I almost felt as if he was courting me all over again.

Once inside the main museum building, I followed Charles as he made his sure way through the labyrinth of halls and rooms, finally climbing a wide set of stairs until we were standing almost nose to nose with an airplane.

A little monoplane, silver, suspended from the ceiling on slender wires so that it appeared airborne, as if gliding on a nation's collective memory. That jaunty *Spirit of St. Louis* painted in bold letters across the nose.

Below, crowds of schoolchildren, families on holiday, a few stray men, gazed up at it. A schoolteacher read aloud the words from a plaque beneath it:

"On May twenty-first, 1927, Charles Lindbergh completed the first solo nonstop transatlantic flight in history, flying the *Spirit of Saint Louis* three thousand six hundred and ten miles from Long Island, New York, to Paris, France, in thirty-three hours, thirty minutes."

I studied Charles as the teacher spoke; his face did not betray any emotion. He gazed at his plane with that clear, determined look of his, unchanged despite the fact that the boy was finally an old man. But his skin did flush, faintly. I wondered what he was thinking; what he was seeing. Did he look at this plane—an antique now, almost a toy, inconceivable that it had once represented the most modern of technology—and wonder at himself, at his bravery, at the impudence of that boy? Did he wish himself back to that time? Did he wish it had never happened?

I gazed at it, and couldn't help but think of the launch site in Florida, and Mission Control in Houston; of the hundreds of men, the computers, the constant contact between the earth and the spaceship—the final destination, the moon itself, always in sight. Then I thought of Charles, flying alone in a fog most of the time with no clear view out of his side window. And with no one to talk to, no one to monitor his position, his coordinates, his vital signs. He had no one but himself to rely on; no one but himself to blame if something went wrong.

And I knew, as I had always known but somehow forgotten to remember in these past years, that I could never have done it, that no one else could ever have done it. That I would never know anyone as brave, as astonishing—as frustrating, too, but that was, I was forced to admit finally, part of his charm—as the slightly stooped elderly gentleman standing beside me in the shadows, listening while schoolchildren read of his exploits. The man who was, for better, for worse, my husband. The man who I loved, in spite of himself.

"No," I said softly, so as not to call attention to us.

"No, what?" He turned to me, startled out of his own contemplation.

"No, I'm not sorry I married you."

"Oh." After a long moment, he smiled, almost in surprise; as if recognizing in me a long, lost friend.

Then he turned back to look at his plane. And he reached for my hand, as he did.

CHAPTER 21

A*CUTE PROMYELOCYTIC LEUKEMIA*—that was the diagnosis. For months, Charles had been tired—so uncharacteristic for him. He'd lost weight, sweated profusely at night. With his attention to detail, his methodical way of dealing with things, he made a list of his symptoms, monitored them over time, then checked himself in for tests.

He called me, late one evening in 1972. I was in Darien, relaxing in the living room, a fire burning in the fireplace. Charles spent fifteen minutes asking how the weather was, if I had enough firewood stacked, were the raccoons getting into the trash cans, if I had remembered to get the mail in. He wanted to know if I had eaten an early dinner (much better, in his view), or would I dine late, how much it had cost, and reminded me to enter the amount in my accounting book.

All that settled, there was a pause on the other end of the phone line. Through my kitchen door I heard the sound of cocktails being made; the tinkle of glassware, the cracking of ice cubes. Impatiently, I glanced at the clock over the fireplace; I didn't want to spend this precious time on the phone.

"Charles, if that's all—"

"I have cancer. Acute promyelocytic leukemia. The doctors

were very forthcoming in their prognosis, at my insistence. It is in the early stages, and they recommend radiation treatment."

"My God." I plopped down on the davenport as if someone had kicked my legs out from under me.

"I know this is an inconvenience, but could you come into the city tomorrow?"

"Where are you? When did you get in? I thought you were in the Philippines!"

"At Columbia-Presbyterian. I arrived two days ago. Can you get in touch with Dr. Atchley? Apparently he's not on call today."

"Yes, I believe so." Even though he couldn't see me, my face glowed.

"Could you please ask him for the name of the best oncologist in New York? I think my doctors are adequate, but given the diagnosis, I would feel it shortsighted not to get another opinion."

"Of course, Charles—are you . . . are you all right? I mean, of course you're not. But how are you taking this?" Although I knew how. After forty-five years, I knew.

He was making a list of the things he wanted to ask the doctors. He probably already had contacted Pan Am to rearrange his schedule. I was sure he had his battered traveling bag, with its small medicine kit and a couple of changes of old clothing that he planned to wash out in the bathroom sink, for he didn't believe in unnecessary baggage. Although none of his clothing—island clothing; threadbare shorts and tennis shoes—would be appropriate for New York in March. I would have to bring him some things from here.

"I'm fine. I've known for a few hours now, so I've had time to absorb it."

"A few hours? That's all you need?" And despite the sick, cold terror filling the pit where my stomach used to be, I laughed.

"Yes." His voice was stern now; he did not understand my laughter.

"Charles, try not to worry. It may be the wrong diagnosis. Let's just wait until the doctors here see you."

Now he was annoyed; he snarled into the phone, "It's not the wrong diagnosis. I asked for a medical book and researched the symptoms myself. My hope is that it will respond to the radiation, as many cancers do."

"All right. Do you want me to—I don't know, what else can I do?"

"Nothing. I don't want you to come here until tomorrow because I don't like you driving in the dark. Please don't tell the children. There's no reason to worry them and of course we don't want any publicity. If anyone asks, just say I have a virus I caught in the jungle."

"I will. Charles, I—have a good night. Try to get some sleep. I'll be there in the morning."

"You, too. And enjoy your evening."

I hung up the phone, and laughed again.

The door to the kitchen swung open and Dana greeted me with a merry smile on his face, a tray of cocktails in his hand.

"Do you want to see a show tomorrow in the city? A patient of mine offered tickets to *A Little Night Music*. Finally, I've wanted to see this for—What? What's wrong, Anne?"

I shook my head, and tried to catch my breath, but let out a ragged sob instead. "It's Charles. He just called. Dana, he—he's sick. Leukemia. I don't remember what kind. But he's in the city and he asked me to ask you—to ask *you*, of all people!—if you could recommend—"

But I broke down, unable to say the words, falling into Dana's familiar arms. He held me to his chest, and clucked soothingly before settling down with me on the sofa.

I laid my head on his shoulder, waiting for my tears to dry. And I tried not to think about my husband.

CHARLES RESPONDED WELL to the initial treatments, and we had a few good months. Months in which we were finally together, as I had desired, so long ago. But I couldn't help but remember the old adage: *Be careful what you wish for.* I was the caretaker, now; the healthy one. And Charles was not a compliant patient; he envied me my strength when he couldn't even climb a staircase without needing a nap. He wanted to keep up his hectic schedule but when he no longer could, he goaded me into his newest project: the extensive editing of my diaries for publication. I'd stopped writing them, years ago—after the war. But observing Charles's urgent interest in them now, I couldn't help but think he was writing his own obituary using *my* words. Rearranging them, pruning them until they portrayed someone I no longer recognized.

But there came a time when there was no use pretending; his body stopped responding to the treatments, and we finally told the children. After a terrible month in the hospital during which it became apparent that his white cells were just as stubborn as the rest of him, he said, "I want to go home to Hawaii. I want to go home and die in peace."

Dana told him it was suicidal. "You won't make it," he said bluntly. "You're much too weak, and it's a hell of a long flight."

"I'm going to die anyway. I want to die at home." Diminished as he was, lying in the hospital bed, his painfully thin body barely making an outline beneath the blanket, Charles set his jaw in that determined way of his and looked, fleetingly, like the hero in the photographs of '27. Even though I had tears in my eyes, because the head oncologist had just informed Charles he only had days to live, my heart did that crazy, balletic leap as I gazed at his still-handsome face. The flesh, wasting away, gave up the strong lines of his face in only greater relief. His hair—thin even before the radiation—was the snowiest of white, which, when he was healthy, contrasted with the permanent ruddiness of his skin after so many years outdoors—first in the open cockpits of airplanes, then in the Pacific during the war; finally after these last decades spent in jungles and rain forests and remote, untamed beaches.

His physical beauty, our physical attraction—that had never faded. In bed, we had always been able to understand each other. If only he hadn't stopped coming to it, years ago.

I shook my head. It was wrong to think such thoughts now. I listened as Charles argued with Dana, who finally gave up and barked at Jon, standing like a tall, watchful Norse god, to make whatever the hell arrangements he had to.

Finally, after everyone else had gone—the platoon of doctors, the boys back to their hotels—I kissed Charles good night. "Do you want me to stay?" I asked, suddenly weary beyond reason. I could have slept on the floor, I was so exhausted, pummeled by the last few days.

"No," he said, frowning. "That would be unnecessary. I will be perfectly fine, and you will sleep better in a bed."

"All right." I gathered up my purse and coat, stopping to wave good night from the door. Now, alone save for the IV bags and machines, he struck me as helpless, small—he, who had been a giant all my life. But he did not give me any indication that he needed my company; he opened a book—a medical book—and put his glasses on, pushing them halfway down his nose. Licking his index finger, he turned a page.

Walking down the hall, I was so weighed down by my weariness that I wondered if my legs would hold out until I reached the elevator. I was almost there when I felt a hand on my arm.

"Mrs. Lindbergh?"

"Yes?" A young nurse, with red hair, was holding some papers in her hand. She bit her lip, then looked worriedly down the hall, back toward Charles's room.

"I shouldn't do this. I know I shouldn't, it's very wrong. But you—I loved your book, you see. It means so much to me, I thought you should know about these."

Then she thrust the papers into my hand, and ran off down a hall. Confused, I put the papers into my purse, assuming they were medical release forms. Then I got into the elevator, hailed a taxi, stumbled up to my hotel room—I had long since given up my apartment—and called down to room service for a drink.

It was only after it arrived that I remembered the papers. Sipping my gin, I took them out of my purse and smoothed them on my lap. These were no medical forms. They were letters—no, copies of letters, the words slightly smudged from the mimeograph machine. And they were from Charles. I recognized the handwriting, small, slanted purposefully to the right, although it was spidery now. The letters were short, uncharacteristically brief for usually, Charles wrote very detailed letters. They were letters of farewell, of finality, of shared remembrances and hopes, no longer to be fulfilled.

They were not addressed to me.

AND NOW, FINALLY, we have reached our destination, the end of our journey together. He is awake once more, aware of my presence, and he coughs; I hear the nurse walking softly toward his closed door but I beat her to it.

"I'd like a few more minutes alone with him, please."

"Oh, of course, Mrs. Lindbergh!" And she retreats, eyes brimming sympathetically.

"Charles, it comes down to this. I deserve to know why. It's not just the women—that, I could almost understand. But the children—why these other children? How many?" I thrust the letters in his face, and he brushes them away with his frail hand.

"Seven. I fathered seven other children."

I stagger at the number; until I heard it, they hadn't seemed real, these others. His bastards. For a moment, I can't catch my breath.

"How many years, Charles?" I finally ask, still breathless. "How many years have you kept them from me? What do they look like? Do they look like you?" For some reason this is important; I need to know they do not look like our children. My children.

"I don't know. I suppose they do. It began—sometime in the fifties." He closes his eyes, as if remembering.

"So that's why you were always gone. That's why you never wanted me to come with you, that's why you kept me hidden away, too."

"Not at first. I *was* working. I met Greta at Pan Am in Berlin. The others, through her. It was a lonely time. You were preoccupied with the children, as you should have been. You were home. You were—"

"Old," I finish for him, and he does not contradict me.

"Our children, you did a good job with them. *You.* I wanted—another chance, perhaps."

"Why didn't you give our children that chance? They would have welcomed it. All you had to do was ask. Instead, you chose to fly away, to leave us. To have these other families. For the last time, Charles—*why?*"

He doesn't answer, and I don't know what else to ask, what else to say. I am only a woman, a woman with so much to do; even as I've been pacing this room, grasping for one last chance to understand the man I married, I've been thinking ahead to all the people I'll need to call, the statements I'll have to make, the practical business of sorting and filing and putting things in order.

Right now, I simply cannot absorb this, the enormity of it, what it means to my children, what happens next. The rage I've nurtured for years against him is finally gone, leaving me empty—and terrified of what will replace it; I can't imagine an emotion big enough, terrible enough.

We are silent, and his breathing is so heavy that I fear he has fallen asleep again. But then I feel his hand—icy, the tips of his fingers already puckered—on my arm, gripping it desperately, fearfully. He opens his eyes, and I see that he is just like any other man would be at this moment—a man frightened, sorrowful, regretful. Tears pool in his lower lids, then trickle down his cheeks; his lip trembles, and he whispers, "Please, please, forgive me, Anne. Forgive me, before I die."

And the words are on my lips; words of confession, which would double as his absolution. I know I have it in my power to forgive him because I, too, have sinned. Finally I am his equal; we are equal in our betrayal of each other.

But I have not sinned like he has. I have never betrayed my children. I have only betrayed him.

"It's too late now," I reply, denying him the comfort I alone can give. It's taken me forty-five years to earn this moment—and I wish, desperately, that it had never come. "You've hurt us all, beyond measure."

"You won't—you won't tell the children?"

Oh, my children! My loves, my life. "No, no, I will never tell them. I will never burden them with that. Never!"

"I don't want this to be how you remember me," he begs, his voice cracking again, catching on the broken pieces of our shattered memories.

"Then you should have thought of that, before."

"I only ever wanted to be your hero. These other women, I didn't care what they thought of me. But you—"

"I didn't need a hero. I never needed a hero. I needed to be loved."

"I came back." The tears are falling down his cheeks. "I *always* came back to you."

"Then that will have to be enough, won't it?" I ask us both, and he nods, and I understand there are no more words. No more explanations. Bending down, I take him in my arms; he's so light, so fragile. He reminds me of Elisabeth, when she was ill.

We match our breaths together, rising and falling as one. "I love you," I tell Charles Lindbergh, the last thing he will hear in this world. Such an ordinary phrase.

For an ordinary couple, after all.

Charles sleeps again, a deep, engulfing slumber that appears to consume what's left of his flesh; he is melting into the bed, his mouth sagging, his skin papery. He sleeps like that for two more hours, until, surrounded by his son and his wife—

He awakes with a start, a gasp, his eyes open, fixed on that distant spot on the horizon, and he inhales sharply, then exhales.

And then is no more.

There is a sharp intake of breath as we lean toward this man, this giant, but he is flesh and bones, finally, just like the rest of us. Land and I look at each other, too shocked for tears; Charles Lindbergh was mortal, after all.

As the doctor comes into the room, stethoscope in hand, I walk away, shaking, although my eyes are dry. I wonder how to begin living the rest of my life without him; without the answers to the questions I will never stop asking.

I spy, on a corner table, Charles's old traveling bag; already I am hungry for reminders of him. Smiling, I pick it up. However did it last so long? It's in tatters; the calfskin worn and shiny, the rusty clasp held shut with safety pins.

For some reason, I open it just to smell his scent one last time, finger his old clothes—a polo shirt he's had since his sixtieth birthday, a present from Reeve. Those horrid, scratchy wool socks he always insisted on wearing, even with tuxedos—oh, how I tried to get him to change! A photograph—I pull it out, instantly on my guard. I'm not sure I can stand any more surprises. But it's so unlike Charles to travel with a photograph that I have to see. *Unnecessary weight,* I can hear him bark, as I open the hinged frame.

"Oh!" For in my hand is the photograph of a young woman. It only takes me an instant to recognize her as me.

So young—dark hair, not gray; no lines or wrinkles. The woman in the photo is a girl, really; a thin, solemnly smiling girl, not the grinning idiot of all those early newspaper photographs. This smile—this careful, cautious smile—is the one that reflected my truest self. Especially back when I was so young as to be unformed; afraid of everything because nothing truly terrible had happened to me, yet.

And in my lap is a baby.

My firstborn; the blond curls, the cleft chin, the big blue eyes. With a shock of remembrance that pulls me to my knees, I recall the day Charles took this photograph. He had just gotten a new Kodak, and was forever snapping at everything—when he wasn't taking it apart and putting it back together, fascinated by all the intricate parts.

That day, I was holding the baby, squirming in a towel. Charlie had just been bathed, and he was smiling, reaching toward me, when Charles snapped the picture.

I don't want any reminders, Charles had declared after that terrible May. *We need to forget.*

Yet he has carried this photograph on every journey, every flight since; even to war and back. I picture Charles in the jungle, trying to sleep on a cot or maybe on the ground; oceans away from home, bombs overhead, just one soldier among many, wanting to remember something good, something decent—something to remind him why he is there.

Or, perhaps, something that might allow him to welcome death.

Through eyes blurred with tears—healing, welcome tears—I look back at the still figure on the bed; rising, I walk over and place the photograph in his arms. And I bow my head, touching my cheek to his, thanking God for this—this unexpected gift of a glimpse into Charles's heart; the heart he had tried to hide from me, all these years.

This answer to all my questions.

All the king's horses and all the king's men, I begin to croon softly, just as I used to do to the babes in my arms, all of them. *I thought they'd never be able to put the Lindberghs together again.*

Gently, Land reaches over the bed to close his father's eyes.

As he does so, I pray that at last, Charles has found what he has been looking for, all his life.

CHAPTER 22

AM FLYING.

Alone, unafraid, high above the blue of Long Island Sound.

I went to visit the daughter of an old friend, who still had an estate with a private airfield. At her father's behest, she had kept an airplane, a four-seat monoplane, in a barn, all these years. Once, the wheel of that plane had fallen off. Once, a girl too young, too stupid to be afraid, trusted a boy to bring her home safely, and he had. And she had thought that he would, for the rest of their lives.

So did he.

I thanked Harry Guggenheim's daughter Diane, a slim, nervous, middle-aged woman now. Harry had died a few years previous. While he always asserted that his friend Slim was no anti-Semite in public, in private Harry had stopped returning his calls.

"Are you sure you want to do this, Mrs. Lindbergh? You haven't flown in a long time."

"I know. But I have to."

"You remember everything?"

"I don't know, but I suppose I'll find out."

"How are you doing? Without him?"

"Well. Well enough."

"Father always said he lost him a long time ago." Harry's daughter shook her head. "Before the war. But then he always said, 'Damn, if I don't miss him, still.' Did he believe it all, Mrs. Lindbergh? Did Colonel Lindbergh believe what he said, back before the war?"

I hesitated, torn between wanting to placate the daughter of a kind, loyal friend, and the truth.

"If you knew him," I finally said, "you would know Charles Lindbergh never said anything he didn't mean."

"That's a shame." Diane shook her head, slowly, mournfully. Then she looked at me with a pitying smile. "But you, we never believed that you—"

"Well, I did. I'm tired of people pretending that I didn't. I was just as wrong as he was. More so, because I didn't speak out for my own beliefs. I borrowed his, as wrong as I knew they were. I'm no better than the Germans. The Germans who sat by and didn't say anything, all those years."

"Oh, no, Mrs. Lindbergh, you're not like them! I'll never believe it. My father never believed it!" My old friend's daughter wouldn't help; she wanted to absolve me, and I didn't want to be absolved.

"I'm sorry, Diane. Truly sorry, for the pain we caused you and your family. The pain *I* caused you, and so many others."

"It was so long ago." She shrugged. So did I. Unlike men, women got less sentimental as we aged, I was discovering. We cried enough, when we were young; vessels overflowing with the tears of everyone we loved. All the tears I cried when my son was taken. But I hadn't shed one tear since my husband died.

"Father always said you were the brave one." Diane laughed down at me in astonishment; she was a head taller than I was. "He

said that the colonel never knew fear, he never understood consequences. You did, but you went along with him, anyway. That
was bravery."

"Or idiocy," I replied, then I climbed—stiffly, every joint
aching—into the cockpit. I pulled my goggles over my head,
fleetingly aware of how ridiculous I looked—a graying grandmother wearing old-fashioned flying goggles. Then I shrugged it
off, fastened the safety harness, flipped a switch, and opened up
the throttle.

Slowly I began to taxi, surprised, at first, by how the propellers cut my vision; I'd forgotten that, about old planes, with the
propellers on the noses instead of the wings. Gradually, it all did
come back; I pulled on the stick, accelerating, holding my breath,
and then it happened—that lovely, balletic, suspended moment,
and I had no fear. Why should I be afraid? I was nearly seventy
years old, and had begun giving too much consideration to the
various ways an elderly person can die. Crashing in an airplane
seemed a reasonable alternative to most of them.

But I will not crash, not this cloudless, windless day. I am in
total control of my aircraft, taught by the best pilot there ever
was, and I keep a gentle tug on the stick, nosing the plane up, up,
up, over the house—Diane is just a doll now, waving her hands
over her head—over the trees, catching the wind, and then soaring out over the ocean. My ears pop, and I realize I have forgotten
to bring any chewing gum, and for a moment I inhale the sharp,
cool scent of spearmint—the flavor of gum that Charles always
had on him.

The engines are so whiny, so loud—I've forgotten how loud!
Even in an enclosed cockpit, they aren't muffled, at least not to
my sensitive elderly ears, and I marvel that we were able to carry
on any kind of conversation on that endless afternoon, when we
were burning off fuel.

I bank the plane due left, flying north now, recognizing some of the houses below; the dunes, the outline of the beach, although of course things have changed since the last time I flew over this spot. There are more houses, smaller and closer together; strip malls; highways now, segmenting the land into neat, orderly squares.

I have a moment where I want to fly inland to see what else has changed, but then I remember why I'm aloft in the first place, and head the plane out over the water.

The white waves keep up their steady, relentless assault against the shore, and I nose down a bit lower, trying one more time to imagine what it was like for him flying alone with only this cold, hard slab of water beneath him for almost the entire trip to Paris. I can't; after all these years, I still can't put myself in his place and see myself doing what he did. I still can't stop admiring that boy's bravery, his astonishing daring. I still can't stop marveling that this same boy chose me; and I'm glad that I can't, for we should rejoice in being seen, needed. Loved.

But it's not the foundation on which to build a life, a marriage, and it never should have been. I wish I hadn't taken so long to understand this in life, although I suppose I should be happy that at least I was able to imagine it on the page.

Peering over the propeller to my right I see it, a lighthouse on a strip of land curling out into the water, and I know I'm almost there. I reach into my pocket.

He dictated, in one of his last lists, that I was to be buried next to him in Hawaii. He never asked me if this was my wish, and I never told him that it wasn't. I let him die thinking that he would lie beside me; I let him die thinking I was honored that he had chosen me, and me alone, for this privilege.

But I will not be buried next to him. When I die, I told my son on the long, sobering flight back from Hawaii, after we laid

Charles in the ground beneath several slabs of stone, his grave crudely marked so that strangers couldn't find it, I want to be cremated. And I would like my ashes to be scattered, among various places dear to me—my garden in Darien; the shores of my family's summer home in Maine; over the sound, at a point about two miles offshore.

About where I am flying right now. I peer out the dirty side window and see the lighthouse far below, and a calm, blue harbor of water. Right—here—

I pop open the window with my elbow, bracing myself against the onrush of cold air, and I kiss his wedding ring, then let it fall from my hand, hoping that the weight of the gold will allow it to cut through the currents and fall over the waters of the sound, near where we honeymooned.

Near where the ashes of our firstborn were scattered.

I still don't understand why Charles did what he did; why he had to father other children, have other families. Perhaps we both kept looking for our lost child. I did, by scanning the faces of every little boy I saw, every little boy about eighteen months with blond hair, blue eyes. By searching in my surviving children's faces when they were around that age, looking for some gesture or laugh that might remind me of him.

Maybe this was Charles's way of looking for Charlie; by trying to replace him, over and over and over.

Whatever his reasons, I don't want to lie next to him when I'm gone and I'm not sure if my children understand. I know that if I explain what their father did to me—to them—they might. But I won't do that. I won't do that to him. I won't do that to them.

I won't do that to the generations of schoolchildren who will learn about him in history books, and marvel, and be inspired to try astounding feats of their own. I won't do that to the brave, primitive monoplane hanging in the Smithsonian, ever empty, ever waiting for him. Just as I once was.

I'll keep his secrets for him.

I bank the plane, and I close my eyes, just for a moment, and I think of Dana, back in the city. He is a good man. A kind man. We ended our physical affair a few years ago, tamping the flame into a warm, comfortable friendship—much like a marriage, I suppose. But I know that if I asked him to he would leave his wife for me, no questions asked.

But I won't ask him, or anybody else, and it's not out of any misplaced widow's loyalty.

Dana taught me what it was like to be loved, to be equal. But Charles taught me how to be alone, long before I ever wanted to be.

But now, I do. Now, I'm ready.

I turn back toward land; the airplane has no radio, of course, so there's no way for me to be in contact with anyone on the ground. And unlike Charles, I want to be. Charles was of the air, but I am of the earth. Most of us are.

I'll never forget what he taught me. I'll never be rid of his legacy; for the rest of my life, I know, I'll be invited to dedicate statues, airports, schools, in his name. *I* will be invited; not those other women stashed away overseas, and I suppose for this, I should be grateful.

I will take my duties seriously, just as seriously as I once navigated as his crew. I will be the bridge between who Charles was, and who he was assumed to be. The keeper of the flame. The guardian of his reputation, for much of it deserves to be remembered. And it's up to me, as the aviator's wife who was once an ambassador's daughter, to decide how much.

I will go wherever I'm invited, whenever I'm asked in his name, alone. I will leave there, alone.

I will fly, alone. Wearing my own pair of goggles, my view of the world just as unique, just as wonderful, as his was, but different. Mine.

Alone.

The horizon is blurring into the darkening sky, and I need to get back, before the day is gone. There are people back on the ground, waiting for me.

But if I don't get back before the sun sets, I can always look to the sky and navigate by the stars. That is one of the many things he taught me, back when I longed to be taught. If I ever get lost now, on my own, I won't panic, I won't flail. I know how to find Polaris, and I can always steer by that.

For it is the one star in the sky whose bright, unwavering gaze reminds me most of him.

WHEN I FIRST HAD THE IDEA TO WRITE a novel about Anne Lindbergh, I found that people all had the same reaction: a gasp of recognition, followed by the inevitable, "Oh, I *love* the Lindberghs!"

So I went off to write the book—and ponder the question that wouldn't let me sleep at night as I began to corral all the research into a manageable novel: "Just what *do* we all love about the Lindberghs?"

There's the name recognition, of course; everyone has heard of them, from either history books or their collective body of writing. But as I began to assemble the threads of the story I wanted to tell, I realized that while everyone has heard of Anne Lindbergh, the nature of that recognition varies widely. The majority of people know vaguely about Charles's importance in the history of aviation, but not many really understand the astonishing courage it took to do this at the time; the extraordinary significance of this feat to the world as we now know it.

And while other parts of the Lindberghs' shared history might be individually recognizable—"Wasn't their baby kidnapped?" "I always heard he was a Nazi." "She was a writer, wasn't she?"—I began to realize how very few people were familiar with the truly operatic scale of Anne Lindbergh's life and marriage. This became my motivation: to tell her *entire* story; to try to understand the nature of this celebrated but mystifying marriage between entirely original individuals.

Most important, I wanted to make Anne the heroine of her own story, finally—as in memory (both her written accounts and the public's perception), she is far too often overshadowed by the dominant personality that is Charles Lindbergh.

And, of course, he is a dominant personality in my story; it is impossible to make him anything but! He was a fascinating man, but a deeply flawed one; in the end, not the hero Anne—and the world—fell in love with, back when he was "Lucky Lindy."

But while this is the story of a marriage, it's primarily the story of a woman; a deeply intelligent, courageous, resilient woman. The things I learned about Anne Morrow Lindbergh as I read her diaries and biographies! The timid intellectual who, through marriage to the hero of the age, found she wasn't so timid, after all. Actually, she was fearless; as the first American woman to earn a glider pilot's license, she allowed her husband to hurtle her off the edge of a mountain like a slingshot. Through sheer determination, she became a confident navigator, one of the first licensed radio operators; she also became her husband's copilot, the only person the most famous aviator of all trusted to steer him around the world on record-breaking exploratory flights.

This was the Anne whose story needed to be told, for few people today know anything about the pioneering aviatrix Anne.

But then there was the tragic—and more familiar—Anne. The woman who, along with her husband, was more hounded by the press than anyone in modern history, with the possible exception of Princess Diana. The Anne who had to wear disguises in order to go to the theater; the woman who was unable to answer her own front door because of all the strangers wanting to get a glimpse of her.

The Anne who, after her firstborn was kidnapped and murdered—tragically, publicly—had to suffer, until the end of her life, countless strangers claiming that they were her dead child. The Anne who had to grieve over this loss in private, because her husband forbade her to do so in public—or in his presence.

The Anne who never once saw her husband cry for his lost son.

And what about the frustratingly compliant Anne? The woman who tried to justify her husband's isolationist (some say Nazi) leanings prior to World War II? The woman who saw what was happening to him, saw how wrong he was, but who hadn't yet discovered she was strong enough to contradict him?

And then the ultimately resilient Anne; the woman who had to build an entire life for herself and her children when Charles all but abandoned them in his increasing unrest after the war. The woman who learned to talk back, to say no, to tell her own story, famously, in the beloved *Gift from the Sea*. The woman who had a surprising adulterous affair in middle age.

The Anne who, despite her public image as the model of a docile wife, refused to be buried next to her husband of forty-five years. And the husband who, despite his public image as the hero of his age, had three secret families—including seven additional children.

But did *Anne* know? Ah, that's the question! She never spoke or wrote of this Charles Lindbergh. The Charles in her diaries is the Charles she wanted us to remember; the idol, the pure, heroic boy. I discovered that the diaries published in her lifetime were heavily edited by both Anne and Charles near the end of his life; even then, Charles was trying to shape *his* image using *her* words.

But I think she did know. And that in discovering this ultimate betrayal, she finally understood her marriage and her husband.

She also recognized that she had been the strong one, all along. For the kidnapping truly broke Charles Lindbergh beyond repair; it can be seen as the explanation for all that he did after—the long absences, the tyrannical behavior toward his children and wife, the obsessive building and abandoning of homes, the restless search for causes. And finally, the secret families.

Whereas Anne—that shy ambassador's daughter—was the one strong enough to hold her family together. She was the one who survived this epic journey intact, able to love and, ultimately, to forgive.

So. That question: *Why do we all love the Lindberghs?*

Because of *Anne*, I realized when I finished writing *The Aviator's Wife*. Anne—tender, courageous, resilient Anne—is the reason we all "love the Lindberghs."

NOW, FOR THE INEVITABLE truth versus fiction discussion! One thing I have learned after writing three historical novels is that there will always be readers who want to know what parts I imagined, and what parts actually happened. My answer, always, is: It's the emotional truths that I imagine; the relationships, the reasons these historical figures do the things they do. I truly believe that the inner life can be explored only in novels, not histories—or even diaries and letters. For diaries and letters are self-censored even at the moment of writing them; it's impossible to be absolutely honest with oneself.

For those who do care about the historical record, however, I will share the following:

The first flight that Anne and Charles take together in my book, unknown to anyone but themselves, is fictional. That is, there is no record of this flight; the first recorded instance of Anne flying with Charles is the second flight mentioned, the one she takes with her mother and sisters in front of the press.

The flight in which the plane turns upside down, losing a wheel on takeoff, is a compilation of many of the early flights before their marriage; they did actually lose a wheel on takeoff during a flight in Mexico after their engagement was announced, so I incorporated that into this fictional flight.

The basic details of their other historical flights, mentioned in this book, are taken from actual accounts.

The timeline of the kidnapping sequence is as historically accurate as I could make it, while I acknowledge there are many details that I left out. Again, this is a novel, not a blow-by-blow account; I was more interested in the emotion, the personal drama, than I was in giving a history lesson.

The basic timeline for the rest of the book is, again, historically accurate. The historical figures we meet are people Anne and Charles did know; major events that occur, such as the rally in Madison Square Garden, Charles's record during the war, the visitation with the Apollo astronauts, actually happened.

Some may wonder why I didn't mention every book Anne wrote, or every flight they took, or every move they made. Each life is made up of a thousand stories; it's the novelist's job to pick and choose which ones will make a compelling novel. This means that some stories will inevitably be left out or not as explored as thoroughly as some might wish.

And finally, I leave you with this: As a historical novelist, the most gratifying thing I hear is that the reader was inspired, after reading my work of fiction, to research these remarkable people's lives further. That is what historical fiction does best, I think; it leaves the reader with a desire to know more. I hope my novel accomplishes this, and I highly recommend the following books that I found very useful: Anne Morrow Lindbergh and Charles Lindbergh's collected published diaries and books, including *Gift from the Sea* and *The Spirit of St. Louis;* A. Scott Berg's monumental biography, *Lindbergh;* Susan Hertog's biography, *Anne Morrow Lindbergh, Her Life;* and Reeve Lindbergh's memoir, *Under a Wing.*

ACKNOWLEDGMENTS

CHARLES HAD ANNE FOR HIS CREW; I have many wonderful people who support and navigate me through my journey, as well. First and always I must thank my wonderful editor, Kate Miciak, who pushes me to do my best with every book. And I have nothing but gratitude and friendship for my literary agent, Laura Langlie.

To the smart and hardworking professionals at Random House, I say, once again, thank you from the bottom of my heart: Libby McGuire, Jane von Mehren, Susan Corcoran, Kim Hovey, Gina Wachtel, Robbin Schiff, Sharon Propson, Kristin Fassler, Leigh Marchant, Benjamin Dreyer, Loren Noveck, Randall Klein, and Loyale Coles. Thanks also to Bill Contardi for all his work on my behalf.

There are so many other book-loving people who never fail to surprise me with their support and friendship, among them Bridget Piekarz, Nicole Hayes, Margie White, Sue Kowalski and Jane Stroh from The Bookstore in Glen Ellyn, and Becky Anderson from Anderson's Book Shop. Thank you all.

And what kind of modern author would I be if I failed to give a shout-out to all my new friends on Twitter and Facebook? Thank you all for making life interesting!

Finally to my family, especially Dennis, Alec, and Ben: thank you, as always, for putting up with me.

MELANIE BENJAMIN is a pseudonym for Melanie Hauser, who has written two contemporary novels. As Melanie Benjamin, she has written *Alice I Have Been* and *The Autobiography of Mrs. Tom Thumb*. She lives with her husband in Chicago, where she is always searching for an interesting story to tell.